Cassie Ford watched with great in~~terest~~ ~~as a taxi cab~~ outside the house in Ca~~mberwell~~ into Walworth all that of~~~~ of luggage emerged from ~~~~

''Ello,' said Cassie. ''~~~~ don't get many people in t~~~~

'No,' said the woman. ~~She seemed~~ quite friendly. 'Me and me 'ubby and brother-in-law 'ave come to live 'ere. I'm Mrs Harper.'

'Oh, you're welcome of course,' said Cassie. She had dreamy brown eyes, the deceptive smile of an angel, and a vivid imagination that frequently got out of hand.

'Me dad used to drive a royal taxi once,' she began, at which point the taxi drove off. It was then that Cassie saw the covered birdcage on the pavement.

'What's that?' she asked, liking to know about everything.

'That's Percy, me parrot,' said Mrs Harper, taking the cover off the cage and revealing a bird of brilliant colours.

'Hello, saucy!' said Percy.

'Oh, ain't he lovely,' replied Cassie. 'A talking parrot. I wouldn't mind changing 'im for my cat.'

'Sorry, love,' said Mrs Harper, and she picked up the cage and went into the house.

It was some time later that the parrot began to say other things – things that seemed very odd, and that finally helped Boots and the Adams family solve a mystery of their own.

MISSING PERSON

Mary Jane Staples

CORGI BOOKS

MISSING PERSON
A CORGI BOOK : 0 552 14230 1

First publication in Great Britain

PRINTING HISTORY
Corgi edition published 1994

Set in 10½pt Linotype Plantin by
County Typesetters, Margate, Kent

Corgi Books are published by Transworld Publishers Ltd,
61–63 Uxbridge Road, Ealing, London W5 5SA,
in Australia by Transworld Publishers (Australia) Pty Ltd,
15–25 Helles Avenue, Moorebank, NSW 2170,
and New Zealand by Transworld Publishers (NZ) Ltd,
3 William Pickering Drive, Albany, Auckland.

Reproduced, printed and bound in Great Britain by
Cox & Wyman Ltd, Reading, Berks.

To Doris, George and Les.

Chapter One

It was haunted, a certain house in Caulfield Place off Browning Street, Walworth.

Well, that was what the street kids said.

True, a gruesome murder had taken place there in 1914, but that was sixteen years ago. So mums and dads told their kids not to go around making up stories about it after all this time.

It's still haunted, said the kids to each other.

'Well, it looks 'aunted, don't it?'

'All them empty winders starin' at yer.'

'Like the ghost is waitin' to grab yer. It was a witch that got done in, yer know, and witches always come back to 'aunt yer.'

The house had been empty for four years. The last occupants, a family called Cook, had moved out in a hurry in 1926 on account of disturbances. Now, suddenly, on the third Saturday in May, 1930, new occupants were arriving. The landlord had had furniture moved into the house two days ago, and a woman had come along to hang new curtains that did away with the blank stare of the windows.

Street kids watched as this same woman and two men in their thirties arrived outside the house in a taxi. The two men alighted and began to unload the luggage stacked beside the cabbie. Out stepped the woman, wearing a costume and a flowery hat. She looked at the house.

'Well, this is it, Wally,' she said to one of the men.

'Good,' said Wally. Both men were in caps and workmen's clothes. The hovering kids glued their eyes to the scene.

''Ere, Alfie,' whispered one to another, 'ain't yer goin' to tell 'em it's 'aunted?'

'No, you tell 'em.'

'No, you're oldest.'

'Well, it don't look so 'aunted now it's got curtains up, so nobody need tell 'em.'

The men, carrying two suitcases each, advanced to the front door. One man, placing a case on the step, opened the door with a key, and in they went. The woman, who looked in her late twenties, reached into the taxi and pulled out a covered birdcage, set it down on the pavement, and then lifted out a laden shopping bag. At this moment a girl came walking down the Place from Browning Street. Long raven-black hair hung down her back, resting on the sailor's collar of her blue and white frock. Seeing the taxi, she quickened her steps. Up she came.

''Ello,' she said to the woman, whose good looks were slightly florid, as if she was on friendly terms with gin.

''Ello, ducks,' said the woman, who was now settling with the cabbie. Out came the bloke called Wally. He heaved out one more suitcase, the last.

''Ello,' said the girl again. He smiled at her. ''Ave you come to visit, only we don't get many people in taxis.'

'No, me and me 'ubby and brother-in-law 'ave come to live 'ere,' said the woman, as Wally carried the case and shopping bag into the house.

'Oh, you're welcome, of course,' said Cassie Ford. Cassie was fourteen and a half, with dreamy brown eyes, a vivid imagination, the deceptive smile of an angel and a natural feminine aptitude for getting her own way. She had left St John's Church School at Easter, and was now waiting for a promised job as an apprentice in a florist's shop at Peckham. 'Me dad used to drive a royal taxi once,' she said informatively, at which point the cabbie, having pocketed fare and tip, drove off. Cassie then noticed the covered birdcage standing on the pavement. 'Excuse me, what's that?' she asked, liking to know about everything.

'That's Percy me parrot,' said the woman, who seemed willing to be neighbourly.

'Crikey, can I 'ave a look at 'im?' asked Cassie.

'I don't see why not, I've got a minute or so to spare,' said the woman. 'I'm Mrs Harper.'

'Oh, how'd you do, Mrs 'Arper, I'm Cassie Ford, I'm friends with Freddy Brown who lives down here.'

'There y'ar, then, Cassie, that's Percy,' said Mrs Harper, taking the hood off the cage, and revealing a bird of brilliant colours.

'What's up, Fred, what's up?' it asked.

'Crikey, it's a talkin' parrot,' said Cassie, and the street kids edged up to take a look. Cassie stooped to gaze into the bird's cocked eye.

'Hello, saucy,' said Percy.

'Oh, ain't he lovely?' said Cassie. 'I've got a cat, yer know, but he don't talk. Well, not out loud. D'you like cats, Mrs 'Arper? Only if you do, I wouldn't mind changin' Tabby for Percy, if you like.'

'Sorry, love, but I don't like, and I'd better take 'im in now. There, listen to that, me 'ubby's callin' me.' Mrs Harper picked up the cage and carried it to the gate.

Cassie, not as backward as the kids in coming

forward with information, said, 'Oh, did yer know it's 'aunted?'

'What, me birdcage?' Mrs Harper laughed.

'No, yer house,' said Cassie.

'Lor' lovaduck,' said Mrs Harper, 'then I'll 'ave to hide me head under the sheets at night, won't I?' She laughed. 'Toodle-oo, love.' Into the house she went, and the door closed.

Cassie skipped along to the Brown family's house, the skirt of her short frock swinging around her stockinged knees. She let herself in by pulling on the latchcord, and her voice travelled gaily through the passage and danced lightly into the kitchen.

'Coo-ee, Freddy, it's me.'

'That's done it,' said Freddy Brown, in his sixteenth year, ''ere comes me Saturday afternoon fate. Tell 'er I'm in hospital somewhere, Mum.'

Too late. Cassie was in. Freddy had made her his best mate four years ago, since when she'd become one of the family, good as. She'd also turned Freddy into a sounding-board for her imaginative flights of fantasy, while acquiring a girlish affection for him. She insisted last Christmas that he kiss her under the mistletoe. Freddy said mates don't kiss, they shake hands. Besides, you're only fourteen, he said. I'll ask my dad to wallop you if you don't kiss me, said Cassie. So he kissed her on her Cupid's bow, Cassie with her eyes shut tight. She was probably thinking of herself as the Sleeping Beauty. Then she asked him if he'd liked it. You tasted of oranges, said Freddy. Yes, I just ate the orange that was in me Christmas stocking, said Cassie, and asked if he liked chocolate. Well, I won't say I don't, because I do, said Freddy. All right, I'll eat a bit of me Christmas chocolate bar, said Cassie, then you can kiss me again. Me dad says I'm nice when I taste of chocolate. All right, said Freddy, let's have a taste of chocolate, then.

Dancing into the kitchen on the wings of new-found ambition, Cassie said, 'Oh, hello, Mrs Brown, how'd you do, Mr Brown.'

'We've missed yer lately, Cassie,' said Jim Brown with a grin, 'not havin' seen anything of yer since one o'clock.'

'Oh, don't you remember, I 'ad to go home and have me dinner,' said Cassie.

'My, so you did, but that was an hour and a half ago, love,' said Mrs Brown, the most amiable mum in the neighbourhood. 'That's a long time not seein' anything of you.'

'We nearly died of all the quiet,' said Freddy.

'Oh, did I ever tell you me Aunt Lettice nearly died once, when she was nearly run over by the Queen's six white 'orses that were out gallopin' in Windsor Park?' said Cassie. 'A lord saved 'er just in time, and Aunt Lettice would've lived happy ever after with him, only 'is lady wife wouldn't let 'er. Are you goin' out, Mrs Brown?'

'Yes, love, that's why I've got me hat on,' said Mrs Brown. 'Mr Brown's takin' me round the shops.'

'Oh, and me and Freddy's goin' down the market,' said Cassie.

'First I've heard of it,' said Freddy, who had a job at a scrap metal yard owned by Sammy Adams and managed by his dad.

'By the way,' said Cassie, 'there's people movin' into that empty house two doors away, the one that's 'aunted.'

'Cassie, it's not 'aunted,' said Freddy, 'it's only what the kids say.'

'Well, I'm only sayin' what they say,' said Cassie.

'I heard from the rent collector that some people from Hoxton were goin' to move in,' said Mrs Brown.

''Oxton's East End,' said Mr Brown, 'which ain't Walworth.'

'Oh, I'm sure they'll fit in all right,' said Mrs Brown in her usual placid way. 'Not ev'ryone in the East End is a tea leaf, I'm sure.'

'It's a lady and her 'usband and 'er brother-in-law,' said Cassie, 'and she's got a talkin' parrot.'

'Well, don't look at me,' said Freddy, 'it's not my fault.'

'I didn't say it was,' said Cassie.

'Well, you two talk about it, Freddy, while I leg it up the Walworth Road with yer mum,' said Mr Brown, and off he went with his plump and equable better half.

'Cassie, what d'you want to go down the market for?' asked Freddy.

'Well, me dad just give me sixpence for bein' an angel,' said Cassie, 'and as I already had tuppence-ha'penny, that makes I've got eightpence-ha'penny. How much money d'you 'ave?'

'Wait a tick,' said Freddy suspiciously, 'what d'you want to know for?'

'Well, could yer lend me fourpence, so's I'll 'ave a bob?' asked Cassie. 'Then we can go down the market and see if we can buy a parrot for that.'

'D'you mind if I say I ain't goin'?'

'Why not?' demanded Cassie.

'I don't want a parrot,' said Freddy, 'specially not a talkin' one. Me dad'll tell yer his sister, our Aunt Milly, 'ad one once and it talked them all out of 'ouse and 'ome.'

'Freddy, I'll keep ours for us,' said Cassie.

'Listen, Cassie,' said Freddy, 'you can only get pets

down the market on Sunday mornings, and anyway, I don't know you could buy a parrot for just a bob. An ordin'ry canary costs one-and-six at least.'

'We can try,' said Cassie, 'there might be a sale on, and I'll pay you back what you lend me on me birthday, when some relatives usually send me postal orders.'

'I ain't lending yer, Cassie, not for any parrot.'

'Yes, you are,' said Cassie.

'No, I ain't, and me mind's made up,' said Freddy.

'Well, you can soon unmake it,' said Cassie, practised in the art of helping him to do just that, 'specially as I've just remembered there's a pet shop at Camberwell Green.'

'Blow that for a lark,' said Freddy, who wondered if his life was his own whenever Cassie was about.

'We can ride there on your bike,' she said.

'I wasn't actually thinkin' of goin' to Camberwell Green, not this afternoon I wasn't.'

'Well, we can still go,' said Cassie, 'it's nice and sunny. Get one of your mum's cushions for me to ride on.' She always rode astride Freddy's carrier with a cushion under her bottom on the grounds that if she didn't it left her bottom with a pattern all over it. Freddy, of course, asked how could she know that, because she couldn't see it. I've never seen me own bottom in all me life, he said. Never mind that, said Cassie, I just know when me bottom's got a pattern on it. 'Come on, Freddy, let's go straight away.'

'I ain't goin' to any pet shop at Camberwell Green,' said Freddy.

'Yes, you are,' said Cassie.

'Not to buy a parrot, I'm not,' said Freddy.

'Yes, you are.'

'No, I ain't, and me mind's made up definite,' said Freddy.

He should have saved his breath, because five minutes later he was cycling along the Walworth Road towards Camberwell Green, with Cassie perched on the cushioned carrier.

Chapter Two

Camberwell Green on this skittish May afternoon was a moving picture of people and shoppers, a mixture of lively cockneys from the immediate area and lower-middle-class families from the upper reaches of Denmark Hill. The mixture was good-natured and as breezy as the weather. Saturday afternoons always represented a cheerful beginning to the weekends, when most people had some money in their purses or pockets and a visit to the pawnbrokers on a Monday morning was happily distant as far as hard-up cockneys were concerned.

There was a family in the pet shop, where birds chirruped in their cages, white rabbits nibbled in their hutches, and hamsters sniffed in search of goodies. Robert Adams, known to his family and friends as Boots, had his wife, son and daughter with him. Thirty-three, an ex-sergeant of the Royal West Kents, he had an excellent war record and distinguished looks. Tall and long-legged, he was in a grey suit. He invariably wore grey, either of a medium or charcoal shade, and very little about his appearance suggested he had been born a cockney and known years of hardship during the time he had lived with his mother, sister and brothers in the heart of Walworth. As for his speech, all its cockney elements had been drummed out of him while he was receiving a grammar school education. Those were the years when the street kids called him Lord Muck. Now he was the general manager of the thriving family firm, Adams Enterprises Ltd, founded by his brother Sammy, a businessman of drive and initiative.

His wife Emily, formerly the girl next door, was a thin woman of thirty-one her peaky looks offset by her wealth of dark auburn hair and her brilliant green eyes. Their son Tim was a lively eight-year-old, and their adopted daughter Rosie was a sparkling fifteen. With hair the colour of ripe corn, deep blue eyes, and extraordinarily enchanting looks, Rosie was a young girl who already had the air of a young lady. Life was a delight to her. She loved Emily, her adoptive mother, and she loved Tim. But it was Boots, her adoptive father, who meant most to her. Boots she adored. However, she had never made the mistake of being sugary, clinging or possessive. She had always been a girl of fun to him, a talkative and teasing daughter.

They were in the shop to buy a hamster for Tim, who had declared, in so many words, that his life wouldn't be worth living without one. I don't like the sound of that, said Boots. Nor me, said Emily. It's doleful, said Rosie. We'd better buy you one, said Boots. Crikey, I'll live for ever if you will, Dad, said Tim. All right, lovey, said Emily, let's go and make sure you live for ever.

They were inspecting several of the smooth-haired little rodents all sniffing around in a wooden hutch.

'They're doing a lot of twitchin',' said Tim, who had his dad's dark brown hair and grey eyes.

'That they are,' said the proprietor. 'If they weren't all of a twitch, they'd be goners. The more they twitch, the healthier they are. It's their noses, y'know, young 'un. They've all got well-bred noses, that lot. They come of well-bred parents. That's mum there, and that's her old man. And that's Toots, that's Tilly, that's Totty and that's Tipsy. Likes his drink, that one.'

'Would you like one that goes to a pub, Tim, or one that stays at home?' asked Boots.

'Eh?' said Tim.

'What a question,' smiled Emily. 'Typical of your dad, Timmy.'

'Oh, I don't know, Mummy,' said Rosie, fetching in a spring coat of royal blue and a round white hat. 'I mean, if Tim fancies the one called Tipsy, he'll want to know if he has to take it to a pub or not.'

'You and your dad, what a pair,' said Emily. 'Is your mind made up yet, Tim lovey?' Emily was still a recognizable cockney. 'I think you've got your eyes on Tipsy, 'aven't you?'

'I'd have to teach him not to drink beer,' said Tim.

'No beer,' smiled the proprietor, 'just strong water.'

'What's strong water, Dad?' asked Tim, enjoying the pleasure of lingering over his choice.

'The kind that comes out of a tap and stands up in a glass,' said Boots.

'Yes, that's the stuff,' said the proprietor.

'There you are, Tim,' said Rosie, 'it's the kind that comes out of our own tap.'

'I bet I could teach Tipsy to drink that,' said Tim, at which point Cassie and Freddy entered the shop.

'Well, look who's here,' said Emily. Cassie and Freddy were both well-known to the family. Freddy's elder sister, Susie, was married to Boots's youngest brother, Sammy, and Cassie's eldest sister, Annie, was married to Freddy's brother, Will.

'Hello there,' said Boots, whom Cassie regarded as an uncle. Freddy also saw him more as an uncle figure than a once removed brother-in-law.

'Oh, 'ello, Uncle Boots, how'd you do, Auntie Em'ly and ev'ryone, what a nice day, I'm sure,' said Cassie with enthusiasm.

'Oh, how'd you do, Cassie,' said Rosie, smiling, 'how'd you do, Freddy, you're together as usual.'

'Yes, I'm still Freddy's best mate,' said Cassie. Freddy rolled his eyes. 'We've come to see if there's any live talkin' parrots. Queen Mary's got hundreds, did yer know that, Uncle Boots? She keeps them in a conservat'ry at Windsor Castle.'

'Where they talk the roof off,' said Freddy. Rosie laughed. Everyone liked Cassie and Freddy.

'You're lookin' very pretty today, Cassie,' said Emily, who wouldn't have been as thin as she was if her appetite had been healthier.

'Yes, I'm pretty most days,' said Cassie, 'me dad says so. Doesn't Rosie look nice, Aunt Em'ly? Rosie, 'ave you come to buy a talkin' parrot too?'

'Well, no, Cassie, I haven't,' said Rosie, 'we've got Tim and Daddy. They do nearly all the talking in our house, and I don't think they'd like competition from a parrot. We're here to help Tim choose a hamster.'

Tim was offering a finger to the little creatures, all of which had had a sniff and had turned it down. The proprietor, having heard there was a possible customer for a parrot, brought a caged specimen to the counter.

'One talking parrot,' he said.

'Freddy, look,' said Cassie excitedly. It was a colourful specimen.

'What is it, a bob's-worth of parrot?' asked Freddy.

'Gertcher,' said the parrot.

'Crikey, it talked, I 'eard it,' said Cassie, and advanced on the bird. It cocked an eye at her.

'Gertcher,' it said again.

18

'Mind your manners,' said Rosie.

'It's a nice colour,' said Emily.

'Dad, what about my hamster?' asked Tim.

'I'm gone on Tipsy myself,' said Boots.

'Can I have it, then?'

'All yours, old chap,' said Boots. 'And a hutch as well,' he said to the proprietor. 'And a bottle of hamster beer until we get it teetotal.'

'Dad, the man said not beer,' protested Tim, 'he said strong water.'

'Daddy, you're a yell,' said Rosie.

'An amateur comic, more like,' said Emily.

'Gertcher,' said the parrot.

'Freddy, it really talks,' said Cassie.

'Yes, but if that's all it can say, ask if it can read and write,' said Freddy.

'Oh, can it, mister?' asked Cassie of the proprietor.

'Not yet,' he said.

'I hope it's not backward,' said Rosie.

'Bright as a button,' said the proprietor, transferring Tipsy to a new hutch.

'I just want one that talks,' said Cassie. 'Me and Freddy can teach it to say poetry, like *The Pied Piper*.'

'Not if I can 'elp it,' said Freddy.

'Mister, how much is it?' asked Cassie.

'It's a five-bob bird, believe me,' said the proprietor, 'but I'll sell it to you for three-and-six.'

'Crikey, three-and-six?' breathed Cassie in shock. 'Freddy, is 'e serious?'

'Are you serious, mister?' asked Freddy, and Boots and Emily exchanged smiles.

'Well, I wouldn't call three-and-six serious,' said the proprietor, 'I'd call it a bargain, and I can find you a cage for four bob, fully furnished.'

'Freddy, 'e's makin' me feel faint,' said Cassie.

'Mister, me and Freddy's only lookin' for a shilling one.'

'Sell you six packets of birdseed for that,' said the proprietor.

'Crikey, I bet I could buy six packets from Queen Mary for a penny if I went to Windsor Castle,' said Cassie. 'Well, she knows me dad. Well, I think she does, I think they met once. Mister, I suppose you don't 'ave a talkin' parrot for just a shilling, do you?'

'Gertcher,' said the three-and-sixpenny bird.

'Sorry, little lady,' said the proprietor.

'Oh, all right,' said Cassie resignedly, 'me and Freddy'll just 'ave to save up for an expensive one.'

'I'm not goin' to,' said Freddy, 'but I've got a feelin' I will.'

Boots, settling for the hamster and the hutch, remembered a murder trial at which he, Freddy and Cassie had all been witnesses. Cassie had faced up to the ordeal like a young trouper.

'I think it's time I treated you, Cassie,' he said.

'Oh, you treated me once before, Uncle Boots, with a box of choc'lates,' said Cassie. 'It was after that trial at the Old Bailey. You treated Freddy as well.'

'That was ages ago,' said Boots. 'I think a new treat's overdue, don't you, Em?'

'Well overdue,' said Emily.

'Right,' said Boots, 'one talking parrot and a cage, Cassie, how will that do?'

Cassie nearly fell over in her bliss, but found enough excited breath to inform Boots he'd go to heaven one day, but not till he'd lived happy ever after with his family for a hundred years. I'll have whiskers down to my knees, said Boots. And a bathchair, said Rosie. And no teeth, said Emily. And a bald head, said Tim. Oh, no, said Cassie, you'll still look nice,

Uncle Boots, and with lots of teeth, and I'll come and look after you sometimes.

Emily laughed. Rosie smiled. She could have said that if Boots needed anyone to look after him when he was old, it was going to be herself. She was attending West Square Girls School now, and sixth-formers from the adjacent boys' school were really giving her the eye now that she was over fifteen. She wasn't in the least interested in any of them. Her family filled her life.

'Right,' said Boots to the proprietor, 'put Gertcher in a new cage, the fully-furnished four-bob one.'

'Oh, couldn't I call it Gertie?' asked Cassie. 'Is it a girl, mister?'

'Leave off,' said the parrot.

'Freddy, did you 'ear that, it talked some more,' said Cassie in delight.

'I think it's just told you it's not a girl,' said Freddy.

'Oh, I don't mind, I quite like boys, me cat's a boy,' said Cassie.

'I wish you 'adn't said that,' remarked Freddy.

'Why?' asked Rosie.

'Her cat's barmy,' said Freddy.

Cassie took no notice of that. She was watching the proprietor transferring the parrot to a new posh-looking cage that had a perch, a seed tray and a water well. Apart from trying to nip the man's finger and having a bit of a go at the perch, the bird accepted its move without turning the shop upside-down. Once settled on the perch, it looked silently around, as if trying to decide if it had anything worthwhile to say. Apparently not, for it said nothing.

To help Cassie in her guardianship, the proprietor gave her some helpful tips plus a list of printed instructions on how to keep the bird happy and make

21

it love her in four quick lessons. Cassie assured him she was easy to love, her dad said so. And I can say so meself, she said. And so can Freddy, can't you, Freddy?

'I ain't listenin' at this exact minute,' said Freddy.

The purchase completed, including a cover for the cage, Cassie delivered kisses of thanks all round, and they all left the shop, Cassie carrying the cage. With the hood on, the parrot had gone quiet, thinking it was bedtime. Freddy took hold of his bike, which he'd left propped against the shop front, and informed his mate she'd have to balance the cage on her head for the ride home. Cassie at once set her mind to finding an alternative.

'Well, here you are at last, we thought you must be buyin' up the shop for Tim,' said a new arrival. It was Boots's mother, Mrs Maisie Finch, known to her family as Chinese Lady. Mr Edwin Finch, her second husband, was with her. He was a worldly and well-travelled man of fifty-six, and an agent for the British Government. He was desk-bound at present, working on codes and cyphers. Chinese Lady was a cockney woman, fifty-three, and like most of her kind she saw everything in clear black and white, being dismissive of all shades of grey. She had an upright walk, a resilient character, a matriarchal attitude towards her sons and daughter, and a wifely respect for her husband, who in turn regarded her as an admirably incurable Victorian, and altogether a woman he cared for.

'Look who found us in the shop, Mum,' said Emily.

'Bless us,' said Chinese Lady, 'it's Cassie and Freddy.'

'Oh, how'd you do, Mrs Finch,' said Cassie, 'how'd you do, Mr Finch.'

'A pleasure, Cassie,' smiled Mr Finch, who had rubbed elbows with Walworth's cockneys during his years as a lodger with Chinese Lady, and had come to admire their robust nature and the cheerful way they fought hardship.

'Tim's got his hamster, I see,' said Chinese Lady, 'and what've you got, Cassie?'

'It's a talkin' parrot; Uncle Boots treated me.' Cassie was a little breathless in her excitement of ownership. 'Well, Freddy and me couldn't afford it ourselves, so Uncle Boots paid. It wasn't just because I'm pretty. Well, I don't think it was, more because 'e's nice, I think, and I told 'im I hope he lives happy ever after with 'is fam'ly and keeps all 'is own teeth.'

'Don't mind Cassie, Mrs Finch,' said Freddy, 'she likes goin' on a bit. It's turnin' me a bit grey, but me mum thinks I'll live.'

'Well, we don't want to lose you, Freddy,' said Chinese Lady, 'and nor do we want to stand about on the pavement when we're supposed to be in Lyons havin' a pot of tea and some buttered buns. Would you and Cassie like to come with us?'

'Oh, yes, please,' said Cassie. 'Can I bring me parrot?'

'Yes, come on, bring it,' said Rosie.

'Cassie, you can leave it with the shopkeeper,' said Freddy.

'It might prefer Lyons and a buttered bun,' said Boots.

'Oh, d'you think so?' asked Cassie.

'Let's give him a go, shall we?' said Boots, and off they all went, although Chinese Lady informed Mr Finch that it was just like Boots to think of having a parrot sit at the table with them. I expect he'll want it to have a cup of tea with us, as well as peck at a bun, she said. Well, Maisie, said Mr Finch, human behaviour being what it is, we have to allow there's a first time for everything. Chinese Lady said she'd never brought Boots up to make a spectacle of himself in a Lyons teashop. Emily, hearing that, laughed.

'Oh, he caught this sort of complaint when he was young, Mum,' she said, 'and nobody's been able to cure him.'

'More's the pity, then,' said Chinese Lady.

Rosie, walking with Boots, whispered, 'Daddy, you're fun, and I don't want anyone to cure you.'

'Too late now, poppet, in any case,' said Boots.

'Oh, good,' said Rosie.

The parrot, when Cassie removed the hood in Lyons, didn't seem to think much of the place or the company. Cassie sat with the cage on her lap, encouraging the bird to say something. It cocked a supercilious eye at her.

'Come on, Cecil,' she said, 'would you like a bit of me bun when it comes?'

'You're calling him Cecil?' said Rosie.

'Yes, I like Cecil.'

'Cassie, nobody in Walworth calls anyone Cecil,' said Freddy.

'Nor my hamster,' said Tim, the hutch on the floor beside his chair.

'Cassie, what made you want a parrot?' asked Emily.

'There's a lady that's moved into the empty house near Freddy's,' said Cassie. 'She's got a parrot, and an 'usband and brother-in-law.'

'Oh, that house has been taken now, has it?' said Emily. Most of the family knew its history.

'Yes, and it's 'aunted, yer know,' said Cassie.

'Cassie, that's only what the kids say,' said Freddy.

'Oh, all right,' said Cassie blithely. 'Cecil, you 'aven't told us if you'd like a bit of me bun.'

Cecil emitted what sounded very much like a burp.

'What was that for?' asked Tim.

'Indigestion,' said Boots, 'and that's before he's even seen a bun.'

Mr Finch cast an eye about in search of a Nippy. The teashop was fairly full, all Nippies busy. Chinese Lady asked Freddy what his new neighbours were like. Freddy said they'd come from the East End.

'H'm,' said Chinese Lady, who considered East End people not as respectable as they could have been.

Up came a Nippy with a pencil and pad. Mr Finch smiled at her.

'Can I take your order, sir?' she asked.

'Push off,' said Cecil.

And he said the same thing to Cassie's family when she finally got him home.

Chapter Three

'Oh, no you don't, get off!' cried Miss Tilly Thomas, an unmarried young woman of twenty-six mindful, at this moment, of her virginity. And since she had recently seen a revival of the bloodcurdling Victorian melodrama, *Maria Martin And The Red Barn*, at the Elephant and Castle Theatre, she chose her next words in the manner of a Victorian virgin. 'Unhand me, d'you 'ear, you villain?'

'Come on, what's a kiss and a bit of slap-and-tickle, eh, me beauty?' said the villain of the moment, the man who rented the house in which she lodged in Brandon Street, Walworth. Burly bachelor George Rice reckoned he was entitled to a bit of what he fancied with his female lodger. After all, hadn't he let her have her two rooms cheap, just six bob a week? And treating her to some lovey-dovey was doing her a favour. She wasn't getting any from anyone else, stuck as she was at her sewing-machine at all hours, making clothes for her customers. What a figure, what a bosom, a real bit of all right she was. With his hands on her shoulders, he pulled her close. He bellowed then, for he received a punch in his paunch from her right knee. 'Oh, yer bleedin' vixen!' he gasped, letting go of her shoulders to clasp his wounded *avoirdupois*.

'Serve yer right,' said Tilly, 'I'm a – oh, yer swine!'

He'd grabbed her again.

'I'll learn yer,' he growled, 'and then treat yer to a bit of what I fancy. Come 'ere.' He tightened his hold. Tilly, endowed with an abundant figure and no lack of vigour, kicked his shin with the pointed toe of her shoe. The pain crucified his leg for a suffering moment and he let go again, hissing with torment. 'I'll 'ave yer for that, I bleedin' will,' he gasped. Tilly picked a vase off her bedroom mantelpiece, and hit him with it as he came at her once more. It broke and shattered as it connected with his hard head. The blow staggered him and floored him. He rolled over, then sat up and clutched his bruised head. 'Sod yer,' he said in mangled fashion, 'that's yer lot, that is, yer fat ungrateful bitch.'

'Fat? 'Ow dare you, you 'orrible ape!' Tilly was furious at being called fat, when she simply had a fine, fulsome figure which she carried off well at her height of five-feet-eight. 'It's not your lot, mister, I tell you that. No, I ain't finished with you, I'm goin' out now to find a copper. I'll give you assault me proud integrity.'

'Copper my bleedin' eye,' growled George Rice, getting totteringly to his feet, 'you just done me grievous bodily 'arm, you 'ave, and I could get yer six months for it. Ruddy 'ell, there's blood as well.'

'Think yerself lucky I didn't knock yer 'orrible 'ead right off,' said Tilly ferociously.

'Yer finished 'ere. Finished. Out yer go. You got tomorrer to pack, then out yer go first thing Monday, bag an' baggage. Got it?'

'I wouldn't stay 'ere, not if you paid me a fortune,' said Tilly, 'so put that in your pipe and smoke it. Now get out of me bedroom, or I'll do you real injury with me poker.'

Growling, scowling, but wary of the poker, George

Rice took himself and his bleeding head down to his kitchen. Tilly closed the door, put the poker back and sat down on the edge of her bed. She was shocked, but not downhearted. She had all the resilience of a born cockney. She'd left the family home in Peckham six months ago, mainly because she couldn't get on with her step-mother. Her mum had died four years ago, and Tilly had stayed with her widower dad, her two sisters being married, while she herself was undergoing a prolonged courtship by Frank Golightly, a decent enough bloke who was always planning a wedding date without ever actually fixing it. She worked for a dressmaker, but if it hadn't been for her dad, who needed someone about the house, she'd have left her job and forced Frank to fix a date. Then her dad was silly enough at the age of fifty-one to fall for a woman of thirty, and a bit of a tart in Tilly's eyes. Dad had a fairly secure job with the council's parks department, and that tart of a woman saw him as some kind of insurance, of course. Dad married her only a month after meeting her, and Tilly, high-spirited, was at loggerheads with her right from the start. To begin with, she was always showing her legs, especially if any of Dad's men friends were present, or even Frank for that matter. Secondly, she soon made Tilly feel surplus to requirements, and it wasn't long before Tilly told Frank she was leaving home, and that they might as well take the plunge and get married. Frank said he wasn't quite set up for that, not quite yet. Probably in another six months, he said. Blow that, said Tilly, it's now or never. We'll see, said Frank, but in any case you can't leave home, he said, it'll make your step-mother think you don't like her. I don't, said Tilly. She's a nice woman, said Frank. All right if you like them tarty, said Tilly. Don't say things like that, said Frank, it ain't nice, nor kind. You've got to stay, he said. Excuse me, said Tilly, but is that an order? Well, you're me fiancée, said Frank, and I naturally expect you to observe me feelings and wishes. That got Tilly's goat. I was your fiancée until a minute ago, I ain't now, and here's your ring back, which you can pop down me step-mother's permanent cleavage and tickle her bumps with it, she said. You can follow it with your eyeballs, she said, seeing they're nearly always popping out.

Frank thought she was joking and he forgave her for her unkind wordage. Tilly wasn't joking, and nor was she in need of being forgiven. She left home a week later, moving to Walworth, having found two upstairs rooms in the house rented by George Rice in Brandon Street. She also left her job and started up on her own with the aid of a sewing-machine, a dummy and a lot of natural talent. She had to work hard because Walworth customers never had too much money to spare for new clothes, but she got by, and in any case hard work had never discouraged her. She was a strong young woman.

George Rice had been breezy, pleasant and friendly for the first few months. Then he began to get ideas. Tilly recognized the symptoms – those of a man who thought he had to be God's gift to a woman living on her own. He'd made several passes at her, all of which she rebuffed. Tonight, just as she was about to get undressed for bed, he'd invaded the room. What an 'orrible villain. Tod Slaughter could have taken him off all right. Tod Slaughter had played the part of the fiendish squire, William Corder, in that Victorian melodrama.

Well, George Rice had finished up with a cracked head, and she had finished up resolved to depart his door and never return. She'd look in the newsagent's window tomorrow and see who had rooms to let.

Cassie spent most of Sunday morning trying to extend her parrot's vocabulary, but all it said in that time was a terse 'Gertcher'. She tried again after dinner, with the cage on the kitchen table. Her dad, Harold Ford, known as the Gaffer, sat watching her, a grin on his face. For the umpteenth time she begged Cecil to say something. Cecil simply looked supercilious. The Gaffer, a widower, suggested she'd got herself a dud parrot.

'No, I 'aven't, Dad, he's just not used to us yet.'

'What made yer call 'im Cecil?'

'Well, there was a Lord Cecil once, wasn't there?'

'It's familiar, Cassie, familiar, I'll say that much. Try callin' 'im that, and see if he answers up.'

'Oh, yes,' said Cassie. 'Here, Lord Cecil, say 'ello, Your Ladyship.'

Lord Cecil tucked his beak into his plumage and fiddled about.

'He don't seem to be much of a lord,' said the Gaffer.

Cassie frowned. Her eighteen-year-old sister Nellie was entertaining her young man in the parlour. Her sixteen-year-old brother Charlie, along with some of his mates, was making life burdensome for everyone in King and Queen Street. Cassie suddenly realized she hadn't seen anything of Freddy all day. A parrot was all right, but it wasn't the same as Freddy. Crikey, he might be giving some other girl a ride on his bike this minute, he might even be up the park with her, when he could be helping to get Cecil talking.

Putting the cover on, she picked up the cage and darted from the kitchen.

'Where you off to, Cassie?' called the Gaffer.

'Round to see Freddy,' said Cassie from outside the door.

'Well, you be back by teatime, pet.'

'All right, Dad. Can I bring Freddy to tea?'

'Course you can. And yer parrot as well.'

Cassie scampered through the passage and out of the house, carrying the cage.

'What yer got there, Cassie?' bawled one of several street kids.

'Me dad's dustbin!'

'You're daft, you are, Cassie Ford!'

Cassie, turning at the corner of the street, whisked out of sight of the kids. When she reached Caulfield Place, she made straight for Freddy's house. Pulling the latchcord, she let herself in.

'Freddy, you home?' she called.

'No, not now,' called Freddy, 'I'm out.'

'Come on, Cassie, come through,' called Sally, Freddy's sister, 'don't take any notice of young Clever Clogs.'

Cassie was at the kitchen door by then, anyway. In she went, with the cage. Sally, a typically lively cockney girl when she wasn't putting on the style as a shop assistant, had a friend with her, Mavis Richards from Cotham Street. Both girls were in their Sunday best, ready to go out.

'Oh, 'ello, Sally, how'd you do, Mavis, don't you both look posh?' said Cassie, rarely less than a blithe young spirit, even when her eyes were at their dreamiest. 'Freddy, where you been all day?'

'Well,' said Freddy, 'I was in bed till quarter-past eight, then I got up and 'ad a wash, then I got dressed and 'ad me breakfast, then I 'elped with the washin'-up, then I cleaned me bike – 'old on, is that that parrot you've brought?'

'Yes, it's Cecil, 'e wanted to come,' said Cassie.

'I suppose he asked to, did 'e?' said Freddy.

'Well, 'e didn't exactly ask,' said Cassie, ''e just looked as if 'e wanted to.'

'Show, Cassie, show,' said Sally, so Cassie placed the cage on the table and took the hood off. Cecil perked up at the sudden onset of light and did a cheeky one-step on his perch. His colourful plumage drew admiring cries from Sally and Mavis.

'Oh, ain't he pretty?' said Mavis.

'Gertcher,' said Cecil.

'Crikey, he talks,' said Sally.

'Yes, but 'e hasn't said a lot today, not a tremendous lot,' said Cassie, 'so I've come to let Freddy 'elp me with 'is talkin'.'

'Cassie, I ain't keen on spendin' me Sunday afternoon talkin' to a parrot,' said Freddy.

'Come on, Cecil,' said Sally, clicking her fingers, 'say something else, like who's a pretty boy, then.'

'Gertcher,' said Cecil.

'Oh, stuck-up, are we?' said Sally.

'I think 'e's got royal blood,' said Cassie, 'I think he'd say a lot to the King and Queen if me and Freddy took 'im to Buckingham Palace.'

'Can't he say some of it 'ere?' asked Mavis.

'He better 'ad,' said Freddy, 'because I'm not takin' him to Buckingham Palace, and that's a fact.'

'We can take 'im on the bus,' said Cassie. 'Sally, d'you know if the King and Queen's in today?'

'Well, no, I don't,' said Sally, 'they don't always let me know about what they're doin'.'

Mavis giggled.

'Cassie, I ain't goin' on any bus with that parrot,' said Freddy.

'I wonder if that lady that's moved into the 'aunted

32

house takes 'er parrot on the bus or for a walk?' mused Cassie.

'It might surprise you,' said Freddy, 'but lots of people don't take their parrots for a walk or a bus ride. And I've told yer, that house ain't 'aunted, it's only what the kids say.'

'Still, I wouldn't live in it meself,' said Mavis. 'What's yer parrot doin' now, Cassie?'

'Just a shuffle,' said Freddy.

'Well, that won't get 'im very far,' said Sally. 'Come on, Mavis, let's go now.'

'Where you goin'?' asked Cassie, who never liked to be in an uninformed state.

'Round to Mavis's,' said Sally.

'What's at Mavis's?' asked Cassie.

'Mavis's brother,' grinned Freddy.

'You said it, I didn't.' Sally smiled and off she went with Mavis.

'Freddy, where's yer mum and dad?' asked Cassie.

'In the parlour, 'aving a quiet life,' said Freddy.

'All right, I don't mind,' said Cassie graciously. 'You and me can stay in the kitchen and teach Cecil to talk a bit more, then you can come 'ome and 'ave tea with us.'

'Cassie, I ain't sittin' in here with the parrot,' said Freddy.

'Yes, you are, you're a nice boy really,' said Cassie. 'Come on, you can sit next to me and we'll teach Cecil together. Let's first try and make 'im say – Freddy? Oh, where's that blessed boy gone?'

The blessed boy was sneaking out through the front door. Hearing him, Cassie gave a little yell and went after him. She caught him as he reached Browning Street. Freddy, however, was adamant that he wasn't going to talk to a daft parrot all afternoon. But five minutes later, of course, he was sitting with her at the kitchen table, and Cecil was giving both of them the once-over out of a beady eye. Freddy, not a bad loser, grinned at the bird.

'Watcher, mate,' said Cecil.

Cassie gave a girlish yelp of delight, then frowned a little. Well, it sounded as if Lord Cecil was more of a cockney parrot than a royal one.

Crack! Mrs Lizzy Somers, thirty-one years old, the wife of Ned Somers and the mother of two girls and two boys, hit a blinder with the willow cricket bat off the bowling of her eldest brother, Boots. The red leather ball soared over his head and landed in the vegetable bed far up the garden and well beyond the long lawn.

'What happened?' asked Boots.

'Yes, who did that?' asked Rosie.

'Me,' said Lizzy. Well, she'd played street cricket in Walworth when a schoolgirl, proving a natural terror with a bat, even if she'd never been able to bowl for toffee.

'A six, Mum, you 'it a six!' yelled her eldest son, nine-year-old Bobby.

'Sacre bleu,' said Boots, showing off his French.

'Don't mention it,' said Lizzy. She wasn't dressed for cricket, she was dressed in fine printed cotton, colourful and summery, but once she had a cricket bat in her hands she gaily reverted to tomboyish thumping, whacking and smiting. She and Ned and their family had been invited to tea at her mother and stepfather's large house in Red Post Hill, off the south end of Denmark Hill, and Boots had said come early for some garden cricket. Lizzy, Ned, thirteen-year-old Annabelle and Bobby were all playing, along with

34

Boots and family, and Miss Polly Simms. Lizzy's younger children, seven-year-old Emma and five-year-old Edward, were sitting at the garden table with Chinese Lady, playing snakes-and-ladders with her. 'Come on, bowl up,' said Lizzy.

'Do it again, Mum, smash another six,' said Bobby.

'Watch your legs, Mum, I think Uncle Boots's blood is up,' said Annabelle.

'Some hopes he's got of hittin' my legs or my wicket,' said Lizzy.

Boots did a lazy-looking run, deceptively lazy, for when he delivered the ball it whizzed through the air and fizzed off the turf. Lizzy did a little scream of outrage and swung her bat vainly at the ball. It broke the stumps.

'Oh, dear, Auntie Lizzy, what a shame,' said Rosie, 'I think you're out.'

'Not likely,' said Lizzy, chestnut hair gleaming in the sunshine, brown eyes defiant and challenging. 'I wasn't ready.'

'Who said that?' asked Ned.

'I did,' said Lizzy. Boots stood with a grin on his face.

'But, Auntie Lizzy,' said Tim, 'your stumps are all knocked over.'

'Lizzy, you're out,' said Polly, long-standing family friend.

'I'm afraid so,' smiled Mr Finch.

'Not likely,' said Lizzy again, 'I wasn't ready for that sneaky cannonball. It was supposed to be a slow one. Stand the stumps up again, Tim.'

From the garden table, Emma called, 'The phone's ringing.'

'I'll go,' said Mr Finch, and entered the house through the kitchen. The telephone in the hall was ringing its demanding note. He answered it. 'Hello?'

'I wish to speak to Mr Finch,' said a man's voice.

'You're speaking to him.'

'Good. You are Mr Edwin Finch?'

'Yes.'

'Formerly Herr Paul Strasser of Frankfurt-on-the-Maine in Germany?'

Mr Finch stiffened, then said quietly, 'That's an odd question. I think you have the wrong man.'

'Ah, so sorry. Goodbye.' The line went dead, but Mr Finch hung on for a few seconds before replacing the phone. He was too experienced an agent not to accept that espionage held its surprises, alarms and dangers for all who engaged in it. Someone knew he had once been a German agent, someone he was certain did not work for the British Government. Well, what would come next? Another phone call, probably, and then a suggestion relating to blackmail? He wondered about that, but had a smile on his face as he returned to the garden.

'Who was it?' asked Chinese Lady.

'A colleague,' said Mr Finch.

'On a Sunday?' said Chinese Lady, who had always thought he worked for the Foreign Office in a kind of diplomatic capacity.

'Some colleagues can't leave work alone, Maisie, not even on a Sunday,' said Mr Finch. 'What's going on out here now?'

'Bedlam,' said Chinese Lady.

Boots had foxed Lizzy so diabolically with his bowling that she'd knocked the wicket over. By falling on it. Now she was chasing Boots all over the garden, trying to hit him with the bat. But that kind of thing was all part of the game when the Somers family were playing Boots and his family at garden cricket.

36

Rosie, shrieking with laughter, thought how spiffing it was to be alive. Mr Finch thought how fortunate he was to have acquired a ready-made family with so much zest for life. Odd phone calls were by the way.

Cassie was getting just a little fed-up with Lord Cecil or just plain awkward Cecil. She complained to Freddy that the blessed bird hadn't spoken a word since saying hello to him. Freddy remarked it hadn't been hello, it had been watcher, mate. Yes, fancy a royal parrot saying that, said Cassie with a frown. And then nothing else in over an hour, she said. Freddy said she'd got to face up to the fact that Lord Cecil wasn't much of a talker. Cassie had a thought. I know, let's take Cecil along to that lady that's got a parrot of her own, she said, I bet she'd know how to get Cecil to talk lots. Freddy said they couldn't go knocking on her door on a Sunday afternoon.

'Course we can,' said Cassie, 'it's what doors are for, to be knocked on.' There was something in that. Well, there was as far as Walworth front doors were concerned. Walworth front doors were neighbourly, they liked being knocked on, except by rent collectors or tallymen. 'Come on, Freddy – oh, 'ave you met the lady yet, Mrs 'Arper?'

'I've seen 'er, I ain't exactly met 'er,' said Freddy. 'Me mum spoke to her this mornin', just to be neighbourly, and she said she was unexpected polite for someone from the East End, considerin' all the tea leafs that 'ang about there. Mind, Mum didn't mean she looked like a tea leaf 'erself.'

'Well, then, you ought to go and say 'ello, Freddy, it's only what you should do with new neighbours,' said Cassie. 'I'll come with you, and Cecil as well. You'd best brush your hair first, before you put your cap on.'

Freddy stood his ground as far as his hair was concerned, but he did put his cap on. It wasn't much use trying to tell Cassie he wasn't going, it would only help to turn him grey a bit quicker. Along they went to the house in question, two doors away, with Cassie carrying the caged parrot. It was Cassie who knocked on the door. It had an old latchcord, but she thought she'd better not use it.

Mrs Harper opened the door. She was in quite a nice blouse and skirt, a woman in her late twenties with fair shingled hair. She wasn't bad-looking, it was her rather florid complexion that was slightly spoiling.

'Yes?' she said, but not unkindly.

'Oh, how'd you do, Mrs 'Arper,' said Cassie. 'This is me friend, Freddy Brown, 'e lives at number four, and wants to say 'ello to you. Go on, Freddy.'

'Afternoon, Mrs 'Arper,' said Freddy.

'Afternoon,' said Mrs Harper.

'We thought we'd come and tell you I've got me own parrot now,' said Cassie.

'So you 'ave,' said Mrs Harper, with a bit of a smile.

'Yes, it's Cecil,' said Cassie. 'He's a talkin' parrot, but 'e's hardly talked at all today.'

'Well, girlie, I don't go much on parrots that don't talk,' said Mrs Harper. 'Percy keeps me company.'

'I told Freddy you called 'im Percy,' said Cassie.

'That's 'is name all right.'

'D'you think you could let Percy meet Cecil?' asked Cassie. 'That's if you're not terrible busy and Mr 'Arper wouldn't mind.'

'Me 'usband and 'is brother 'appen to be out,' said Mrs Harper, 'so all right, you can come in for a bit. Mind, I don't entertain much on account of me 'eadaches, which catch me something chronic at times.'

'Oh, 'ave yer got one now?' asked Cassie.

'No, I've been all right today, so you can come through, you don't seem the kind to kick up a racket. What did yer say yer names was?'

'I'm Cassie and he's Freddy. We're mates.'

'All right, come in.'

They stepped in, Mrs Harper closed the door and they followed her through the passage into the kitchen. It was sparsely furnished with a table, four chairs, a dresser and a built-in larder. The range wasn't alight, but there was a gas oven in the scullery. On the dresser stood a birdcage, in which a parrot was perched. It cocked an eye at the boy and girl.

'What's up, Fred, what's up?' it said.

'There, that's Percy,' said Mrs Harper.

'Lovaduck,' breathed Cassie, 'did you hear 'im talk to us, Freddy?'

'Made me Sunday afternoon, that did,' said Freddy, who felt he'd be a lot better off taking a ride on his bike. Cassie placed her birdcage on the table, and Mrs Harper brought Percy from the dresser to say hello to Cecil.

'Let's 'ope the feathers don't fly,' she said.

The birds, actually, seemed quite uninterested in each other. Percy, however, cocked a flirtatious eye at Cassie.

'Hello, sailor,' he said.

'Crikey, ain't he quick to say something?' said Cassie.

'Gertcher,' said Cecil.

'Well, listen to that, they're both talkin',' said Cassie. 'Freddy told me they would if they met, Mrs 'Arper.'

'I don't recollect that,' said Freddy.

'Mind, I thought of it first,' said Cassie. 'Cecil, ask Percy what 'is name is.'

Cecil wasn't having any of that sociable stuff. Percy might have been a canary for all he seemed to care. He preened his feathers in a mood of indifference, then suddenly lifted his beak and said, 'Push off.'

'There, did you 'ear that, Mrs 'Arper?' said Cassie triumphantly.

'He's a parrot all right,' said Mrs Harper, and lit herself a fag.

Percy hopped about and Cecil chewed his plumage again.

'Cassie, he's doin' a lot of that,' said Freddy. 'It looks like he's got fleas.'

'Parrots don't 'ave fleas, specially not Cecil,' said Cassie. 'Cecil's a royal parrot, yer know, Mrs 'Arper, it's best to call 'im Lord Cecil.'

'I'll remember that if I meet 'im in the street,' said Mrs Harper, and spread a smile over the boy and girl, much as if she liked their company.

'What's up, Fred, what's up?' asked Percy.

'Nothing's up, yer daft bird, so 'old yer noise,' said Mrs Harper.

'Have Mr 'Arper and 'is brother gone up the park?' asked Cassie, thinking there wasn't much else to go to on a Sunday afternoon, except the parlour. That's if you were courting, like her sister Nellie was.

'No, they've both gone out, ducks,' said Mrs Harper.

'Well, if me and Freddy and Cecil could stay a bit, Cecil might do a lot of talkin' with Percy,' said Cassie hopefully.

'Gertcher,' said Cecil.

'Hello, sailor,' said Percy.

'There, ain't they gettin' on fine together?' said Cassie.

'I think I'll go for a ride on me bike,' said Freddy, at which Cassie stood on his foot.

'Much as yer welcome to stay,' said Mrs Harper, issuing fag smoke, 'I've got things to do before me old man and 'is brother get back.'

'Oh, all right,' said Cassie. 'Freddy's thinkin' of takin' me and Cecil up to Buckingham Palace on a bus, anyway.'

'No, I ain't,' said Freddy.

'We might bring Cecil and come and knock again, Mrs 'Arper,' said Cassie.

'Ruddy 'ell,' said Cecil.

'Eh?' said Freddy, and Cassie blushed for her parrot and his royal lineage.

'Oh, I 'ope you'll excuse 'im, Mrs 'Arper,' she said, 'it must be all the excitement. Well, me and Freddy best say goodbye now, and thanks ever so much for lettin' Cecil meet Percy.'

Percy said something unintelligible then, and Mrs Harper ushered the boy and girl out.

'It was nice meetin' yer both,' she said, opening the front door for them, 'and if you knock again and I don't 'ave one of me chronic 'eads, you can come in and 'ave another talk with Percy. Toodle-oo, duckies.'

The door closed.

'What did Percy say when we said goodbye, Freddy?' asked Cassie, birdcage cuddled to her chest.

'Search me,' said Freddy. 'Well, it sounded something like, "I'll hit yer".'

'Freddy, parrots don't hit people, so why should it say that?'

'I hope you won't mind,' said Freddy, 'but I don't 'ave the answer to that. Mind you, mate, it could've been an East End swear word. My dad says they've got swear words in places like Hoxton and Shoreditch that no-one else 'as ever heard of.'

'Freddy, don't call me mate, you daft boy,' said

41

Cassie. 'Anyway, Mrs 'Arper didn't swear. She was quite nice really, and you 'ave to admit Percy helped Cecil to do some talkin'. Shall we get a bus to Buckingham Palace now? Then we can – Freddy, where you goin'?'

'Anywhere except to Buckingham Palace with a potty parrot,' said Freddy, running.

Cassie rushed after him.

Cecil, shaken about in his cage, took umbrage.

'Ruddy 'ell,' he said.

Chapter Four

Knock, knock.

'Who the hell's that?' said Dan Rogers of Caulfield Place. It was Monday morning and coming up to eight-thirty. He had his job to go to any moment and was at his wits' end in how he was going to manage it. 'Stay there and don't break anything,' he said to Bubbles, nearly four, and Penny-Farving, nearly five. They were creating minor havoc over their breakfast, as usual. He answered the front door and found himself looking at a young woman in a light-brown costume and a round brimmed hat. The costume jacket shaped a very full bosom. On the doorstep stood two large suitcases.

'Oh, 'ello and good mornin',' said Miss Tilly Thomas. 'You Mister Rogers that's got a notice in the newsagent's window about rooms to let?'

'That's me,' said Dan, thirty-one, broad-shouldered and rugged. 'You after rentin' them?'

'If they suit me,' said Tilly, looking him over to see if an aptitude for villainy was detectable. 'Sorry if I've called a bit early—'

'Think nothing of it. Come in. It's the upstairs back and middle, and they'll suit you a treat. Here.' Dan hauled the suitcases in himself and placed them in the passage. 'I need a friendly face around. Seven-and-six a week, that all right? Thought it would be. Come through and meet the kids, and be a great help. The girl who usually comes in to keep an eye on them 'as fractured her ankle. 'Ighly inconvenient, believe me. Come on, come through.'

'Excuse me, I don't like bein' rushed,' said Tilly.

'Nor me, but I'm bein' rushed this mornin',' said Dan, and breezed his way to the kitchen with her, she just a little suspicious of all this quickfire stuff. At the kitchen table sat two little girls, both fair, both angelic-looking and both in long frocks. One was gurgling up warm milk from a china mug, the other was eating toast and marmalade. 'Well, there they are,' said Dan, 'that's Bubbles and that's Penny-Farvin'. Might I enquire your own name?'

'I'm Miss Thomas—'

'Violet Thomas?'

'No, Tilly. Look, if you don't mind—'

'There's no problem,' said Dan, glancing at the mantelpiece clock. 'The rooms are yours. Glad to 'ave you. I'll see you when I get back from me work this evenin'. Look, would you mind keepin' an eye on Bubbles and Penny-Farvin' till then? They'll show you where their food is. Can't stop longer meself, I'm late already. It's this girl, y'see, the one who can't get 'ere today. It's turned me Monday mornin' upside-down, so you can bet you're welcome. Well, I'll leave you to it. You'll find the rooms fully furnished. Back and middle. Did I say that? 'Ave to push off now—'

'Here, 'old on,' said Tilly, 'what d'you take me for, a nursemaid?'

'Can't talk now,' said Dan, 'but we'll 'ave a chat this evenin'. Can't tell you how much I appreciate you keepin' an eye on the kids. Make yerself a pot of tea, if you want. So long, Bubbles, be'ave yerself, Penny-Farvin', and be nice to the lady, both of you.' He picked his cap off the dresser and put it on.

'Wait a minute, not so fast,' said Tilly, 'I 'aven't come 'ere to—'

'See you this evenin', thanks for everything,' said Dan, and disappeared at speed. Tilly chased after him.

''Ere, come back!' she yelled. Out he went through the still open front door. 'Well, of all the nerve, what's he think I am, a performin' monkey?' She stopped at the gate, checking her impulse to chase him up the street. What an old-time Flash Harry, he ought to be run over by elephants, he ought. He'd landed her with his kids. Well, she didn't have to take them on, she could walk out. But she'd have to take her suitcases with her and traipse around Walworth looking for other lodgings. Blow the man. And come to that, where was his wife, the mother of the little girls?

A woman came out of the adjoining house and picked up a can of milk from the doorstep. She glanced at Tilly.

'Mornin', ducky,' said Mrs Harper.

'Mornin', said Tilly brusquely.

'Nice day,' said Mrs Harper, her florid complexion pale with morning.

'For some,' said Tilly, but only to herself, and the neighbour disappeared. Tilly went back into the house. The kitchen was alive with little shrieks, and she found the small girls throwing bits of bread at each other. Young Bubbles showed a face sticky with marmalade. 'What's goin' on?' asked Tilly.

'She pushed a bit of 'er toast and marm'lade in me face,' said Bubbles.

'What d'you do that for?' asked Tilly of Penny-Farving.

''Cos I don't like 'er face,' said Penny-Farving.

'I don't like 'ers, eiver,' said Bubbles.

'What's your names?' asked Tilly.

45

'I'm Penny-Farvin', she's Bubbles,' said the four-year-old angel.

'No, your real names,' said Tilly, feeling she really was stuck with the pair of them.

'Dunno,' said Bubbles.

'I forget,' said Penny-Farving.

'Where's your mum?' asked Tilly.

'Dunno,' said Bubbles.

'We don't want 'er,' said Penny-Farving, 'we've got our dad. We like our dad.' She eyed Tilly in curiosity. 'What you 'ere for?'

'Ask me another,' said Tilly. 'I'm daft, I suppose. Is there some gel who usually looks after you?'

'Yes, Alice 'Iggins from down the street,' said Penny-Farving. She and Bubbles both had the blue eyes of angels.

'She's umployed,' said Bubbles informatively.

'Unemployed, I suppose you mean,' said Tilly. 'Your dad mentioned she'd fractured 'er ankle.'

'Yes, and it's 'urting,' said Penny-Farving, 'so she can't come. She takes us for walks. You goin' to take us?'

'Well, I'm not goin' to sit about all day,' said Tilly, who'd have shown a bit of motherliness if their father hadn't put her into a temper.

'You'll 'ave to do the breakfast fings first,' said Bubbles.

'Beg yer pardon?' said Tilly.

'It's what Alice does first,' said Penny-Farving.

Tilly surveyed the table. It might have looked all right when it was first laid, even though there was no cloth. It looked a mess now, probably due to these two little angels being against keeping anything tidy. It seemed that breakfast had consisted of porridge and toast.

'Who 'asn't eaten their porridge?' she asked.

'Dad,' said Bubbles.

'He didn't 'ave time,' said Penny-Farving.

'Poor man,' said Bubbles.

'Well, 'e was late,' said Penny-Farving.

'All right, I'll do the washin'-up,' said Tilly, 'but I'm goin' up to look at the rooms first. Afterwards, as I've got to go out, I'll take you with me. You can put all the things in the sink while I'm upstairs.'

'Us can?' said Bubbles.

'Us can't,' said Penny-Farving, 'our dad says 'andles come off cups when we put them in the sink.'

'Besides, we're only little,' said Bubbles. 'Could you tell us yer name?'

'Tilly.'

'We ain't met a Tilly before,' said Penny-Farving.

'Well, there's only one like me,' said Tilly. A daft one, she thought, because she was taking on the responsibility of looking after them for the day. But just wait till their father came home from his job. She'd scorch him. 'Stay there,' she said, and went upstairs to look at the rooms on offer. The back room was really quite pleasant, furnished like a sitting-room, and there were even shelves with books. The window overlooked the yard, and immediately opposite was the window of the upstairs back room of the adjoining house, the house from which the common-looking woman had emerged to pick up her morning delivery of milk. Cheap curtains framed the window, and above them she saw the cord of a blind hanging. She turned away, checked that there was a gas ring available for cooking, and then made her way to the middle room. She stopped to open a door and found the upstairs lav, complete with a small handbasin. The

47

middle room proved to be the bedroom. It looked quite attractive, and a very nice eiderdown covered the bed. Well, she couldn't complain about either room, they represented lodgings a lot better than her abode with George Rice, the paunchy old goat who'd got above himself.

One thing, she'd never had to fight Frank Golightly off. He'd always behaved like a regular gent, and hadn't even touched her proud bosom, which might not have objected to a squeeze or two. Frustrating that had been sometimes. A gel didn't mind a fiancé enjoying a bit of lovey-dovey with her bosom. Crikey, Frank had been courting her for four years and never undone a single button of any of her blouses. Funny thing, she hadn't missed him a bit in all of the six months she'd been in Walworth. All the same, she was twenty-six now, and there ought to be some exciting bloke ready to enter her life or she'd wake up an old maid one day. Dressmaking was all right, but she hadn't been born to make a lifelong career of it. Blow that for a lark, twice over and with knobs on.

A crashing sound swept up from the kitchen, startling her out of her reverie. Down she went, and in a hurry. In the kitchen the two little angels were on their feet, blue frocks long to their ankles, blue eyes gazing at a porridge bowl lying shattered on the stone floor of the scullery.

'Blessed fing,' said Penny-Farving.

'I dropped it, that's all,' said Bubbles, 'and look what's 'appened.'

'No wonder your dad told you not to carry things to the sink,' said Tilly.

'Yes, it's 'cos I'm too young,' said Bubbles.

'I dunno why fings break so easy,' said Penny-

Farving, 'Bubbles only dropped that a little bit. You goin' to smack 'er?'

'I'll leave that to your dad,' said Tilly.

'Our dad don't smack us,' said Penny-Farving indignantly, 'he likes us, we're 'is little sausages.'

'Glad to 'ear it,' said Tilly. 'All right, where's a brush and pan?'

'On there,' said Penny-Farving, pointing to the scullery copper. On top of it were the brush and pan. 'We can't reach ourselves.'

Tilly brought the brush and pan into play, and emptied the shattered remains of the porridge bowl into the yard dustbin, at which precise moment the front door opened to a pull on the latchcord and a hearty voice was heard.

'Dust-oh! Comin' through!'

A hefty dustman clumped through the passage to the back door on the other side of the kitchen. He stopped to look through the open kitchen door at the scene in the scullery. He grinned broadly beneath his large leather headgear that covered his hair, his neck and his shoulders.

''Ello, me little pickles, is that yer Aunt Gertie lookin' after yer today?'

'No, it ain't, you saucebox,' said Tilly, 'I'm nobody's Aunt Gertie.'

'She's goin' to live wiv us in upstairs rooms,' said Penny-Farving, 'she's Tilly.'

'Pleased to meet yer, Tilly,' said the dustman, 'like a ride on me dustcart come Sunday?'

'Blimey O'Reilly,' said Tilly, 'a gel can 'ardly wait, can she?'

'I can 'ardly wait meself,' grinned the dustman, 'yer a fair old treat to me mince pies after all the kipper bones on me cart.'

Penny-Farving giggled.

'We're not keepin' you, are we?' said Tilly.

'I wouldn't mind keepin' you, love, corblimey I wouldn't,' said the hearty dustman. 'Say in the private apartments of me palace.'

'Flattered, I'm sure,' said Tilly. 'Well, don't break your leg emptyin' the dustbin.'

'Ain't she a caution, me little pickles?' grinned the dustman. 'Well, must git on, yer know, or I'll never git the baby washed.' He made short work of carrying the dustbin out.

'Has 'e got a palace?' asked Bubbles.

'Yes, in Peabody's Buildings, probably,' said Tilly, 'but 'e's not gettin' me there. Well, let's get everything cleared up, then I'll take you both out.'

The dustman came back with the empty bin. He stopped for another look at Tilly.

''Ow about if I leave me visitin' card?' he said.

'Push off,' said Tilly, 'you're frightenin' the canary.'

'What a caution,' grinned the dustman. He put the bin in its place in the yard and left the house chortling.

'We ain't got a canary,' said Penny-Farving.

'Well, never mind,' said Tilly, 'your sister's got a sticky face and we'll make do with that for the moment.'

The little girls giggled. Tilly cleared up and washed-up. Then she found a fairly clean flannel and washed Bubbles' face. After which, she took a new look at the girls. Crikey, their long old-fashioned frocks. They made them look like young Victorian frumps. Little girls needed short frocks and white socks. She asked them what they were wearing under the frocks.

'Nuffink,' said Bubbles.

'Nothing?'

'Knickers,' said Penny-Farving.

'Same to you,' said Tilly, 'but thank gawd for some things. No vests?'

'Nuffink,' said Bubbles.

'That dad of yours needs talkin' to,' said Tilly. 'All right, I'll just take me baggage upstairs, then we'll all go out.'

'Ain't she kind?' said Penny-Farving to Bubbles.

'I like goin' out,' said Bubbles.

Tilly, having deposited her suitcases in the bedroom, took the girls into their own bedroom, the upstairs front. The bed wasn't made and the room generally looked a little untidy. If that father of theirs thinks I'm going to make beds, he's got another think coming.

She combed the girls' hair, and then took them out. She headed for the East Street market, and the girls trotted along with her. They gave her a trying time in the market, darting about, dodging about, disappearing and reappearing, while she made her way to a vegetable stall run by Joe Hardiman.

'Now look 'ere,' she said to them, 'just stay close to me skirts, because if you disappear I'll send the market copper to look for you.'

'Can you buy us an apple each?' asked Bubbles.

'Well, all right, I will as long as you don't disappear,' she said, so they kept close to her skirts the rest of the way to Joe's stall. Joe said hello and asked what he could do for her. Tilly bought some vegetables while pointing out she'd got new lodgings and that his son Tom had promised to collect her sewing-machine and her dressmaking model from her old lodgings and deliver them on a barrow to her new address. Joe said he'd get Tom to do that first thing in the afternoon.

'Who's them little girls that arrived with yer, Tilly?' he asked.

'Me new landlord's daughters,' said Tilly, turning. ''Ere, where've them young terrors gone?'

Bubbles and Penny-Farving had disappeared again, and Tilly spent the next ten minutes fuming and searching. She'd been landed with them, become responsible for them and now, blow it, she'd lost them. She supposed they knew their way home, but they were still too young to be wandering about on their own. Bother it, she thought, why should I have a heart attack?

She elbowed her way through a morning crowd of shoppers. Most kids were at school, some little ones in the market with their mums. But there was no sign of the blue-eyed angels in their old-fashioned frocks.

''Ere, where yer goin' wivout us, Tilly?' The voice came from behind her. She whipped round and there they were, little girls who looked as if they didn't have a care in the world.

'You pair of Turks, where've you been?' she asked.

'We been 'ere, in the market,' said Penny-Farving.

'You went and got lost,' said Bubbles accusingly to Tilly.

'Me? I got lost? I'll drown the both of you in a minute,' said Tilly. 'Didn't I tell you to stay close to me skirts?'

'Penny-Farvin', what's she cross for?' asked Bubbles.

'I dunno,' said Penny-Farving.

'What's that you've got in your 'ands?' demanded Tilly of both girls.

'Apples,' said Penny-Farving, 'we've got one each.'

'You bought them yourselves, did you, without waitin' for me to?'

'We couldn't buy them, we didn't 'ave any money,' said Penny-Farving.

'Our money's at 'ome in our money-boxes,' said Bubbles.

'Lord 'elp us, d'you mean you nicked them?' asked Tilly.

'Well, they was nearly fallin' off the stall, and the man wasn't lookin',' said Penny-Farving.

'Pinchin' apples at your age? Well, I'm now goin' to take you back to the stall, d'you 'ear?' said Tilly. 'And you're goin' to show me which stall.'

The blue-eyed angels looked at each other. Their expressions said it all. What's she fussin' for?

'Oh, all right,' said Penny-Farving, and Tilly marched them back to the stall in question, which they pointed out to her. The middle-aged stallholder, Alf Cooley, eyed the little girls benevolently.

''Ello, back again, are yer, Penny-Farvin' and little Bubbles? And who's the lady I'm seein' yer with if it ain't Tilly Thomas that's been a customer of mine these last months? 'Ow's yer good-lookin' self, Tilly me gal?'

'Oh, you know these two angels, do you?' said Tilly. 'Well, they've got something to tell you, Alf.'

'No, we ain't,' said Penny-Farving.

'Nor me, eiver,' said Bubbles.

'Yes, you 'ave,' said Tilly. 'Go on, own up.'

'Oh, bovver it,' said Penny-Farving. 'Oh, all right. Me and Bubbles took an apple each.'

'Oh, yer did, did yer?' said Alf Cooley. 'Was that when me back was turned?'

'Yes, you wasn't lookin',' said Bubbles.

'Quick as a flash, were yer?' said Alf. Penny-Farving giggled. Bubbles looked at her feet. 'All right, show us what you took,' said Alf, and they showed him. 'Two of me best New Zealand pippins, is it? Well, you got good taste for the time of the year. But don't do it again, me angels, or I'll fall out with yer.'

'Half a mo',' said Tilly, 'they're goin' to put those apples back or pay for them.'

'But I've 'ad a bite of mine,' said Bubbles.

'And we ain't got any money,' said Penny-Farving.

Tilly tried an expression of frowning disapproval, but it wasn't a great success. In a manner of speaking, it hardly broke surface. Well, she was a good-hearted young woman generally, and these imps were so young. It was their father who was to blame in not teaching them what was right and what was wrong.

'All right, I'll pay,' she said, 'and you can owe me.'

'No worries, Tilly,' said Alf, 'I'll let 'em off this time. We've all been kids, we've all done a bit of swipin' down London markets on account of our mums and dads bein' 'ard-up.'

''Ere, d'you mind not includin' me?' said Tilly.

'Granted with pleasure, I'm sure,' said Alf. 'Well, there y'ar, me little angels, one free pippin each gratis and for nothing, but don't do it on me again. Try Ma Earnshaw's fruit stall next time.'

'Blimey,' said Tilly, 'you're as bad as they are.'

'Well, wasn't I a kid meself once, like I just said? Besides, I know their dad. Reg'lar decent bloke.'

'Well, if you know 'im, that's your 'ard luck,' said Tilly. 'Wait till I see 'im again meself.'

'Wish yer luck, Tilly,' said Alf, 'but what're yer doin' out with 'is little 'uns? 'Ow did yer come – oh, 'ello, top of the mornin' to yer, missus,' he said to an arriving customer, 'what can I do for yer shoppin' basket?'

'Come on, you two,' said Tilly, and led the girls away.

Once back in the house, she spent the next few hours unpacking her cases, sorting out clothes and other belongings, going downstairs at regular intervals to make sure the terrors were still alive, reading the occasional riot act and pushing home the top bolt of the front door so that they couldn't go out and get themselves run over. At twelve-thirty she prepared a meal from food in the larder and sat down to share it with them at the kitchen table.

In the afternoon, Tom Hardiman, the twenty-year-old son of stallholder Joe Hardiman called on her, with his barrow. He let her know that George Rice, a street corner bookie who was always too smart to be copped by the law, had refused to let him in to collect the sewing-machine and the dressmaking model.

''Ad a growl all over 'is clock, Tilly, and 'e was wearin' 'is 'obnailed boots as well.'

'Right,' said Tilly, ''old on a tick and we'll go round together.'

She took the girls with her, and to their delight Tom gave them a ride on his barrow all the way to the house in Brandon Street. Tilly also took a rolling-pin. George Rice answered her knock on his door.

'Git off me doorstep,' he said by way of openers.

'I've called for me sewing-machine and me dummy,' said Tilly, with Tom beside her.

'Yer out,' said Rice, 'you ain't lodgin' 'ere no more, so you ain't entitled to enter me abode without me permission, which you ain't gittin'. That clear?'

'She's got a right to collect what's 'er own,' said Tom.

'What she left 'ere is what I got a legal right to claim as mine,' growled Rice, still upset not only at being rebuffed but at the painful damage that had been done to his head. It was still sorely painful.

55

'You goin' to stand aside and let us in or do I 'ave to show you me passport?' said Tilly, with the girls watching from the barrow.

'What passport, yer daft bitch?'

''Ere, watch yer mouth, mate, when yer talkin' to a lady,' said Tom, a gallant young costermonger.

'A lady? So's my bleedin' canary, I don't think,' said Rice. 'Listen,' he said to Tilly, 'ten passports ain't goin' to git you past my door, let alone one.'

'Here's mine,' said Tilly, and her hand came from behind her back and a solid wooden rolling-pin with an injurious look showed itself to George Rice's large hooter. Remembering what she'd done to him with her knee, then a vase, and, further, what her fireside poker might have done, his hooter suddenly felt in mortal danger. 'That's me own personal passport, mister,' said Tilly, 'so are you goin' to stand aside or not?'

'Oh, yer crazy bitch,' bawled Rice, 'ain't you got no respect at all for people's life and limbs?'

Tilly poked him in the paunch with the rolling-pin. Expressions of glee appeared on the faces of Penny-Farving and Bubbles, still sitting in the barrow. Rice himself was far from gleeful. The rolling-pin looked as if it was about to land on his sore head. He backed away.

'That's better,' said Tilly.

'Take yer bleedin' sewing-machine,' bawled Rice, 'and I 'ope it falls on yer ruddy feet.'

'Poor bloke, 'e's all upset now, Tom,' said Tilly. 'Come on, let's go up.' Tom, grinning, went upstairs with her, and between them they brought the sewing-machine down. With its treadle it was heavy, and the little girls scrambled out of the barrow to make room for it. Tom then went upstairs again and brought down the dressmaking dummy, something that fascinated Penny-Farving and Bubbles. With Rice having retired to his kitchen, Tilly and Tom made a peaceful departure. Reaching the house in Caulfield Place, Tilly helped Tom to load the sewing-machine on his back, and he took it upstairs for her. She followed with the dummy, then paid Tom for his time and trouble.

'Yer welcome, Tilly,' he said, and departed with his barrow.

'Now, you gels,' said Tilly, 'let's 'ave a pot of tea.'

'Can we 'ave cake as well?' asked Penny-Farving.

'Is there some?' asked Tilly.

'Course there is,' said Bubbles, 'Dad always makes sure there's cake. 'E says it's good for us.'

'It's in a tin,' said Penny-Farving.

It was. Half of a baker's Madeira. Well, that father of theirs at least didn't keep them short of food. The larder was quite well stocked. All the same, Tilly promised herself a set-to with him the moment he got home.

Chapter Five

Mrs Higgins, a long-term resident of Caulfield Place, could be very informative about all the others, and having met the new neighbour, Mrs Harper, coming down the Place from Browning Street, she had taken the opportunity to introduce herself and enjoy a bit of a gossip.

'I 'ear you come from 'Oxton, Mrs 'Arper.'

'Well, that's right,' said Mrs Harper, 'but I'm Shoreditch-born, yer know.'

'Oh, we won't 'old that against yer,' said Mrs Higgins, 'none of us can 'elp where we're born. Take my old man now, 'e was born on a tram in Bermondsey, a week earlier than expected. They had to stop the tram and the passengers all 'ad to get off, and 'is mother, poor woman, was never more embarrassed. But she never 'eld it against 'im, and I 'aven't, either, and it was natural that when 'e was old enough 'e got 'is job as a tram conductor. Is yer 'usband from 'Oxton too?'

'Yes, we was both livin' in 'Oxton together, bein' 'usband and wife. His firm moved 'im to Camberwell, with 'is brother-in-law, who works for the same firm, so we've all come 'ere to live.' Mrs Harper spoke like a new resident wanting to be neighbourly. 'It seems a nice quiet street, there ain't much noise from them printin' works nor them drug mills, and we ain't 'ad any of our winders broke yet by any of the street kids.

58

I remember once in Shoreditch there was a shop that 'ad all its winders broke.' Her father's boot and shoe repair shop, that was the one, but she didn't say so.

Broken windows weren't meat and drink to Mrs Higgins, so she said, 'Yer brother-in-law don't 'appen to be married, Mrs 'Arper?'

''E's a widower, poor soul.' Mrs Harper let sorrow sigh. 'Lost 'is wife four months ago. Pleurisy took 'er. So me and Wally, me 'ubby, took pity on 'im, and 'e's livin' with us for a while till 'e gets over 'is sad loss.'

'It's 'ard on a man, gettin' widowered,' said Mrs Higgins, 'they can't look after themselves like women can. Me old man couldn't even boil an egg if I left 'im to it. Oh, 'ere's Mr Rogers comin' 'ome from 'is work.'

Dan Rogers was striding down the Place from Browning Street. He wore a peaked black cap and a dark grey suit. His broad shoulders and chest tapered to a good waist and supple hips. He had some shopping with him in a brown paper carrier bag. His rugged face creased in a smile as he approached the two women.

'Oh, 'ello, Mr Rogers,' said Mrs Higgins from her gate, ''ave yer met Mrs 'Arper, yer new neighbour?'

'How'dyer do, can't stop,' said Dan. He knew that if he did stop and gave an ear to Mrs Higgins, she'd take hold of it and not let go until she'd worn it out. He nodded to the new neighbour who'd moved in next door to him and the girls. 'Got to get indoors and feed me girls,' he said, and went on.

'That's Mr Rogers that lives on the other side of you, Mrs 'Arper,' said Mrs Higgins. 'You'll probably get to 'ear 'is two little girls playin' in 'is yard, next to yours. They ain't old enough for school yet.'

'Seems to me I 'ave 'eard 'em,' said Mrs Harper.

'They're out in the yard a lot, are they?'

'Well, it's on account of not 'aving their mum around,' said Mrs Higgins. 'Me youngest daughter Alice that's not got a job yet usually looks after them durin' the day, but the poor girl's got a fractured ankle that's keepin' her in bed, and—'

'I'll be on me way, if yer'll excuse me, Mrs 'Iggins,' said Mrs Harper, 'there's supper to get for Wally and 'is brother, seein' they'll be back from their work soon. Been a pleasure talkin' to yer.'

What a boring old faggot, she thought, as she made her way to her house. Still, it was as well to know the two little girls next door were out in their yard a lot.

Tilly was in the kitchen with Penny-Farving and Bubbles when their father walked in. She'd had to stop them playing with the old sewing-machine that stood in the bay of the window. Few Walworth families lacked a sewing-machine, usually of Victorian vintage. These irrepressible little terrors, playing about at their own machine, were quite likely to run the needle into their fingers. The arrival of their father was a relief to Tilly, and also an opportunity to have a go at him.

'Hello,' he said cheerfully, 'how's it been?'

'Yes, you might well ask—'

'Hello, me little sausages,' he said to the girls, 'behaved yerselves, have you? The nice lady's looked after you, has she? That's good, so how about a smacker?' He picked up each girl in turn and delivered smackers on their noses. They giggled. 'I can't tell you how grateful I am, Miss – let's see, what was your name now?'

'Miss Thomas,' said Tilly, 'and I've spent the day gettin' grey hairs on account of—'

'Bless you, Miss Thomas, you've been a treasure,' said Dan breezily. 'Can't thank you enough. Hope you've settled in and found the rooms comfy.'

'Now look 'ere—'

'Got some problems?' said Dan. 'Don't worry. As soon as we've had supper, I'll 'elp you sort them out. I like the idea of having someone else around. Did I say that this mornin'? Well, no harm sayin' it again, it's a real pleasure to have a lady lodger.'

''Old on,' said Tilly, 'I'm not 'ere for your benefit—'

'You just make yerself at home, Miss Thomas, and consider yerself one of the fam'ly.'

'Not likely,' said Tilly, 'and if you don't let me get a word in edgeways, there'll be ructions.'

'She 'it a man wiv the rollin'-pin, Dad,' said Penny-Farving.

'Yes, we seen 'er,' said Bubbles, and gazed admiringly at Tilly.

'Deserved it, did he?' grinned Dan. 'Where'd she hit him? On our doorstep?'

'No, down in Brandon Street,' said Penny-Farving. 'She give us a ride on a bloke's barrow.'

'I'll do the talkin',' said Tilly, 'I've got a lot of it to deliver to your—'

'Well, don't let's worry,' said Dan, 'we can have a chat after supper. What d'you say to some saveloys and mash, me little sausages?' He opened the carrier bag he'd placed on the table. 'Got some here, and enough for you as well, Miss Thomson, if you'd like to join us.'

'Thomas, not Thomson,' said Tilly, frustrations beginning to boil. 'You're makin' a supper of saveloys and mash for your girls?'

'You bet,' said Dan, fishing out a dozen wrapped saveloys.

'We like sav'loys,' said Bubbles.

'What about veg?' asked Tilly. 'What about greens?'

'Ugh,' said Penny-Farving.

'We don't like greens,' said Bubbles.

'Hate 'em, don't you, me angels?' said Dan.

'You can't leave greens out of their meals,' said Tilly, 'it ain't good for children not to 'ave any greens, they'll get rickets or something.'

'That a fact?' said Dan. 'Well, Bubbles, it looks like you and Penny-Farvin' might have to eat a bit of cabbage now and again, say on Sundays.'

'I'll be sick,' said Penny-Farving

'Me too,' said Bubbles, 'and on a Sunday as well.'

'All right, no greens on Sundays, then,' said Dan. 'Some other day, eh?' He unwrapped the saveloys, and their skins gleamed redly. 'Like to join us, Miss Thomas? Tell you what, let's forget Miss Thomas, it's a bit stuffy.'

'She's Tilly,' said Penny-Farving.

'That'll do,' said Dan. 'Well, fancy some saveloys and mash with us, Tilly? Won't take long to heat the saveloys. I boiled some potatoes last night, I'll bring 'em back to the boil now and then mash 'em with some milk and butter.'

'Butter? Butter?' Tilly's brown eyes showed the heat of exasperation. 'You don't 'ave to use butter to cream mashed potatoes. Milk and marge are good enough for anybody.'

'Well, that's a fair point,' said Dan, still so breezy and cheerful that Tilly wanted to dot him one. 'But we're not exactly hard-up. I'm the foreman-mechanic for Soper's lorries off the New Kent Road. It's a good job, well-paid on account of my qualifications and responsibilities, and there's more and more lorries comin' on to the roads these days, y'know.' He moved into the scullery, taking the saveloys with him, on a plate. Penny-Farving and Bubbles followed him, watching as he tipped the saveloys into a pan and placed it in the gas oven. He struck a match and lit the jets, then closed the oven door. Tilly came into the scullery. 'Internal combustion's goin' to push horse-drawn transport right off the roads, Tilly,' he said, lifting the lid of a saucepan and inspecting last night's boiled potatoes that were immersed in water. 'D'you know anything about internal combustion?'

'Yes, it's smelly and 'orrible,' said Tilly, and opened the door to the yard. 'Go and play in the yard for a bit, you gels.'

'Can Dad come wiv us?' asked Bubbles.

'Not now 'e can't,' said Tilly.

'Oh, all right,' said Bubbles, and into the yard she and Penny-Farving went, to play with an iron hoop. Tilly closed the door.

'Now, Mr Rogers,' she said. Dan had lit the gas under the saucepan. 'About today. I ought to set a dog on you for landin' me with the responsibility of lookin' after your daughters. Talk about takin' advantage of me good nature, I was never more imposed on. It was downright—'

'Believe me, Tilly, I was never more pleased meself to see a helpful young woman on me doorstep,' said Dan.

'Will you stop interruptin' me?' said Tilly. 'I'll 'it you in a minute. Look 'ere, it's not that I don't like kids, but you've got two young gels there that's bein' brought up like little terrors. They're in and out of mischief all the time, and they even pinched apples off a stall down the market this mornin'. Just how old are they?'

'Bubbles is nearly four, Penny-Farvin' nearly five,' said Dan. 'What made 'em pinch apples?'

'What made 'em? You did,' said Tilly. 'You 'aven't taught them what's right and what's wrong, nor 'ow to behave. They were throwin' bits of bread at each other over breakfast after you left. And what's more, you 'aven't even taught them to dress properly. They don't put any vests on, which means they could catch their death in winter.'

'D'you wear vests?' asked Dan.

'Kindly don't be personal,' said Tilly.

'Well, I daresay—'

'I 'aven't finished yet,' said Tilly. 'Normally, I'd mind me own business, but 'aving been landed with your gels all day, I feel I'm entitled to say a thing or two, if only for their sakes.'

'Well, you go ahead, Tilly, I like you for it,' said Dan, taking a look at the potatoes heating up in the saucepan. 'And I'm a good listener. Regardin' mashin' the potatoes, I'd use marge to cream them if there was any, but I've only got butter. The fact is, Bubbles and Penny-Farvin' don't go much on marge.'

''Aven't you heard anything I've said?' asked Tilly. ''Ave I been talkin' to meself? Those gels of yours need lookin' after properly. Where's their mother?'

'In a circus,' said Dan.

'In a what?'

'Circus. A travellin' one.'

'I'm hearin' things, I am,' said Tilly. 'You've got two young daughters and you let your wife travel around in a circus?'

'On a tightrope,' said Dan, 'and in spangles and tights, but she ain't exactly me wife.'

'What d'you mean, not exactly?'

'Well, between you and me,' said Dan, 'I can't recollect we ever got married.'

'Are you sayin' you're not married to your children's mother?'

'It's not something I tell everybody,' said Dan. The water in the saucepan began to bubble. He turned off the gas, picked up the saucepan and tipped the contents into a colander over the sink. The water drained away and he put the potatoes back into the saucepan. He began to mash them with a fork. 'Do us a favour, Tilly, bring us the milk, pepper and butter from the larder, would yer?'

Tilly exhaled breath to stop herself exploding, marched into the kitchen and returned with the required ingredients. Dan showered pepper over the potatoes, added butter and milk, and set to again with the fork. The whipped mash began to turn creamy.

'Am I expected to believe you're not married to your gels' mother?' she asked.

Dan said they'd meant to marry, but on the first occasion they had to cancel the ceremony because Elvira forgot to turn up. She was doing her tightrope act in Birmingham. On the second occasion, they postponed it because Elvira was in hospital giving birth to Penny-Farving. Dan said he thought they forgot about making new arrangements. Well, Elvira was away a lot, and when they did get together, there were always other things to do.

'I bet there were,' said Tilly, 'and I suppose the next thing that 'appened was Bubbles. I don't know 'ow a grown-up man and woman could be so irresponsible. It ought to be against the law, people bringing children into the world without gettin' married.'

'Well, Elvira didn't seem too bothered about holy wedlock,' said Dan. 'She was a lot more bothered each

65

time her condition kept her off her circus act.'

'Me heart bleeds for her,' said Tilly. 'Is that 'er name, Elvira?'

'Professional monicker,' said Dan, taking a look at the saveloys. 'Elvira Karona, the 'Ungarian tightrope marvel. Her real name's – let's see, Gladys Hobday or something like that. I met her when her circus was pitched on Hampstead Heath six years ago, and she took a fancy to me, which surprised me no end, seein' I've never been a handsome Harry. But what an eyeful she was in her spangles and tights, and on top of that there was all her Hungarian passion. It made me feel I'd fallen into a hot bath.'

'Don't be disgustin',' said Tilly. 'And don't be daft, either. She's not 'Ungarian, she's a Gladys Hobday, and it's time she did what was right, it's time she married you and became a mother to the gels.'

'She doesn't go much on domestic stuff,' said Dan. 'Her dad was a fairground sword-swallower, and her mother told fortunes, so she had a bit of a gipsy unbringing. Anyway, let's have supper, shall we?'

'When was she last 'ome?' asked Tilly.

'About ten months ago,' said Dan.

'D'you mean she 'asn't seen her children for nearly a year?'

'I suppose you could say she's married to her tightrope,' said Dan, sounding so airy-fairy about it that Tilly felt he ought to be hit with a sack of coal until he came to his senses. He opened the scullery door to the yard and called the girls in for their supper.

Tilly decided she might as well sit down and eat with them. There was a lot of unfinished business about, and for the sake of the girls someone ought to make Dan Rogers see that he'd got to take their mother in hand and marry her, even if the woman then went back to her bloody tightrope.

Dan put a mound of creamy mashed potato and three hot saveloys on each of four plates. Bubbles and Penny-Farving immediately set about skinning their saveloys with their fingers. Having done that, they wiped their fingers on their frocks and began to tuck in. Tilly didn't say anything, but she gave Dan a telling look.

'What's up?' he asked.

'Can't you put bibs on your gels for them to wipe their fingers on?' she asked.

'Where's your bibs, girls?' asked Dan.

'What bibs, Dad?' asked Penny-Farving.

'Don't 'ave any bibs,' said Bubbles.

'Yes, you do,' said Dan.

'Blessed old bibs,' said Bubbles. 'You get them,' she said to her sister.

'No, you,' said Penny-Farving.

'You're oldest,' said Bubbles.

'I'm even older,' said Dan with a grin. He got up, pulled open one of the dresser drawers, fished around and came up with two white linen napkins that were creased and crumpled but clean. 'Here we are,' he said. He tucked one down the neck of Penny-Farving's frock and the other down the neck of Bubbles' frock. The crumpled napkins rested untidily on bodices.

'They want ironing,' said Tilly.

'Alice Higgins does our ironing,' said Dan.

'How old is she?'

'Sixteen,' said Dan, 'and out of work, so I pay her ten bob a week to look after the girls and the housework. I'll pop along to her house after supper and see how she is.'

'It would make more sense if you popped along to a certain circus and brought Gladys 'Obday home,' said Tilly.

'Who's she, Penny-Farvin'?' asked Bubbles.

'I dunno,' said Penny-Farving.

'I asked the gels their real names, Mr Rogers,' said Tilly, 'and they told me they couldn't remember. Children shouldn't be brought up not knowin' their proper names.'

'What's your proper name, Penny-Farvin'?' asked Dan.

'Olga,' said Penny-Farving, and pointed her fork at Bubbles. 'And she's Carla.'

'They're foreign names,' said Tilly.

'Hungarian, I suppose,' said Dan.

'I could say a lot to that, but I won't,' said Tilly, 'except I'd like to know why this bright pair told me they couldn't remember.'

'Oh, we're always forgettin', ain't we, Bubbles?' said Penny-Farving.

'Yes, and we remember later,' said Bubbles.

Tilly refused to be captivated by the precocious little angels, whose father obviously spoiled them. She listened as they regaled him with far-fetched accounts of how they'd spent the day, accounts that included downright fibs, recognizable as such. But he didn't pull them up, he simply laughed. As soon as she'd finished her meal, Tilly thanked him for it, then said she had work to do.

'Work?' said Dan.

'I do 'ome dressmakin',' said Tilly, 'and I've got some orders to get on with.' She had decided that the unfinished business had to stay unfinished as far as she was concerned, or her good nature might make a fool of her. She would be a fool if she interested herself in

68

the welfare of his young girls, she'd find herself committed. He was old enough and resilient enough to sort out his own problems. Besides, she wanted to discover if there were any single men in this neighbourhood who might find her attractive enough to offer her some enjoyable social occasions. 'So I'll go up to me rooms now, if you don't mind – oh, before I do, you might like to think about me makin' some nice dresses for your little gels. Those long frocks of theirs make them look like little old ladies.'

'D'you think so?' said Dan. 'I had an idea they gave them a look of Alice in Wonderland.'

'The pictures in the book I read once didn't show Alice in any long frocks,' said Tilly.

'She don't like our frocks, Bubbles,' said Penny-Farving.

'Is she cross wiv us again?' asked Bubbles.

'No, course I'm not,' said Tilly, 'but if your dad likes to give me an order for dresses, I'll make nice pretty ones for both of you.'

'Take an order now,' said Dan.

'Is that serious?' asked Tilly.

'You bet,' said Dan.

'Two dresses each?'

'They'd like that,' said Dan, 'and so would I.'

'All right,' said Tilly, 'I'll let you know 'ow much I'll charge. By the way, what about me rent and a rent book?'

'I'm not askin' any rent for today,' said Dan, 'I owe you for today, Tilly. Can't tell you how obliged I am. Tell you what, come Saturday and you can pay your first bit of rent then. Say half a crown, and then seven-and-six Saturday week and onwards. How's that?'

'Well, I won't complain about that,' said Tilly, and made for the door. She turned and said, 'But listen, don't try and take advantage of me good nature tomorrow. I won't 'ave any time to look after your gels tomorrow.'

'Understood, Tilly,' said Dan breezily.

'Good evenin' to you, then,' said Tilly, and found a smile for the girls as she left.

Upstairs she did some more sorting out so that she could settle down to a few hours work at her sewing-machine.

She heard Mr Rogers and the girls in the passage thirty minutes later.

'Come on, then,' she heard him say, 'let's go and see how Alice's fractured foot is.'

'Can Tilly come wiv us?' That was Penny-Farving asking the question.

''Fraid not, angel, she's busy.'

'Oh, dear, poor woman,' said Bubbles.

Tilly smiled. She heard the front door open and close, and the house became quiet. She closed her own door, then sat down at her sewing-machine in front of the back room window. The evening sun danced on the crowded rooftops of Walworth.

Chapter Six

The balmy May evening had brought Boots and Mr Finch out into the garden. Boots, having finished mowing the lawn, put the machine away in the shed. At the same time, his stepfather finished his diligent work with a hoe, and they sat down together at the garden table. They both looked as if physical exercise in the open air agreed with them, although it hadn't done very much for their gardening clothes. Ancient trousers, suffering wear and tear, stayed up as much by force of habit as by such help as old belts were able to give. And their open-necked shirts looked long past retiring age.

Rosie appeared on cue, carrying a tray on which stood two bottles of light ale and two glass tumblers.

'Refreshments, Daddy, with Mummy's compliments,' she said, placing the tray on the table. 'She says you're both deserving, but I have to tell you that Nana says you both look sights.'

'We've all got problems,' said Boots, 'but take a bow for bringing the refreshments, poppet.'

'Oh, I'll make do with five bob extra pocket money for next month,' said Rosie.

'Sounds a reasonable offer, Rosie,' said Mr Finch.

'Five bob's reasonable?' said Boots.

'Yes, aren't you lucky I'm not a grasping girl?' said Rosie. 'Shall I undo the beer stoppers for you?'

'Not if you're going to charge me for that as well,' said Boots.

'Should I charge him, Grandpa?' asked Rosie.

'Why not?' smiled Mr Finch, thinking the girl a picture in the warm evening light. Rosie, he thought, would be a quite beautiful young woman by the time she was nineteen. And her personality was totally engaging. There she was, a teasing smile on her face. She had combed out her wavy hair to let it hang down her back, a blue ribbon around it. Her attire was simple, a white button-up blouse and a short blue skirt. Rosie would always go for simplicity, not frills and flounces. 'It's an art, Rosie, freeing stoppers from beer bottles. Yes, you should charge.'

'All right, say another five bob, Daddy,' she said.

'Hold on,' said Boots, 'it's your granddad's turn to fork out.'

'No, this is just between you and me,' said Rosie, picking up one of the bottles. 'Another five bob will make it ten bob in all. No, say seven-and-six, then you'll make a profit of two-and-six. That'll mean we'll both be in the money. Can't say fairer, can I? There.' She twisted the stopper free, and did the same with the second bottle. Froth rose and put a light brown foamy cap on each bottle. 'Shall I pour, Grandpa?'

'Don't say yes, Edwin,' said Boots, 'or it'll cost me another five bob. Go and help yourself to a lemonade, Rosie, then come and join us.'

'Oh, don't you want to have men's talk?' asked Rosie.

'We'd like some young lady's talk as well,' said Boots, 'as long as there's no charge.'

'Oh, I never charge for talking,' said Rosie, and sped back into the house.

Boots and Mr Finch poured their ale and drank thirstily, counting themselves as deserving cases after their gardening stint. They chatted in the easy way of

72

men always completely at home in each other's company. Rosie rejoined them, a glass of fizzy lemonade in her hand. She sat down, a lithe girl of natural grace. Boots observed her, the fun girl of his life. She had always been that. He wondered how long it would be before he lost her by reason of marriage. Rosie would never be less than very special.

'You've something on your mind, Rosie?' said Mr Finch, noting her thoughtful expression.

'Yes, I'm afraid so, Grandpa,' said Rosie.

'Something serious?' said Mr Finch, who had not forgotten Sunday's strange phone call.

'Well, yes,' said Rosie. 'It's a message from Nana. She said if both of you don't give your disreputable gardening trousers to the dustmen, she'll burn them. She said that never in all her born days has she seen more disgraceful trousers, except on ragged hooligans. She said they'd even look disgraceful on a scarecrow.'

'Ah,' said Mr Finch.

'H'm,' said Boots.

'H'm won't do you any good, Daddy,' said Rosie, 'you'll have to think of something better than that. You too, Grandpa. I can't go and tell Nana you just said "ah" and Daddy said "h'm". She wants action, like both of you taking your trousers off this very minute and putting them in the dustbin.'

'Tell her we've all got worries,' said Boots.

'No, that won't work, either,' said Rosie.

'All right, kitten,' said Boots, 'try telling her that your Grandpa and I are working on it.'

'Some hopes if you think she'll swallow that,' said Rosie. 'She told me your gardening trousers are a shame and disgrace to the whole family, and the neighbours as well.'

'There's a problem,' said Boots. 'Not about putting our trousers into the dustbin, that's easy enough. But what about the disgrace and shame to the family – and the neighbours – if the dustmen give them back?'

Rosie shrieked with laughter. Then she jumped up and ran indoors.

'There'll be no quarter given, Boots, when Rosie delivers that message,' said Mr Finch.

'Well, get ready to field the brickbats,' said Boots.

'I'm fond of my relics,' said Mr Finch.

'I feel married to mine,' said Boots, and refilled his glass. They sat waiting, and Rosie came out again after five minutes.

'You're both in real trouble now,' she said, 'Nana's taken umbrage.'

'Is she bringing it out here?' asked Mr Finch.

'No, she's saving it up until you both go indoors,' said Rosie, sitting down again. 'She said you're both disgraceful music hall comics, and then she asked Mummy what there was to laugh about. Mummy said she wasn't laughing, she was having a fit about Nana being married to one of the comics and herself to the other. She said she and Nana just had to live with it, that it was the sort of cross lots of wives had to bear. Nana said just wait till I see the pair of them. Oh, lor', Daddy, I think you and Grandpa are really going to catch it. You'll be safest if you stay out here all night.'

'Something has to be done,' said Mr Finch.

'Right, you're the patrol leader, Rosie,' said Boots. 'Sneak up to our rooms, get hold of a fairly decent pair of trousers for each of us, then sneak back here with them.'

'Got you, Daddy,' said Rosie, and away she went. She reappeared from around the side of the house after a while, carrying two pairs of trousers. Boots and Mr

Finch retired to the shed, took off their relics and put on the presentable replacements. They came out and gave the relics to Rosie, who promised to hide them.

'They're old and cherished friends of ours,' said Mr Finch.

'Yes, I know, Grandpa,' said Rosie, and away she went again, a girl of quicksilver. When she reappeared once more, she looked victorious.

'They're out of Nana's reach?' said Boots.

'Oh, not half,' said Rosie, 'and I don't suppose she'll burn them now, in any case. I cut them up with Mummy's dressmaking scissors and put them in the dustbin. D'you think that was a good burial for old and cherished friends?'

'Say that again,' said Boots, coming to his feet.

'Well, they were a bit past it – oh, crikey, is that you looking like thunder and lightning? Oh, help.' Rosie ran, Boots in pursuit. Over the lawn she ran, and around the kitchen garden, little shrieks escaping. Boots caught her as she travelled over the lawn again. She swung round, flushed and laughing.

'Minx, you plotted that with your Nana,' he said.

'Yes, I know, Daddy. Well, Nana has to win sometimes.' Boots laughed and shook his head at her. Rosie impulsively hugged him, thinking as she often did that her happiest moments were always those she shared with her adoptive father.

'Anything else up your sleeve?' asked Boots.

'No, nothing,' she said, 'except you owe me seven-and-six for my money-box.'

From the open kitchen door, Tim called.

'Someone wants you on the phone, Grandpa.'

'Who is it, Tim?' asked Mr Finch, getting to his feet.

'A man,' said Tim, and Mr Finch entered the

75

house, Sunday's phone call on his mind. In the hall, he picked up the receiver.

'Hello?'

'George here, Edwin.'

'Problems?' said Mr Finch. George Duncan was a close colleague.

'Not really. The file you took home with you to study, can I rely on your bringing it back tomorrow?'

'Of course. I intended to, in any case.'

'Good. Sorry to have bothered you at home, old man.'

'No bother,' said Mr Finch, and said goodbye. The doorbell rang. He answered it. General Sir Henry Simms, very military-looking with his spruce iron-grey moustache and his straight back, smiled at him. Still on the active list at the age of fifty-six, his looks were deceptive at first glance. He was no old-fashioned, hidebound soldier. He was a very reasonable and percipient one, with a dry sense of humour. He'd become a family friend, mainly because of his great liking for Boots, to whom his daughter Polly was incurably attached.

'Good evening, Edwin,' he said, 'I rang Boots earlier about coming over.'

'Yes, I know,' said Mr Finch. 'Come in and have a light ale with us in the garden.'

'Lead me to it,' said Sir Henry, and followed Mr Finch through the house to the garden. Passing through the kitchen, he said hello to Emily.

'Oh, pleased to see you, Sir Henry,' said Emily, just a little flustered, despite being a woman who was rarely like that. But she sometimes found it difficult to believe this distinguished man had actually become a family friend. He and Lady Simms had even been to Sunday tea, with their daughter Polly, and Sir Henry and Polly had both joined in the garden cricket. Chinese Lady frequently said she just didn't know how it had come about, it wasn't any of her doing, Boots had sprung it on her some months after the wedding of Sammy and Susie, and only a few days after Polly Simms had come back from darkest Africa. Kenya, said Mr Finch. It's all darkest Africa to me, said Chinese Lady. Boots just casually mentioned he'd invited them, which put her into the kind of state that shouldn't be allowed. That only oldest son of mine, she said, I wouldn't be surprised if he came home one day to say he could raise the dead, then ask if there was any tea in the pot.

Boots, standing beside the garden table when Mr Finch appeared with Sir Henry, moved to greet the General. Rosie was at her father's elbow.

'Not interrupting anything, am I, Boots?' said Sir Henry, shaking his hand.

'Only a discussion with Rosie on how I came to owe her seven-and-six,' said Boots.

'How are you, Rosie?' asked Sir Henry genially.

'Oh, one up on Daddy, I can tell you that, Sir Henry,' said Rosie, who never lost any of her composure, however exalted the company. She was very much like Boots in that respect, even though she wasn't his natural daughter. She didn't question how it was that he'd come to be a friend of the aristocratic Sir Henry when he'd only been a sergeant during the war. It simply seemed something that had happened. Sir Henry and his daughter Polly had actually attended her fifteenth birthday party a few weeks ago. Lady Simms, Polly's step-mother, would have been there too if she hadn't had to go up to Yorkshire to visit her sick father. Sir Henry and Polly joined in the garden cricket and later, after tea, in all the compulsory party games, when Polly discovered what a yell it was to participate in Forfeits as devised by Boots. She demanded that Chinese Lady lock him up, and Chinese Lady said she'd given up trying to make a gentleman of her eldest son. Boots said he'd always preferred to be a common or garden bloke. I'm a leg man myself, said Uncle Sammy. Same thing, said Boots. Count me in, said Uncle Tommy. Chinese Lady said you're all reprobates, and Sir Henry said he was one himself. Rosie thought him a very nice man. He'd come this evening to see Boots about something.

'Rosie,' said Boots, 'would you like to fetch another bottle of ale and a glass?'

'Love to,' said Rosie, 'and I'll do it for nothing.' Off she went, and the three men sat down. Sir Henry drew a large folded brown envelope from his jacket pocket and passed it to Boots.

'It needs filling in, Boots, and signing,' he said. 'If you'll then let me have it back in a day or two, I'll see it arrives on the right desk accompanied by a recommendation from me.'

Boots drew out a comprehensive form relating to enlistment in Officers' Reserve. Sir Henry had been after Boots for years, on the grounds that there would be another war with Germany sometime during the Thirties, and Boots had finally agreed to apply. He'd been given to understand that if such a war did break out, he would probably take command of a training camp for recruits. However, what Sir Henry actually had in mind for him was a position on his staff, for Sir Henry, providing he was still active, was intent on securing command of a corps.

Boots skimmed through the four-page form, noting the information he had to supply.

'Frightening?' smiled Mr Finch, who shared Sir

Henry's expectations of another war, even though few other people did; not after the carnage of the Great War. Mr Finch knew, however, that it was a consideration in the minds of certain elite German military men, as it was in the ambitions of Adolf Hitler and his National Socialist Party, now known as the Nazi Party.

'Not frightening, no,' said Boots. 'Challenging.' He put the form back in the envelope as Rosie reappeared with a fresh bottle of ale and a tumbler.

'What's that, Daddy?' she asked.

'Who's asking questions?' smiled Boots, who would choose the time to tell his family.

'Oh, sorry, Daddy, nosy me. Shall I go and have ladies' talk with Mummy and Nana?'

'You can still stay and have men's talk with us,' said Boots.

'Love to,' said Rosie, 'I'll go and stick on a moustache. Oh, Mummy's putting Tim to bed and wants us to go up and say goodnight to him first. There, Sir Henry.' She unscrewed the stopper of the bottle.

'Thank you, Rosie,' said Sir Henry, understanding why Polly adored this girl.

'Will you excuse me while I go with Daddy?' asked Rosie, and off she went with Boots. When they reached the stairs, she said, 'Love you, Daddy, so I'm not charging you for opening Sir Henry's bottle of beer.'

'Well, love like that, kitten, does wonders for my pocket,' said Boots.

Dan Rogers, who had somehow found himself and his daughters trapped by gossipy Mrs Higgins, managed to eventually break free. Alice Higgins had been a bit desolate about her fractured ankle, heavily encased in plaster. It was making her housebound. But she'd suggested to Dan that he could ask Cassie Ford, that funny but likeable friend of Freddy Brown. Cassie was still waiting to be apprenticed to a florist. Dan, who knew Freddy and Cassie, said yes, he'd ask Cassie if she'd stand in for Alice, and he knocked on the Brown family's door after leaving Mrs Higgins talking to thin air. Cassie, however, wasn't with the Browns, Freddy had taken her to the pictures, saying she needed a change from her potty parrot. Dan said he'd call at Cassie's house sometime tomorrow. Mrs Brown wished him luck, saying Cassie was a very capable girl and did a lot of housework for her widower dad every day. She'd probably be happy to look after Bubbles and Penny-Farving until Alice was back on her feet. It's a very trying time for you, Mr Rogers, she said, with your wife away with a travelling circus. She thought it was also disgracefully hard on a husband and father, but didn't say so. Mrs Brown, that most agreeable woman, rarely let words of criticism escape her lips, and she wouldn't have upset Mr Rogers for the world, him being such a happy-go-lucky man.

Tilly heard the girls enter the house with their father, at a time when she thought they should have long been put to bed. But no, she wasn't going to interfere, and certainly she wasn't going to offer to put the girls to bed herself. Mind your own business, that's what you've got to do, Tilly Thomas, she thought. On the other hand, she might just do him a good turn by keeping on at him about getting married to the girls' mother. That would be a good turn for the girls as well. Otherwise they'd grow up illegitimate, which would be downright shocking.

She heard him come up with the girls a little later,

the girls noisy. And they were noisier still when they were in bed, giving little shrieks of laughter at things their dad was saying. They'd never get to sleep if he didn't act sensible with them. Eventually, however, she heard him say goodnight to them. Then he paused on the landing to call to her.

'Everything all right, Tilly?'

Her door was ajar.

'Yes, thanks,' she called back, and got up and closed the door, just in case he took it on himself to come in.

'Hope you sleep well tonight,' he called, and went downstairs.

Tilly resumed her work. Twilight turned to dusk and she lit the gas mantle. Sitting down again, she noticed light showing at the windows of the kitchen next door. She could see the windows over the yard wall. A man appeared and drew the curtains.

Tilly resumed work at her sewing-machine.

Bubbles and Penny-Farving went soundly to sleep.

Dan made himself a pot of tea and listened to his new wireless set. He thought about his girls and their wandering mother.

I suppose I ought to get married or I'll give my kids a bad name. Still, we're happy as we are, and their mum chucks things about. She's taught herself to have an Hungarian temperament. Silly woman. But I'm daft meself. It was her spangles and tights that did it. What legs.

He grinned at the wireless set.

Dan Rogers really was a happy-go-lucky bloke.

The woman known as Mrs Agnes Harper woke up in the night, in the bedroom that lay between the kitchen and the parlour. What had woken her? Whispers and rustles. Where from? Everywhere, or were they mostly from the kitchen? She thought they were, except it wasn't as if she was sleeping just outside the kitchen door. It couldn't be Percy. Once his hood was on he never made a sound.

It was one of the men, of course, or both of them. What had they come downstairs for? You couldn't always tell with their kind, secretive and close. They'd only confided so much to her, the rest they were keeping to themselves. But they were clever all right, coming here to use this house of all places, and she'd been willing to help.

And why shouldn't she? She was the daughter of a German immigrant and an East End cockney woman. Her father, a cobbler, had been building up a modest little business doing boot and shoe repairs until the war came along. Not long after it broke out, an anti-German mob smashed up his little shop in Shoreditch and left him lying near to death before the police arrived. He managed to stay alive, but was still a bit of a cripple. She'd never forgive that mob.

More whispers and rustles. Hold on, Agnes me girl, is it one of the men shuffling about and trying to make up his mind about slipping into bed with her? They had good bodies, both of them, and one of them might be thinking of helping himself to what he fancied. Well, come on, then. Wait a tick, it might be both of them shuffling about and whispering who's going to have first go. I'm not having that, I don't mind one of them, but two would make me look like a tart from Whitechapel.

She slipped from the bed, the lino cool beneath her feet, and in her flannel nightgown she quietly opened her bedroom door. The darkness of the passage confronted her, and the rustles reached her ears more clearly. Her body turned a little cold, but she felt her way to the kitchen and pushed the door open. The whispers and rustles fled into the darkness, and the silence that followed seemed to offer a ghostly hello to her. She knew then that no-one was there. No-one human. Icy fingers ran down her back.

Oh, did yer know it's haunted?

The remembered words of that girl slid into her mind, and she rushed blindly back to her room and into her bed, pulling the sheet and blanket up over her head. It took her some time to get to sleep again. When she next woke, light was streaming in, lovely light that made her laugh at her imaginings, the kind a kid could suffer in night darkness.

'Yer daft woman,' she said to the ceiling.

She heard the men about upstairs. They'd have breakfast, then go out and not come back until evening, much as if they'd been at work all day.

They'd made a good job of fixing a blind to the upstairs back window.

Chapter Seven

They were up, Dan Rogers and his angels, and so was Tilly. She was having breakfast, a cheap but satisfying meal of a poached egg on toast, to be followed by an apple. Down below were the sounds of Bubbles and Penny-Farving larking about over their own breakfast.

Tilly wondered if the carefree father had made arrangements for anyone to come in and look after the girls for the day.

She heard him then, coming up the stairs, his footsteps quick.

'Tilly, you there?'

The enquiry was followed by a knock on her door.

'All right, come in,' she called, and Dan came in, his blue serge suit fairly commonplace, but fitting him well. Dan kept his overalls at his place of work.

'Mornin', Tilly,' he said cheerfully. She eyed him suspiciously.

'What're you after, Mr Rogers?'

'Call me Dan.'

'What're you after, Mr Dan Rogers?'

'Just thought I'd let you know I'm off to me job now,' smiled Dan.

'Good,' said Tilly, 'it's nice to know you're responsible enough to 'ave a job. Well, don't let me keep you. Mind, while you're at work do some thinkin' about that woman who thinks she's 'Ungarian. You owe it to them young gels to drag 'er off 'er tightrope and to turn 'er into a proper mother.'

'All right, love, I'll—'

'Don't call me love,' said Tilly, who was looking a treat. The splendid top half of her figure was wrapped up in a clinging yellow jumper. 'I don't want any familiarity.'

'Wouldn't dream of it,' said Dan. 'Anyway, I thought I'd let you know I've been talkin' a bit of turkey to Bubbles and Penny-Farvin'. They know they're not to go out, except in the back yard, which saves me havin' to say a prayer for them. They'll stay indoors, bless 'em, so I'm relieved I don't have to ask you to look after them. Still, if you could just listen out for them in case one of them falls down the stairs or gets her head stuck between the banister rails, I'd be much obliged. That's all, then, have to go now. Thanks, Tilly, I'll—'

'Oh, no you don't,' said Tilly, getting up to put herself between him and a quick sneaky departure, 'you're not leavin' me landed with the same responsibilities like yesterday.'

'It's only if one of them looks like she might break a leg—'

'Nothing doin',' said Tilly.

'All right, understood,' said Dan, and slipped by her in a flash. Down he went and out of the house, and Tilly was left fuming again.

The offices of Adams Enterprises Ltd, situated on the first and second floors above their shop a little way from Camberwell Green, were fully staffed. There were three companies, the affairs of Adams Fashions and Adams Scrap Metal being looked after by the parent company, Adams Enterprises. Boots, general manager, held the administrative reins securely and competently, while Sammy provided the driving force that ensured a profitable turnover year after year. That in turn ensured all the Adams' families were comfortably off.

Sammy was currently in favourable consideration of an offer for Adams Scrap Metal Ltd. He was in Boots's office, giving his eldest brother the good news. The offer had come from Johnson and Company Ltd, a rival firm well-known in the trade. Boots, however, wasn't too sure it was good news, and said so.

'Come off it,' said Sammy, 'prices are near to rock-bottom.'

'Not quite,' said Boots.

'No difference, old cock,' said Sammy, 'considerin' the offer is forty thousand quid.'

'Yes, well under four thousand for each of our twelve yards,' said Boots, 'and we own the freeholds of eight of them. Sammy, for the first time since you launched yourself into business, I think you're making a mistake. All the yards are returning a steady income.'

'At a minimum profit,' said Sammy.

'Fair enough under present circumstances,' said Boots, 'but if there's a crisis in the affairs of Europe, our yards will be a collective goldmine. Hang on to them, Sammy.'

'You feelin' your age?' said Sammy.

'Not yet, Junior,' smiled Boots. 'Are you feeling a need for a large chunk of cash in your pocket?'

'Being as I am, a married bloke with a fam'ly, I've got expenses of a ruinous kind,' said Sammy, happy husband of Susie and doting dad of three-year-old Daniel and one-year-old Bess. Remembering his years of poverty and striving, he meant to give his kids the best that he and Susie could afford.

'You're thinking, are you, of investments that'll look after the expenses of a superior education for Daniel, Bess and any others that come along?' said Boots.

'Susie being a lady, despite being brought up in Peabody's Buildings, I'm in favour of makin' sure they all turn out to be a personal credit to her,' said Sammy.

'What does Susie say to that?' asked Boots, who seemed quite good-humoured about everything, despite having voiced opposition to an acceptance of Johnson's offer.

'Well, I'll be frank,' said Sammy, 'she's against Eton or Harrow.'

'She probably knows neither of those would get past Chinese Lady.'

'I wasn't thinkin' of askin' our revered Ma's opinion,' said Sammy. Boots raised an eyebrow. Sammy raised a grin. 'My mistake,' he said.

'Granted,' said Boots.

'I'll admit Susie speaks kindly about your old school, West Square,' said Sammy.

'I'm fond of Susie,' said Boots.

'You're fond of the fact that Rosie and Annabelle are attendin' West Square these days,' said Sammy. 'Point is, would it educate Daniel into bein' smart enough to own a City bank when he's old enough? I put that to you candidly.'

'And I put it to you, Sammy, has Daniel said he'd like to own a City bank?'

'Who wouldn't?' said Sammy.

'Some of us,' said Boots. 'It means striped trousers, a frock coat and a top hat. And aspirins in the afternoon.'

'All the same, old cock,' said Sammy, 'I take it you appreciate my feelings as a parental dad wishful to see his kids don't end up pushin' a barrow.'

'Sammy old love,' said Boots, 'your present salary would take care of the expenses of a superior education for any of your kids.'

'Presently two,' said Sammy.

'You've got four in mind,' said Boots, who'd have liked another son and daughter himself.

'Which coincides with Susie's ideas,' said Sammy. 'But there's other expenses, like fur coats for her.'

'Susie doesn't want fur coats,' said Boots, 'any more than Emily does.'

'Also,' said Sammy, 'I 'ave in mind wages for gardeners and suchlike.'

'I see,' said Boots, his smile lurking, 'you're thinking about being lord of a manor, are you?'

'The fam'ly's got a lord of the manor,' said Sammy. 'That's you.'

'Talking about fur coats, the family won't want to see you in one, complete with a fat cigar. Nor would Chinese Lady stand for it.'

'Perishin' dustbin lids,' said Sammy, 'me in a fur coat and a fat cigar? Come off it. Susie wouldn't open the door to me in the evenings.'

'There's another point of view,' said Boots.

'All right, out with it,' said Sammy.

'It concerns the people who run our yards.'

'Well, good on yer, mate,' said Sammy, 'that's a point of view all right, and I'm not denying it.'

'We've got our yard managers and their employees to think about,' said Boots.

'Might I mention that if Johnson's buy us out lock, stock and barrel, it's not for the purpose of closin' the yards down?' said Sammy.

'And might I mention in turn that Susie's dad manages our Old Kent Road yard, and that her brother Freddy is one of the employees?' said Boots. 'What happens if Johnson's take over?'

'Good question,' said Sammy.

'Needs a good answer,' said Boots, 'or Susie might use her shares to vote against selling.'

The issue had been a thousand shares, and Sammy had given Susie fifty of his as a wedding present.

'Hold on,' he said, 'that's got to be disallowable, me lawful wedded wife votin' against me.'

'Lawful wedded wives don't always take a lot of notice of what's disallowable,' said Boots.

'Lawful wedded wives sometimes need a bunch of flowers and some kind advice,' said Sammy. 'In any case, I'm not in favour of Jim and Freddy bein' made surplus to requirements by Johnson's, so I'd contract for Jim to remain in charge and Freddy's employment to be guaranteed. Further, there'll have to be a shareholders' meetin' when we're ready to lay full details of a satisfact'ry offer on the table. Meanwhile, as I'm up to me ears in work, I'll leave you to nod off. Shame about you feelin' your age, Boots.'

'I think I'll last the week out,' said Boots. He took a phone call as Sammy left, and when that was over he checked on the shareholdings of Adams Scrap Metal. Sammy held three hundred and fifty, he himself two-fifty, Tommy and Lizzy a hundred each, and Chinese Lady, Emily, Vi and Susie fifty each. No wonder Sammy, with four children in mind, was keen. He'd net fourteen thousand quid. And he only needed Lizzy and Tommy to vote with him for the sale to go ahead. Boots had a feeling that to sell would be a mistake, but the temptation might be irresistible to Lizzy and Tommy. They'd pocket four thousand pounds each. A comparative fortune. Further, Adams Enterprises and Adams Fashions would remain untouched.

But how would the family feel if, in a few years time, Adams Scrap Metal was suddenly worth three times as much as Johnson's were offering? In that amount of time, the country might be re-arming itself. Come to that, with the market in scrap currently depressed, why did Johnson's want to buy? They had their own yards, their own headaches in respect of scraping out a profit. Were they looking ahead too?

I'd say a little investigation is required, thought Boots, and made a phone call to Mrs Rachel Goodman, who had been the one and only girlfriend of Sammy's when he was young. Rachel, at home, answered the call.

'It's Boots here, Rachel.'

'My life, what a pleasure, ain't it?' said Rachel, who had attended a finishing school but was still a Jewish cockney at heart and could talk like one.

'How would you like to meet me at Simpson's in the Strand tomorrow and have lunch with me?' said Boots.

'I'm hearing what I'm listening to?' said Rachel, whose affection for the Adams' family ran deep. She could still sigh over Sammy sometimes, and Boots always had the effect of melting her. 'Chinese Lady's only oldest son is inviting me to lunch?'

'For the pleasure of your company, of course,' said Boots, 'but I won't say I'm not going to ask you a favour.'

'My dear, ask me a hundred favours,' said Rachel, 'I'm only a weak woman who can't say no to you or Sammy or Tommy. What time shall I meet you?'

'I'll book a table for twelve-thirty,' said Boots, who

knew that behind all Rachel's natural warmth and outgoing charm lay a mind as sharp as a needle. 'Is that convenient?'

'For lunch with you, lovey, any time is convenient.'

'Tomorrow, then, at twelve-thirty,' said Boots.

'Will you tell Sammy?'

'Not much,' said Boots. 'Sammy regards you as his private property outside of his marriage.'

Rachel's warm laughter arrived from the other end of the line.

'I should question that?' she said.

'See you, Rachel,' said Boots.

He went into Emily's little office. Emily was now secretary to the company, and worked until a quarter to four each day, when she then left to meet Tim from school and to take him home. Boots advised her in his disarming way that he was lunching with Rachel in town tomorrow.

Emily, not disarmed, said, 'Oh, you are, are you, my lad? What's goin' on?'

'A matter of business,' said Boots.

'With Rachel, that lush beauty?' said Emily. 'Some hopes. I'm puttin' my foot down.' There had been a time some years ago when she had behaved like a lukewarm wife, but when she realized he might give his most intimate affections to Polly Simms, she found that her innermost feelings weren't lukewarm at all. Boots attracted women without even trying. Most, on first meeting him, gave him a second look. A tigress was born in Emily in her determination to keep him. 'You and your girlfriends,' she said, but she let go a smile. There was nothing she could do about women giving him the eye and edging up on him. What she did do and was still doing was to let him know she cared for him too much to ever play second fiddle.

'Lucky for you I trust you,' she said. She could have said she didn't trust Polly Simms, or even Rachel for that matter, but she didn't. Chinese Lady had told her more than once that Boots would never lose his head over any woman as long as he knew he had a caring wife.

'Well, you're busy and I'm busy,' said Boots, 'and I'll leave it until tonight to tell why I'm having lunch with Rachel. I'll just say I need the help of a woman with brains.'

'What about my brains?'

'You're using them every day at your work,' said Boots. 'Rachel's are going spare. There's my phone ringing. Get your head down, Em.'

''Appy is the day,' said Emily.

Mrs Higgins, standing at the gate of her house in Caulfield Place, saw two new neighbours turn in from Browning Street. The Harper brothers, one the husband of Mrs Harper, that's who they were. The street kids, of course, regarded the Harpers with curiosity, on account of believing their house was haunted. Kids. They'd believe anything, most of them. Still, it had been horrible, that murder, old Mrs Chivers with her throat cut from ear to ear, so people said, and the police had never found the murderer.

'Evenin', gents.' Mrs Higgins addressed the two men as they reached her gate. They were stalwart men, with good looks, their caps and working clothes very respectable. Just home from their work, she supposed. They smiled at her as they passed by.

'Good evening,' they both said.

'Been a nice day,' said Mrs Higgins, who'd have liked a bit of a gossip with them, even if they had come from the East End. They were different, East End

92

people. They teemed, that's what they did. Well, they bred like rabbits in all them tenements and rows of flat-fronted houses, and the kids ran about ragged and bare-footed, and the women screeched like fishwives. And some of the men would murder a woman just for her handbag. Well, that was what she'd heard. She'd bet Jack the Ripper had been born and bred in Shoreditch.

The two men entered their house and went up to their bedrooms. The woman known as Mrs Agnes Harper came out of the kitchen and called up to them.

'Yer back, then. Yer meal's nearly ready. Say ten minutes. You 'earing me up there?'

'Yes,' called the man Wally.

'I did the shoppin', and got the padlock you wanted,' she said.

'Good.'

'Did I 'ear you say thanks?'

'Many thanks.'

'Pleasure, I'm sure,' said Mrs Harper, and returned to the kitchen, where she had a little nip of gin to keep her spirits up. The other man walked into Wally's room.

'A coarse woman,' he said.

'But a useful cover,' said Wally.

'Expendable, however?'

'If necessary,' said Wally.

Dan Rogers, arriving home, couldn't find either of his daughters. But he heard Tilly's sewing-machine going. Up he went and knocked on her door.

'Tilly Thomas?'

'She's at 'ome, you can come in,' called Tilly.

Dan entered, and there they were, Bubbles and Penny-Farving, sitting together in the fireside armchair. Tilly, at her dressmaking work, was facing the window, the light dancing on her dark brown hair.

''Ello, Dad,' said Bubbles.

'Ssssh,' breathed Penny-Farving, 'it's no talkin'.'

'You can take them away, Mr Rogers,' said Tilly.

'Listen, me little sausages,' said Dan, 'what're you doin' up here?'

'Can we tell Dad, Tilly?' asked Penny-Farving.

'I'll tell 'im meself,' said Tilly. 'First, you did it on me again, Mr Rogers, you—'

'On me honour as an old Boy Scout, I'm an innocent party,' said Dan.

'I bet,' said Tilly. 'You sneaked off like a slippery Sam, leavin' me to keep an eye on your gels, and don't think—'

'I was in a hurry, I can't say I wasn't, but I've never sneaked off in me life,' said Dan.

'There's always a first time,' said Tilly, 'and don't start that interruptin' stuff all over again. It ain't polite. Your gels gave me all kinds of 'eadaches this mornin', yellin' in the yard, knockin' the dustbin over and chasin' someone's cat. That woman next door knocked and said if I didn't bring them in out of the yard, she'd chuck washin'-up suds all over them. So this afternoon I brought them up 'ere and made them sit quiet or suffer smacked bottoms.'

'She give us a banana each, though,' said Penny-Farving.

'She told us she'd give us anuvver one each if we stayed quiet,' said Bubbles.

'We like bananas,' said Penny-Farving.

'We don't like smacked bottoms,' said Bubbles.

'Have you had yours smacked, then?' asked Dan.

'They nearly 'ave, once or twice,' said Tilly, 'but that's more your duty than mine.'

'No, it's not, Dad don't ever smack our bottoms,' said Penny-Farving, slightly indignant.

'No comment,' said Tilly.

'It seems to me I owe you again,' said Dan. 'I did tell 'em not to be a worry to you.'

''Ave you ever heard of water off a duck's back?' asked Tilly. 'Well, you've got two ducks, and there's both of them.'

'All the same, thanks a lot for takin' them under your wing this afternoon,' said Dan.

'It was to save meself from bein' driven to drink,' said Tilly. 'They're all yours now, Mr Rogers, and I 'ope you did a bit of serious thinkin' today. Wait a tick, you gels.' She went to the cupboard serving as a larder and found two bananas. She gave one each to the girls. 'There, you didn't do too bad this afternoon. Off you go with your dad now.'

'Oh, fanks,' said Bubbles.

'We'll sit wiv you tomorrer, if you like,' said Penny-Farving.

'All I'll see of you tomorrow will be when I measure you for your new frocks,' said Tilly. 'I've got calls on customers to make tomorrow, Mr Rogers, if you'd kindly remember that.'

'I'm hopin' to get a girl called Cassie Ford here tomorrow to keep an eye on things,' said Dan. 'Well, thanks again, Tilly, you're a sport. Come on, sausages, let's go down and see about a bit of supper, eh?'

Down they went, and peace and quiet made a welcome visit to the upstairs back.

At seven-twenty that evening, the door of Mrs Brown's house opened to a pull on the latchcord, and a familiar voice floated through the passage.

'Coo-ee, Freddy, can I come in?'

'No, not tonight,' called Freddy, 'I'm in bed with a broken leg.'

A fat lot of good that did him, because Cassie was in the kitchen almost before he'd finished speaking. Sally was out with friends, but Freddy's mum and dad were present.

'Oh, good evenin', Mrs Brown, and how'd you do, Mr Brown?' said Freddy's blithe spirit. 'Freddy, you 'aven't broken your leg, you're standin' up. Can you come 'ome with me and spend the evenin' helpin' Cecil to do more talkin'? He still isn't sayin' much.'

'Give 'im a drop of port,' said Freddy.

'Well, I must say a drop of port livens me up myself,' said Mrs Brown, 'but I don't know I've ever heard what it does to parrots.'

'Probably knocks 'em off their perch,' said Mr Brown.

'We don't 'ave any port except at Christmas,' said Cassie. 'Come on, Freddy, let's go and talk to Cecil. Me dad says you'll be very welcome – oh, did I tell you he said it's all right for me to be your girlfriend now I'm over fourteen?'

'Yes, you told me,' said Freddy, 'but we're still mates.'

'No, me dad says girls can't be mates when they're over fourteen.'

'Blokes can,' said Freddy.

'Well, I'm not a bloke,' said Cassie, 'I'm a girl.'

'Which I like you for, Cassie,' said Mr Brown.

'Yes, I do too,' said Cassie.

The front door knocker sounded.

'I'll go,' said Freddy, and found the caller was Mr Dan Rogers, a friendly and cheerful neighbour, who looked as if he could play a good game of rugby football. 'Oh, 'ello, Mr Rogers.'

'How's yerself, Freddy?' smiled Dan. 'I wondered if your long-standin' mate Cassie Ford was here.'

'She mostly is,' said Freddy, 'it's 'er second 'ome, you might say, and she's 'ere now.'

'Could I have a word with her?'

'Come in,' said Freddy. He took Dan through to the kitchen, and Dan said hello to his neighbours. Mrs Brown gave a little touch or two to her hair. She liked Mr Rogers. He was what Walworth women called manly, which was how most Walworth women liked their men, as long as they didn't break up the furniture. It was nice Mr Rogers had a lady lodger now, seeing his wife had as good as deserted him.

'Mind if I have a word with Cassie, Mrs Brown?' asked Dan.

'Oh, 'elp yourself, I'm sure, Mr Rogers,' said plump Mrs Brown.

'How'd you do, Mr Rogers, I'm just visitin' Freddy,' said Cassie.

'Makes a change,' said Freddy.

'You know my little girls, Cassie?' said Dan.

'Oh, yes, nearly like twins, ain't they?' said Cassie.

Dan said he was a proud dad of nearly twins, that Alice Higgins had been looking after them while he was at work, but she'd fractured her ankle and couldn't leave her house yet. Was it possible Cassie could look after Bubbles and Penny-Farving until Alice was on her feet again? He'd be happy to pay her two bob a day.

''Ow much?' gasped Cassie.

'Two bob,' said Dan.

'Crikey,' said Cassie, brown eyes dancing, 'me sister Nellie only gets two-and-six a day workin' in a fact'ry, and I do 'appen to be disengaged, Mr Rogers. Well, I am for the time bein' and I'm good at lookin' after children. And cats and parrots. What time shall I come in the mornin'?'

'Could you manage eight-fifteen, just before I go off to me work?' asked Dan. 'The girls would be having their breakfast then.'

'Oh, easy,' said Cassie, 'and if you like I could take them to me own 'ome and let them talk to me parrot while I did a bit of 'ousework for me dad. It would be like – well, like—'

'Killin' two birds with one stone,' said Freddy.

'Freddy, that don't sound right or nice,' said Mrs Brown.

'Oh, Freddy can't 'elp his other self, Mrs Brown,' said Cassie.

'What other self, lovey?' asked Mrs Brown.

'His funny one,' said Cassie. 'Oh, he's quite nice really, it's 'is other self that makes 'im sound a bit peculiar sometimes.' Freddy rolled his eyes and his dad grinned. 'Mr Rogers,' said Cassie, 'I'll be ever so pleased to look after Bubbles and Penny-Farvin', ain't they dear little girls? I remember me dad sayin' I was a dear little girl once.'

'Once,' said Freddy.

'Well, Cassie,' smiled Dan, 'I'd say you'd be a valuable young lady to me if you'd take the job on till Alice is better.'

'Oh, I'm valuable to everybody,' said Cassie.

Dan coughed.

'That's 'er other self talkin',' said Freddy. ''Er other self's off its chump. So's 'er parrot.'

'Course it isn't,' said Cassie. 'In the mornin' tomorrow, I'll take Bubbles and Penny-Farvin' to see it, shall I, Mr Rogers?'

'They'll like that, Cassie,' said Dan, 'and I'll try to get home a bit early, say by five o'clock. Can you manage to look after things till then?'

'Oh, Cassie's a good girl, Mr Rogers,' said Mrs Brown, 'she manages things about her dad's house very competent.'

'Well, bless you, then, Cassie,' said Dan.

'Oh, a pleasure, I'm sure,' said Cassie. She wanted to ask him what it was like living next door to a haunted house, but kept her curiosity in check for once.

'See you in the mornin' before I go,' said Dan, and left after thanking Mrs Brown for letting him talk to Cassie.

'Crikey, me a nursemaid sort of,' breathed Cassie, 'and bein' paid two bob a day. I could buy another parrot as company for Cecil.'

'Barmy,' said Freddy.

'Anyway,' said Cassie, 'you comin' 'ome with me to talk to Cecil or not?'

'Not,' said Freddy. Mr Brown and his better half smiled. They knew what was coming next, even though Freddy repeated himself. 'Not,' he said again, firmly negative.

'We'll go now,' said Cassie.

'Might I be so bold as to say I definitely ain't?' said Freddy.

'Come along,' said Cassie, and when they left the house a minute later she suggested they first knocked on Mrs Harper's door to ask after Percy.

'What for?' questioned Freddy. 'In case 'e's got flu?'

'No, just to be polite,' said Cassie. 'Mrs 'Arper did say we could bring Cecil to talk to Percy again sometime, so we ought to be polite.'

'Cassie, did yer know there's other things a bloke can do besides bein' polite to a woman that's got a parrot?'

'You mean like kissin' girls?' said Cassie. 'All right, as soon as we get 'ome you can kiss me.'

'Cassie, blokes don't kiss their fourteen-year-old mates.'

'Well, you kissed me at Christmas,' said Cassie, 'and I'll 'it you if you keep callin' me your mate. Come on, let's knock.'

It was Percy's florid-faced owner who answered the door.

'Well, 'ello, it's you two again,' she said.

'Yes, it's me and Freddy,' said Cassie, 'and we wondered if Percy's all right.'

Mrs Harper, who had just enjoyed a post-supper drop of gin and was accordingly a little mellow, said, 'You can come in for a tick and say 'ello to 'im, if yer want.'

'Oh, thanks,' said Cassie, and she and Freddy followed the woman through to the kitchen. Percy, his cage uncovered, greeted them with a squawk.

'What's up, Fred, what's up?'

'There, yer see, right as rain 'e is,' said Mrs Harper.

'Yes, don't he speak up friendly?' said Cassie. 'Is he a comfort to you, Mrs 'Arper?'

''E enjoys a chat with me now and again,' said Mrs Harper, 'and with me 'usband Wally too.'

''Ello, Percy, ain't you nice?' said Cassie.

'Who's a pretty girl, then?' asked Percy.

'Me,' said Cassie, tickled pink.

Freddy, hearing noises upstairs, asked, 'Is yer 'usband doin' some decoratin', Mrs 'Arper?'

'A bit,' said Mrs Harper.

'Me and Freddy's goin' to do some more talkin' to Cecil,' said Cassie. 'We could take Percy with us, if yer like, and bring 'im back later.'

'If yer don't mind, dearie, I'll keep Percy 'ere with me,' said Mrs Harper.

'Oh, all right,' said Cassie graciously, 'we'll bring Cecil Saturday afternoon then, when Freddy's 'ome from work.'

'On Saturday,' said Freddy, 'I think I'll be cycling to somewhere.'

'No, you won't,' said Cassie. 'Goodbye, Mrs 'Arper, goodbye, Percy.'

'Yes, so long,' said Freddy.

Percy responded in garbled fashion.

'What was that 'e said, Mrs 'Arper?' asked Cassie, as the woman ushered them out.

'Just 'is way of sayin' goodbye, ducks,' said Mrs Harper.

When they were out in the street, Cassie said, 'Did it sound like goodbye to you, Freddy?'

'No, it sounded the same as before,' said Freddy. 'Like, "I'll hit yer".'

'Freddy, I already told you, parrots don't hit people.'

'Well, as Sammy Adams told me once, everyone's got some small mercies to be thankful for,' said Freddy.

'I expect you're ever so thankful for me,' said Cassie.

The man Wally came down to the kitchen.

'Must that boy and girl come into the house?' he asked.

'I'm surprised you askin' a question like that,' said Mrs Harper. 'It won't do not to be neighbourly or to act like we've got something to 'ide. London people always keep an open door for neighbours.'

'Yes, you have a point,' said Wally.

101

'Glad yer think so,' said Mrs Harper. Seated, her hitched skirt was offering him a look at her legs, which were quite handsome.

'Of course.'

Percy said something. A slight smile appeared on Wally's face.

''E's got that from you,' said Mrs Harper, 'but it's all Chinese to that boy and girl.'

'Good. I'd be sorry to have to wring its neck.'

'Don't get cantankerous,' said Mrs Harper.

'Of course not.' Wally put a hand on her uncovered knees and lightly patted them. She stiffened with pleasure. He smiled again, then went back upstairs.

'Tilly?' Dan knocked and put his head round the door.

'Did I say come in?' asked Tilly, enjoying a cup of tea in the armchair.

'Just a friendly call to let you know Cassie Ford's goin' to look after the girls from tomorrow,' said Dan.

'Well, I'm thrilled, ain't I?' said Tilly. 'But suppose I'd been 'alf undressed?'

'Well, lucky old me, I'd have said.'

'Feelin' saucy, are we?' said Tilly. 'Just watch yerself, I've met other blokes like you. Still, it's a relief you've got someone to keep an eye on them angels. But you're always goin' to 'ave problems unless you yank Gladys Hobday off 'er tightrope, put 'er in a sack and bring her 'ome to be a mother to Bubbles and Penny-Farvin'. And marry her into the bargain.'

'Well, it's an idea, I suppose,' said Dan.

'An idea? Are you short of a bit of common? It's what you've got to do.'

'I'm givin' it serious thought, Tilly.'

'You don't look serious, not with that grin all over your face.'

'Sorry about that, Tilly, me face gets like that sometimes.'

'Ha-ha,' said Tilly.

'Dressmakin' goin' all right?'

'It's got to, it's me livin',' said Tilly.

'Well, if you fall on hard times,' said Dan, 'I've always got a quid or two to spare, so just ask.'

'Excuse me,' said Tilly, 'but I pride meself on me integrity, which don't allow me to go borrowin', not while I've still got something I can pawn. Still, that don't mean I'm unappreciative of such a kind offer, which I thank you for, and ain't it time you put your angels to bed?'

'Ruddy sheets and pillows,' said Dan, 'I must've had a hard day, I've forgotten about puttin' them to bed. Excuse me.' He disappeared. She heard him calling as he went down the stairs. 'Bubbles! Penny-Farvin'! Bedtime, me little sausages. Come out wherever you are.'

What a case, thought Tilly. He'd forget one day that he had two daughters.

Chapter Eight

It was only a few minutes past eight when Cassie knocked on Dan's front door, pulled the latchcord and went in.

'Mr Rogers? It's Cassie, I'm 'ere,' she called.

'Come through, Cassie.'

Freddy's sprightly young mate went through and entered the kitchen, where Bubbles and Penny-Farving were having breakfast and Dan was finishing a cup of tea.

'Oh, 'ello, everyone,' said Cassie. 'Mr Rogers, I've come a bit early because I'm ever so sorry but me dad says it'll be too much for me to look after Bubbles and Penny-Farvin' all day. He says 'e don't mind for the mornin' and seein' to their midday meal. I can do that each day, 'e says, but not the afternoons as well.' The Gaffer, in fact, had thought, not unreasonably, that all day every day would be asking too much of his fourteen-year-old daughter. 'I'm ever so sorry.'

'Understood, Cassie, don't worry,' said Dan, 'your dad's probably right, and I daresay I was askin' a bit much of you. Anyway, sit down with the girls, and I'll just pop upstairs for a quick minute.'

Up he went. Tilly, putting the kettle on her gas ring for her breakfast tea, heard him coming. He knocked.

'Miss Thomas?'

Miss Thomas? I don't like the sound of that,

thought Tilly, it's like the kiss of doom, coming from a bloke who's usually a cheerful Charlie.

'Come in,' she said, and Dan showed himself.

'Mornin',' he said, and a smile appeared. Watch him, Tilly told herself. 'Fresh as a daisy you look,' he said, which she did in a green skirt and a dazzling white blouse. 'Thought I'd just pop up and tell you that Cassie Ford's arrived to keep an eye on the girls.'

'Kind of you to let me know, Mr Rogers.'

'Don't mention it,' said Dan. 'Oh, there's just one thing, she can only stay till the girls have had their midday meal. Her dad thinks it'll be too much for her to look after them all day. Fair enough, I suppose, seein' she's only fourteen. Anyway, I'll tell the girls to behave themselves durin' the afternoon, and perhaps you'd do me a favour again and listen out for them, in case they pull the ceilin' down. Can't tell you how much I appreciate—'

'Oh, you crook,' breathed Tilly, 'you're doin' it on me again. I see it all now, why you advertised for a lodger, you 'oped a soft touch would turn up. Well, I ain't a soft touch, I've got me livin' to earn—'

'Yes, course you have,' said Dan, loading his voice with deep manly sympathy, 'and I admire you for it. Believe me, I wasn't lookin' for any soft touch in a lodger, and I'd stay and talk to you about it, but I must get crackin', I've got a crew of motor mechanics to supervise, and me guv'nor's already allowin' me to get in a bit late on account of the girls. I'll just leave it to you to listen out for them after Cassie's gone, and you've got all me thanks in advance – oh, and there's no charge for any rent at all this week. Got to rush now.'

He disappeared.

'Come back, you lousy geezer!' yelled Tilly. She

picked up a closed Oxo tin that was full of buttons, and dashed out to the landing. There he was, nearly at the foot of the stairs. She threw the tin down at him. It struck his left shoulder, the lid sprang off and the tin fell on the passage floor, scattering buttons. 'Oh, yer swine, now look what you've done!'

Dan had disappeared again. He was in the kitchen, telling his girls to stay in this afternoon and conduct themselves like true-blue angels, and letting Cassie know where food for the midday meal was. Out he came again. Tilly pounced, her weapon this time an umbrella. By the time Dan managed to get out of the house he was close to being in a wounded condition. Miss Tilly Thomas was a young woman who had a vigorous way of chastizing any man who had fallen from grace in her eyes.

Out from the kitchen came Cassie and the girls.

'Oh, 'ello, how'd you do, are you Tilly?' asked Cassie.

'That's me,' said Tilly, breathing a little hard.

'Is it rainin'?' asked Bubbles, seeing the umbrella.

'No, it's just a bit stormy,' said Tilly. 'Pleased to meet you,' she said to Cassie.

'Oh, pleasure, I'm sure, and I'm Cassie.'

'Are you sure you can manage these two angels, Cassie?'

'Well, I don't 'ave any bother managin' me cat and me parrot,' said Cassie. 'Or Freddy,' she added.

'Who's Freddy?' asked Tilly.

'Me young man,' said Cassie. 'Well, he will be when 'e's older. He lives just a few doors away. Did yer know that Mrs 'Arper, your neighbour next door, 'as got a parrot, like I 'ave?'

'I suppose I know now,' said Tilly.

'Cassie's takin' us to see 'er parrot this mornin','

said Penny-Farving. 'Can I give it a bit of what's left of me toast and marmalade, Cassie?'

'No, it don't eat toast and marmalade,' said Cassie. 'You make sure you eat it all up yerself. Bubbles, what're you doin' with your glass of milk?'

Bubbles had brought her glass of warm milk with her.

'Blowin' in it,' said Bubbles.

'Crikey, you'd best not do that,' said Cassie. 'Me Aunt Fanny's little girl used to, and one day the milk all blew up in 'er face and drowned 'er. Well, it would 'ave if Aunt Fanny hadn't turned 'er upside-down and shaken all the milk out of 'er.'

'Oh, 'elp,' said Bubbles and stopped blowing.

Tilly, calming down, smiled. Young Cassie seemed quite capable of keeping Bubbles and Penny-Farving out of trouble.

'Well, I'll leave you to it,' she said, 'I've got some buttons to pick up.'

'Oh, Mr Rogers said 'is angels had got to do that,' said Cassie. 'He told us the tin fell out of your 'and, and that pickin' the buttons up for you would be something for the girls to do.'

'I don't mind, I like buttons,' said Penny-Farving.

'I don't mind eiver,' said Bubbles.

'All right,' said Tilly. It wouldn't do them any harm. 'Well, good luck, Cassie. I'll keep an eye on the angels this afternoon.'

'Mr Rogers'll be ever so pleased if you would,' said Cassie.

I bet he will, the crook, thought Tilly. I'll give him make a soft touch out of me. I'll knock his head off next time.

Boots and Rachel met at Simpson's in the Strand.

Long-standing friends, their affection for each other was singularly warm. Accordingly, it was a pleasure to meet for lunch. However, since neither the rib of beef nor the saddle of mutton could be said to be kosher, Rachel chose a grilled Dover sole. Boots chose the roast beef. Rachel asked for a white wine. Boots, dismissive of recommendations laid down by connoisseurs as to what wines should be drunk with what dishes, said he'd share the bottle of white with Rachel.

'My life,' murmured Rachel, when the waiter had taken their orders, 'I should be having lunch with Chinese Lady's Lord of Creation?'

It was a fact that Chinese Lady often referred to Boots acting like the Lord of Creation. Boots never commented on this, any more than the Lord of Creation would. It was also a fact that because of her long association with the Adams' family, Rachel could freely use the nickname given by Boots, Lizzy, Tommy and Sammy to their mother.

'Is it going to be too much for you?' asked Boots.

'Oh, I shan't pass out,' smiled Rachel. 'All the same, this is the first time I've ever dined privately with you.'

Boots looked around. Simpson's, very English, very Edwardian and very handsome, was full of lunchtime patrons.

'Publicly, I'd say,' he said. 'But there you are, Rachel, long time both married, long time never seen at lunch together.'

'Long time? That's not implying we're old, is it? You're not, and I'll fight any suggestion that I am.' Rachel, her glossy hat a triumph, was all velvet brown eyes and velvet voice. Rachel could purr when in a loving mood. In her twenty-eighth year, she was a quite beautiful brunette, a director on the board of

108

Adams Fashions and a prominent shareholder. All that, of course, made her a part of Sammy's business life. She still carried a torch for Sammy, but was too sensible a woman and too faithful a wife to ever let the flame scorch either of them. Her close relationship with the family, gentiles without a single prejudice, meant a great deal to Rachel. She was also extremely friendly with Polly Simms, a brittle but fascinating woman who always seemed to be eating her heart out for Boots. While Rachel knew that she herself could never have Sammy, Polly was unable to accept she was never going to have Boots. 'How is Sammy, our live wire?'

'Still full of sparks,' said Boots.

'And Polly?' asked Rachel, just a little teasingly.

'Ask me another,' said Boots, who never gave anything away whenever Polly's name was mentioned. 'In any case, it's my belief that when I'm out with a woman, it's bad form to talk about others.' He smiled. 'Worse when the woman's you, Rachel. Damned if you aren't the best-looking woman in London.'

'Heavens,' murmured Rachel, 'you want to borrow money, Boots?'

'Not a penny,' said Boots.

'Well, then good on yer, lovey, for making my day,' said Rachel, observing him from under thick lashes. Chinese Lady had three remarkable sons, all tall and highly personable, but Boots had become the most distinguished-looking of them. His wife Emily had been a godsend to the family, so Chinese Lady always said, but she could sometimes look painfully plain, and Rachel, in common with Polly, often wondered how it was that Boots, who could surely have taken his pick, had not chosen someone lovely. Perhaps he was the kind of man to prefer a godsend to a picture postcard. Polly would have none of that, and could express herself bitterly to Rachel. She had an angry bee in her bonnet at times, and had said more than once that Boots cheated her by not waiting for their paths to cross. Rachel always responded to that by saying she doubted if an upper-class deb would really have been fired up by crossing paths with a man who had the heart of a cockney, as Boots did. And to that, Polly always said blow you, ducky, for thinking with a small mind, Boots was mine from the moment he put on long trousers and I wore my first silk stockings. Emily pinched him from me.

The trolley containing the salver on which stood the huge roast rib of beef did not arrive beside the table until Rachel's freshly grilled sole was being served. While the waiter, on request, was taking it off the bone, the trolley chef carved the beef for Boots, and Boots slipped him the traditional silver sixpence. Then he and Rachel began to dine in companionable fashion. He introduced the subject of Johnson's offer for the scrap metal business, letting her know Sammy was inclined to accept. As a family man now, said Boots, Sammy thinks he's in need of a large amount of money to cover the cost of installing Susie and the kids in a castle. Say that again, demanded Rachel.

'It's something like that,' said Boots. 'Sammy has the kind of ambitions that snowball.'

'You're pulling one of my remarkable legs,' said Rachel. 'Or both. All the companies still provide Sammy with a challenge. He'd never agree to selling any of them.'

'He might if he fancies himself as some kind of country squire, with Susie serving dinner in a ball gown and his kids riding around on thoroughbred horseflesh,' said Boots.

'I'm dead against that, lovey,' said Rachel. 'It's no secret to you that I consider some part of Sammy belongs to me. Didn't I pay him a penny for every kiss I had from him, didn't I gladly show him my remarkable legs every time I fell over at Brixton roller-skating rink? I should let him disappear into the Cotswolds without a fight? Not on your life. Is the favour you want from me something to do with knocking this offer on its head?'

'That's a clever girl,' said Boots, the light in the restaurant picking out the gleam of cutlery and glass, and the colourful hats of women. Economic depression was never visible in Simpson's.

'Clever but not cocky, that's me, ain't it, me dear?' smiled Rachel, whose husband was a prosperous course bookie.

'A godsend,' said Boots, and let her know he didn't think the sale of the business a good idea at this time, that the market was nowhere near as promising as it might be in a few years. If fortunes were to be made for all shareholders, they should wait a while. Rachel asked what would improve the demand for scrap metal. A certain amount of rearmament, said Boots.

'Come again?' said Rachel.

'That's from the horse's mouth,' said Boots, thinking of Edwin Finch and his knowledgeable opinions on the rise of militarism in Germany.

'But you've never been interested in making a fortune,' said Rachel.

'That doesn't mean I'd favour selling any old time,' said Boots. 'But since no-one's hard-up, we could all afford to wait until rearmament makes the price of brass, copper and lead jump over the moon.'

'Like the cow in the nursery story?' said Rachel. 'I

111

bet the lumpy beast didn't make it. Boots, are you sure you're not at my legs?'

'Not in here,' said Boots, 'but if you'd care to join the family in a game of Forfeits one day, I'll make sure—'

'Never. I'm a respectable wife and mother, and I've heard about your kind of forfeits. Polly told me. But listen, Boots, why should there be rearmament? Pacifism is the thing these days, thank God.'

'Not everywhere,' said Boots, and mentioned there was an aggressive element on the march in Germany. Rachel frowned and said she'd heard stories about certain happenings in Germany. 'There's a fanatic on the loose,' said Boots. 'Now, why do Johnson's want to buy at a time when the demand for scrap metal is so low? Sammy says they've inspected our balance sheets for the last three years, and they know accordingly that the profits have been low. Sammy thinks they're after a London monopoly, but I'm not so sure. The glint of a fortune has made him pie-eyed for once. I need someone to do a little digging for me. I don't have time myself.'

'I'm your digger?' smiled Rachel.

'Do you have time?' asked Boots.

'For you I do.'

'Claim a fee and expenses, Rachel.'

'I should worry about such a thing?'

'A new hat, then?'

'Another lunch?' suggested Rachel.

'You're on,' said Boots, and explained what he wanted her to do, examine the annual returns of Johnson's for the last three years, visit some of their yards, enquire about prices, see what stocks they're holding and find out what she could about their directors. Rachel was not only willing, she liked the sound of the challenge. When the lunch was over, he gave her a lift in his car to her home in Lower Marsh, off Waterloo Road. Just before they parted, she asked him if Emily knew they'd lunched together. 'Tell a wife nothing, and she suspects everything,' said Boots. 'Tell her everything, and she'll make you an apple pie.'

'I wouldn't,' said Rachel.

'Well, perhaps Emily won't, either,' said Boots, 'but when I left the office to meet you, we were still good friends.'

'I believe you,' said Rachel, 'you're an impossible man to quarrel with.' The car pulled up. Boots got out, went round and opened the passenger door. Rachel alighted, not without an acceptable display of grey silk stockings. 'So long, Boots lovey, gorgeous lunch,' she said, and kissed him on his cheek. 'I'll be in touch.'

'Thanks,' said Boots. He smiled. Rachel warmed to him. 'And bless your remarkable legs.'

'Same to you, ain't it?' said Rachel, and away she went, a woman to catch the eye.

On his way back to the offices, Boots drove along the Walworth Road. Its familiarity stirred memories, pre-war memories, when Lizzy went about in patched school clothes and cracked footwear, when they all wore darned socks and Sammy's urchin look belied the fact he was already hoarding pennies and farthings. And Chinese Lady never knew how to make ends meet, but somehow always did.

He indulged his memories by turning into Browning Street, stopping the car on the corner of Caulfield Place, where the family had lived for many years and where the Brown family now lived. The May afternoon was warm and he remembered the smell of horses when days were really hot, a smell that was always seeking to sneak in through open doors and windows. Horse-drawn vehicles formed the bulk of the traffic before the war. This kept the street cleaners busy, and it kept their wives reluctant to let them in after their day's work unless the council hosed them down, which it didn't, not being officially obliged to.

Unrelenting poverty meant a permanent struggle to keep families together, and kids like Sammy had all kinds of ways of earning a penny or two. One way was to capitalize on the prevailing nature of the traffic. The kids would shovel up horse droppings, and when they'd got a bucketful off they'd go to places like Kennington or Camberwell, where there were quite a few houses with gardens. They'd knock on doors and offer their wares to housewives.

'Like some 'orses' durves for yer garden, missus?'

'How much?'

'Bucketful.'

'I can see that, saucy. I mean, how much for it?'

'Tanner?'

'You'll be lucky.'

'Worth a bob, yer know, missus. Good for yer rhubarb. Better than custard.'

'Not for a tanner, it's not.'

'All right, seein' yer look like me young sister that's 'ad her picture in the papers, say fourpence, then. It's all fresh, yer know, it ain't last week's. You can smell it, if yer like.'

'I can smell it from here, thanks. Give you thruppence. Take it round to me back garden and empty it round me roses.'

'Yer robbin' me, missus, at thruppence. But all right, you got a warm 'eart inside yer apron, I can see that, and I don't mind cuttin' me price for yer.'

'And I don't mind givin' you a thick ear, me lad.'

'I s'pose you couldn't give us a currant bun as well, could yer?'

Kids like that, kids like Sammy, usually got a currant bun and no thick ear. Kids like that could also earn a bit for services rendered.

''Ere, missus, look at this, yer kitchen door 'andle's come orf.'

'What d'yer mean, and what yer doin' in me kitchen, anyway?'

'Well, yer front door was open and I thought I'd come in to make sure yer kitchen 'adn't caught fire. Mrs Arbutt's kitchen caught fire only last week in Amelia Street, did yer know? Nearly nasty, it was. About yer doorknob, missus, it just come orf in me 'and. D'yer want me to mend it for yer? I ain't goin' to charge yer anyfing, just tuppence.'

'I ain't got no tuppence for mendin' doorknobs.'

'Funny you should say that, missus, I'm skint meself. All right, just a penny, then, and I'll fix it for yer.'

Then there was the gainful pursuit of picking fag ends off pavements and putting them in a cocoa tin and taking them home. There, a kid would separate the tobacco from the paper, put it in a tobacco tin and sell it to some old geezer for a penny. The old geezer would roll his own fags with it, using Rizla cigarette papers, of which he could get a daffy for a penny.

There was also Sammy's own speciality, a fiendish talent for catching cockroaches, putting one in a matchbox and showing it to a girl at school. The girl would nearly die on her feet. But that wasn't all. Give us a penny, Sammy would say, or I'll tip it down yer neck. Oh, you rotten little beast, the girl would say. I know, Sammy would say, but I've got to do something to keep me old widowed muvver alive. When Chinese Lady was given the horrendous details by one girl's mum, she boxed both Sammy's ears. Sammy couldn't believe he deserved that kind of reward for using his initiative.

Post-war poverty wasn't quite as grim as pre-war poverty, perhaps, but there was still plenty of it about.

'Oh, hello, Uncle Boots, what're you doin' 'ere?'

Boots turned his head. Cassie, carrying a shopping bag, was beside the car.

'Where did you spring from?' he asked, smiling.

'Well, I live round 'ere,' said Cassie, 'don't you know that?'

'Yes, I know it, Cassie.' Boots had a soft spot for the girl. 'I suppose I'm playing truant from my office, and ought to be on my way. But come and sit with me for a couple of minutes.'

'Crikey, love to,' she said. Opening the passenger door, she slipped in beside him, her cotton frock pretty, her long black hair tied with a yellow ribbon. 'Are you just sittin' and thinkin'?' she asked.

'Well, yes, I was, Cassie. How's the parrot?'

'Well, he's ever so healthy-lookin', Uncle Boots. 'Is feathers look lovely, but he's still not a very good talker.'

'Talking's important, of course,' said Boots.

'Yes, I like talkin' meself,' said Cassie. 'I don't know why Freddy goes deaf sometimes when I'm bein' important. I'm 'is girlfriend now, yer know.'

'Well, that's important,' said Boots.

'Yes, I expect Freddy'll realize that when 'e's a bit older,' said Cassie, who had had a fairly hectic morning looking after Bubbles and Penny-Farving. 'I've just been to the Maypole to get some groceries for me dad. Uncle Boots, would you like to come 'ome

116

with me and see Cecil and 'ave a cup of tea?'

Boots smiled. He'd have liked two more children, a brother for Tim and a sister for Rosie. A girl like imaginative and ingenuous Cassie.

'Thanks, Cassie, but I must get back to my office.'

'Well, I could take you to see Mrs 'Arper's parrot, if you like,' said Cassie. 'It's only down there, near the house where you used to live, and she's quite nice about lettin' me see Percy. That's 'er parrot's name. He doesn't half say funny things, like "Hello, sailor," and "I'll hit yer." Fancy a parrot sayin' that.'

'Well, it's a funny old world, Cassie,' said Boots, 'full of funny old people and funny old parrots. But I still don't have time to see Mrs Harper's. Never mind, I can at least drive you home.'

'Crikey, ain't you a sport, Uncle Boots?'

'Sometimes, I hope,' said Boots, and drove away. Going up King and Queen Street, he remembered his many ventures into the East Street market when he was young and Chinese Lady, always so busy herself, prevailed on him to do some bargain shopping for her.

Cassie interrupted his thoughts. 'Oh, look, that's 'er, Uncle Boots, that's Mrs 'Arper, the lady with a talkin' parrot.'

Boots saw the woman on the other side of the street, coming from the market. She was wearing a costume and a brown hat with two old-fashioned green feathers.

'Well, she seems all right, even in a funny hat,' he said, driving on. Arriving at Cassie's home in Blackwood Street, he asked her how she was off for pocket money. Cassie said she was earning some this week by minding the children of a Mr Rogers in the mornings. But as she wouldn't be paid till Saturday, she was sort of poor at the moment. So Boots gave her a shilling.

Cassie, wide-eyed, asked what a whole shilling was for.

'To help you feel a bit richer, Cassie, and for being you.'

'Yes, I'm quite nice, ain't I? I 'ope Freddy realizes it.'

'He's a lemon if he doesn't,' said Boots. ''Bye, Cassie.'

Cassie, watching him drive away, thought oh, lor', I didn't really thank him properly for the shilling.

Boots reported to Emily when he reached the offices.

'Rachel's goin' to investigate Johnson's?' said Emily.

'Just an idea of mine, Em.'

'Why can't you just have a talk with Sammy?'

'Because at the moment, old girl, Sammy only wants to be told what he wants to hear. I need some information, the kind that'll put his mind back on the straight and narrow.'

'But suppose the information makes the sale look good?' asked Emily.

'Then I'll have to rubbish it a bit,' said Boots.

'What?' Emily looked shocked. 'Boots, you wouldn't, you've been honest all your life.'

'Have I, Em? Who said?'

'Well, I don't count what you got up to in the Army and in the war. Boots, Chinese Lady would 'ave fifty fits if she thought you hadn't been the soul of honour in any dealings with Sammy.'

'Bless the old lady,' said Boots, 'who knows better than she does that there are always problems, and that most of us have to work our way around them?'

'Don't get clever,' said Emily. 'Did you enjoy your lunch with Rachel?'

'Rachel's always entertaining,' said Boots.

'Well, just remember one thing,' said Emily, 'it's me you're married to.'

'Well, that's the way I like it,' said Boots, making a move.

'Half a tick,' said Emily, 'I was just thinkin'.'

'What about?'

'You won't want a big supper this evening, not after your lunch at Simpson's, I bet,' said Emily.

'True,' said Boots.

'But tomorrow evening I could make a nice apple pie for afters,' said Emily. 'Apple pie's your fav'rite.'

'So are you, Em,' said Boots, and laughed.

Chapter Nine

As soon as Dan was home from his work, Tilly came down to the kitchen.

'How old are you?' she demanded.

'Come again?' said Dan.

'How old are you?'

'Thirty-one,' said Dan.

'Then you should've grown up years ago,' said Tilly, sumptuous figure vibrant with aggression. 'You must've been retarded to take up with that dotty female on a flyin' trapeze—'

'Tightrope,' said Dan.

'And you must've been brain-damaged to 'ave children by 'er without marryin' 'er. What a daft case of infantile delinquency. There's twelve-year-old kids in Walworth that've got more sense. But just because that barmy woman landed you with them gels, don't think you can land me with 'em every day. You get 'er home here.'

'She'll break the furniture up,' said Dan. 'Elvira's a bit—'

'Elvira my foot,' said Tilly. 'You get 'er home. Your gels 'ave got to 'ave a full-time mother. They gave Cassie the run-around this mornin'. When she took them to 'er home, they managed to knock 'er parrot and its cage off 'er kitchen table, and 'er cat nearly got the bird. Then when she took 'em down the market, they pinched three bananas off Ma Earnshaw's stall,

Ma Earnshaw with 'er eagle eyes and all. And this afternoon I've 'ad to 'ave them up with me to keep them out of the yard and rollin' the dustbin about. Gels of four and five rollin' a dustbin about, I never 'eard the like.'

'They're lively, I'll say that much,' said Dan, 'but I can see I need to talk to them.'

'I've 'eard you talkin' to them,' said Tilly, 'like a soft cream doughnut. I'm sorry to say so, but they need a smack, and it's you that's got to do it.'

'Smack me little angels?'

'Yes, if you don't want them to turn into little 'orrors permanent,' said Tilly.

'Ruddy elephants,' said Dan, 'can't have that, can we? What're they doin' now?'

'Nothing,' said Tilly.

'Nothing?'

'They're tied to the armchair,' said Tilly.

'Who tied them?'

'I did,' said Tilly. 'Now, never mind about Gladys Hobday breakin' up your furniture if you bring her home, because I'll break it up meself if you take any more advantage of me good nature.'

'Blimey,' said Dan, 'you're a bit of a wild Hungarian yerself, Tilly.'

'You barmy coot, will you stop talkin' about Hungarians? Do like I said, go and yank the gels' mother off 'er tightrope and bring 'er back 'ere, or I'll go and find other lodgings.'

'I hope you won't, Tilly,' said Dan, 'you're already like one of the fam'ly.'

'Don't make me fall about,' said Tilly. What vexed her most about this cheerful Charlie was his failure to marry the girls' mother and legitimize them. It was all very well to keep dark about not being married, but

121

that skeleton in his cupboard would come to light one day. 'Do yer duty by the gels. I'll go up now and untie them, and it's up to you to see that when they come down the stairs they don't break their necks.'

'Thanks, Tilly, anyway, for keepin' an eye on them,' said Dan. 'Accept an appreciative little gift with me gratitude and compliments.' He picked up a white paper bag from the table and handed it to her. Tilly, opening it, saw a box of chocolates. She put the bag back on the table at once.

'Kind of you, I'm sure, Mr Rogers,' she said, 'but it's bribery, and I ain't that sort of lady, I don't accept chocolate that's meant to turn me into a nursemaid to your gels, thanks all the same.'

'Believe me, Tilly—'

'Nice try, Mr Rogers, but if you come up tomorrow mornin' and ask me again to listen out for the gels, I'll 'ave a try meself at throwin' you down the stairs. Stop runnin' away from your responsibilities.'

Dan ran a hand through his hair as she left the kitchen. What a woman. She was more Hungarian than Elvira. Elvira, with her temperament, was a danger to the furniture. Tilly was a danger to life and limb. That figure of hers, it must be full of coiled springs forever waiting to get sprung.

All the same, his grin arrived and spread.

Bubbles and Penny-Farving came down from Tilly's upstairs back looking in need of a wash and brush-up to tell their dad that Tilly had tied them to a chair. Bubbles said it wasn't very nice, and Penny-Farving said she supposed they'd been naughty.

'And were you?' asked Dan.

'Dunno,' said Penny-Farving.

'I think the pair of you gave young Cassie a hard time this mornin',' said Dan. 'I heard that for starters

122

you knocked her parrot and cage off the table, and then helped yerselves to bananas from Ma Earnshaw's stall. Why'd you do that?'

'We wanted one each for us and one for Cassie,' said Bubbles.

'But you've both got pocket money, so why didn't you pay for them, you monkeys?'

'We forgot,' said Bubbles.

'Did Cassie make you take them back?'

'Bubbles ate 'ers,' said Penny-Farving, 'and when we give one to Cassie, she ate it.'

'She did, did she?' said Dan.

'So I ate mine,' said Penny-Farving.

'I've got an idea she didn't know you hadn't paid for them,' said Dan.

'Not till afterwards, when she asked,' said Penny-Farving.

'She made us go and pay for them then,' said Bubbles. 'Dad, they cost a penny each.'

'Well, hard luck,' said Dan, 'and I'm goin' to have to smack the pair of you.'

'Crikey, you ain't, Dad, are you?' gasped Penny-Farving.

'It's got to be done,' said Dan. 'After supper.'

'Where you goin' to smack us?' asked Bubbles.

'On your bottoms.'

'Oh, 'elp,' said Bubbles.

'I'm goin' to sit on mine,' said Penny-Farving.

Later, just as Dan was about to dish up the supper of fresh haddock, the front door knocker sounded. He answered it. Mrs Harper was on his doorstep.

'Is this yours?' she asked, showing him a dustbin lid.

'I don't know, Mrs Harper, is it?'

'Yes, it is,' she said. 'I don't know 'ow them little

terrors of yours managed it, but they chucked it over the wall into me yard. I've got to ask you, Mr Rogers, to stop 'em playin' about out there. The noise they make goes right through me 'ead. Now take this lid back.'

Dan took it and Mrs Harper departed in a state of umbrage. Dan was forced to tell his young daughters that if they misbehaved themselves tomorrow at any time, he'd hand them over to a policeman.

Bubbles giggled.

'Think it's funny, do you, Bubbles?' said Dan.

'Yes, I like policemen,' said Bubbles.

Somehow, she and Penny-Farving escaped smacked bottoms.

Tommy Adams was just thirty. His wife Vi would be thirty in August. They lived in a quite nice house in Grove Lane, Camberwell, with a small garden. Tommy had a mortgage on the property. There were two children, five-year-old Alice and three-year-old David. Tommy also had a car, supplied by the firm. He was up in the world, and so was Vi, which pleased her mum, known to her relatives as Aunt Victoria. Aunt Victoria had always thought Vi, her only child, had been born to be up in the world.

Tommy, arriving home from his work as manager of the garments factory belonging to Adams Fashions, tickled Alice, tickled David and kissed his wife. In Tommy's opinion, Vi always deserved a kiss, being the most equable and easy-going wife a bloke could wish for. Wives like Vi never argued about the love, honour and obey bit. Lizzy, Emily and Susie, on the other hand, all thought it had been invented by some ancient archbishop whose wife left him to do his own cooking while she went off to do the dance of the seven veils in ancient Rome nightclubs. For her part, Vi thought Tommy easy-going himself and the most soft-hearted of Chinese Lady's three sons. She had to remind him sometimes not to let Sammy take advantage of him. Tommy always said that when his kid brother was able to take any kind of advantage of him, he'd eat the mangle. But Sammy, of course, was always doing it by making Tommy do the work of two managers instead of employing an assistant.

'Sammy been on the phone to you?' asked Tommy.

'No, should he 'ave been?' said Vi.

'Well, you've got some shares in the fam'ly scrap metal business,' said Tommy, 'and Sammy's after sellin' the company. If it comes off, it'll mean four thousand quid for my shares and two thousand for yours. Six thou in all, Vi. We could buy one of those big 'ouses in South Norwood with an acre of garden, pay a gardener to do the hard work and a maid to look after the 'ousework. How about that for a posh leg-up?'

'All that money?' said Vi. 'Tommy, I'd get a temp'rature. Besides, I don't want any maid runnin' my house. She'd get bossy and give the children looks every time they sat on a cushion. And I wouldn't know how to give 'er the sack.'

'Still,' said Tommy, 'six thousand smackers.'

'It's too much,' said Vi, 'it's got to be a joke. We couldn't handle money like that.'

'I don't know it would actually hurt,' said Tommy, 'and we could make a religious job of tryin' to get used to it. Mind, it's nowhere near settled yet. Sammy wants everything in writing, and when he's satisfied with what's on paper, we'll all 'ave to attend a meetin' in Sammy's office and vote on it.'

'What does Boots say?' asked Vi.

'He's tryin' to slow Sammy down. He says if we let the company go, it's gone for ever. Then there's all the workers that run the yards. Boots ain't too keen on them bein' handed over lock, stock and barrel with everything else, specially as the company owns the freeholds of some of the yards. Sammy says that's why the offer's as good as it is. Forty thousand.'

'Forty?' Vi went faint. 'It's nearly criminal, anyone 'aving that much money.'

'No-one's goin' to have it all, Vi. It'll be divided up among the fam'ly shareholders.'

'Yes, but it's still makin' me dizzy,' said Vi.

'Even Sammy's got a touch of that,' said Tommy. 'Boots 'asn't. Well, you know Boots. 'E was born with immunity.'

'Well, he never runs after money like Sammy does,' said·Vi.

'But it's Sammy who's made the businesses what they are,' said Tommy, 'right from when 'e first started Adams Enterprises and saw to it we all had shares in each company. Sammy's sharp, but he's also fam'ly-minded. We've all got our own 'ouses now, and cars. We're up in the world all right, Vi, even without what we'll get if the scrap metal company is sold.'

'I'd like to hear for myself what Boots 'as to say before I do any votin',' said Vi.

'Hold on,' said Tommy, 'you and me'll vote the same way, won't we?'

'Well, of course, lovey,' said Vi, 'you'll vote your way and I'll vote my way, it's the same for both of us.'

Tommy grinned.

'Same privilege?' he said.

'Same privilege, Tommy.'

'I've just found something out,' said Tommy.

''Ave you, Tommy?'

126

'Yes, I've just found out you're not just a pretty face.'

Vi smiled.

'Will the meetin' be soon?' she asked.

'Sammy'll let everyone know.'

'Well, I think it's all goin' to keep me awake tonight,' said Vi, fair-haired and soft-eyed.

'I'll be with yer, Vi.'

'Doin' what?' asked Vi.

'Well, if you're goin' to stay awake,' said Tommy, 'we might as well do something mem'rable.'

Vi laughed.

'Go and do something mem'rable with your son and daughter,' she said, 'like standin' them on their heads to stop them racketin' about.'

Lizzy discussed the possible sale with Ned. Ned said it was entirely up to her to decide how she voted. They're your shares, Eliza, and it'll be your money if the sale goes through. Our money, said Lizzy. What money you've got is ours, so what money I might have is ours. We're married in case you've forgotten. All the same, said Ned, there's no reason why you shouldn't have your own nest egg. It'll be a family nest egg, said Lizzy. Four thousand pounds, she thought, crikey. That's if the company's sold. She'd already wondered what could be done with it. She and Ned and their children really had all they needed because of Ned's well-paid job as manager of a wine merchant's store in Great Tower Street. They didn't need a larger or posher house. The one they'd always had was the kind she'd dreamed of having during the years when a girl could only dream. No, if she used some of the money, she'd use it for Ned, who'd been a loving husband, a good dad and a generous provider.

There'd been ups and downs, of course, but Ned was the one who'd made her dreams come true. So she'd thought of using some of the money to get a local builder to enlarge the attic and fit it up as a posh billiards room with easy access. Ned was gone on billiards and another game called snooker. He sometimes played at a City club in his lunch hour. Converting the attic would cost a lot, of course, but the idea was favourite with her at the moment, although she was keeping it to herself.

'That Sammy,' said Chinese Lady, presiding in her upright way at the supper table, 'what's he want all this money for?'

'His family,' said Boots.

'Sounds reasonable,' said Mr Finch.

'Am I goin' to get some?' asked young Tim.

'Someone might find you ten bob,' said Emily.

'Well, I won't say no to that, will I, Dad?' said Tim.

'You'll be a mug if you do,' said Boots.

'There, look what the talk of money's already doin' to a boy who didn't ought to be thinking about more than pennies,' said Chinese Lady. 'Might I ask if anyone's heard that Sammy's hard-up?'

'I haven't, Nana,' said Rosie, 'but I know I was hard-up myself until I earned that seven-and-six from Daddy.'

'Talked it out of me, you mean,' said Boots.

'If you don't mind,' said Chinese Lady, 'I want to know if Sammy's suddenly got hard-up.'

'I shouldn't think so, Mum,' said Emily, 'not when he's spent all his life makin' sure he wasn't.'

'Then what's he want all this money for?' demanded Chinese Lady.

'His family,' said Boots.

'You've already said that,' remarked Chinese Lady. 'D'you mean he's got money himself, but keeps Susie and his children short of it? I hope that youngest son of mine's not turnin' into a miser, I don't hold with havin' any misers in this fam'ly.'

'It's nothing like that, old lady,' said Boots. 'I think he simply fancies buying a dukedom and making Susie his duchess.'

Chinese Lady stared. Mr Finch emitted a slight cough, which was his usual way of warning her not to take Boots too literally.

'Sammy fancies what?' she said.

'Being a duke, Nana,' said Rosie.

'Or a country squire, say, with a butler,' said Boots. Rosie smothered a giggle.

'I'm hearin' things,' said Chinese Lady.

'I've been hearin' them since my weddin' day,' said Emily.

'Well, it's no good me talkin' to your husband,' said Chinese Lady, 'he'll only say more things that don't make sense. So p'raps you'd better ask him if he's bein' serious or not.'

'Are you bein' serious, Boots?' asked Emily.

'I think Sammy is,' said Boots.

'Grandpa, do dukes wear crowns?' asked Rosie.

'Ducal crowns?' said Mr Finch. 'I think so.'

'Crikey, will we have to bow to Uncle Sammy, Nana?' asked Tim.

'If I catch anyone in this house bowing to that youngest son of mine, I'll send for the doctor,' said Chinese Lady. 'But you can all be sure there's not goin' to be any dukes or country squires in my fam'ly while I've still got breath in me body. Nor misers, neither. Wait till I next see Sammy, I'll give 'im something to think about. Besides, there's our other

129

relatives, Susie's dad and her brother Freddy. I'm not havin' them put out of work by this firm that's after gettin' their hands on one of the fam'ly businesses. I wouldn't be able to look Susie's mum in the face. Em'ly, Tim's got his elbows on the table.'

'Elbows off, Tim,' said Emily.

'And ask Boots what he's smilin' about.'

'Dad's not smilin', Nana,' said Tim.

'Well, he looks as if he is,' said Chinese Lady.

Rosie couldn't have agreed more. Boots always did look as if there was a smile lurking about somewhere.

Susie was speaking to Sammy.

'Sammy, I've been thinking. You can't sell all the yards, you've got to keep one, the one that employs Freddy and my dad.'

'But, Susie, I can contract for them to—'

'Sammy, I'm talkin' to you.'

'Yes, I'm hearin' you, Susie.'

'But you're not listening. I said we're not to sell all the yards.'

'In a deal like this, Susie, it has to be all.'

'Sammy, my dad and Freddy won't want to work for Johnson's, they like workin' for us.'

'Well, I'm flattered, Susie, but—'

'I don't want any buts, Sammy.'

'Well, nevertheless, Susie—'

'Sammy, you weren't brought up to use words like that. Even Boots doesn't say nevertheless. Only people on the wireless do. Suppose someone like Mr Greenberg heard you say nevertheless? He'd think it meant you could see round corners, and no-one trusts people who can see round corners. Sammy, you talk quite nice mostly. Not like Boots, of course. Well, he's got a natural way of bein' lordly without actually soundin' stuck-up.'

'Listen, if anyone can see round corners, Boots can.'

'No, he can't, he wouldn't want to. It's a sneaky sort of thing. Anyway, when I'm talkin' to you, Sammy, don't say nevertheless. It means you're goin' to try and do what I don't want you to do.'

'Susie, when it's a matter of business—'

'You've got to keep that one yard, Sammy.'

'Well, as I mentioned, Susie, in this kind of a deal—'

'Bother the deal,' said Susie. 'Who needs it?'

'But wouldn't you like a country mansion?'

'Sammy, I don't like feelin' I'm talkin' to a brick wall. I've got you and the children, and a house that's as good as a mansion.' Their house on Denmark Hill was large, handsome and much admired. 'And I don't want to go and live in the country away from everyone.'

'I'll do some thinkin', Susie.'

'That's better,' said Susie.

Sammy wondered how he could get around the problem. Well, I don't have a brainbox for nothing, he thought, and it's not every day that a fortune's looking me straight in the eye.

Tilly went out that evening to take a finished skirt to a customer in Penrose Street, opposite the East Street market. The customer, happy with the skirt, paid for it, and Tilly began the walk back to her lodgings. Approaching the pub on the corner, she saw a woman emerge. Her hat was a little askew, and she had a tipsy smile on her face. Agnes Harper had been treating herself to a lively hour in the pub. Tilly recognized her as the next-door neighbour of Mr Rogers.

''Ello, dearie,' said Mrs Harper, mellow with well-being, ''ow's yer good self?'

'Fine, thanks,' said Tilly.

'I'd treat yer to a port and lemon, but I'd best get back 'ome now.'

'I don't drink, anyway,' said Tilly.

'Do yer good, a little drop of this and that,' said Mrs Harper, her speech slightly slurred. ''Andsome woman like you. Would yer like to walk 'ome with me?'

Tilly, hardly taken with the woman, could think of all kinds of things she'd rather do.

'I've got some calls to make,' she said.

'Oh, got some men friends, 'ave yer, ducky?' said Mrs Harper and winked.

'Not that kind,' said Tilly.

'I never 'eard there was different kinds,' said Mrs Harper, 'I thought they was all the same.' She swayed a little.

'I must get on,' said Tilly. She crossed the road into East Street.

'You are drunk,' said the man the neighbours knew as Wally Harper, husband of Agnes Harper.

''Ere, I 'eard you say that,' she said, taking her hat off and looking at it in bleary fashion. 'But I'll ask you to repeat it, as I don't know I like it.'

'You are drunk.'

'Well, fancy that, ain't I a naughty girl?'

'People notice such things.'

'Well, course they do,' she said, 'and they don't 'old it against a woman who likes a little drop of this and that. At least, they don't round 'ere or in the East End, I don't know about where you come from.'

'You are not being paid to get drunk but to keep house for us.'

'All right, keep yer shirt on. I ain't drunk, anyway. Never been one over in me life, just a bit jolly. 'Ow's Percy?'

'Talking.'

'Been 'aving a chat with 'im again, 'ave yer?' she asked.

'He's an amusing bird. Sit down.'

She sat down, and the two men made coffee for her and themselves. She was quite sober when she went to bed later.

Chapter Ten

Cassie arrived at ten past eight the following morning, Friday. She was her usual sprightly self, not a bit put out by all the tricks her young charges had got up to yesterday. Dan apologized for their behaviour. Cassie said he didn't have to, that she had just the same kind of trouble with Freddy, and that it never got her down.

'Me dad asked where their mum was,' she said.

'She's away a lot,' said Dan.

'Oh, lor', poor woman, fancy bein' away all that much,' said Cassie. 'Never mind, Mr Rogers, I'll look after them this mornin' and see to their midday meal.'

'Would you keep them out of the yard?' asked Dan.

'Oh, I'll take them 'ome with me again,' said Cassie, 'and make sure they don't try to feed me parrot to me cat.'

'If they do, take them to the Zoo and feed them to the lions,' said Dan.

'Oh, 'elp, I don't want to be fed to no lions,' said Bubbles.

'Nor me,' said Penny-Farving.

'Behave yourselves, then,' said Dan, and went up to knock on Tilly's door.

'Keep out,' called Tilly.

'I'm off now,' called Dan. 'Just thought I'd let you know me little angels are goin' along to Mrs Higgins after Cassie's left. Mrs Higgins has promised to have them for the afternoon.'

'That won't solve anything,' called Tilly. 'You can't marry Mrs 'Iggins. Go and fetch Gladys Hobday 'ome. Good mornin'. Oh, I measured the gels for their new dresses yesterday, and I'll be startin' them in a day or so.'

'Good as one of the fam'ly, you are, Tilly.'

'Hoppit,' said Tilly.

With Cassie having taken the holy terrors to her home, Tilly had a busy and undisturbed time at her sewing-machine. At one stage, when she was holding a child's dress up to the light to inspect the stitching, she experienced the feeling that eyes were watching her. She turned her gaze to the window, and there, at the opposite window, framed by the curtains, was the face of Mrs Harper, her expression wooden. It changed, however, as Tilly caught sight of her, and a neighbourly smile appeared. She waved to Tilly. Tilly nodded and managed a smile of her own. The face disappeared. The knob of the blind cord did a little jig as a withdrawing head of hair brushed it.

I think I've got a nosy neighbour, Tilly said to herself.

All went well for Tilly until three-thirty in the afternoon, when she had to go down and answer a knock on the front door. Mrs Higgins stood there, with Bubbles and Penny-Farving.

''Ere we are, Miss Thomas,' said the good lady, 'I've brought the children back.'

'Beg your pardon?' said Tilly.

'It's us,' said Penny-Farving.

'Yes, I told Mr Rogers I'd 'ave them till half-past-three,' said Mrs Higgins. 'Now I've got to do me shoppin' and I don't want to leave them with Alice,

135

not while she still can't get about much on 'er feet. They've been behavin' themselves except for tryin' to put our cat through me mangle. Ain't they a pair of little loves? Well, I'd best get down the market now.' Off she went, and in went Bubbles and Penny-Farving to gaze up at Tilly with angelic smiles.

Lord have mercy on my soul, thought Tilly, I'm going to strangle their dad this evening.

Cassie was waiting on the corner of Browning Street when Freddy arrived there on his way home from work. His dad was with him. Mr Brown said hello to Cassie and walked on, leaving Freddy to have Cassie to himself, which might be a trial to the lad and might not. It would depend on how Freddy handled her.

'Oh, 'ello, Freddy,' she said, 'fancy it bein' you.'

'Well, I've been me all day,' said Freddy. He grinned. 'And yesterday as well.'

'Would you like a kiss?' asked Cassie, looking dreamy.

'A kiss? What for?' asked Freddy, walking with her down Browning Street.

'Well, you've just come 'ome from work,' said Cassie, 'and I don't suppose anyone's kissed you at your scrap yard.'

'No, well, there's not a lot of kissin' goin' on in the yard,' said Freddy.

'Oh, that's good,' said Cassie, 'I don't want to 'ave to worry about you bein' unfaithful. King Edward was ever so unfaithful to Queen Alexandra, so me dad told me once, and it turned 'er hair white with worry and she used to have to dye it to hide 'er worry. Oh, look, here's Mrs 'Arper.'

Mrs Harper was approaching at a brisk walk.

''Ello,' she said, 'you two again?'

'Oh, a pleasure, I'm sure,' said Cassie. 'I see you don't 'ave your nice parrot with you, Mrs 'Arper.'

'I see you don't 'ave yours, either, ducky,' said Mrs Harper, summoning up a smile.

'No, I don't take 'im out a lot,' said Cassie. 'Me sister Nellie says it's not what parrots are used to. She's just got 'ome from 'er work and is doin' the supper.'

'Well, yer don't say,' said Mrs Harper.

'Cassie will if you let 'er,' said Freddy with a grin, 'she does a lot of sayin'.'

'Got a tongue in 'er head, 'as she?' said Mrs Harper. 'Well, good for her. Now I've got to go and buy a packet of tea before me 'ubby and 'is brother get 'ome.'

'Excuse me, Mrs 'Arper,' said Cassie, 'but has your 'ouse been 'aunted since you moved in?'

Mrs Harper, remembering her disturbed night, tightened her mouth.

'Cassie, don't be daft,' said Freddy.

'I just thought I'd ask,' said Cassie.

Mrs Harper shook herself.

'Well, like I mentioned,' she said, 'I'll just 'ave to 'ide me 'ead under the blankets if the old lady's ghost starts walkin' at nights, won't I? So long now.' And away she went. Cassie called after her.

'Could we bring Cecil to 'ave another talk with Percy sometime, Mrs 'Arper?'

'Sometime,' called Mrs Harper, 'sometime.'

'There, Freddy,' said Cassie, 'you and me can take Cecil in again on Saturday afternoon.'

'Now look, Cassie,' said Freddy, as they approached his house, 'I ain't spendin' me Saturday afternoons keepin' you company with two potty parrots. Me mind's made up for good.' They reached his front door. 'You comin' in to say 'ello to me mum? Talk to yourself,' he added. Cassie, using the latchcord, was already in. Following on, he thought someone must have told Mrs Harper about the murder that had happened years ago, that it had been an old lady that got done in. People ought to keep quiet about that sort of thing when talking to new tenants of the house. Not that Mrs Harper had seemed bothered. She'd treated Cassie's question as a bit of a giggle. Except she had frowned a bit at first.

Tilly had had a brainwave. Collecting offcuts of various materials, she had given them to the girls, together with lengths of string, and told them to make themselves large rag balls that they could play with and throw at each other without doing any damage. When Dan arrived home they were in the kitchen, sitting at the table, still striving after an hour and more to complete large rag balls. Offcuts were scattered over the table and on the floor.

''Ello, Dad,' said Penny-Farving, 'look what Tilly give us so we can make a big rag ball each.'

'We've been ever so good,' said Bubbles.

Dan kissed them both and said, 'That's the stuff, little sausages. Um, did Tilly say anything when Mrs Higgins brought you home?'

'No, she just give us funny looks,' said Penny-Farving.

'But when she took us up to 'er room, she said there was goin' to be a war.' Bubbles offered this piece of information generously.

'Is there goin' to be a war, Dad?' asked Penny-Farving, doing some string-tying.

'Hope not,' said Dan. 'I'll just go up and have a word with Tilly.'

Up he went. He knocked.

'Come in,' said Tilly.

He opened the door and went in. The armchair cushion, flung, arrived in his face. That was followed by a bolster from Tilly's bed, except that she didn't fling it, she wielded it, bashing his face and head with it.

'Oh, my bleedin' soul—'

'Take that.' Bash. 'And that.' Wallop. 'And that!' Thump.

'Tilly—'

'I'll give you Tilly, I'll give you something for your bleedin' soul – take that and some more as well!' Wallop.

Dan tripped and fell over the armchair. Down came the wielded bolster, bashing him. He grabbed it, pulled at it, and Tilly fell on top of him. They rolled off to the floor, Tilly's legs up in the air. A consolation factor made up for the bashing as long legs, shining stockings and delectable underwear made a spectacular impact on his eye.

'Mother O'Reilly, mind my eyesight, Tilly.'

'Oh, yer gawpin' oaf, look at me clothes!'

'Well, I am lookin', ain't I? And can I help it?'

'Oh, yer lecher!' Tilly jumped up, took hold of the bolster and set about him again, while he was on the floor. 'You ought to be boiled in oil, you did. Try this for your eyesight!' Whack, whack.

What a woman. That figure of hers held a healthy percentage of vim and vigour. Dan rolled away from the thumping bolster, and came up on his knees. Wallop. Down he went again. It was war all right. Dan, not a bloke to lie about and get slaughtered, made another grab. Tilly, muffling a yell, fell on top of him again, and Dan rolled her over. Her skirt and slip ran upwards.

'Now look,' breathed Dan, 'can we—'

'Oh, me legs!'

'It's a lot more than that—'

'I'll do for you, Dan Rogers! I never met such evil eyes as you've got. Pull me skirt down, d'you 'ear?'

Dan got up. Tilly sat up. She covered herself, then took hold of the bolster again. Dan put his foot on it.

'Can't we talk?' he asked.

Tilly came to her feet, face flushed, eyes flashing new danger signals.

'You did it on me again, you let Mrs 'Iggins land the gels on me this afternoon,' she said.

'It wasn't what I meant,' said Dan, 'I told them to look after themselves until I got home.'

'That's criminal thinkin',' said Tilly. 'You can't leave little gels like them to look after themselves. Little gels like them could set fire to the 'ouse.'

'I'll admit, it's been a bit difficult since Alice fractured her foot,' said Dan.

'Oh, yer daft loony,' said Tilly, 'can't you get it into your thick 'ead that their mother's got to come and take care of them?'

'Awkward, y'know,' said Dan,' 'she's not cut out for 'ome life, bein' what you might call an artiste.'

'You might call 'er that,' said Tilly, 'I've got other names for 'er. Where's 'er circus right now?'

'I think it's due to pitch near Margate for a short season.'

'All right, you go there, then, and I'll do you a favour by comin' with you next Sunday,' said Tilly, with a ferocious kind of determination. 'We'll take a wooden mallet with us for knockin' her on her 'ead. When she's unconscious, we'll tie her up, wrap her up and cart 'er back to London on a train.'

'I don't think she'll like that,' said Dan. 'It's her temperament. Have I told you about her temperament? It's all due to her gipsy upbringing and her feelin' that she was once a Hungarian dancer.'

'Did she come from 'Ungary, then?' demanded Tilly.

'No, she thinks she's a reincarnation case,' said Dan.

'Oh, she does, does she?' said Tilly. 'Well, we'll see if a few taps of the mallet will knock 'er brains about a bit and wake 'er up to the fact that she's nobody but Gladys Hobday. Now, you just find out if that circus is really goin' to be at Margate.'

'I'll give it a bit of thought.'

'You'll give it more than that,' said Tilly, 'or I'll 'it you with a brick next time you get my goat. Specially if you interfere with me clothes and offend me integrity. 'Ere, what's that cross-eyed look of yours all about?'

'Can I help still havin' mem'ries of what caught me mince pies only a few minutes ago?' said Dan not unreasonably.

Tilly made a dive for the grounded bolster. Dan made a dive for the stairs. The heavy bolster came hurtling down after him. It struck him in the middle of his back.

'Got yer!' called Tilly triumphantly from the landing.

What a woman. Why, he thought, couldn't a meek and mild one have taken the lodgings? One who wouldn't have minded keeping an eye on the girls until Alice was back? But when advertising for a lodger, a bloke couldn't actually put down that his preference was for a female meek and mild, and fond of children. As it was, he'd let himself in for another wild Hungarian.

'Dad, what was you doin' with Tilly upstairs?'

asked Penny-Farving as he entered the kitchen.

'Just a bit of a talk,' he said.

'It didn't sound like that,' said Bubbles, her odd-shaped rag ball growing in size.

'There was a lot of bumps,' said Penny-Farving.

'Were there, me angel? Well, never mind, no worries.'

'Just as well you put that blind up,' said Mrs Harper, as she served supper to the men.

'Why?' asked the man called Wally.

'There's a woman lodger next door that sits in the window of the upstairs back. She looks to me like she's usin' a sewin'-machine. She can see right across.'

'We'll start using the blind,' said Wally. 'The gas mantle must be lit and the blind pulled down as soon as it becomes dark each night. The light can be turned out later.'

'Well, you're the brains round 'ere, I suppose,' said Mrs Harper.

'You are still valuable to us,' said the other man, 'providing us with a respectable front.'

'One day next week we will all go out together,' said Wally.

'I'll wear me best 'at,' said Mrs Harper.

She woke up again that night. But, gritting her teeth, she shut her ears to the whispers and rustles, and went back to sleep. Nothing would get her out of the bed, not until sane daylight broke.

Cassie arrived promptly in the morning, and Dan gave her three shillings, a shilling for each morning so far. Cassie went dreamy with delight and assured him she liked looking after Bubbles and Penny-Farving.

'That's nice to hear,' said Dan, relieving Bubbles of her porridge spoon. She was using it in an attempt to beat her slice of toast to death.

'Oh, they're little loves really, Mr Rogers,' said Cassie.

'Are they?' asked Dan, an over-indulgent dad but not so blind as to accept Cassie's comment at face value.

'Well, now and again they are,' said Cassie. 'I'll take them to me home again and then down the market, shall I? Then I can do some shoppin' for me dad that I said I would.'

'Cassie, would you make sure they don't pinch fruit off stalls?'

'If they do, when me back's turned, shall I give them a smack?' asked Cassie.

'Yes, you do that,' said Dan, who always shirked handing out smacks himself.

'But, Dad, you don't like us bein' smacked,' protested Penny-Farving.

'Sorry, sausage, I'll 'ave to grin and bear it,' said Dan. He told Cassie he'd be back home in time to prepare the midday meal himself, as it was Saturday, and off he went to his job.

Tilly heard him leave the house. For once he hadn't come up to deliver his usual load of bland codswallop. Well, that was something to be thankful for. It was more than enough to know she'd saddled herself with the responsibility of persuading him to marry the girls' mother, or at least to drag the woman home and make her do her duty. Crikey, she'd really set about him yesterday evening. Well, he'd earned it, except it was horrible to remember she'd finished up nearly standing on her head.

★　　★　　★

Mid-morning, and Miss Polly Simms was climbing the stairs to the offices of Adams Enterprises. Polly was now thirty-three, and as vivacious and brittle as ever, her grey eyes and her smile often self-mocking. A supple and slender woman, she still wore the hair style of a flapper, a Colleen Moore bob whose curving points always seemed to lightly caress her cheeks. She was a school-teacher. Friends as upper-class as she was found it hysterical that she actually worked, and as a teacher of the lower classes. She was at West Square Girls School, attended by Rosie and Rosie's cousin, Annabelle. She had taught at Rosie's primary school, and had subsequently made shameless use of her father's influence to secure the post at West Square. She always saw Rosie as the daughter she might have had by Boots if Emily hadn't got her hands on him first.

An ambulance driver during the Great War, Polly could never forget those horrendous years, nor the sound of the guns, nor the men of the trenches, of whom Boots had been one. Her attachment to him was incurable. Perhaps because she had never had him she would always want him.

She knocked on the door of his office and went in without waiting for his response. Boots, at his desk, turned his head. Seeing her, he took on a slightly wary expression. His feelings for Sir Henry Simms's extrovert daughter were of a kind he kept closely guarded.

'Polly?'

Polly, closing the door, said, 'Good morning, you swine.'

'Now what have I done?' asked Boots.

'Had lunch at Simpson's with Sammy's old girl-friend, Rachel Goodman,' said Polly. 'You low-down snake in the grass, when have you ever invited me to a high-class lunch in town?'

'I've had the pleasure of lunching with you several times in the pub across the road,' said Boots.

'Burning arrows, I'm not talking about a sandwich and a gin and it in a pub,' said Polly, 'I'm talking about an intimate lunch in the West End, with violins playing. If you're thinking of having an affair with Rachel, I'll come round to your house and smash all your windows.'

'Emily won't like that,' said Boots, 'she'll phone for a policeman.'

'Damn Emily,' said Polly, striking in a stylish hat and spring coat. The day was fresh. 'I'm meeting Rachel for lunch at the Ritz today.' She and Rachel had established a warm friendship, due in the beginning to their affinity with the Adams family. 'I phoned her this morning to confirm the time, and we had a hen party over the line. Until, that is, she told me about lunching with you. End of hen party.'

'Didn't she tell you it was a business lunch?' said Boots.

'She tried to,' said Polly, 'but there's no such thing as a woman having a business lunch with a man like you. When I get to the Ritz, I'm going to spoil her ravishing beauty by scratching her eyes out.'

'I'll smack your bottom if you do,' said Boots.

'Promises, promises, that's all I've ever had from you,' said Polly.

'That's why we're still good friends,' said Boots. His phone rang, and Polly stood fuming while he attended to the call. The curse of it was that fuming was no real help to a woman whose prevailing desire was to get him into her bed and eat him. Putting the phone down, he said, 'Now where were we, Polly old love?'

He was looking up at her with his smile close to the surface, as if even at her most furious he couldn't help being amused by her. She swooped, she put her mouth to his and kissed him out of sheer frustrated want. She felt his immediate response, but then he wrecked the moment by breaking the kiss.

'Must you?' she said.

'I think we're out of order,' said Boots.

'Well, bloody good show,' said Polly.

'It's hardly the time and place, Polly.'

'Where, then, and when?'

'Let's see,' said Boots, still giving nothing away, 'it's the monthly garden cricket and tea party next Sunday, to which you're coming as usual. I'd suggest after tea and in the garden shed.'

'God help you, d'you think that's funny?'

'It will be, if we fall over the mower,' said Boots.

Polly's sense of humour saved her from smashing up his phone. She burst into laughter, at which point one of the general office girls knocked on the door and came in with Boots's morning coffee. She checked as she saw Polly.

'Oh, shall I bring another coffee, Mr Adams?'

'Not for me, thanks,' said Polly.

'All right,' said the girl, and placed the coffee on Boots's desk, the while taking in Polly's elegance.

'Thanks, Gwen,' said Boots, and the girl left.

'I'm going now,' said Polly, 'I've got this appointment to strangle Rachel. But about next Sunday.'

'What about it?' asked Boots.

'Smash the mower up and get it out of the shed before I arrive.'

'I'll have to mow the cricket pitch first,' said Boots.

'God knows why I love you,' said Polly, 'I must be right off my chump.'

'Join the club,' said Boots.

'Here's my seal of membership,' said Polly, and kissed him again before leaving.

During the afternoon, Mrs Harper answered a knock on her door.

'What, you two again?' she said.

'Yes, it's me and Freddy,' said Cassie.

'I don't know why it's me as well,' said Freddy, 'I was supposed to be somewhere else.'

'It's Cecil too,' said Cassie, showing the covered birdcage. 'Can we bring 'im in to see Percy, Mrs 'Arper?'

'Not now, dearie, I've got company,' said Mrs Harper. The men were in the kitchen. 'Some other time. Toodle-oo.' She closed the door.

'Oh, bother, Cecil won't 'alf be disappointed,' said Cassie. 'Shall we take 'im up the park, Freddy?'

'What for?' asked Freddy.

'He can look at the flowers. He likes flowers.'

'Oh, 'e said so, did 'e?' asked Freddy, walking up the Place with his eccentric and imaginative mate.

'Well, I showed 'im the flowers Nellie's young man brought, and asked 'im if he liked them,' said Cassie. ''E didn't say anything, but he nodded 'is head.'

'Why didn't he say anything?' asked Freddy.

'He was eatin' 'is birdseed,' said Cassie, 'and 'e never speaks with 'is mouth full.'

A girl, fifteen-year-old Flossie Dicks, came walking down the Place from Browning Street. She gave Freddy a come-on smile.

''Ello, Freddy, ain'tcher gettin' 'andsome?' she said. Then she almost fell over Cassie's foot. ''Ere, who did that?' she demanded.

'You hurt my foot then, kickin' it like that,' said

147

Cassie, who had attempted to trip her up. 'If you do it again, Flossie Dicks, I'll kick you back.'

'Like to see you try,' said Flossie, but went on her way just in case Cassie did start kicking.

'Cassie, what d'you do that for?' asked Freddy.

'She's flirty, that's why,' said Cassie, 'and you're not to talk to 'er. Are we goin' up the park, then?'

'No, to your home,' said Freddy, 'so that you can get rid of Cecil. Then I'll take you up King and Queen Street and buy you a toffee-apple.'

'Crikey, d'you love me, then, Freddy?'

'Ask me when I'm thirty,' said Freddy.

'Oh, all right,' said Cassie.

Over lunch with Polly in town, Rachel had been taken to task for daring to dine with Boots at Simpson's. Stick to your weakness for Sammy, Polly said, or I'll draw blood. Rachel assured her it had only been a business lunch. Rats to that, said Polly, I've already told Boots it's impossible for any woman to have a business lunch with him.

'I should do you down with Boots?' murmured Rachel.

'Well, old thing, I can only say I feel the pain of a knife in my back. Don't be surprised if I suddenly pour my glass of wine all over your lap. What was the business about?'

'Oh, simply a little commission from Boots, Polly love. Nothing to give you even a small twinge.'

'I don't have small twinges over Boots, darling, only fiery ones.'

'How we suffer from our frustrations,' said Rachel. 'Is there a way out?'

'Yes,' said Polly, 'we could shoot each other.'

Chapter Eleven

The waggons of Blundell's Circus, some motorized and some horse-drawn, trawled their way around the Elephant and Castle and into the New Kent Road, gathering up the dust of a dry May. They were heading for Margate.

At four o'clock, Tilly returned from a visit to the market, her shopping bag full. She opened the door by pulling on the latchcord. Bubbles and Penny-Farving, playing with kids in the street, called to her.

''Ello, Tilly, can we come and be wiv yer?'

Tilly dodged the question by quickly entering the house and closing the door. Dan, keeping his eye on the girls from the parlour, came out into the passage.

'Like a cup of tea?' he asked.

Tilly, sensing a cup of tea was going to turn into a bribe, said, 'Sorry, can't stop, Mr Rogers, I've got shoppin' to unload and things to do.' She began to climb the stairs.

'I'll bring you one up,' said Dan, looking casual and manly in a shirt and belted trousers.

'Well, if you come up with a cup of tea and start askin' favours of me,' said Tilly from the top stair, 'I'll get me bolster off the bed again and lay you out.'

Dan, looking up at her from the foot of the stairs, grinned.

'Compliments to yer, Tilly,' he said.

'What d'you mean, compliments?'

'Well, from where I am,' said Dan, 'you're a sight for sore eyes.'

Tilly's legs and skirt whisked out of vision as she hastily put herself on the landing. She looked down at him from over the banister rail.

'You ought to be locked up for indecent gawpin',' she said. 'Don't you 'ave no respect for me integrity?'

'For your integrity, Tilly, I couldn't 'ave more,' said Dan, 'not after all the help you've been, but I can't help bein' naturally compliment'ry about what you look like up there when I'm down here.'

'Just a moment,' said Tilly. She put her shopping bag on the floor, went into her bedroom and came out again, carrying the washstand pitcher. She held it out over the banisters and turned it upside-down. Water sheeted. Dan, however, suspecting something was going to be dropped on his head, shifted himself out of the way fast. The water splashed and ran over the bottom stairs.

'Strike a light,' he grinned, 'no sooner a word than a blow.'

'Missed, did I?' said Tilly. 'Well, drowning's too good, anyway, for a bloke with eyes like you've got. I don't like bein' unkind, but you've got evil eyes, Mr Rogers.'

'Well, blow me,' said Dan, a pained expression on his rugged face, 'I never knew it was evil just lookin' at a woman.'

'Well, it is, the way you look,' said Tilly, 'and you'd best get it into yer head that I'm a girl who can stand up for 'erself.'

'Don't I know it,' said Dan. 'Every time you stand up for yerself, I finish on the floor. But there's no hard feelings, Tilly, I respect what you're standin' up for, specially as I'm a husband and father.'

'Here, give over, you're not a husband,' said Tilly, staying behind the banisters and keeping her skirt and legs out of sight.

'Well, no, not yet,' said Dan, 'but I feel I'm goin' to be. I feel you're right, I've got to marry the girls' mother.'

'Well, hoo-blimey-hooray,' said Tilly, 'now you're talkin' like a man instead of a soft cream doughnut, and not before—'

She was interrupted as the front door opened to another pull on the latchcord, and in tumbled a hurrying Bubbles and Penny-Farving, slightly grimy from their street play.

'Dad, Dad,' cried Penny-Farving, 'it's her, she's comin'!'

'Who's her?' asked Dan.

'Our muvver,' said Bubbles, and she and Penny-Farving tucked themselves behind their dad's legs. In through the open door came a woman of thirty, carrying a medium-sized suitcase. She was wearing a dark blue hat and a cherry-red coat, the coat trimmed with astrakhan. It was tightly waisted with a flared knee-length skirt. Long lace-up black boots sheathed her black-stockinged legs. Her face was made up to give her a painted prettiness, and her figure was of a bold hour-glass kind. She came to a theatrical stop in the passage, the skirt of her coat executing a little swirl. She put the suitcase down and darted a glance at the little girls seeking to hide themselves.

'Ah, are zey my children, zat pair wiz dirty faces?' she asked.

Lovaduck, thought Tilly from above, that's her, that's Gladys Hobday trying to sound like a Hungarian? Looks like a tart from here.

151

'Come out, me angels,' said Dan, 'she's not goin' to eat you.'

The girls peeped apprehensively. The woman shook her head at Dan.

'Zat is not ze way wiz girls, to let them 'ave dirty faces,' she said.

'Well, now you're here, you can do something about it,' said Dan.

The woman, giving him a disdainful look, said, 'I am not hearing zat.'

'Go into the kitchen for a bit, me sausages,' said Dan, and the girls seemed only too glad to lose themselves. 'I've been thinkin', Elvira, it's time you gave up the circus to look after the girls.'

'Pooh, you silly man, zat is not for me, zat is for someone who does not mind washing dirty faces and grubby clothes. I am ze famous Elvira Karola, ze 'Ungarian wire-walker. But I 'ave stepped out of my caravan to come and see you, to forgive you for getting me wiz child – ah, twice, you naughty man, so zat I am thinking I must marry you. But no, it is not for me, it would not please all ze men who admire me.'

'Blow pleasin' them,' said Dan, 'it's time you and me did what's right for the girls, not what's right for you.'

That's the stuff, thought Tilly, go it.

'Again I am not hearing zat,' said the woman.

'Well, hear this,' said Dan, moving through the passage and closing the front door. 'Now you're here we'll fix up to get married at the town hall as soon as I can arrange it.'

'No, no, you are crazy,' said the woman. 'But I am still fond of you and will spend ze night wiz you, zen take ze train in ze morning to catch up wiz ze circus at Margate.'

'No, no dice,' said Dan. 'We're goin' to get married for the sake of the girls, and you're goin' to look after them.'

The woman let a hiss escape.

'Stupid man! I am to look after your children? I, ze magical Elvira?'

'They're your children as well,' said Dan.

'Ah, what a stupid way to make love to me, by giving me ze children I did not want!'

'Hold on,' said Dan, 'you did your share of draggin' me into bed.'

'Ah, love is terrible,' sighed the woman. 'You are so good in bed, Dan, but zat does not mean we should marry. Ze circus is to go to France late zis summer, and cannot go wizout ze great Elvira Karola, which is me.' She caught sight of Tilly then, for Tilly had moved to stand on the top stair. 'Who is zat fat woman up zair?'

It was Tilly's turn to let a hiss escape.

'That's Miss Thomas, our lodger,' said Dan, 'but she ain't fat, not from here she ain't, nor from anywhere.'

'Ze cow 'as been listening,' said the Hungarian marvel. 'Let *her* look after ze girls. Does she know 'ow famous I am?'

'No, I bloody-well don't,' said Tilly, and down the stairs she came, hot with outrage, to confront the woman. The hour-glass figure and the sumptuous figure locked bosom to bosom. Well, almost they did. Only three inches separated them. 'You ain't Elvira Carry-oolala or whatever,' breathed Tilly, 'you're Gladys Hobday, and if I was Mr Rogers I'd give you a bloody good 'iding.'

''Ow dare you!' hissed the tightrope wonder, and smacked Tilly's face.

'That's done it,' said Tilly, and boxed the woman's ears. The mask dropped.

'Oh, yer bleedin' bitch!' screeched Gladys Hobday.

'Steady,' said Dan, 'I don't want to send for the fire brigade.'

Gladys smacked his face this time.

'Get this fat cow out of 'ere!' she hissed.

'Well, I never,' said Tilly, 'ain't you 'orrible? Mr Rogers, you'll 'ave to lock 'er up till she comes to 'er senses and does what's right. You owe it to yer little angels. Lock 'er up for long enough and she'll 'ave time to take a good look at 'erself. There's got to be a woman there somewhere, and a mother too.'

'I'll bleedin' murder you, yer saucy bitch!' yelled Gladys.

'How about if we all calm down over a pot of tea?' suggested Dan.

'Bugger a pot of tea, and 'er as well,' said Gladys, 'I'm gettin' out of this crummy hole.' She reached for her suitcase. Tilly kicked it over. Gladys, spitting, turned on her. Dan shoved himself between them. He received a furious swipe from Gladys and a blow from Tilly.

'Gawd blimey,' he said, 'd'you want me to knock yer heads together?'

'Lock 'er up,' said Tilly, 'it's your only chance.'

'Well, Elvira,' said Dan, 'I put it to you—'

'She's Gladys, not Elvira,' said Tilly, 'and if you'll remember that, you'll come down to earth and not let 'er treat you like a dog's dinner.'

'Let me get at that cow,' panted Gladys, 'I'll bleedin' kill 'er.'

'Shut up,' said Dan, 'I don't like hearin' a woman talk like that.'

'Bloody 'ard luck,' said Gladys, and made a dive for

154

her suitcase, lying on its side. Tilly executed a tigerish spring and put a foot on it. The kitchen door opened just a little and a small face showed itself. A small voice was heard.

'Dad, is she chuckin' fings?' asked Penny-Farving.

'Not yet, sausage, you sit with Bubbles,' said Dan. Penny-Farving vanished.

Gladys was trying to yank the suitcase free, bending to the task.

'Now's yer chance,' said Tilly to Dan, 'smack 'er bottom.'

'Not my style,' said Dan. 'Still, now she's here I suppose I ought to make her stay and see reason.'

'She'll 'ave to stay if she's got no clothes,' said Tilly, and Gladys, with a screech, bolted for the front door. Tilly got there first and barred the way. Gladys cannoned into her and bounced off. She opened her mouth to scream, and Dan clapped a hand over her lips.

'Don't let's 'ave a lot of noise, Elvira,' he said.

'Best thing is to take 'er into your room,' said Tilly. 'Then get all 'er clothes off, put them in your wardrobe and lock it.'

'You serious?' said Dan.

'It's the best thing,' said Tilly. 'She won't fancy runnin' off back to 'er circus without a stitch on. She can stay in bed and you can talk to 'er till she realizes she's got to stop muckin' about on a tightrope and be a mother to 'er gels.'

'It would take me a week to get all her clothes off,' said Dan, one arm holding Gladys fast, and his right hand still over her mouth.

'Well, Mr Rogers,' said Tilly, 'for the sake of all the good that'll come from turnin' her into a 'ome-lovin' woman, I'll do it for yer. It won't take me more than

155

ten minutes in private, unless she's got a padlock on 'er corset.'

'I'm not sure – oh, blimey!' Dan let go of Gladys. She'd managed to sink her teeth into his hand. She yelled then.

''Elp! Police!'

''Old her!' shouted Tilly, but Gladys rushed into the parlour. Tilly went after her. Dan heard a thumping bump and a strangled yelp from Gladys.

'Talk about a quiet weekend,' he said, and went in. Gladys was on the floor, on her back, Tilly kneeling astride her hips. Gladys's legs were kicking, her skirts all over her hips. Dan recognized the legs as those he'd seen so often in circus tights. He also recognized that a battle was taking place. They weren't skinny women, either of them, they were both full-bodied, and it was obvious they could do each other a lot of damage. Gladys was biting and clawing, Tilly working to subdue her. Dan heard something rip and tear.

'Oh, yer naughty woman,' breathed Tilly, 'that's me second-best blouse you've just done in.'

'Sod yer,' panted Gladys.

Dan sighed, reached and hauled Tilly off the dishevelled Gladys. Gladys, not a high-wire act for nothing, was up in a flash. Lashing out with a booted foot, she caught Dan on the side of his left calf. It collapsed him, and Tilly went down with him, landing on top of him. Gladys, spitting, dashed out, picked up her suitcase, opened the front door and shot through like an expelled cannonball made of indiarubber. Her loosened hat danced on her head as she made a beeline for Browning Street.

'You wet week, you've let 'er get away,' panted Tilly.

156

'I happen to 'ave a broken leg,' said Dan. 'Get off me.'

Tilly rolled off and sat up. Dan, on his back, did some more gawping. His lady lodger's button-up blouse was split wide open, revealing a deep valley.

'What a chump,' breathed Tilly, 'we 'ad her floored and you let her scarper.'

'It wouldn't have worked,' said Dan, 'she'd have smashed up all me bedroom furniture and the windows as well. It's her Hungarian reincarnation that does it. Look, would you mind doin' yer blouse up? It's givin' me more eye problems.'

Tilly looked down at herself. Above her exposed corset top, fulsome upper curves peeped, and hardly in a coy fashion.

'Oh, me gawd,' she said, 'did it with 'er claws. Nearly tore me second-best blouse off. I'm chargin' you for a new one, and d'you mind takin' them evil eyes of yours for a walk somewhere?' Tilly gathered her ripped blouse together. 'Mind, I'm not sayin' you're evil all through. There's some good in you, or you wouldn't be the kind of dad you are to the gels, which makes me wonder what made you take up with that 'orrible female.'

'I think her circus tights did it,' said Dan, 'they went all the way up to her spangled corset.'

'Don't be disgusting,' said Tilly, 'and what're you still lyin' there for?'

'I'm worn out,' said Dan, 'and in any case, I don't feel like gettin' up now that the bird's flown. And I've got a gloomy idea that's the last I'll see of me red-hot Elvira.'

'If that woman wasn't your gels' mother, I'd call it good riddance,' said Tilly. She got up, and Dan followed. He rubbed his hurt leg. 'But you can still catch 'er in 'er caravan at Margate, can't you? Take a mallet with you, like I said, and one of them wandering preachers that do Bible readings. Hit 'er with the mallet, just enough so that she won't know if it's Christmas or Easter, and then get the preacher to marry you. I'll 'ave to come with you, because you won't get her home by yerself. I'm sorry to say this, Mr Rogers, but while you look like a man with a man's muscles, you're as wet as a paper bag that's been out in the rain all night. Otherwise, you'd 'ave put that woman over your knees and pasted 'er.'

'I'm not sure it's right, a bloke pastin' a woman,' said Dan.

'It's right with a woman like Gladys Hobday,' said Tilly. 'I don't know why I'm puttin' meself out tryin' to help a bloke as unsure as you are. Blow my eye and Betty Martin, why am I botherin' when I've got me livin' to make?' Her wrecked blouse parted again. Dan blinked. 'Them eyeballs of yours'll drop out one day,' she said.

'Look how about that pot of tea?' suggested Dan. 'Then I'll be puttin' Bubbles and Penny-Farvin' in their Saturday bath – um, unless you'd like to do it.'

'Gawd 'elp us,' said Tilly, 'for a bloke who lets a woman like Gladys Hobday walk all over 'im, you've got a lot more gall than you ought to 'ave. All this week you've been tryin' to make a nursemaid of me, and now you've got the nerve to suggest I might like to bath the gels. Nothing doin'.' Tilly knew she had to fight to keep her independence, and her options. She was thinking of opting tomorrow for a visit to Ruskin Park in her Sunday best. She had a tall dark handsome man in mind, a highly eligible bloke who might give her the eye. She was in need of a man friend, one with a bit more go than Frank, her ex-fiancé. I could let myself go with someone tall dark and handsome, she thought, I've been a virgin long enough, and I'd give it up for a promise to marry me.

Penny-Farving put her head in.

''As she gone, Dad?' she asked.

'Yes, she's gone,' said Dan.

'Cor, what a relief – Dad, what's Tilly showin' 'er bosom for?'

'Her blouse got accident'lly torn,' said Dan, and Tilly did her best to cover herself.

'Oh, did our muvver chuck somefing at 'er?' asked Penny-Farving, and Bubbles appeared. She asked a hesitant question.

'Is she still 'ere, Dad?'

'No, she's gone,' smiled Dan.

'Oh, good,' said Bubbles.

Tilly ground her teeth in anger at a woman whose little girls had reason not to like her.

'Let's have a pot of tea and the jam doughnuts I brought in from Hall's the bakers,' said Dan.

'Oh, bless yer, Dad,' said Penny-Farving.

'Excuse me,' said Tilly, 'I've got to go up and change me blouse. Don't forget about Margate and the gipsy's caravan, Mr Rogers.'

'What a thought,' said Dan.

Tilly disappeared.

On Sunday morning, Dan popped up to knock on his lodger's door.

'All right, come in,' called Tilly.

Dan, entering, smiled and said, 'Mornin', Tilly.' She was at her machine and wearing a floral dress. She turned her head and eyed him with now familiar suspicion.

'I don't like that smile of yours,' she said.

'Sorry about that,' said Dan. 'Just thought I'd come and ask if you'd like to join us for Sunday dinner. I'm doin' roast beef. Fancy sittin' down with us?'

'You can cook?' said Tilly.

'I've had to learn to,' said Dan, 'and I think I'm passable.'

'You shouldn't 'ave had to learn,' said Tilly, 'you've let that woman get away with murder. Are you still daft about 'er?'

'Daft?'

'Infatuated.'

'I've got to admit, she sent me cockeyed in her tights and spangles,' said Dan.

'I don't like to 'ear a man talkin' lustful,' said Tilly, 'so kindly shut up about 'er tights. Anyway, if you're still daft about 'er, I suppose you'd like 'er for a wife, even if there's no sense to it. All I can say is that it's got to be for the sake of the gels. So don't sit in corners, go after 'er, and don't forget about givin' 'er a good 'iding. Never mind she's a woman, a good 'iding ought to do wonders for 'er, and it'll make more of a man of you.'

'You sure?' said Dan.

'Course I'm sure,' said Tilly, 'so gird up yer manly armour and do what a man ought to do with that selfish Gladys Hobday. All right, I'll come down and 'ave Sunday dinner with you, for which invite many thanks. But I'm goin' out after dinner to meet someone.'

'Well, good for you, Tilly,' said Dan, not knowing she was dealing in wishful thinking. 'I'm pleased for yer, you bein' a proud-lookin' woman.'

'Proud? What d'you mean, proud?'

'Only that you're a fine figure of a woman,' said Dan breezily, 'and I've got a feelin' you'd bring the house down in tights and spangles.'

160

Tilly let go a little yell and looked round for something to throw at him. Dan wisely disappeared.

Tilly enjoyed the dinner, and couldn't fault the cooking. In return, she made a contribution in a domestic sense by seeing to it that Bubbles and Penny-Farving exercised proper behaviour at the table. She also played the major part in clearing the table and doing the washing-up, the little girls frisking around her skirts as she worked at the scullery sink. Dan used the tea towel to dry the dishes, whistling as he did so. Tilly thought it very airy-fairy of him to always be so cheerful when he ought to be applying himself seriously to his problems.

Afterwards, she went up to her bedroom and changed into a very nice costume and blouse. She put on some light make-up, then her best hat, and out she went. She took a tram ride to Ruskin Park, the afternoon bright with sunshine. In the park, she joined the cockney and lower-middle-class promenaders, keeping her eyes open for someone tall, dark and handsome. She couldn't have said they were there in their hundreds, so after a while she sat down on a vacant bench and watched as the immediate world passed by. She spotted a tall man, jacket over his arm, hat in his hand, sauntering along with the air of a bloke on the casual look-out for someone who might make his day. She thought him in his early thirties. He stopped as he caught Tilly's glance. A friendly Sunday afternoon smile appeared on his face.

'Mind if I take the weight off me feet?' he asked.

'Well, it's not my bench,' said Tilly, and he smiled again and sat down beside her.

'Not seen you here before,' he said.

'That's funny,' said Tilly, 'I 'aven't seen you, either.'

'Oh, I'm nobody much,' he said, and Tilly wondered if this could be the beginning of a welcome friendship. She wouldn't mind, he was a personable bloke. Not that she'd ever made a habit of being picked up. But you could meet people in parks in a way that was more acceptable than having some street corner Romeo try his luck. 'Have you been waitin' long?' asked the friendly stranger.

'Beg yer pardon?' said Tilly.

'Don't mention it,' he said. 'Where'd you conduct the business?'

'Do what?' said Tilly.

'Well, whatever you call it,' he said, winking.

'You're askin' funny questions,' said Tilly. 'I do dressmakin', but I don't call it a business.'

'Dressmaking's a new one on me,' he said, giving her figure a very friendly look. 'Anyway, how much?'

'What d'you mean, 'ow much?'

'With your kind of looks, I could go to ten bob,' he said, 'but I hope it's not too far, I'm a bit short of time this afternoon.'

Tilly caught on then, and umbrage made her vibrate.

'You disgustin' beast, I've never been more insulted in all me life.'

'Come on, gorgeous, let's go and do a bit of dressmakin' together, if that's what you call it,' he said, winking again.

'If you don't hoppit,' said Tilly, 'I'll bash your 'ead in.'

'But aren't you a friend of Gloria's?' asked the disgusting bloke.

'Who's Gloria?' fumed Tilly.

'She always sits there on a Sunday afternoon,

waitin' for custom,' he said. 'She calls it havin' a tea party.'

'That's done it, that 'as,' said Tilly, and got up and clouted him with her handbag. People stopped to stare. Tilly finished her short meeting with a tall stranger by delivering a kick on his shin, which nearly crippled him and made him think twice about taking certain things for granted. Then she helped herself to a quick flushed walk to the park gates, from where she walked all the way back to her lodgings to give herself a chance to cool off.

It was a relief to find Dan Rogers and his girls were out. She was sure that if he'd appeared, he'd have noticed she still hadn't quite cooled off, that she was still outraged. But the saucy devil had slipped a note under her door.

'Have taken the girls for a bus ride, be back about six. If you're back first, with your bloke, make yourselves a pot of tea in the kitchen, then enjoy it in the parlour, where there's a comfy sofa.'

Men.

In the garden of the house in Red Post Hill, cricket was in progress and noisily so. Chinese Lady always had all the families there once a month in the summer. It was her way of making sure the young ones, as much as their parents, knew the importance of belonging, and that family loyalty was what the Lord asked of everyone. Come rain or shine, hardship or good fortune, family togetherness was what counted. Then there was Miss Simms, Sir Henry's daughter, whose eyes fastened on Boots so much when she thought no-one was looking. Bless the woman, I like her, thought Chinese Lady, and it's best to keep her a family friend, because it's harder for a family friend to do something she knows she shouldn't.

Chinese Lady sat at the garden table outside the kitchen, keeping an eye on the little ones sitting with her. There were four of them, Alice and David, children of Tommy and Vi, together with Daniel and infant Bess, children of Sammy and Susie. Lizzy and Ned's offspring, Annabelle, Bobby, Emma and Edward, were all joining in the cricket, and so, of course, were Rosie and Tim, the beloved of Boots. Yes, he can be as airy-fairy as he likes, thought Chinese Lady, but that only oldest son of mine has got the kind of fatherly weakness for his son and daughter that does him credit. Fatherly weakness that's strong in a man is highly creditable, it's put there by God. Emily likes him for it, which she should, because he gives them so much of his time. Mind, he's still like a music hall comic sometimes. I don't know where he gets it from, not from me, nor his late dad. The war ought to have cured him, specially when he was blinded, but it didn't. It's ingrained, that's what it is. Man and boy, he's always said things that never mean what a body thinks they do. Still, he's been a good husband to Emily, and if I know him like I should he won't make a fool of himself over Miss Polly Simms, nor over any other woman that gives him looks, like Mrs Fletcher next door. If he ever did, I'd make him wish he'd never been born.

The cricket was chaotic. Polly, her stumps spreadeagled by a wicked ball from Boots, was indulging a tantrum, yelling at him that fire and brimstone were too good for a man who thought he was Mars and delivered thunderbolts. He's always doing that to me, said Lizzy. Oh, what a shame, said Rosie, but you're still out, Aunt Polly. All the young people called her Aunt Polly now. I don't mind being out, said Polly, but I do mind being nearly broken in half by your fiend of a father, Rosie. Emily old thing, she said, can't you get your husband to stop thinking he's the god of war? Emily, who always watched Polly like a hawk, but had never caught her putting a foot wrong, said she might as well talk to her mangle as to Boots.

Polly, willowy in a white shirt-blouse and cream skirt, laughed. Once engaged in garden cricket with these families, she became as boisterous as they always were. She had never known people with so much enthusiasm for life and so much affinity with each other. Their origins were cockney, and the cockney nuances in the speech of some of them were frequently perceptible. With others, like Tommy and Vi, unaffected cockney accents still prevailed. Yet Polly was drawn to the whole brood as if by a magnet, their rousing enjoyment of these occasions irrepressible and infectious. Vivacious herself, she quickly became one of them. And she would have been one of them in every sense if she stood in Emily's place.

'Would someone like to tell me if Polly's out or not out?' enquired Boots.

'Out!' yelled Tim, who was in his dad's team.

'Not out!' yelled all the young people who were in Polly's team.

'Never mind, sports, I'm out,' said Polly, relinquishing the bat to Lizzy.

'Boots,' said gentle Vi, 'don't you think you ought to bowl underarm to all the ladies?'

'Ladies?' said Sammy. 'What ladies?'

'Uncle Sammy,' said Rosie, 'Nana's listening to you.'

'So am I,' said Susie, her hair the colour of golden corn in the bright light of the June sun.

165

'I think I tripped up,' said Sammy. 'Unconscious, like. All right, Boots, bowl underarm to all the ladies.'

'If he bowls underarm to me,' said Lizzy, 'I'll knock him silly for insultin' me.' Lizzy was, of course, a batsman of renown.

'There you are, Boots,' called Ned, 'that's no lady, that's my wife.'

The young ones yelled with laughter.

'Ned Somers,' called Chinese Lady, 'I heard that.'

'Sorry, old lady,' said Ned, 'I had one of Sammy's unconscious moments.'

'I'll see to you when I get you home, Ned Somers,' said Lizzy. 'Now, come on, Boots, stop standin' about lookin' like Lord Muck waitin' for the muffin man. Bowl up.'

Boots, in cricket shirt and flannels, hair a little ruffled from exercise, wore his usual good-humoured expression.

'Sure I'm not interrupting the conversation?' he said.

'Worse than that, Daddy,' said Rosie, 'you're holding up the cricket.'

'Hit him, someone,' said Lizzy.

Boots laughed, and Polly thought, burning arrows of fire, am I never going to have that man? And Rosie thought, oh, I don't think I'll ever love anyone more than Nana's only oldest son.

He bowled to Lizzy and she cracked the ball to the far corner of the garden.

'Good shot, Lizzy,' smiled Mr Finch, fielding at long-stop, not far from the kitchen.

'Phone's ringing, Grandpa, phone's ringing,' called young Alice.

'Coming,' said Mr Finch, and deserted his post to enter the house through the kitchen. With the place empty of people, the ringing had a loud and demanding note. In the hall, a moment of suspicion made him hesitate. Then he picked the phone up and lifted the receiver.

'Yes, hello?' he said.

'Oh, hello, I think that's you, Mr Finch,' said Rachel from the other end of the line.

'And I think that's Rachel,' he said. Her voice always had a distinctive musical element.

'Yes. How's the family?'

'Playing cricket in the garden,' said Mr Finch.

'My life, they'll never grow up,' said Rachel.

'We're all trying not to.'

'So am I,' said Rachel. 'Is Boots there, can he be torn from his cricket?'

'I think so,' said Mr Finch.

'Is Sammy there?'

'Yes, with his family.'

'Well, dear Mr Finch, this is actually a business call that's just between me and Boots for the moment, even if it is your Sabbath.'

'I see. Point taken, Rachel. Hold the line.' Mr Finch went back through the kitchen and called to Boots from the door.

'Can you spare a moment, Boots?'

'Only too pleased,' said Boots, 'I've just been hit for two sixes by my lady sister.'

'Some lady,' said Bobby, 'that's my dad's wife.'

'Em'ly, smack that boy's bottom,' said Lizzy.

'Why, what've I said?' asked Bobby.

'Who's on the line?' asked Boots of his stepfather as he entered the kitchen.

'Rachel,' smiled Mr Finch. 'A business call.'

'The lady's a charmer,' said Boots, and went through to the hall. He picked up the phone. 'Rachel?'

'Hello, Boots lovey, d'you mind that it's Sunday?'

'Not a bit. I like Sundays.'

'I mean phoning you on a Sunday.'

'I like that too,' said Boots.

'There's a sweetie,' said Rachel. 'I wanted to give you a report on what I've found out so far concerning Johnson's. There are three directors, John Johnson and Frank Johnson, brothers, and Rolf Berger. They own all the shares between them. But they're not doing very good business, their last two balance sheets show a loss. You said your own company's only making a small profit, so what's the point of Johnson's buying you out?'

'Ask me another,' said Boots.

'I wasn't actually asking,' said Rachel, 'I was being rhetorical.'

'Rhetorical? Don't use that word in front of Chinese Lady,' said Boots, 'she'll think you've picked up some naughty French. I put it down to your finishing school.'

'Yes, ain't I educated, ducky?' said Rachel. 'But you can talk, after what your school did for you. I've heard about all the kids calling you Lord Muck. Anyway, back to business, as I don't want to keep you from your cricket. And I only want to say I'm going to call on some of Johnson's yards tomorrow to see what they've got on offer and at what prices.'

'This is what I call an act of faithful friendship,' said Boots.

'It's a loving friendship, ain't it?' said Rachel, and her laughter purred over the line.

'I like that too,' said Boots, and they spoke their goodbyes.

Emily asked who'd been on the phone, and Boots said a faithful friend.

'One of your old Army mates?' asked Emily, with the cricket still going on.

'No, a different kind of old mate,' said Boots. 'Rachel Goodman,' he murmured.

'Am I goin' to have to hit you with something?'

'Well, Em old love, I'll let you know if I think you should.'

'Boots, you're sly, you are.'

'Is that good or bad, Em?'

'Wicked, mostly,' said Emily.

The cricket ended, and Chinese Lady made everyone sit down for tea in the garden. It was a chattering tea, every tongue adept at wagging, and the garden echoed to lifted voices, laughter, giggles and arguments. Polly sat with Lizzy and her family. She had always got on well with Lizzy, and she liked Ned. He too was an old soldier.

After tea, when the lowering sun brought a touch of balmy evening to the garden and the young ones were chasing about, Polly sauntered across to the shed.

'Aunt Polly, what d'you want in the shed?' called Tim.

'I've got an appointment,' called Polly.

'Who with?' asked Annabelle.

'With the lawn mower,' said Polly, which tickled some of the young and slightly mystified some of the grown-ups.

It made Boots smile.

Chapter Twelve

Sammy, on his way to the firm's one and only shop in the West End – Oxford Street, to be precise – entered a turning off Waterloo Road and pulled up outside the yard belonging to Eli Greenberg, the well-known rag-and-bone merchant who was also well thought of. Sammy got out of his car and Mr Greenberg came out of the green-painted shed that served as his office. His yard, much of it under cover, contained mountains of household articles, from frying-pans to bedsteads. He wore, as usual, a round black hat, green with age and a long serge overcoat with capacious pockets. His curling beard, flecked with grey, received a caress from his hand as he sighted Sammy.

'Sammy, my poy, what a pleasure, ain't it?'

'I ain't denyin' it, Eli, old cock,' said Sammy, and shook hands with his old friend who had always been an invaluable business help. 'Seeing I was on my way to our Oxford Street emporium, I thought I'd pop in and see how you were.'

Mr Greenberg, now a married man with three healthy stepsons, said 'Vell might you enquire, Sammy, vell you might. Ain't my good vife's boys eatin' me out of house and home?'

'It's hard, Eli, I know, and I daresay it hurts as well,' said Sammy, 'but what's a hole in your pocket when there's a good wife warmin' your bed and doin' your washin' for you?'

'True, Sammy, true, consolations ain't to be sniffed at,' said Mr Greenberg, 'but the emptying of a poor man's pocket is a sad thing.'

'Granted,' said Sammy, 'but as long as we've both got enough to keep the bailiffs from cleaning us out, there's no point in committin' suicide.'

'Vell, there's alvays friendship, my poy, even if it does cost money sometimes. Now, vhile you're here and have a few minutes to spare, come into my office and I vill speak to you about if I should beggar my poor self by buying a small brewery to be run by Hannah's sons.'

'That kind of discussion is meat and drink, Eli,' said Sammy, 'and I wouldn't be the bloke I am if I didn't participate with a willing heart and without chargin' you for me advice.'

'Ain't that music to my ears, Sammy, vhen ve both know some varm hearts come expensive?'

'I concur, Eli. I also agree. Lead the way.'

They've forgotten to let the blind up, thought Tilly, at a little after ten. Does that woman think I'm sitting here to get a look at her private bedroom life during daytime? Or is she at a bottle?

Tilly put that unneighbourly thought out of her mind, and, seated at her machine, absorbed herself in her dressmaking. The blind at the window facing her across the adjoining back yards stayed down.

Downstairs, Cassie was talking to her charges. She was going to take them out, round to her own home again, and then for a walk, having discovered they couldn't do as much damage out of doors as when they were in. She'd bring them back for their midday meal, and when they'd had that she was going to take them to Mrs Tompkins across the street. Their dad had arranged for Mrs Tompkins to keep a kind eye on them for the afternoon.

'All right?' she said.

'We don't mind,' said Bubbles.

'Ev'ryone looks after us a bit,' said Penny-Farving.

'Except our muvver,' said Bubbles.

'Yes, I'm sorry about that,' said Cassie, 'it's a shame she can't get 'ome more often.'

'No, it's not,' said Penny-Farving.

'We don't like 'er comin' home,' said Bubbles.

'She shouts at our dad,' said Penny-Farving.

'Oh, poor woman,' said Cassie. 'Never mind, you can come home with me now, but first we'll go and knock at the 'ouse of the lady next door. You've seen my parrot lots, but you 'aven't seen Mrs 'Arper's, and she just might let you this mornin'. Come on.'

When Mrs Harper answered Cassie's knock, her eyes alighted immediately on Bubbles and Penny-Farving.

'What're them little terrors doin' on me doorstep?' she asked.

'Oh, they're quite nice little girls really, Mrs 'Arper,' said Cassie in her blithe way, 'and they'd like it ever so much if they could come in and see Percy.'

'Oh, they would, would they?' said Mrs Harper, florid face looking a bit sour. 'First thing them nice little girls 'ud do would be to turn 'is cage upside-down.'

'Oh, they wouldn't do that, Mrs 'Arper, I'd see they didn't,' said Cassie.

Mrs Harper gave that some thought.

'Well, all right, bring 'em through,' she said, 'but take 'old of them and don't let go of them.'

'Come on,' said Cassie to the girls, and she took hold of their hands and went through to the kitchen with them, where she did the honours herself by introducing them to Percy. Percy eyed them brightly, and Mrs Harper eyed them warningly.

'Go on, say 'ello to 'im,' said Cassie.

''Ello, Percy,' said both girls. Percy responded in peculiar fashion.

'I'll hit yer,' he said.

Well, that was what it sounded like to Cassie.

'Mrs 'Arper, why's he say that?' she asked.

'Say what?' said Mrs Harper.

'That 'e'd hit us,' said Cassie.

Mrs Harper laughed.

''E don't mean it,' she said.

'Hello, sailor,' said Percy, 'give us a kiss.'

'There y'ar,' said Mrs Harper, ''e likes yer.'

'Can I tickle 'im?' asked Penny-Farving.

'Best not,' said Mrs Harper, 'you might poke 'is eye out and 'e'll bite yer finger off.'

'Who's a pretty girl, then?' said Percy, and Dan's two angels giggled.

'Well, you can say goodbye to 'im now,' said Mrs Harper, 'I'm a bit busy.'

'Goodbye, Percy,' said the angels.

'I'll hit yer,' said Percy, or something like that.

'What a funny parrot,' said Cassie. 'Cecil's sort of more serious. Well, thanks ever so much, Mrs 'Arper. Come on, you two.'

Mrs Harper saw them out with a fairly amiable goodbye. Well, it was best to be neighbourly.

Tilly had enjoyed an unbothered day. She'd done some uninterrupted sewing and some shopping. She'd had a sandwich and a pot of tea at midday, and now, at fifteen minutes to four, she was cutting material with her dressmaking scissors. On the model in a corner of the room was a finished blouse. She had a skirt to make now, and when that was done she would begin the dresses for Bubbles and Penny-Farving. The mental note she made of that took hold of her mind. Bother it, she said to herself for the first time that day. She'd heard the little girls downstairs when they were having their midday meal with Cassie. How two girls as young as they were could make so much noise had to be heard to be believed. High spirits. It was in their favour, she thought, that they could be high-spirited when they were so neglected by their mother. They were little girls running wild. If that dad of theirs didn't do something about taming Gladys Hobday, he'd be faced with the problem of always needing someone to look after them. 'Someone' could be a succession of different faces and different attitudes.

They had left the house with Cassie at one o'clock, however, and now they were on Tilly's mind. She frowned. Glancing, she saw that the blind was up in the window opposite. She shook herself, and began to use her scissors again. She heard the front door open and the chattering voices of Bubbles and Penny-Farving. The door closed and she heard them go into the parlour. They'd get up to something in there if no-one was with them.

Blow it, thought Tilly, why should I worry? They're not my kids, they're Gladys Hobday's, a freak of a woman who's barmy about spending her life balancing on a tightrope. What a loony that man is, falling for a tarted-up hussy just because she looks good in tights. Oh, Lord, there they go, Bubbles and Penny-Farving, jumping and yelling. Next thing they'll be trying to walk a tightrope themselves, in the parlour.

Crash. Something had gone.

Down went Tilly, sighing.

In the parlour, Bubbles and Penny-Farving were looking at a vase on the lino. It was in pieces.

'That ain't very clever, is it?' said Tilly.

'It fell off the window ledge,' said Penny-Farving.

'She did it,' said Bubbles.

'No, I didn't, you did,' said Penny-Farving.

'It just fell off,' said Bubbles.

'Well, whoever did it can pick the pieces up,' said Tilly. 'No, you'd better not or you'll manage to cut your fingers off. Aren't you supposed to 'ave someone lookin' after you?'

'Yes, we been across to Mrs Tompkins,' said Penny-Farving, 'but she sent us 'ome.'

'She said we was tryin' to tie 'er kettle to 'er cat's tail,' said Bubbles.

'And were you?' asked Tilly.

'We emptied it of water first,' said Penny-Farving.

'Tilly, could yer make us a cup of tea?' asked Bubbles, long frock dusty, face needing a wash.

'Only if you promise to sit quiet,' said Tilly.

'Can we do it upstairs in your room?' asked Penny-Farving.

'Do what upstairs?'

'Sit quiet,' said Penny-Farving.

'You can try it first at your kitchen table,' said Tilly. She took them into the kitchen, made them sit down and then put the kettle on. She noted how tidy the kitchen and scullery looked. That was Cassie's doing. Now there was a very nice girl, a typical daughter of Walworth in having been brought up to make herself useful at the tender age of fourteen. God alone knew what Bubbles and Penny-Farving would be like at fourteen. Well, at least they were fairly quiet now. They each had a box of water-colour paints out and a painting book, and were actually absorbing themselves.

Tilly made the tea, gave them a cup each and poured one for herself. And finding what was left of a baker's cake in the larder, she gave them each a slice. By which time, when her back had been turned only while she looked into the larder, they had managed to paint each other's faces a bright green.

'You imps,' she said.

'Don't Penny-Farvin' look funny?' said Bubbles.

'So do you,' said Penny-Farving, and they giggled.

'Right,' said Tilly, 'you can sit there with green faces and drink your tea and eat your cake. Then when your dad comes in, p'raps 'e can see how funny you both look.'

'Yes, won't 'e laugh?' said Bubbles.

'Dad's always laughin',' said Penny-Farving.

Tilly counted silently to ten, and that saved her from telling the girls some home truths about that cheerful Charlie. She stayed there in the kitchen and made them apply themselves sensibly to their painting. She ended up sitting between them, mothering them, and when she realized what she was doing she told herself she'd been victimized into the role by the absent figure of their father.

She was there when he came in from his work, pleasantly attired in his suit with no signs of motor oil about him, and carrying a shopping bag.

'Hello,' he said, 'that's nice of you to be sittin' with the girls, Tilly.'

''Ello, Dad,' said Bubbles, and she and Penny-Farving lifted their green-painted faces.

Dan looked, blinked and shouted with laughter.

Tilly, who had spent a couple of hours of her precious working time with the girls, rarely let the fact that she was a lady hold her back from doing what she felt a woman had got to do. She jumped up. Dan, reading the danger signals, said a hasty something about needing to go upstairs. He disappeared, leaving the shopping bag on a chair.

'Stay there, you two,' said Tilly, and went after him. He was up the stairs and into the landing lav before she could catch him, and he locked himself in. Tilly banged on the door.

'Come out, you coward!'

'D'you mind if I don't, Tilly?'

'Yes, I do mind. Come out. I've got things to say to you.'

'What things?'

'I'm not shoutin' them at you through the key'ole. Come out.'

'You can say them quietly,' said Dan, 'I've got good hearin' and I'm a good listener.'

'Don't make me laugh, you never listen at all. Them gels of yours are runnin' wild. They tied a kettle to the tail of a neighbour's cat this afternoon. Mrs Tompkins', they said.'

'Yes, she offered to 'ave them for the afternoon.'

'Well, she sent them back 'ome, and that's cost you a smashed vase in the parlour and me two hours of me dressmakin' time. And now they've got green paint all over their faces.'

'Yes, I saw that,' said Dan, keeping himself safely locked in.

'Oh, yes, and funny, wasn't it? Loads of laughs. But the gen'ral picture's not funny.'

'Well, Tilly, if you could just wash their faces—'

'What? If I could do what?'

'There's a face flannel and soap in the scullery.'

'Oh, yer saucy comic! Dan Rogers, if you don't

come out of there and take a wallopin' like a man, I'll break the door down.'

'Elvira tried that once,' said Dan.

'Never mind – oh, blow yer,' said Tilly, suddenly hating to think her aggressiveness put her on a par with that circus act. 'Them gels are all yours, and so are yer problems.' And she went into her room, closing the door with a bit of a bang. She heard him come out quite soon after and she heard him go down the stairs. And half a minute later she heard shrieks of laughter in the kitchen.

He just didn't seem to care that his girls were illegitimate and were without any kind of mother.

Blow the man.

'Freddy, I've been thinkin',' said Cassie that evening. They were out walking.

'Thinking's supposed to be good for yer,' said Freddy.

'Yes, me dad told me that once,' said Cassie.

'Funny it don't seemed to 'ave 'elped you much, Cassie.'

'Course it has,' said Cassie, 'I'm the most thinkin' girl that was ever born. Anyway, when I was thinkin' at supper this evenin', it made me mention to me dad that 'e's got a niece that's nineteen and lost 'er job a while ago. The fact'ry she worked in in Camberwell got burnt down, and it won't be rebuilt for ages. I said p'raps Dad's niece could come and look after Bubbles and Penny-Farvin' every day if Mr Rogers could afford to pay 'er a wage. Dad said well, ask Mr Rogers first. So when we get back, we'll do that, Freddy, we'll knock and ask 'im.'

'Stone the crows,' grinned Freddy.

'What d'you mean?' asked Cassie.

'Well, that's good thinkin', Cassie, which don't 'appen all the time with you. Well, not a lot. Still, once in a while is promisin', I'd say.'

'Fancy you bein' compliment'ry like that,' said Cassie. 'D'you think it bodes well?'

'Do I think what?'

'Freddy, don't yer know what bodes well means?'

'No, I work with me dad in one of me brother-in-law Sammy's scrap metal yards.'

'That don't mean you shouldn't know what bodes well means,' said Cassie.

'All right,' said Freddy, 'what does it mean?'

'Well, it could mean that later on you and me might live 'appy ever after,' said Cassie.

Freddy looked at his girl mate. In her printed dress and the boater she'd always worn during her years at school, she was a happy-go-lucky dreamer. And crackers as well. But he liked her.

'I was actu'lly thinkin' of goin' in for football later on,' he said.

'Oh, all right,' said Cassie.

They called on Mr Rogers when they got back, and Cassie told him about her dad's niece. Dan said he liked the sound of a regular weekly help, and would pay a wage of twelve bob for five-and-a-half days.

'Tell yer dad that, Cassie,' he said.

'Yes, I will,' said Cassie. She and Freddy were in the parlour with him, and she jumped a little at a crashing sound in the kitchen. 'Crikey, Mr Rogers, what's that?'

The answer to that came from Penny-Farving. She called from the kitchen.

'Dad, a chair's fell over.'

'All right, stand it up again,' called Dan.

Tilly's voice floated down from the landing.

'Who's breakin' the 'ouse up?'

'It's all right, Miss Thomas,' called Freddy, 'it's just a chair fell over in the kitchen.'

'If you believe that, you'll believe anything,' called Tilly, and went back into her room.

'Anyway, thanks, Cassie, for thinkin' of the girls,' said Dan.

'Oh, pleasured, I'm sure,' said Cassie, 'and I just remembered, me dad wondered if you took 'is niece on, if you'd stamp 'er card as an employee, like.'

'You bet I will,' said Dan. 'See you in the mornin', Cassie.'

'Oh, yes,' said Cassie. 'I'm goin' to take Freddy 'ome with me now so's we can talk to our parrot.'

'Pardon me, but I ain't goin',' said Freddy.

'Course you are,' said Cassie, 'then I'll let you play football later on when you're older.'

'So long, Freddy,' smiled Dan.

'I ask meself, what's the use?' said Freddy.

On their way to King and Queen Street, they met Mrs Harper coming out of the Jug and Bottle, the off-licence attached to the pub in Browning Street.

''Ello, dearies.' Mrs Harper was very amiable. Well, she had a bottle of gin in a straw bag, and was going to have a drop or two to give herself a cheerful evening. The men were no real company. ''Ow's yer young selves, eh?'

'Well, Cassie's still goin' strong, and I'm still alive,' said Freddy, 'so we ain't complainin'.'

'He's a joker, that lad,' said Mrs Harper to Cassie.

'Yes, but I always do the best I can with 'im,' said Cassie. 'Has Percy 'ad a nice day?'

'Well, 'e's got 'is birdseed and no worries,' said Mrs Harper, 'so 'e ain't complainin', neither. Toodle-oo duckies.' Away she went, happy with her gin.

Going on with Freddy, Cassie told him she'd taken Bubbles and Penny-Farving to see Percy that morning, and he'd said the same thing again.

'What same thing?' asked Freddy.

'He said he'd hit us,' said Cassie.

'Strike a light,' said Freddy, 'what with all the barmy people about, it's a bit much that there's barmy parrots as well.'

'Cecil ain't barmy,' said Cassie.

'Not much,' said Freddy.

Chapter Thirteen

'Um, Tilly?' said Dan, knocking on her bedroom door. It was only fifteen-minutes-to-eight.

'I'm in bed,' she called. She wasn't. She was dressing. She had her underwear on and was fixing the hooks and eyes that ran down the front of her white corset.

'Oh, right,' said Dan, and opened the door and put his head in. Tilly uttered a little shriek, and Dan goggled. What a woman. Her legs and thighs were actually superior to those belonging to the temperamental reincarnation of a Hungarian dancer. Morning light ran up and down her shining stockings. 'Oh, sorry.' The apology served no purpose. The bed bolster arrived smack in his chops. And again. He retreated fast and just escaped having the slammed door flatten his hooter.

'I'm on to you, you lecher!' The hissed words reached his ears through the door. 'Wait till I'm dressed, then I'll come down and poke your eyes out, you 'ear me?'

'Don't do that, Tilly. Honest mistake. Thought you were under yer blankets. I just came up to tell you there's no worry about the girls today. The woman who runs our works canteen—'

'Your what?'

'Our works canteen, the kind they've got at some tram depots. I get my break from one till two, so I'll

182

be poppin' home to pick up the girls and take 'em back with me. Our canteen lady finishes at two and she only lives round the corner from our works, so she'll take them home with her and I'll collect them when I finish me labours. I don't want them to be landed on you again. Can't thank you enough for all the help you've been – um, sorry I um – well, sorry. Mind you, Tilly, I think you'd look even better in tights and spangles than Elvira—'

The door opened. Tilly in a dressing-gown appeared, hands gripping one end of the bolster. She swung it. It collided with Dan's face again, and the blow nearly knocked him backwards over the banisters.

'How'd you like your eggs fried?' panted Tilly, and went for him again. Dan ducked and ran. The bolster, of course, followed him down the stairs, as it had before, Tilly chucking it at him. It landed on the floor of the passage. He stopped and looked up at her.

'No hard feelings, Tilly, hope you 'ave a nice quiet day,' he said.

'Hope you break your leg,' said Tilly.

Dan grinned.

What a woman.

He'd written to Gladys – no, Elvira – last night and set out plainly what he thought was owing to Bubbles and Penny-Farving. Married parents, that was what he and she owed them. All right, he'd written, he and she needn't live together, he wouldn't force her to do that, knowing her life was with the circus. But they ought to get married for the girls' sake, and he was hoping to arrange for a young woman to come in every day on a permanent basis to see that Bubbles and Penny-Farving had some kind of mothering. They were running wild. He hoped she would answer his letter and agree to a wedding ceremony, a quiet one. Could she answer fairly quickly?

He addressed the letter to Miss Elvira Karola, c/o Blundell's Circus, Margate, Kent.

'Sammy, have you thought any more about keepin' the one scrap yard for the sake of Freddy and my dad?' asked Susie, just as Sammy was leaving the house.

'Susie, I'm workin' on it,' said Sammy.

'You sure you are?' said Susie.

'Now, Susie, do I ever tell you porkies?'

'Sometimes, Sammy, you tell me things that don't always mean what I think they do.'

'Me, yours truly?' said Sammy, a well-set-up and personable businessman whose blue eyes looked as honest as the day was long, which was saying something considering the number of competitors he'd left floundering in his wake. 'You're thinkin' of Boots, me treasure. Even when he says pass the salt, you get a feelin' he means it's goin' to be foggy tomorrow.'

'Yes, I adore Boots,' said Susie a little wickedly.

'You can't,' said Sammy, 'I forbid it.'

'Oh, you do, do you, Sammy Adams?'

'You bet I do, Mrs Adams,' said Sammy, 'I've got to hold you to love, honouring and obeyin'.'

'Ha-ha,' said Susie, and Sammy winked, kissed her and set off for his office.

It was a quite beautiful June morning, in this, the twelfth year of peace since the Great War had come to an end. The devil, however, was still exacting his price from victors and losers alike, so much so that one could have said there had only been losers.

Unemployment, economic depression, anarchy, the rise of Stalin and the emergence of Hitler, both acolytes of the devil, all contributed to the woes and sufferings of people in Europe and elsewhere. Secret societies and secret services were more active than ever.

Nevertheless, the morning was so beautiful that Mr Finch, a secret service gentleman himself, phoned a colleague in a department in Whitehall and informed him he was taking the day off.

'Well, good luck, old man, do you have an outing and a fast filly in mind?'

'I've an outing in mind, yes,' said Mr Finch, 'but with my wife, not a fast filly.'

'Allow me in haste to point out I meant a visit to the races at Lingfield and a fiver on Merry Maid in the three-thirty.'

'Allow me, George, to accept your apology.'

'Very decent of you, old man. Enjoy yourselves.'

'We will,' said Mr Finch. Accordingly, he and Chinese Lady prepared for their outing, Chinese Lady quite delighted by the idea of a motorcar ride into the country, even if she would have preferred to travel by horse and cart. What she actually had in mind was a pony and trap, but all such conveyances were horses and carts to her. She still didn't trust motorcars. Well, even though Edwin was a very reliable motor driver, that didn't mean the engine wouldn't blow up.

Mr Finch came out of the house some time after ten to check the petrol gauge of his Morris car and to place Chinese Lady's umbrella in the back. Chinese Lady was apt not to trust the weather, either. She was going to do a little country shopping and the umbrella was a precaution.

A car pulled up on the other side of the road as Mr Finch approached his Morris in the gravelled drive. It tucked itself up behind a grocer's parked delivery van. Its occupants glimpsed Mr Finch. Chinese Lady put her head out of their bedroom window.

'Edwin, where did you say we were goin'?' she called.

'Farnham, Maisie. For lunch at the Red Lion Hotel.'

'Oh, yes, there should be some nice shops in Farnham,' said Chinese Lady, and withdrew her head to put her Sunday hat on.

They left ten minutes later, making for Merton, Epsom and Leatherhead. The Morris hummed along amid a fair amount of traffic, which became lighter once they reached Leatherhead, from where they took the road to Guildford. The countryside was green with early summer, the Surrey Hills arousing a comment in Chinese Lady.

'I must say, Edwin, I used to think Hampstead 'Eath quite countrified, but it was never like this.'

'Hampstead Heath, of course, is somewhat urbanized, Maisie.'

'Is that a government word, Edwin? I don't like government words, specially as Boots always says they cost taxpayers money. I will say he does talk sense sometimes. My, doesn't everything look pretty? We do have some very nice scenery in this country.'

'Our small island, Maisie, has an infinite variety.'

'Mind you,' said Chinese Lady, looking very nicely dressed in a lightweight costume and her Sunday hat, 'I like seein' trams and buses and London markets – Edwin, what're you tryin' to do?'

'Overtake the slowcoach in front,' said Mr Finch.

'You don't need to do that,' said Chinese Lady, 'we're not in any hurry and we don't want a wheel to fall off.'

'There's traffic behind, Maisie,' said Mr Finch. The car in front was dawdling, its passengers probably just enjoying a leisurely outing, he thought. He overtook on a straight stretch, much to Chinese Lady's discomfort. She simply didn't trust the feeling of the Morris moving fast. Mr Finch, however, accomplished the manoeuvre smartly and quickly. The other traffic behind moved up on the slow car.

'I'm sorry people don't drive horses and carts like they used to when I was younger,' said Chinese Lady.

'Alas for progress, Maisie,' smiled Mr Finch, 'it causes the disappearance of much that we hold dear.'

'Yes, like modesty,' said Chinese Lady, 'which I've always held in natural respect. When I think of them 1926 fashions and my daughter and daughters-in-law showing their legs like they did, well, that was when young women simply didn't 'ave no modesty at all.'

'Fashions can be a revelation, Maisie.'

'I don't like that word, Edwin.'

'I note your disapproval,' said Mr Finch, smiling. His wife was never going to be less than incurably Victorian. He motored through the little villages of Surrey towards Guildford, rarely clocking more than thirty miles an hour in indulgence of her preference for safe travel. The traffic behind, having passed the slow car, caught him up, and two or three motorists overtook him, making Chinese Lady frown.

'I don't know why some people are in a hurry to break their necks,' she said. 'I must say you drive quite nice yourself, Edwin.'

'Thank you, Maisie. Are you enjoying the outing and the countryside?'

'Yes, ever so much,' said Chinese Lady, and her enjoyment was very apparent after they left Guildford behind and were travelling along the Hog's Back with its panoramic views of Surrey in the sunshine of June. Passing the Hog's Back Hotel, Mr Finch suggested that after lunch and shopping in Farnham, they could, on their return journey, stop at the hotel for a pot of tea. Chinese Lady said well, that sounds very nice, Edwin.

When they reached Farnham, he signalled a left turn before he pulled into the carriage yard of the old-established Red Lion Hotel, and following cars passed them.

In the Red Lion, Chinese Lady enjoyed an excellent lunch with her worldly husband. They dined leisurely, and followed that with what Chinese Lady considered was country shopping. That was leisurely too, so that when they stopped at the Hog's Back Hotel on their return journey, Chinese Lady was more than ready for a welcome pot of tea. She also fell in with Mr Finch's suggestion that some buttered toast would go down well with the tea. She thought the latter, when poured from a silver pot, was extremely high-class, but no more satisfying as a reviver than that which she had poured a thousand times from an old glazed pot during her years of penury in Walworth. She said so, but immediately assured Edwin that it was still a lovely treat to take tea here.

Mr Finch smiled. An intelligent man, a university graduate and widely travelled, he had seen much of the world and run up against the idiosyncrasies of many different peoples. All the same, he considered Chinese Lady worth a mention in the journal of any traveller. He had come to know she was what the English called 'a character'. Her cockney origins had endowed her with fortitude and resilience, and also with a belief that proper behaviour and a proper way of speaking made people respect you. Most of all she believed in the omnipotence and infallibility of the Almighty, and that marriage and the family had been ordered from Above.

At fifty-three, she was still pleasant to look at, and grey had not yet touched her brown hair. Further, she still had a quite proud walk, which stemmed from the days when, as a striving young wife and mother, she carried herself in very upright fashion to show that although she was poor she was also respectable, with nothing to be ashamed of. Mr Finch was extremely fond of her, although they were far apart intellectually. But, then, he had never found that a drawback in his relationship with her, first as her lodger and later as her husband. His admiration for what she and her family had achieved had no ifs or buts about it.

'Are you ready to go now, Maisie?' he asked when the buttered toast was no more and the pot empty.

'If you don't mind, Edwin, I'll just go to the Ladies' first.'

'I'll settle the bill and then wait for you outside, by the car,' he said.

But when she reached the car several minutes later, he wasn't there. She looked around. There were other parked cars, one with its bonnet up and a tall man in tweeds tinkering with its works. But there was no sign of Edwin. He must have gone to the Men's, she thought. So she waited. Five minutes went by, and as he still hadn't appeared she went back into the hotel and to the restaurant, thinking he had perhaps forgotten he was to meet her outside. He was probably still sitting at the table. But he wasn't, he was nowhere in the restaurant. She went outside and back to the car again. But he was still missing. A little worried and a little confused, Chinese Lady approached the gentleman who was still tinkering with his car. She asked him if he had seen her husband. She described Edwin and how he was dressed.

'So sorry, but no, I don't think I have seen him,' said the gentleman. 'All I have seen out here was a car driving out as I drove in ten minutes ago.'

'Oh, that wouldn't of been anything to do with my husband,' said Chinese Lady. 'That's our motorcar over there.'

'When I arrived, my plugs were spluttering,' said the gentleman, 'and I've been out here cleaning the points since then. Apart from that car which passed me as I drove in, I've noticed nothing else. Certainly, I'm sure I haven't seen your husband. But he must be around somewhere. Why not ask the receptionist? She's very helpful. I'm staying here a few days myself.'

'Thank you, I'll do that, I'll ask her,' said Chinese Lady, and carried herself briskly back into the hotel again. There she asked the receptionist, an attractive and friendly young lady, if she had seen her husband. Again she described him.

'You're not residents here, madam?'

'No, we just came in for a pot of tea and some buttered toast, which was very nice.'

'Oh, yes, I remember now, you came in about an hour ago,' said the young lady. 'Your husband left about thirteen or fourteen minutes ago, and you followed several minutes later, didn't you?'

'Yes, I went to the Ladies' first,' said Chinese Lady, experiencing the first pangs of real worry.

'Perhaps he's gone round to the terrace at the back of the hotel, madam. From there, the views are lovely.'

'Oh, I'll go and look,' said Chinese Lady.

'I'm sure he's out there somewhere, madam.'

'He'd better be, I wouldn't like to think I'd lost him,' said Chinese Lady, making a brave attempt to lighten the moment.

At four-twenty, someone knocked on the door of Boots's office in Camberwell.

'Come in,' he said. He was signing letters.

In came Rosie and Polly, Rosie in her gymslip and school hat, Polly in the kind of plain costume suitable for a schoolteacher, although it took little of her vivacious air away.

'Hello, Daddy, are we interrupting?' asked Rosie.

'Oh, I don't count the entry of light into the darkness of heavy labour an interruption,' said Boots.

'Crikey, listen to you,' said Rosie. 'Did you hear him, Miss Simms?'

It was always Miss Simms during the hours when the relationship was that of teacher and pupil. 'Can he really mean we're the light in his darkness, or does he say that to all the girls?'

'Oh, I think he's just showing off, Rosie,' said Polly. 'It's his age.'

'Poor old thing,' said Rosie. 'Daddy, Miss Simms—'

'Polly?' said Boots.

'Oh, all right, Aunt Polly,' said Rosie. 'She gave me a lift from school in her car, and would have treated Annabelle too, only Annabelle went home early with a bad cold. Anyway, we stopped here to ask if she could take me to her home for tea, and supper later on. She'll drive me home afterwards. Is that all right?'

'I can't think of anything against it,' said Boots.

'Well, bless your Sunday cricket belt,' said Rosie.

191

'And thanks for the loan of Rosie, old sport,' said Polly.

'Don't mention it,' said Boots, always in control of the vibrations that were present in his relationship with Polly. 'Pop off, then.'

'Heavens,' murmured Polly, 'now we're a couple of corks, Rosie.'

Boots's phone rang. He picked it up.

'Hello?'

'Mr Adams,' said the switchboard girl, 'it's your mother.'

'Put her through,' said Boots. Polly and Rosie stood by. 'Hello, old lady, what can I do for you?'

'Is that you, Boots?' Chinese Lady sounded uncertain. A telephone was something else she didn't trust.

'Yes, it's me.'

'Is Sammy there with his motorcar?' asked Chinese Lady, speaking from the residents' phone in the hotel lobby.

'No, he's out,' said Boots.

'Then you'll 'ave to go home and get your own, then,' said Chinese Lady, 'and you'll 'ave to come without Sammy.' The dropping of aitches meant agitation was close to the surface, for she rarely dropped any these days. 'I want you to drive down here. I'm at the Hog's Back Hotel, near Farnham, and your dad's gone missin'.'

'Edwin? He's what?' said Boots.

'He's gone and disappeared, that's what,' said Chinese Lady, resolutely trying to keep agitation from breaking out. 'We had tea here, then he was supposed to wait outside for me, at our motorcar. But I just can't find him anywhere, so I want you to come down and look for him. I can't come home without 'im.'

'Listen, old lady,' said Boots, 'are you sure you know what you're saying?'

Rosie quickened at the odd look on his face, and Polly experienced intense curiosity.

'Of course I know what I'm saying,' said Chinese Lady. 'Edwin's gone missin'. I've spent over half an hour lookin' for him. Our motorcar's still here, but he's not.'

'Could he be somewhere in the hotel?' asked Boots.

'No, they've looked. Boots, I'm worried. You'll have to drive down here and be quick.'

'Right, I'll do that,' said Boots, 'and be with you as soon as I can. I hope he'll turn up before I get there. Try to take it easy.'

'Yes, I'll do a dance round the hotel,' said Chinese Lady tartly.

'Chin up, old lady,' said Boots, and rang off.

'Daddy, what's up?' asked Rosie, and Boots briefly explained. Rosie's eyes opened wide, and Polly looked astonished. But she made a typical offer of help.

'I'll drive you there, Boots,' she said. 'My tin can's outside, and it'll save you going all the way home for yours.'

'Yes, we needn't waste any time, Daddy,' said Rosie. 'I'll come as well, and we can all look for Grandpa.'

'My time's my own, if I could just ring my step-mama,' said Polly, which she did, while Boots used the extension in Sammy's office and the second line through the switchboard to call Emily. Emily, of course, found his brief account of his conversation with Chinese Lady too far-fetched to be taken seriously.

'Boots, are you playin' silly devils?' she asked.

'No,' said Boots, 'and you can take it from me that Chinese Lady isn't, either. I'm going now.'

'Oh, Lord,' said Emily, 'you really are serious.'

'Polly's here with Rosie, and we're using her car so that we can leave straightaway.'

'Well, isn't that kind of her?' said Emily, who didn't trust Polly any farther than the end of her nose.

'Can't stop, Em, see you later.'

'I just can't believe – Boots? Boots?' But he'd hung up, leaving her doubtful that Mr Finch could really have gone missing. Nor was she too happy about Polly playing a leading part in the dash to the hotel.

Polly was only too willing to commit herself. Boots might have suggested that Rosie went home, but he knew Emily would prefer him not to make the journey with Polly alone. As for Rosie, she was set on going. She would always rather be with her adoptive father than anyone else, much as she loved Emily.

Polly's open sports car, in which she drove to school daily, stood outside the offices, its leather seats warmed by the afternoon sunshine.

'I'll drive,' said Boots.

'Look, old thing,' said Polly, 'you're a worried man—'

'I'll drive.'

'If you want,' she said, and thought what weaklings women could be when in love. She was quite certain she was the equal of any man alive, but there it was, the weakness that made her play second fiddle to Boots. She slid smoothly into the passenger seat, and Rosie quickly established herself in the back of the car. Boots, in the driving seat, accepted the keys from Polly. He pushed in the ignition key, switched on and pulled the self-starter. The lively engine fired. With the car facing the rise of Denmark Hill, he took a look over his shoulder at traffic coming up from Camberwell Green, then drove off in low gear and put himself in front of it. He was in third as he passed the entrance to Ruskin Park.

Rosie, her school satchel on the seat beside her, said, 'Go, Daddy, go, Nana needs us.'

'He's going, Rosie,' said Polly. Boots was racing up the gentle rise, the engine growling before settling into a busy hum. He estimated it would take him an hour and a half to reach the Hog's Back if they weren't held up by too many lumbering lorries. He headed for Streatham, Sutton and Guildford. The slipstream tugged at Polly's hat and gusted around Rosie's face. Boots overtook slow traffic at speed, the while thinking about Edwin Finch. He was the only one in the family who knew that his stepfather had been a German agent and was now a naturalized British subject, invaluable to British Intelligence. But he was not the kind of man to let his secrets or his work affect him to the point of forgetting who he was. Boots rejected the idea that he had walked out on Chinese Lady to wander about in a mental fog. Some people, unable to cope with certain worries, developed – what was it? Yes, amnesia, a condition that helped them forget their troubles and their own identity. But that did not fit a man like Edwin Finch. He was far too cool a character.

The tailboard of a lorry seemed to be rushing back at the speeding car as they were passing Brockwell Park. Boots pulled out on to the tramlines, and Polly and Rosie held on to their seats as he raced to overtake. An oncoming tram clanged in angry warning. Boots squeezed the car through the narrowing gap and shot ahead of the lorry.

'Breezy,' said Rosie.

'If it's going to be like this all the way, I think I'll get out and walk,' said Polly, but she knew she'd have accepted similar challenges herself in order to make good time.

'Daddy, you don't think Grandpa could have really disappeared, do you?' said Rosie.

'We'll find out the facts when we get there, poppet,' said Boots, 'and let's concentrate on getting there, shall we?'

'Yes, all right, Daddy, not much talking, then,' said Rosie.

'Look after my hat, would you?' said Boots, and took it off and tossed it to her. She put it next to her satchel, and Boots drove with the wind making its assaults on his hair. Polly glanced at his profile. For all his easy-going air, he was not without a touch of steel. The war would have put that there. It had permanently shattered the nerves of some men. It seemed to have made Boots a man of very few nerves. All the same, he was obviously affected by the apparent disappearance of his stepfather. A little frown kept showing itself as he motored to eat up the miles. He took a pipe out of the breast pocket of his jacket and stuck it between his teeth to chew on it. It reminded Polly of the *estaminets* of France and Flanders, places full of Tommies in the evenings, Tommies out of the line and resting, either a fag or a pipe between their lips, creating blue fug while they told earthy anecdotes that brought forth roars of laughter.

Boots went through Streatham in fits and starts because of traffic. When clear of it, he raced for Sutton.

'All right, you two?' he asked, taking his pipe out.

'Yes, I'm fine,' said Rosie.

'And I'm still living,' said Polly.

'Compliments to both of you,' said Boots, and back went the pipe.

They were on the route taken by Mr Finch and were tangling with home-going traffic, buses and cars. Rosie and Polly said very little. Well, under the circumstances, small talk was out of place. Thoughts were on Chinese Lady and her vanished husband.

Chapter Fourteen

Sammy was back at his desk, studying details of a new business proposition. Gwen Fuller from the general office, a homely-looking but quite engaging girl, knocked on his door.

'Come right in,' called Sammy.

Gwen, entering, said, 'Mister Sammy, Mrs Em'ly Adams wants you to phone 'er.'

'Can't be me fatal charm, seein' she's me sister-in-law,' said Sammy.

'No, she didn't say anything about your fatal charm, Mister Sammy, she just asked if you'd phone 'er as soon as you came in.'

'She wants to speak to me and not her better half, my respected brother?' said Sammy.

'Oh, your respected brother left in a hurry over half an hour ago,' said Gwen.

'In a hurry?'

'Yes, with 'is daughter Rosie and that posh lady, Miss Simms. He didn't say what he was in a hurry about.'

'All right, fair do's, Gwen, tell Nancy to make the call for me.' Nancy Griggs, who operated the switchboard, had been taken on following the departure of Doreen Paterson. Doreen had left to get herself married to her young man, Luke Edwards.

The call to Emily was put through.

'You wanted to talk to me, Em'ly?' said Sammy. 'What can I do for you?'

'I wish I knew, but I'm all confused,' said Emily. 'Boots rang me about forty minutes ago with some story that Mr Finch 'ad gone missin'.'

'Come again?' said Sammy, and Emily recounted what Boots had told her. Emily knew that her in-laws had gone out for the day, and according to Boots they had stopped to have tea at the Hog's Back Hotel on their way home. Chinese Lady phoned Boots from the hotel and insisted that Mr Finch had disappeared while she was in the ladies' cloakroom, after they'd finished tea. She'd asked Boots to drive to the hotel and find her husband for her. 'Sammy, can you believe that? It makes me feel I'm dreamin', and I wanted to ask if you know anything about it.'

'I've only heard from Gwen that Boots left here in a hurry over half an hour ago,' said Sammy, 'and that Polly Simms and Rosie went with him.'

'Yes, they're usin' her car.'

'Let me get this straight,' said Sammy. 'You're tellin' me Boots rang you to say Chinese Lady asked him to drive down to the Hog's Back Hotel because our stepdad's disappeared?'

'Yes, that's it,' said Emily, 'and it's not believable, is it? I've got a headache comin' on.'

'I'll have one meself, if it's true,' said Sammy. 'Did you phone the hotel?'

'Oh, blow, no, I didn't,' said Emily. 'I should 'ave, but I'm not thinkin' straight.'

'I'll do it,' said Sammy. 'Polly's drivin' Boots and Rosie in her car, you said?'

'Boots said to save him comin' home to use his own.' Slightly acid, Emily added, 'Polly just happened to be in the office with Rosie. Very convenient, I must say. I'm here at home with Tim, waitin'.'

'I'll phone the hotel and see if I can speak to Chinese Lady,' said Sammy. 'Then I'll call you back. Till then, make yourself a cup of tea.'

'Not much else I can do,' said Emily, and rang off. Sammy got through to the switchboard and asked Nancy to ring the operator and find out the number of the Hog's Back Hotel.

'Oxback, Mister Sammy? I never 'eard of any hotel callin' itself that.'

'Hog's Back,' said Sammy, 'Hog's Back. It's near Farnham. Then ring them for me.'

'Very good, Mister Sammy. Hog's Back. What a funny name.'

A few minutes later, Sammy was put through.

'Hello, reception desk, Hog's Back Hotel. May I help you?'

'Hope so,' said Sammy. 'I'd like to speak to Mrs Finch, if she's there.'

'Oh, yes, sir, she's here,' said the receptionist, Miss Penny Jordan.

'I'm her son. I understand that her husband, my stepdad, seems to have disappeared. Am I understandin' correctly?'

'It seems so, sir. We're doing what we can for her while waiting for you to arrive.'

'That's my brother, Mr Robert Adams. I think he's well on his way by now. D'you think I could have a word with my mother?'

'Of course, sir. I'll get the porter to fetch her. I think she's outside. Hold on a moment, please.'

Sammy waited until Chinese Lady came on the line.

'Hello?' she said suspiciously. It wasn't natural to

her, a contraption that didn't allow a body to see the person she was talking to.

'Sammy here, Ma. I'm phonin' about Dad. He's disappeared, I hear, and you're a worried woman.'

'Well, Sammy, you don't expect me to be jumpin' for joy, do you? I just can't make out what's 'appened, Edwin goin' missin' like this. It's been well over an hour now. He was supposed to meet me at our motorcar after we'd had tea here, but he wasn't there and there's still no sign of him. I don't know how many times I've been outside to look for him. Something must of happened, because it's not like him to go off without saying a word. What about Boots, where is he?'

'On his way, Ma. He shouldn't be too long. Look, have the hotel staff made a search for Dad?'

'Yes, they've been very kind and 'elpful,' said Chinese Lady, 'they've searched everywhere, but there just isn't any sign of Edwin. I'm very upset, Sammy.'

'I'm sure you are,' said Sammy.

'But I don't want everyone in the fam'ly to have to worry, I don't want anyone to know about this except you and Boots.'

'Em'ly knows, of course,' said Sammy, deciding not to mention Polly and Rosie at this point. 'It beats me where Dad could've got to, but I've got a confident feelin' things will sort themselves out and that he'll suddenly pop up.'

'Pop up?' said Chinese Lady, agitation making her take umbrage. 'Kindly don't make your stepdad sound like a Jack-in-the-box, he's always been a conservative gentleman. Still, I'm not saying it wasn't thoughtful of you to telephone me, and it's a consolation knowin' Boots is on 'is way. I hope at his age, I can rely on him to find out what's happened to your stepfather.'

'You sit tight, Ma, Boots'll sort it out. Wait a tick, has the car disappeared as well?'

'No, it's still here,' said Chinese Lady, 'which makes it more worryin'.'

'Well, wait for Boots to arrive, he'll go to work on it, Ma.' Sammy spoke with more reassurance than he felt. 'Tell him to phone me at home later. Good luck, and keep your pecker up. So long now.'

'Goodbye, Sammy.'

Sammy then got back to Emily to confirm everything Boots had told her. Emily, upset, asked if it wouldn't be a good idea to tell the police in case Mr Finch had had some kind of brainstorm and might be a danger to himself. Sammy said the best idea at the moment would be to wait until they'd heard from Boots. Emily said Chinese Lady would be going off her head, that she was very fond of Mr Finch. Sammy said they were very fond of each other. Just keep hoping, he said, just leave it to Boots for the time being. And to that Polly Simms, I suppose, said Emily.

'I ought to be with him instead of her,' she said.

'Well, Boots would have preferred you, of course,' said Sammy tactfully, 'you've always had a smart brainbox. Anyway, I expect he'll ring you as soon as he's got some good news.'

'Yes, I've just 'ad all the bad news I want,' said Emily.

'I share your feelings,' said Sammy. 'On top of which, it's not doin' my work a lot of good. Owing to it affectin' my concentration, I'm against havin' a respected senior member of the fam'ly disappear. Ought to be a law forbiddin' it.'

'You're worryin' about the business at a time like this?' said Emily.

'I'm worryin' about it puttin' me off me work,' said Sammy.

'I'm cryin' my eyes out for you,' said Emily, and rang off.

Susie, like Emily, found the news almost impossible to believe. Sammy put her in the astonishing picture as soon as he got home. He said he was still having a job to believe it himself. However, the family had to put their money on Boots, whose mental equipment, said Sammy, was well up to scratch. Susie said it was above scratch, especially in a crisis. Mr Finch has got to be found, she said, he's the only dad-in-law I've ever had. Sammy, she said, you look really worried.

Sammy said he didn't feel too good, and that was a fact. Susie said how could Mr Finch have disappeared just like that? Sammy said ask me another. We'll just have to rely on Boots, said Susie.

'Well, Susie,' said Sammy, 'Chinese Lady mentioned that at his age, she ought to be able to rely on him.'

It was a little before six when Boots reached the hotel, a tall and imposing edifice on the high road known as the Hog's Back, from where it commanded magnificent vistas of the countryside. Pulling in, he brought Polly's car to a stop in front of the hotel, and was out of his seat at once. Polly and Rosie alighted and looked around. The sunny evening offered bright visibility. A uniformed porter, standing at the entrance to the hotel, spoke as Boots approached.

'Are you Mr Adams, sir?'

'Yes. Is my mother, Mrs Finch, in the hotel?'

'She's in the lounge with Miss Jordan, our receptionist, sir. I'll take you through.'

'Thanks,' said Boots. With Polly and Rosie, he
followed the porter into the lobby. There was a man in
reception. The porter nodded to him.

'Good evening, Mr Adams,' said the man, the
assistant manager, 'the hotel will offer you any help
you may require.'

'I'm obliged,' said Boots, continuing on in the wake
of the porter, who brought the arrivals to the residents' lounge. Only two people were there, Chinese
Lady and Miss Jordan. They were seated in arm-
chairs, a small table between them, and Chinese Lady
had a glass of something in her hand. Her best Sunday
hat sat bravely on her head.

She regarded the arrival of Boots with relief.

'This is my eldest son, Robert Adams,' she said to
Miss Jordan, and the receptionist, a slim brunette in
her early twenties, came to her feet.

'Good evening, Mr Adams,' she said, 'I'm so sorry
you've had to drive all this way.'

'Thanks for taking care of my mother, I'm sure
she's appreciated it,' said Boots. Miss Jordan,
impressed by his looks, essayed a smile.

'It's been a pleasure, Mr Adams,' she said,
'although we're all upset by what's happened. If I can
be of help in any way, or if you want anything, just let
me know. I'll be in reception, I'm Miss Jordan.'

Polly's eyes flickered. That was typical of the effect
he had on women. *If you want anything, just ask*. Polly
suspected he had rarely asked for anything to raise a
blush. She knew he had made love to a woman
ambulance driver during the war, a madcap of a
woman. Lily Forbes-Cartwright. But she doubted if
Lily had blushed.

'Thanks, Miss Jordan, I'm grateful,' said Boots, and the young lady left.

Chinese Lady put her glass on the table and stood up. Rosie swooped then to give her a hug and a kiss.

'We're here, Nana, we're all going to help.'

'Well, I'm glad to see your father, Rosie,' said Chinese Lady, and gave Boots a direct look. 'Why have you brought Rosie and Miss Simms?' she asked.

Boots pointed out they were in his office when she phoned, and that Polly offered immediate use of her car, which saved him having to go home for his. Rosie said she just had to come too, because it was so upsetting about Grandpa and the more help the better. Chinese Lady acknowledged Polly then, saying good evening to her and that it was kind of her to let her car be used. Polly said it was the very least she could do.

'Let's sit down and get all the facts,' said Boots.

'I don't want more sittin'-down,' said Chinese Lady, 'I want you to go out and find Edwin.'

'I know you do,' said Boots, 'but first I'd like to hear every detail, so let's spare a few minutes. What's in that glass?'

Chinese Lady frowned.

'I don't know that that's important,' she said, 'but Miss Jordan has been very kind, and when she asked if I'd like something, I said a little port would be welcome.'

'Well, sit down and finish it,' said Boots. 'Rosie, will you go to reception and ask Miss Jordan if she could arrange for someone to bring a gin and Italian for Polly, a whisky for me and whatever you'd like for yourself?'

'I'm flying,' said Rosie, and dashed out.

'We're goin' to sit drinkin'?' said Chinese Lady.

Tart again, she said, 'Then I suppose we'll all do a knees-up.'

'We'll just enjoy a drink while you tell Boots everything,' said Polly gently. Despite being a woman of her times, Polly had a helpless admiration and liking for this Victorian matriarch.

'But I told him everything on the telephone,' said Chinese Lady. However, she sat down again. Although she would never have admitted it, she was, in her own parlance, very admiring of her eldest son's thinking head. Never mind that sometimes he sounded like a music hall comic, he never got into a dither or went in for a lot of wordage like Sammy did whenever something upsetting happened.

Boots pulled up other chairs, and he and Polly sat down. Chinese Lady didn't miss the way Polly hitched her skirt so that her grey silk stockings showed almost to her knees. That was the way of some women these days. If they had good legs they liked to show them. It would have scandalized Queen Victoria.

Rosie returned to say the drinks were coming, then she sat down too, and Chinese Lady, for all that her mind was occupied by her worries, thought oh, dear, young Rosie's doing it too, letting her legs show in her school stockings of black lisle. I don't know what the world's coming to.

'Now, old lady, start from the beginning,' said Boots.

'I don't feel like repeatin' everything,' said Chinese Lady.

'Come on, Nana, I'm sure it'll help,' said Rosie, so Chinese Lady took another little drop of the port and went ahead. She and Edwin stopped for a pot of tea and some buttered toast, which was very nice, she said, and afterwards she'd gone to the Ladies' while Edwin settled the bill. He'd arranged to meet her outside, by the motorcar. She went out several minutes later, but he wasn't there. She looked for him, but couldn't see him, so she went back into the hotel to see if he was still in the restaurant, which he wasn't. So out she went again for another look, but he wasn't anywhere around.

Her account was interrupted then as a waiter brought in a tray containing the drinks. He set them out on the table, a whisky, a gin and vermouth, and a glass of kola water. Boots fished in his wallet.

'There's no charge, sir,' said the waiter.

'My compliments to the management, then,' said Boots, and gave the waiter a tip.

'Thank you, sir,' said the waiter, and left.

Polly took a welcome mouthful of her aperitif, Boots sank his whisky, and Rosie gulped her kola water thirstily.

'Is this a party we're havin'?' asked Chinese Lady.

'No, just a few thoughts,' said Boots. 'Carry on.'

Well, said Chinese Lady, as Edwin simply wasn't anywhere around, she went back into the hotel again and asked Miss Jordan if she'd seen her husband, and Miss Jordan said yes, she'd seen him leave about fourteen minutes ago, and perhaps he was on the terrace at the back of the hotel, looking at the view. So again Chinese Lady went out, but no, he wasn't there. She spoke to Miss Jordan again, and Miss Jordan spoke to a gentleman, one of the managers, who had the hotel searched, while Chinese Lady kept going outside in the hope that Edwin had turned up. After half an hour, she telephoned Boots, since when there still hadn't been any sign of Edwin. She was downright worried now.

'Nana, we all are,' said Rosie, 'but Grandpa's simply got to be somewhere around.'

'Listen, old lady,' said Boots, 'when you were first looking for him outside, did you spot anyone who might have seen Edwin coming out of the hotel?'

'I told you, Boots, Miss Jordan saw him leave,' said Chinese Lady a little fretfully.

'So we at least know he left the hotel,' said Polly, unusually sober.

'Yes, but was there anyone who actually saw him come out?' asked Boots.

'Oh, there was a gentleman who had something wrong with his motorcar and was tinkerin' with it,' said Chinese Lady. 'I spoke to 'im, but he hadn't seen anything of Edwin. Well, from what he said he hadn't been there long enough to see Edwin come out.'

'He'd only just arrived?' said Boots.

'He said ten minutes, and it was longer than that when Edwin came out.' Chinese Lady thought. 'He's puttin' up here, he said.'

'Well, that's something,' said Boots, 'let's see if we can talk to him.'

'I talked to him already,' said Chinese Lady. 'I'd of thought you'd be lookin' and searchin' by now, Boots, instead of askin' questions.'

'Well, you've looked, old lady, and the hotel staff have looked,' said Boots, 'and I don't fancy we'll do much good wandering up and down the road in hope. We need a clue.'

'Oh, you're goin' to play detectives now, are you?' said Chinese Lady. 'Supposin' Edwin went for a little walk while he was waitin' for me? He might of tripped and fallen down a bank somewhere, and p'raps broke his leg.'

'Daddy, I'll go, I'll look up and down the road,' said Rosie. 'Grandpa might just have done that, gone for a little walk and fallen somewhere. I'll do a quick search.' She was quickly up and out of the lounge.

'Mrs Finch, the gentleman you spoke to, what was he like?' asked Polly.

'Oh, he was dressed very nice in a tweed suit and tweed cap,' said Chinese Lady, 'a sort of country gentleman.'

'Not a seedy character, then?' said Polly.

'What, one that might of attacked my husband and robbed him?' said Chinese Lady, bridling at the notion that anyone at all would dare to set about her highly respected spouse. 'Certainly not. He was a very nice gentleman.'

'His description?' said Boots.

'Well, he was as tall as you, but older, in his late forties and 'ealthy-lookin',' said Chinese Lady, and in her downright worry she took another sip of the port.

'Yes, I'd like to talk to him,' said Boots, 'I'll see if reception can help.' He left the lounge, and Chinese Lady sighed.

'Oh, lor',' she said, 'I don't know I've ever felt more troubled.'

'It doesn't make sense, does it?' said Polly, who knew Mr Finch well enough to feel sure he wasn't the kind of man to walk away from life and his family.

At reception, Miss Jordan recognized the description Boots gave of the gentleman in tweeds.

'Oh, that's Captain Arnold, sir, he booked in yesterday and is staying two more days. But he's out now, he left five minutes ago to meet friends in Guildford. I believe he's dining with them.'

'My mother spoke to him outside the hotel not long after my stepfather disappeared,' said Boots. 'He wasn't able to offer any help, but I'd still like to speak to him myself. He arrived not too long after my stepfather came out of the hotel.'

'Yes, Captain Arnold had been out for the afternoon, Mr Adams,' said Miss Jordan.

'Have you any idea of what time he'll be back from Guildford?'

'Not really,' said Miss Jordan.

'Taking advantage of your helpfulness, we could stay on here for a couple of hours if you thought Captain Arnold would be back by then.'

'You're welcome to stay on as long as you like, sir, and to use our amenities,' said Miss Jordan, 'but I still couldn't say when Captain Arnold might be back. But I can say that if he told your mother he'd seen nothing of your stepfather, you can rely on that being the case. He spoke to me about it. He felt concern for your mother. He really was quite sure he'd seen nothing of Mr Finch. All he had seen was a car leaving as he drove in, but I understand it wasn't your stepfather's.'

'He saw a car leaving?' said Boots.

'That was what he told your mother and repeated to me.'

'Then the car would have belonged to one of your residents or visitors?' said Boots.

'I suppose so,' said Miss Jordan, 'although I didn't see anyone leave about that time. Nor did any resident leave his key at my desk.'

'Well, my very helpful young lady,' said Boots, 'I think you may have given us something we need.'

'And what is that?' smiled Miss Jordan.

'A hint of a clue,' said Boots.

'Sir, you think there's a clue about the car that was driven out as Captain Arnold drove in?'

'A hint,' said Boots. Two women entered the lobby and passed through. One stopped, turned back and collected a key from Miss Jordan with a murmur of thanks. Boots, waiting until she'd gone, said, 'That

210

car driving out was the only happening at a time you could connect with my stepfather's disappearance, so it has to be a hint of a clue. Yes, I'd very much like to wait for Captain Arnold.'

'I'll be going off duty at eight,' said Miss Jordan, very much in favour of giving this personable man all the help she could, 'but I'm resident here and I'll tell my relief to give me a buzz when Captain Arnold does come in. Then I'll contact you if you're still here.'

'We'll wait, thanks,' said Boots, and Rosie came back then, quicksilvery in her movements, her round school hat worn on the back of her fair head like a dark blue halo. 'Daddy, I'm sorry, but there simply isn't any sign of Grandpa.'

'Well, it was a shot in the dark, poppet,' said Boots. 'This is my daughter, Rosie, Miss Jordan.'

'How'd you do, Rosie?' smiled the receptionist.

'Oh, it would be a pleasure if things weren't so worrying,' said Rosie.

'Well, the worry's still with us,' said Boots, 'but Miss Jordan's just provided us with a small clue. Let's go back to Polly and your grandma and tell them. Thanks again, Miss Jordan, for all your help.'

'Just ask if you need anything,' said Miss Jordan.

'Ye gods,' murmured Polly a few minutes later, 'you really believe there's a clue in that departing car?'

'I want to know if Captain Arnold noticed who was in it,' said Boots.

'There, I suppose I might of asked him,' said Chinese Lady, 'but I didn't think to.'

'Well, Nana, you didn't know then that you had to think about clues,' said Rosie.

'Rosie, I certainly didn't think your grandpa might

211

just be in the car, which is what Boots is thinkin', if I know your father,' said Chinese Lady.

'How long do we have to wait for Captain Arnold?' asked Polly.

'All evening, if necessary,' said Boots, 'so I suggest we ought to consider having dinner here. Or perhaps I should phone Sammy and get him to drive here to take all of you home. I'll stay, naturally, but Polly and Rosie can go with you, old lady.'

'Nothing doing,' said Polly, 'I'm here and I'm sticking here until we've got a pretty clear idea of how to solve this problem.'

'Boots, I'm not goin' back home until you've found your stepdad,' said Chinese Lady firmly.

'I'm not sure we'll find him here,' said Boots.

'Never mind that, I'm not havin' you send me home,' said Chinese Lady, 'specially not with Sammy. That young man drives his motorcar as if he's tryin' to get to perdition before the gates shut.'

'Daddy, we've all got to stay,' said Rosie.

'Then we've got to think about staying for the night,' said Boots, 'as well as having something to eat, if anyone feels like a meal.'

'I can share a room with Nana,' said Rosie.

'Let me help a little,' said Polly, 'let me make a provisional booking of rooms with reception.'

'Go ahead, Polly,' said Boots, 'and a little later I'll ring Emily and Sammy to put them in the picture about developments and arrangements.'

'I couldn't eat much,' said Chinese Lady, 'but it might be sensible to have a bit of dinner here. It'll help to pass the time till Captain Arnold comes back and we can talk to him.'

Other people entered the lounge as Polly came to her feet.

'Book the rooms definitely, Polly,' said Boots, 'and we'll use them. I don't think we'll want to sit here all evening.'

'I'll ask about dinner as well,' said Polly.

'What about school if we stay all night?' asked Rosie.

'Well, for once, Rosie old thing, rats to school,' said Polly, and went to reception, where the first thing that happened was to be mistaken by Miss Jordan for Boots's wife. Miss Jordan, in fact, addressed her as Mrs Adams. The imps of devilment brought a gleam to Polly's eyes, and had it not been for the prevailing circumstances she wouldn't have thought twice about booking a double room for herself and Boots. As it was, the imps had to be resisted.

Chapter Fifteen

Tilly had had a totally peaceful day. Cassie had taken care of Bubbles and Penny-Farving, giving them their usual outing, and a little after one their father had come home from work and taken them back with him. That made the afternoon particularly quiet, for not a sound disturbed the house. The adjacent house was just as quiet, the blind up at the facing window.

All the same, Tilly felt on edge, suspecting the quietness was like calm before a storm. She heard Dan Rogers arrive home with the girls, and she began to wait then for him to mount one of his usual cheerful invasions of her lodgings. Well, it was obvious he wouldn't want to come home every day to take the girls back to his works and into the charge of that canteen lady, and she didn't think the woman would agree to the arrangement for more than a short time. Not more than a week, thought Tilly, by which time he'd be hoping Alice Higgins would be back on her feet. But he'd be looking for some options.

However, no invasion took place, and Tilly was left alone to prepare her supper and eat it without suffering exasperation or umbrage.

'Freddy,' said Cassie, talking to him at the gate of his house a little after eight, 'I was thinkin' that with the money I'm earnin' lookin' after Bubbles and Penny-Farvin' in the mornings, I could buy another parrot.'

'Cassie, if I thought another parrot would stop you tryin' to send me potty, I'd 'elp you buy six more,' said Freddy.

'I don't want six more, you silly,' said Cassie, 'just one, that's all. He'll be company for Cecil, and 'elp him to talk more.'

'I'll 'ave to profess me profound ignorance about what makes parrots tick,' said Freddy, 'but—'

'Freddy, what makes you talk like that?' asked Cassie.

'Me brother-in-law, Sammy Adams.'

'Crikey,' said Cassie, 'I don't mind meself, but don't talk like it when you go down the market or someone'll chuck rotten cabbages at you.'

'No-one ever did that to Sammy,' said Freddy. 'Anyway, despite me profound ignorance, I've 'eard that if you put two parrots in a cage together they'll knock 'oles in each other.'

'Course they won't,' said Cassie. 'Will they?' she asked uncertainly.

'So I 'eard,' said Freddy.

'You sure, Freddy? Cats fight, but you sure parrots do?'

'So I 'eard,' said Freddy.

'Don't keep sayin' so you 'eard,' said Cassie. 'I had an uncle once who was always sayin' it, and one day me Aunt Priscilla, that was married to 'im, hit 'im with a long wooden box full of old 'orseshoes. Well, she was past patience, like they say.'

'Then what?' said Freddy.

'I think me dad said the funeral was on a Friday.'

'Is that a fact?' said Freddy.

'Yes, so I 'eard,' said Cassie, and giggled. 'Freddy, let's go and ask Mrs 'Arper if parrots fight when you put two together. I bet she'll know. Or she might let us ask Percy 'imself.'

'You go, I'll stay 'ere,' said Freddy.

'Freddy, I don't know why you're so contrary,' said Cassie.

'It's in'erited,' said Freddy.

'Well, take some medicine, then.'

'All right, there's some indoors,' said Freddy, but he might have known he wouldn't get away with that. He landed on Mrs Harper's doorstep with his insistent mate, muttering, 'What's the use?'

Cassie knocked. There was no answer. She knocked again. Still no answer.

'Oh, ain't that a disappointment, Freddy? They're all out.'

'I can't say me disappointment is bitter, Cassie. Like me to take yer for some fish and chips?'

'Freddy, we could use the latchcord and go in,' said Cassie. 'Mrs 'Arper might like us to, in case Percy's gone a bit sick from bein' alone.'

'Cassie, you can't go in,' said Freddy.

'Course we can,' said Cassie. It was a reasonable comment because most Walworth people didn't think anything of going into a neighbour's house to see if everything was all right and if anything new had been bought lately.

'No, we can't,' said Freddy, 'there's no latchcord.'

'Crikey, nor there isn't,' said Cassie, 'what a swizz. Oh, did yer mention fish and chips?'

'Yes, like a treat, would yer?' said Freddy. 'Come on, then.'

Going with him, Cassie said, 'Are yer treatin' me because you like me, Freddy?'

'No, because you're me mate,' said Freddy.

*　　*　　*

Dinner had been eaten in the grand-looking hotel restaurant. Chinese Lady had only pecked at the excellent food, Rosie had eaten fairly well, and Polly and Boots had dined modestly. Their table conversation had been inhibited by what was on their minds, the mystery of Chinese Lady's missing husband. Now they were in the room that she and Rosie were to use for the night. It was close to nine-thirty. Boots had phoned Emily and Sammy to let them know what was happening. Sammy said it made sense to stay overnight if Boots was sure that the military bloke, Captain Arnold, was worth a confab. It will be worth it, said Boots, if he saw who was in the car that passed him. Only if he noticed that our stepdad was in it, said Sammy. Emily said staying overnight made her suspicious of what Polly Simms might get up to. Boots said he wasn't sure if any of them were in the mood to get up to anything, but that if Polly took a fancy to Captain Arnold, well, she was a grown woman and there'd be nothing he himself could do about it. I don't mean this Captain Arnold, said Emily. Anyway, she said, you've got to keep your mind on your stepdad.

Boots had had coffee and brandy brought up for Chinese Lady, Polly and himself, and coffee for Rosie. Chinese Lady said brandy on top of port wasn't what she was used to. Boots said the brandy's medicinal. I don't need any medicine, said Chinese Lady, I need to find Edwin, and Lord only knows where he is by now.

'Daddy, d'you think Captain Arnold might be out all night?' asked Rosie.

'That depends on the company he's keeping,' said Polly.

'I hope he's not that kind of gentleman,' said Chinese Lady.

'Not every gentleman is quite like Boots,' said

Polly, which could have been interpreted as an oblique reference to his strict but exasperating adherence to his marriage vows. Polly regarded that not only as exasperating but ridiculous as well.

'Well, I have tried to bring all my sons up with a sense of proper behaviour,' said Chinese Lady.

'Oh, they're all very proper, Nana,' said Rosie. 'Daddy, suppose Captain Arnold didn't notice who was in that car, and even if he did, suppose Grandpa wasn't in it?'

'Yes, and what I want to know,' said Chinese Lady, 'is why should he have been? He wouldn't have got into anyone's car and let them drive him off when he knew he was waitin' for me.'

'I grant you it's a mystery, old lady,' said Boots.

'Stop callin' me old lady.'

'Let's wait in hope that Captain Arnold can help us,' said Boots.

There was no option but to do just that, and in an atmosphere that was strained and fidgety, although Polly thought Boots hid all his anxieties under a cloak of calm reassurance that at least kept his mother from biting her nails.

Someone knocked.

'Come in,' called Rosie hopefully, and Miss Jordan appeared.

'I'm really sorry for all this trouble you're having,' she said, 'and I'd like to mention two things. First, the manager suggests you might like him to call in the Farnham police.'

'No, not yet,' said Boots. He was against the suggestion. He knew that the one authority likely to take an exceptional interest in the matter was a certain Government department in Whitehall.

'Very well, Mr Adams,' said Miss Jordan. 'Second,

218

you've no overnight belongings. I can find nightwear for all of you, if you'd like.'

'Oh, that we would like,' said Rosie. 'Something borrowed for us ladies, something blue for Daddy.'

'Of course,' smiled Miss Jordan, 'and it will all be fresh and clean. Mr Adams, is there anything else we can do for you?'

'Only to let us know as soon as Captain Arnold gets back from Guildford,' said Boots.

'Yes, I've arranged that with my relief,' said Miss Jordan.

'Well, you're a treasure,' said Boots.

I'll kill him, thought Polly, he'll have that young lady turning cartwheels for him before the night's out.

Bubbles and Penny-Farving were in bed and sound asleep. Dan looked in on them at ten o'clock, saw two young heads resting on the pillows and tucked the bedclothes cosily around their shoulders. Then he knocked on Tilly's door.

'I ain't at 'ome to visitors,' called Tilly.

'If I could have a few words?' said Dan.

'Push off,' said Tilly. 'Oh, all right, what few words?' She opened the door. Her gas mantle had just been lighted, and her hair looked soft against the glow. But her eyes were challenging.

'I just thought I'd let you know I sent a letter to Elvira—'

'Gladys.'

'She never answers to Gladys.'

'She's off her chump,' said Tilly.

'I wrote to ask her if she'd marry me for the sake of the girls,' said Dan, 'and to let it go at that. I felt it 'ud be useless askin' her to come and live with us. She'll never desert her tightrope.'

'She will eventu'lly,' said Tilly, 'old age will make her fall off it.'

'Well, we'll all manage somehow until old age makes her a bit mellow,' said Dan.

'Who's all of you?' asked Tilly.

'Me and the girls,' said Dan.

'You're crazy, you'll never bring them gels up without havin' someone to mother them. All you're doin' is bringing different faces into their lives. They won't ever know who they belong to, and even when Alice 'Iggins starts lookin' after them again, you don't suppose she'll be out of work for ever, do you? She's bound to get a job sometime.'

'Yes, I've been thinkin' about that,' said Dan, a manly figure of cheerful, rugged optimism. 'Would it be too personal to ask what your av'rage earnings are for dressmakin'?'

'Yes, it would be too personal,' said Tilly.

'Still,' said Dan, 'that needn't stop me sayin' I'd be willin' to pay you seventeen-and-six a week if you'd care to look after me girls all the time I'm at work. My job's sound and permanent, and I could find seventeen-and-six for—'

'I can't believe me own ears,' said Tilly. 'So that's your game, is it? Turnin' me into your paid 'elp?'

'I'd include all your food,' said Dan.

'Mr Rogers, I'm naturally a kind and nice-tempered person—'

'Yes, you are sometimes,' said Dan, 'and I won't say you aren't.'

'Sometimes? What d'you mean, sometimes?'

'Well, there's that ruddy bolster,' said Dan.

'You weakling,' said Tilly, 'are you complainin' about one or two little taps?'

'No, just mentionin' them,' said Dan. 'Anyway, how about me proposition? Tell you what, I'll make it a quid a week. Like you said, Tilly, me girls need a bit of motherin' by someone who'll be around every day, and you'll probably still be able to do some dress-makin'.'

'I don't know I ever met anyone with more nerve than you've got, and why I'm standing 'ere—'

'Bubbles and Penny-Farvin' like you,' said Dan.

'That's it, come the old acid,' said Tilly.

'And I like you meself,' said Dan. 'Also, I meant it when I said you'd look even better in tights than Elvira.'

'Where's me fireside poker?' said Tilly.

'Tilly, I hope you ain't goin' to forget you're a lady again,' said Dan.

'It's because I'm a lady that I'm goin' to poke your eyes out,' said Tilly. 'Ladies don't invite blokes with evil eyes to gawp at their legs.'

'On me honour, it was accidental,' said Dan. 'I had no idea you hadn't finished dressin'.'

'Yes, you did, you 'ad a very good idea,' said Tilly. 'Just stay where you are, Mr Rogers, while I pick up me poker.'

'Ruddy hell,' said Dan, and beat a retreat. Tilly closed the door and sat down at her sewing-machine. For some reason she wanted to laugh. That cheerful Charlie, what a joker.

The June night was dark now. She sat in the bright glow of the gas mantle. The window opposite hers was a blankness, and nor was there any light in the kitchen below. She wouldn't be surprised if the people there were all out at the pub. Mrs Harper liked a drop all right, and her husband and brother-in-law probably did too.

Tilly did a thirty-minute stint on her machine before going to bed.

Mr Finch came to, for the second time. On the first occasion, he had been rendered unconscious again. His head was a fiery ache. The chopping blow had been ferociously efficient.

He was on a bed, a large piece of sticking-plaster over his mouth. He was handcuffed, and there was a padlocked chain around his ankles. The light was on, gaslight.

He had come out of the hotel and walked to his car to wait for his wife. A man and a woman got out of a car parked opposite his. The woman had a map in her hand, and she and her companion spread it over the bonnet of the car. She called to Mr Finch.

'I say, old chap, could you help us?'

Mr Finch went across.

'What kind of help do you want?' he asked.

'We're looking for a little place called Upper Hale, south of Farnham, but it doesn't seem to be on the map.'

'It's north of Farnham,' said Mr Finch, and the man moved aside to let him point it out on the map. It was then that the first blow was dealt, a vicious chop to the back of his neck. He blacked out. He was in the car when he first came to, and dusk had arrived. The car was travelling, the man next to him on the back seat, a second man driving, and the woman in the passenger seat. Weakly, Mr Finch lifted his head and attempted to say something. A hand turned him, and the second blow arrived. He blacked out again.

'What luck,' the chopper had said after the car had been driven away from the hotel.

'The luck of the righteous,' said the driver, and laughed. 'To have seen him when we had merely come to look things over, and then to have heard him state his destination.'

'You could say it was the luck of the righteous,' said the woman.

'What else?' said the chopper. 'It stayed with us, he came out of the hotel alone while we were wondering what to do about his wife.'

'What a chase,' said the driver, 'first to Farnham, then to the hotel.'

'I had a satisfying feeling the day was marked out in our favour,' said the chopper.

'The day's not over yet,' said the woman, 'we have to get him safely into hiding.'

'That means not until it's dark, not until it's late enough for London to be asleep,' said the chopper.

'London never sleeps, don't you know that?' said the woman.

'We shall take no risks,' said the driver, 'not after fortune has favoured us.'

'God bless the righteous,' said the woman.

The conversation was in German.

'You are awake?' The man who had felled Mr Finch was standing beside the bed. Mr Finch turned his aching head. With an effort, his eyes examined the room. It had an old familiarity about it. He had lodged for several years in just such a room, and in a house rented by Mrs Maisie Adams, a woman of resilience, who was always striving to rise above poverty. 'You are awake?' The question came again, and Mr Finch looked up at the man, tall and self-assured.

With sticking-plaster over my mouth, he thought, I'm expected to answer?

223

He could nod, of course. So he did.

'I telephoned you not long ago,' said the man. 'Do you remember? I asked if you were Edwin Finch, formerly Paul Strasser of Frankfurt-on-the-Maine.'

Mr Finch's eyes flickered.

'Do you remember?'

Mr Finch nodded again.

'Good. There are other things we want you to remember. However, it's late, so we shall put you to sleep and begin talking to you tomorrow. But first, perhaps, you would like to use the toilet.'

Mr Finch nodded yet again. If he was in need of one other concession, it was the removal of the plaster.

'Very well. We are going to free your mouth and take off the handcuffs and chains, but if you give us any trouble we shall gag you again and probably break your right arm. Do you understand?'

Mr Finch fully understood. He knew the type. Again he nodded. A second man appeared. The handcuffs were removed and the chains unpadlocked. Fingers peeled off the sticking-plaster. Then he was taken to the lavatory next to the room. Back on the bed a few minutes later, the leg chains were re-fixed. His brain was clearing, and he was quite calm. He had his own kind of resilience. He gave himself over to thinking, but was not allowed prolonged reflection, and was forced to accept an injection in his arm that put him to sleep. His last thoughts before the drug laid total claim on his consciousness were of his wife Maisie and the fact that the man had spoken to him in German.

The light was turned out, and not long afterwards the house fell silent.

The waiting had placed an almost impossible strain on

Chinese Lady, and she suffered it with tight lips. She felt Boots ought to have rushed about in a search for Edwin, asking questions of people. There must be some people in the area who had seen her husband, there must be some such people somewhere around. At the same time, however, she was not without faith in her son's conviction that they had to talk to Captain Arnold.

The hours went by, and at ten minutes to midnight, Miss Jordan, who was still up, knocked again. A little ruefully, she informed Boots that Captain Arnold was still not back.

'Although I like the sound of the gentleman,' said Polly drily, 'it's a little inconvenient of him to stay out so long.'

'He's an unconventional type,' said Miss Jordan.

'I don't mind the unconventional,' said Boots, 'I was simply hoping he'd favour an early night.'

'And I was hopin' a lot more could have been done than just waitin',' said Chinese Lady.

'But, Nana, what could we have done when we haven't known how to start?' said Rosie.

'It's a headache to all of us, Rosie love,' said Chinese Lady.

'That car is our one hope,' said Boots, not for the first time, 'especially as we know it was the odd man out.' He had spoken to the manager, and asked him if any guests had vacated their rooms this afternoon, guests who had cars. The manager, checking with Miss Jordan, said no. Well, then, said Boots, did any other people, in addition to his mother and stepfather, stop at the hotel just for tea? The manager, after further checking, said no. It was mostly on Sunday that motorists pulled in for tea. Boots said can I trouble you further by asking if anyone called this afternoon to enquire about rooms without actually making a reservation? Miss Jordan said no to that, which left Boots feeling only Captain Arnold could be of any real help. 'That car,' he said now, 'contained a person or persons who parked here but didn't use the hotel.'

'Well, old thing,' said Polly, 'that's suggesting the person or persons pulled in to sit and wait, don't you see.'

'Wait for what?' asked Chinese Lady.

'Ye gods,' said Polly, 'yes, wait for what?'

'We're keeping you up, Miss Jordan,' said Boots.

'I'll stay up all night, Mr Adams, if that's a help to you,' said the receptionist.

'I'd like to only know one more thing,' said Boots. 'Does your porter station himself at the entrance to the hotel all day?'

'He'll be there whenever guests are expected,' said Miss Jordan, 'but he has other duties that take him away. Why do you ask?'

'I'm wondering if he was at the entrance when my mother and stepfather arrived, and if he saw another car pull in a little while after them,' said Boots.

'I'd have to ask him,' said Miss Jordan.

'I can answer that,' said Chinese Lady. 'He was in the lobby when Edwin and me walked in.'

'Nana,' said Rosie, 'did you notice another car come in after you and Grandpa pulled in?'

'No, I didn't,' said Chinese Lady.

'Were there any cars behind you as you approached the hotel?' asked Boots.

'There was a bit of traffic all the time,' said Chinese Lady. 'Oh, lor', are you sayin—'

'Never mind,' said Boots, not wanting too much to

226

be discussed in front of Miss Jordan. 'What are we left with at the moment?'

'With the hope that Captain Arnold can tell us something about the car and who was in it,' said Polly.

'Just a description of the car would help if it was a little out of the ordinary,' said Boots.

'You'd need the help of the police then,' said Miss Jordan.

'We'll see,' said Boots, glancing at Polly. Such help might come from her father. Sir Henry knew something of Edwin Finch's background, and he was also acquainted with the anonymous figureheads of British Intelligence. Such people, in view of Edwin's work, would almost certainly conduct a search for the car. 'Miss Jordan, as we're stuck at the cross-roads, I think the most practical thing now is for all of us to go to bed and buttonhole Captain Arnold at breakfast. Or does he take breakfast in bed whenever he's had a late night?'

'He's a regular guest here, a bachelor,' said Miss Jordan, 'but I've never known him to take breakfast in bed, however late he's been overnight.'

'We'll wait until morning, then,' said Boots.

'Goodnight, sir,' said Miss Jordan, 'I do hope you all get some sleep.'

It was well after midnight when Chinese Lady finally went uneasily to bed, with Rosie lending her sympathetic company. Boots and Polly retired to their own rooms on the opposite side of the corridor. The rooms were adjoining, and Boots noted a communicating door. Knowing something of Polly and her devil-may-care attitude, he wondered if the communicating door had anything to do with the fact that she had booked the rooms herself. He tried the door. It was locked. He accorded it a brief smile. He undressed and put on a pair of pyjamas. The estimable Miss Jordan had somehow found clean nightwear for all of them. He got into bed, heaping the pillows to help him sit up and think. It would not go out of his mind, the certainty that the car seen by Captain Arnold held some clue to his stepfather's disappearance. And with that certainty was the suspicion that the disappearance had something to do with Edwin's cloak-and-dagger profession. Outside of that, nothing made sense.

About to douse the bedside light, he heard a soft sound. The communicating door opened and in came Polly, wearing a borrowed wrap and a bedtime smile. She looked admirably younger than thirty-three. Her hair style, her vivaciousness and her smooth skin had always favoured her in respect of her years.

'I thought that door was locked,' said Boots.

'Oh, it was, darling, yes,' said Polly, 'but the key was on my side.'

'What's the idea?' asked Boots.

'Nothing important, old love,' she said. 'It's more of a feeling.'

'What kind of a feeling?' asked Boots, eyeing her guardedly as she sat down on the edge of the bed.

'The feeling that you cut short the conversation when you realized you'd arrived at the possibility that someone had been following your stepfather,' said Polly.

'Yes, I think my mother had seen that,' said Boots, 'and I felt it best to say no more in front of Miss Jordan.'

'But that young lady has made herself invaluable,' said Polly. 'It's the way you look at her.'

'I've got that kind of look?' said Boots.

'Don't play "Little Boy Blue" with me,' said Polly,

'you know damn well how to make young women like Miss Jordan go weak at the knees. Hell's bells, don't I do that sometimes when you condescend to look at me?' Her wrap moved. She didn't seem to move herself, but her wrap did. It parted at her thighs, and the sheen of grey silk stockings caught the light. A suspender clip winked. 'God, me at my age, nearly thirty, having my knees give way.'

Boots let 'nearly thirty' pass.

'You're coming undone, Polly,' he said. 'As for the possibility that my stepfather may have been followed, that's something best kept to the family. I'm against having people peering into the family window.'

'You're against anything that might blow your family's washing into the high street,' said Polly. 'God give me patience, how much longer do I have to wait?'

'For what?' asked Boots.

'To get into bed with you.'

Boots, not unaware of how splendid her legs looked in their sleek silk stockings, said, 'Well, Polly old love, much as I care for you, I don't think we'd make a very good job of bedding down together, not while circumstances are as they are, bloody depressing.'

'One day,' said Polly, 'you'll run out of excuses. D'you find it easy to resist me?'

'Is that a serious question?' asked Boots.

Polly eyed the top two buttons of his pyjama jacket, both of which were undone, smiled her brittle smile and said, 'Do you strip well, Boots?'

'Not as well as I think you do, Polly.'

'Then I can't think of anything more serious than my question.'

'I can think of my stepfather being followed here,' said Boots. 'Is that more serious than my saying no, I don't find it easy to resist you?'

'Then look here, dear old sport, can't we get bosom to bosom beneath the sheets?'

'Definitely not,' said Boots. 'Rosie's across the corridor.'

'That's a wounding blow,' said Polly, 'it's crippled me. Aside from that, why should anyone want to follow your stepfather and go off with him into the misty blue? He's only a civil servant, isn't he?'

Polly was ignorant of what her father knew about Edwin Finch.

'There's just a suspicion he might have been followed,' said Boots. 'The rest is a mystery. Shall we get some sleep, Polly?'

'That's all I'm going to get, I suppose,' said Polly. Her brittle smile surfaced again. 'But listen, even Emily should allow a lovely old soldier like you the pleasure of one concubine, and believe me, no concubine would be more of a pleasure to you than I would. But not tonight, it seems. Oh, well, here I am, a scorned woman again.' She kissed him and went back to her room, and the communicating door closed. His mention of Rosie had been a singular deterrent. The girl, perhaps unable to sleep, might just take it into her head to look in on her father to find out if he was sleepless too. Rosie, whenever things weren't right, would always turn first to Boots. It would have been frightful, Polly thought, if the girl had found her in bed with him.

Not for the first time, she took her frustrations to bed with her.

Chapter Sixteen

'Tilly?'

'Oh, me gawd,' breathed Tilly. It wasn't yet eight o'clock and she hadn't finished dressing. She moved fast and put her back against the door of her bedroom in case the sneaky swine caught her in her underwear again. 'Go away,' she hissed.

'No problems, Tilly,' said Dan, talking cheerfully to the door, 'just thought I'd let you know Cassie'll be turnin' up as usual to look after the girls for the mornin'. That reminds me, did I mention to you her dad's goin' to ask a niece of his to do a full-time job with them?'

'No, you didn't mention it,' said Tilly, fumbling at her hooks and eyes. 'Why, you artful old codger, you asked me to do that.'

'Irons in the fire, y'know, Tilly. A bloke has to think of that, specially as Cassie's dad hasn't had any reply yet from his niece.'

'Lord give me strength,' said Tilly, 'I'm first reserve, am I? You've got a hope, Mr Rogers.'

'Call me Dan.'

'Don't try and worm yer sneaky way into me affections,' said Tilly, 'it won't work.'

'Well, you know me, Tilly, sold on Elvira's affections.'

'More fool you,' said Tilly, her corset now nicely in place, her proud bosom comfortably tucked away but not at the expense of its rounded shape. 'That woman's got no affection for anything or anyone except 'er barmy tightrope. I'd tell you not to marry 'er if it wasn't for the sake of yer little angels. Well, that's all, you can go now.'

'Yes, I'll be away as soon as Cassie arrives,' said Dan. 'Just thought – um – well, if you could do me a little favour again and keep your ears open for what me girls might get up to after Cassie's gone, I'd be grateful to me dyin' day.'

'Your dyin' day could be tonight if you land me with Bubbles and Penny-Farvin' again, d'you 'ear? I can't believe you'd do it again.'

'Only for this afternoon, Tilly, take me word,' said Dan, 'I'm confidently hopin' Cassie's dad will come up trumps with his niece tomorrow. Believe me, Tilly, when a bloke's havin' problems, it's a relief I've got a reliable and 'elpful lady like you in me domain. I'll see you as soon as I get home this evenin'. So long now.'

'Come back, you 'orrible ape!' yelled Tilly, hearing him going down the stairs. 'Oh, I'll do for you, once and for all, you 'ear me?'

Dan heard her all right, but kept going.

Tilly fumed.

'Oh, 'ello, Mr Rogers,' said Cassie on arrival.

'Mornin', Tilly,' said Dan.

'How'd you do,' said Penny-Farving.

'We like yer,' said Bubbles.

'That's nice,' said Cassie. 'Mr Rogers, I'm ever so sorry, but me dad 'ad a letter from his niece first post this mornin', and in it she said she couldn't look after yer girls as she 'ad a job comin' up.'

'Never mind, can't be helped,' said Dan, a

philosophical character as well as a cheerful one, 'and I wasn't takin' it for granted, Cassie.'

'Well, p'raps Alice won't be long now gettin' to be your daily help again,' said Cassie, who never looked on the dark side any more than Dan did. ''Ave you got someone for this afternoon?'

'Tilly's promised to keep an eye open,' said Dan. 'Well, more or less, and she's a nice obligin' young lady.'

'And ever so good-lookin',' said Cassie. 'Bubbles, stop breakin' your toast up. It's for eatin', not throwin' at yer sister.'

'But she frew some of hers at me,' complained Bubbles.

'Did you?' asked Cassie of Penny-Farving.

'Only a little bit,' said Penny-Farving.

'Mr Rogers, shall I give 'er a little smack or will you?' asked Cassie.

'Um – well, I'm off now, Cassie, I'll leave it to you,' said Dan, dodging that one by departing. So Penny-Farving received a little smack on her hand from Cassie.

'Crumbs,' said Penny-Farving, 'that nearly 'urt.'

'The next one will,' said Cassie, who had a dreamy imagination, a soft heart and a lot of commonsense hidden away.

Captain Arnold, RE retired, began his breakfast at his favourite corner table at half-past eight precisely. He'd had a late night, not having got back to the hotel until past two in the morning, his friends in Guildford having given him a very convivial evening. He was, however, ready to tackle a good breakfast, his constitution being excellent, and by nine o'clock he had partaken healthily of bacon and eggs and toast and marmalade. He poured himself a final cup of tea.

Miss Jordan arrived at his table.

'Excuse me, sir,' she said, 'but may I introduce you to Mr Adams?'

Captain Arnold looked up and took note of a distinguished-looking chap.

'Morning, Mr Adams,' he said.

'How'd you do,' said Boots. He had left Chinese Lady, Rosie and Polly at a table on the other side of the restaurant, with Polly due to phone the school and give a reason why she and Rosie would be absent today. 'D'you mind if I sit down with you?' he asked Captain Arnold.

'Help yourself, old chap,' said Captain Arnold.

'I'll leave you to each other,' said Miss Jordan, and returned to reception.

'You've something on your mind, Mr Adams?' said Captain Arnold.

'Yes, and I wonder if you can help me,' said Boots. 'First, that's my mother over there, with my daughter. The lady with them is Polly Simms, daughter of General Sir Henry Simms.' Boots thought he might as well mention he had connections.

'Sir Henry Simms?' Captain Arnold looked impressed. 'The corps commander who made himself unpopular with Haig by having a stand-up row with him after the first battle of the Somme?'

'The same,' said Boots. 'His daughter can also hold her own. However, to get to the point. Do you recognize my mother as the lady who spoke to you when you were tinkering with your car yesterday afternoon?'

Captain Arnold, vigorously masculine in appearance, took a look at Chinese Lady, who gave him a little nod.

'Yes, I recognize her, Mr Adams. She was a little worried. Very unfortunate, I thought. Seemed to have mislaid her husband.'

'Not out of carelessness,' said Boots.

'No, certainly not, by George,' said Captain Arnold. 'Bad form if I implied that. Did he turn up?'

'No,' said Boots, and pointed out that they hadn't a clue as to why and how he had disappeared. All they did have was the knowledge that Captain Arnold had seen a car driving out as he drove in. Captain Arnold said that was correct. Boots asked if he had also seen who was in the car. Captain Arnold said he hadn't made that kind of observation of the car, but he thought a man was at the wheel, a woman beside him. Just a brief glimpse. The car was being driven in a hurry, as if the occupants hadn't paid their hotel bill.

'There was a woman?' said Boots.

'I had this glimpse, old chap,' said Captain Arnold, 'and I'd say yes, there was a woman in the passenger seat.'

'Anyone on the back seat?' asked Boots.

'Didn't notice, didn't look. My plugs were oiling up. What's the suggestion, that your father was in the car?'

'My stepfather,' said Boots.

'Does he do that kind of thing?' asked Captain Arnold. 'Go off without notifying his family?'

'No,' said Boots, and asked if Captain Arnold could describe the driver of the car and the woman beside him. Captain Arnold said he couldn't, since he hadn't taken a deliberate look, merely an automatic glance as a fellow might when passing another car that was in a hurry. A momentary image of a man and a woman, that was all he could recollect. How important was it?

'Very important, if my stepfather happened to be in the back of the car.'

'Silly question of mine,' said Captain Arnold. 'Are you up against dirty work at the cross-roads, Mr Adams? If so, don't you need to inform the police? There's a station in Farnham, and your mother must be a desperately worried woman.'

Boots said it looked as if the police might have to be called in. However, had Captain Arnold noticed which direction the car took? Yes, said the Captain, it was turning left to Guildford as it passed him.

'And would you have noticed what kind of car it was?'

'That's an easy one, old chap,' said Captain Arnold, 'I'm a car enthusiast. It was a wine-coloured Austin Cambridge saloon.'

That was something, thought Boots. Most cars, except the specialist kind, were black. Guildford, therefore, was worth a visit. It was a major Surrey city, and a likely place in which to hole up. Assuming Edwin had been in that car, then it was for the purpose of taking him somewhere and doing what to him? I'm going to settle, thought Boots, for an abduction relating to his years in Intelligence. And who would think of looking for him in Guildford? It's a shot in the dark, but we'll go there, and Polly can make use of her fascinating eyelashes. She can ask policemen on point duty if they can remember seeing a wine-coloured Austin Cambridge saloon in yesterday afternoon's traffic. What's a copper worth if his training hasn't sharpened his powers of observation?

'Well, thanks very much, Captain Arnold,' he said. 'Good of you to put up with my questions.'

'Only too pleased, my dear fellow,' said Captain Arnold, and smiled as he added, 'I think you were good enough yourself to wait until I'd finished a very enjoyable breakfast. Damn civilized of you. My regards to your worried mother, and I'm at your service today if you need my help. I take a very poor view of buggers who make off with a lady's husband, if that's what's happened.'

'We'll get to work on the possibility,' said Boots, and returned to his table. Polly was at reception, using the phone there to call the school. Boots took Chinese Lady and Rosie out of the restaurant to the lobby, where they picked up Polly and then went up to his room. There he told them of the small amount of information given to him by Captain Arnold. Chinese Lady, under increasing strain, was dubious about the meaning of a woman being in the car. I can't hardly think that a woman would be wicked enough to help take Edwin away, she said, and how could they have taken him, anyway? Edwin's a strong man and a sensible one.

'But it's all we've got, Mrs Finch,' said Polly, 'the possibility that somehow or other he was persuaded to get into the car and was then driven away.'

'Oh, help,' said Rosie, 'he'd have been furious. Daddy, what do we do now?'

'Go to Guildford and try to find out if anyone noticed the car,' said Boots.

'And if someone says yes, they noticed it passing through yesterday, where will that get us, old sport?' asked Polly.

'It may not have gone all the way through the city,' said Boots, 'it may be parked somewhere.'

'Daddy, we're going to look at every street in Guildford?' said Rosie.

'It's work for the police,' said Polly.

'Well, we'll have a go first,' said Boots, 'but before we do I'd better ring Emily and Sammy.'

He did so, from the lobby call-box. Emily was as dubious as Chinese Lady about Mr Finch having been taken away in some strangers' car, and couldn't think what good it would do to chase about Guildford. Still, she said, I've got to believe in you, Boots, and I know you'll have the sense to go to the police if you feel you're not getting anywhere. And she asked if Chinese Lady was bearing up. Well, you know Chinese Lady, Em, said Boots, she's an old soldier. She's biting her lip and giving me what for now and again, but she's bearing up. Well, I hope so, said Emily, she must be going out of her mind with worry. And what's Polly doing? Lending support, said Boots, and Rosie's a godsend to all of us. That girl's a dear, said Emily, so just find your stepdad and make her happy.

Sammy's response was to tell Boots to go ahead, to do what he thought best, and not to contact the coppers until there was no option. Keep it in the family, he said. My idea precisely, said Boots. What a palaver, said Sammy, our respected stepdad going missing in what looks like a serious way. Makes no sense to me. Get on with it, Boots, Susie sends you her best.

Mr Finch had been given quite a decent breakfast. The woman brought it up to him, telling him to enjoy it while he was still alive. And she spoke in German. Afterwards, the two men addressed themselves to him as he lay on the bed, his legs chained and the handcuffs around his wrist. His mouth was free, however, but he understood the threat he was under. He'd had experience of men like these, with their steely eyes and their incorruptible dedication to whatever cause they were serving. They wouldn't hesitate to cripple him for life or even strangle him.

'You were born Paul Strasser, that is accepted?'

'Yes.'

The man who had struck the chopping blows did most of the talking, and in a calm, dispassionate way. No good would have come of you denying your German origins, he said, for we know all there is to know about you. Is there any need for questions, then? asked Mr Finch. There's need for some, said the chopper. For instance, do you concede you betrayed your Fatherland by going over to the British and taking with you information entrusted to you? Do you concede, in fact, that you're a disgusting traitor?

Mr Finch replied that he would not concede that at all. German Intelligence made a mistake when they sent him to England many years ago, for he quickly found he identified more comfortably with the English than with Germans. To begin to feel more English than German was not a betrayal of Germany, it was an accident of nature. Further, he said, if my original file still exists, you will find I recorded my strong opposition to Germany going to war in support of Austria. There was no need for Austria to go to war herself. Serbia had accepted the Austrian ultimatum and its terms.

'You put that forward as an excuse for playing the traitor?' The question was a contemptuous denunciation.

'I did not play the traitor, I remained faithful to my calling and to Germany right up to March, 1918, when I then decided I could no longer represent Germany. I changed sides, yes, but at a time when I could have contributed nothing that would have helped Germany avoid defeat.' Mr Finch spoke with cool exactitude.

'Your interpretation is not acceptable. However, modern Germany is prepared to forgive you. You are a man of great experience and accomplishments, and modern Germany is a State that has risen from the ashes of defeat and found itself with the potential to become the greatest in the world. Before very long we shall have a new Chancellor, a new leader. It will only be a matter of two or three years.'

'You are speaking of Adolf Hitler,' said Mr Finch, his German measured.

'Our future Fuehrer. Your experience is needed, so is all the information you can give us concerning British Intelligence. You will go to Germany freely in three days time, stay there for a week, during which time you will be interrogated, and then return to become a double agent.'

'Excuse me?' said Mr Finch.

'You will work for British Intelligence in your usual way while acting for Germany.'

Mr Finch said that was impossible and absurd. British Intelligence would be highly suspicous of any agent who vanished for ten days. The second German said he must simply advise his superiors that in a dispirited mood he had left England to return to his native country with the intention of making amends by serving German Intelligence again. However, after only a week he realized he had planted his roots too deeply in England, and another change of heart brought him back again. At least, that was what he would tell his superiors.

Mr Finch said he was inclined to laugh at that because of its absurdity. The senior German said to laugh would cause them intolerable offence. You will go to Germany, in any event, he said. If not freely, then aboard a small German merchant ship at present in London Docks. But when you reach Berlin you will be tried and shot. However, Intelligence, knowing of you and your excellence, would rather you cooperated.

Mr Finch pointed out that by now the British police would be looking for him, that Whitehall would be supervizing the hunt.

They have only three days, said the senior German, the chopper, and that will not be long enough to find you. You were once involved with a lady called Elsie Chivers, a lady who worked for the British Admiralty and helped you with information concerning Lord Kitchener's sea voyage to Russia. We sank the *Hampshire*, and Lord Kitchener was lost to the British war effort. That put you in high esteem with German Intelligence. Unfortunately, you had previously helped Fraulein Chivers to murder her mother.

Mr Finch said absurdity was having a field day.

'You think so?' said the second man.

'I am certain,' said Mr Finch.

'We have seen Fraulein Chivers and interviewed her.'

'The lady is in a home for patients with mind disorders,' said Mr Finch.

'But she has very lucid moments, when truth pours from her lips.'

'It's a peculiar kind of truth if it points a finger at me,' said Mr Finch. He was free to shout if he decided to disregard unspoken threats. But they would smother his mouth immediately, and since he knew where he was, in the heart of Walworth, what good would a single shout do, whoever heard it? Some Walworth people revelled in bawling and shouting, and others got into the habit of taking no notice.

'I think it could be said you were an accessory after the fact.'

'Nonsense,' said Mr Finch.

'Not at all,' said the senior man. 'Fraulein Chivers was acquitted of the murder, but we have enough

241

information to give the police food for thought. Enough, I should say, for them to arrest you and get you committed for trial.'

'More absurdity,' said Mr Finch.

'Not as we see it. Further, Herr Strasser, there's your wife and her family. Would you like us to convey to them the information that you and Fraulein Chivers helped the Germans to drown Lord Kitchener, that you were a German spy throughout the war, and that you were implicated in the murder of Frau Chivers?'

Mr Finch's mouth tightened.

'If I agree to work for you as a double agent,' he said, 'you have no guarantee I will do that. You can't force me to give you the kind of information you want. It might very well be the wrong kind, without you realizing it.'

'Our Intelligence is no more staffed by idiots than the British, Herr Strasser. It would pay you unpleasant dividends if we suspected you of fooling us or double-crossing us. The moment that happened, your wife would receive a detailed account of all that we know about you, and so would the police and your national newspapers.'

Mr Finch sighed.

'You're making things very difficult for me,' he said.

'But of course. We need you, we need your experience and all that you know of British Intelligence, and if you refuse to cooperate, then regretfully we shall destroy your life here.'

'It's a singularly unpleasant form of blackmail,' said Mr Finch.

'Ah, well, you know yourself that Intelligence is not the profession of gentlemen.'

'Do you know where you are?' asked the second German.

'Yes, I know,' said Mr Finch. The room, so like the one that had been his when he lodged with the Adams family, had been used by Elsie Chivers as a place where she used her sewing-machine and kept herself out of the way of her spiteful and embittered mother. He had only been in it once, but that was enough for him to identify it. There was a crack in one of the door panels and another crack in the stone hearth. He knew why these men had brought him here. To remind him of the murder of Elsie's mother, and to let that reminder weaken his resilience. If possible.

'An appropriate choice of ours, would you say?' said the senior man.

'Childish,' said Mr Finch, 'and handcuffs and chains are equally so.'

'Does he think that witty? asked the second man.

'No, it's consistent with his character. He's not a mouse.'

The door opened and the woman looked in.

'Does he want some coffee?' she asked in German.

'Do you?' asked the senior man.

'Thank you, yes,' said Mr Finch.

'Coffee for all of us, fraulein, and prepare lunch for one o'clock.'

'If you say so,' said the woman, and disappeared.

'Well, what is your answer, Herr Strasser?'

'I'm expected to go to Germany to ostensibly redeem myself, and then to change my mind?' said Mr Finch.

'It's expected of you to do what is good for your health.'

'Then I need time to think,' said Mr Finch.

The senior man said they'd give him until tomorrow,

and that it would be as well for him not to misjudge the situation. In the event of a failure to cooperate, information would be laid with his wife and her family to the effect that he was German by birth, that there was a birth certificate to prove it, that he had worked for German Intelligence, with documents and a photograph as further proof, been indirectly responsible for the sinking of the *Hampshire*, and an accessory to the murder of Frau Chivers. The police would also be given information concerning the latter, and that, of course, would make it very uncomfortable for him to remain in England.

'You're very thorough,' said Mr Finch, 'but thoroughness, of course, is a notable German characteristic. I repeat, I need time to think.'

'What you mean, my friend,' said the senior man, 'is that the British authorities need time to find you. It won't happen. There's nothing for them to work on. As you say, we have been very thorough. However, there it is, you have until tomorrow to decide. Note that you will not be left alone, one of us will always be with you. My colleague will sleep this afternoon and keep an eye on you all through the night. We will be rough with you if you cause any trouble. Do you understand?'

'Perfectly,' said Mr Finch.

'He's a cool character,' said the second man.

'That is why the new Germany will need him,' said the senior man.

Tilly did some shopping in East Street Market, and while there she ran into Cassie and the girls. The girls were each munching an apple.

'Apples, eh?' said Tilly. 'Bought or pinched, Cassie?'

'Oh, I've smacked pinchin' out of them,' said

Cassie, 'and treated them. They've been real little angels this mornin', except when they tried to open me parrot's cage and give 'im to me cat. I might 'ave to sell me cat. D'you want to buy 'im for sixpence, Tilly?'

'Not this week, Cassie,' smiled Tilly. 'You're doin' a good job lookin' after Bubbles and Penny-Farvin'.'

'I'm tryin' me best,' said Cassie, 'even if I do feel a bit worn out by the end of a mornin'.'

'They need a mother,' said Tilly.

'Don't want our muvver,' said Penny-Farving, 'she frows fings.'

'It's a shame Mr Rogers is married to a difficult woman,' said Cassie.

'I think they're divorced,' said Tilly, feeling that was the best thing to say.

'That's not very nice for the girls,' said Cassie, keeping an eye on them as they inspected a heap of cardboard boxes under a stall. 'And Mr Rogers is such a nice man. I think 'e'd look nice on a horse.'

'On a horse?' said Tilly.

'Yes, 'e's got a sort of cowboy look,' said Cassie. 'Well, I'll take Bubbles and Penny-Farvin' back to their home, then see if Mrs 'Arper will let them meet 'er parrot again.' She pulled the girls out of the cardboard boxes.

'So long, Cassie,' said Tilly, 'and behave yerselves, you gels.'

'Oh, you lookin' after them this afternoon?' asked Cassie.

'Seems like it,' said Tilly, keeping to herself her intention to break their father's leg, whether he had a cowboy look or not.

''Ello, what's all this?' asked Mrs Harper, having

245

answered Cassie's knock to find the girl had those two noisy brats with her.

'Oh, how'd you do, Mrs 'Arper,' said Cassie, 'I wondered if Bubbles and Penny-Farvin' could come in and talk to Percy again.'

'Well, dearie, I'd be pleasured to 'ave you all come in,' said Mrs Harper, floridly expansive in her neighbourliness, 'but I've got me old man Wally ill in bed, and 'is brother 'ome with 'im, 'aving just got the sack from 'is job. 'E's talkin' about us goin' back to 'Oxton, which ain't very agreeable, not when Wally and me is settlin' down nice 'ere. Anyway, ducks, I ain't able to entertain visitors just now. Some other time, p'raps.'

'Oh, all right,' said Cassie, 'and we 'ope Mr 'Arper'll soon be better. Oh, I was goin' to ask if parrots fight when you put two in a cage together.'

'Yes, course they would,' said Mrs Harper, 'there's only room for one parrot in one cage.'

'But suppose one was a lady parrot?' said Cassie.

'She'd soon kick 'er old man out,' said Mrs Harper. 'Well, I must get on, dearie. Toodle-oo for now.'

'Goodbye,' said Cassie, and the door closed on her.

Chapter Seventeen

'Must I?' asked Polly.

'I'll hold the fort,' said Boots.

'You mean you'll just sit here in the car,' said Polly. She had asked three traffic-duty policemen one after the other if they had noticed a wine-coloured Austin Cambridge saloon car yesterday afternoon. None of them could recollect seeing it. Now a fourth officer was visible at a junction. There was a fair amount of traffic in Guildford, including a good percentage of vehicles that were still horse-drawn. These included old-fashioned traps that probably belonged to people from the outlying countryside.

Boots had been driving around side streets, hoping to spot the car while trying to convince himself it was reasonable to assume the people he was looking for had his stepfather somewhere in Guildford. Chinese Lady was very dubious about that. Rosie, a staunch ally of her father, went along with all his assumptions and suggestions. Polly, while high on adrenalin at simply being in company with Boots, felt they were chasing a needle in a haystack.

Boots had passed the junction and pulled up close to the kerb. Polly sighed.

'All right, I'll take a turn, I'll go,' said Boots.

'No, I will, let me,' said Rosie, and was quickly out of the back seat she was sharing with Chinese Lady.

'Mind how you go, Rosie,' called Chinese Lady.

Rosie dashed across to the policeman on point duty. She waited until he indicated she could address him.

'Oh, sorry to bother you, Mister Police Officer,' she said, giving him the smile of a young lady who'd been waiting all her life to talk to a traffic cop, 'but did you happen to see a – yes, a wine-coloured Austin saloon car in yesterday's traffic?'

The policeman, holding up two facing lines of vehicles, while motioning other lines through, cocked a paternal eye at the engagingly attractive schoolgirl.

'Well, now I come to think of it,' he said, 'I noted an over-loaded brown lorry and a Green Line bus, and I've got an idea I also saw a dustcart.'

'Oh, that's no good,' said Rosie, 'my father won't thank you for that.'

'I'm 'eart-broken,' said the bobby. He brought the moving flow of traffic to a halt and released the stationary vehicles. Rosie, on the little island with him, waited just in case he had real information up his sleeve. 'What's this partic'lar car done, miss? Robbed your dad's bank?'

'Daddy doesn't have a bank of his own,' said Rosie, 'he uses Lloyds.'

'Well, you can tell him I now recollect some such car as mentioned,' said the amiable bobby. 'I recollect it tried to slip through as if it was in a hurry, but I waved it down, made it stop and pointed a reprovin' finger at it.' He used a hand to keep the moving traffic on the go. 'Why's your dad interested?'

'Oh, he wants to get in touch with the people in it,' said Rosie, quickening. 'Did you see who was in it?'

'A gent and a lady in front, two gents in the back,' said the constable. He reversed his hand signals. 'Would your dad like them arrested?' he asked, a twinkle in his eyes.

'Oh, no, thanks,' said Rosie, 'we only wanted to know if they were in Guildford yesterday. Thanks ever so much, Mister Police Officer, I like you.'

'Same to you, miss,' he said, and kept a line of vehicles stationary as she ran back to Boots's car. She got in.

'Rosie, that bobby told you something,' said Polly.

'Yes, you were there quite a bit, Rosie love,' said Chinese Lady.

'Well, you see, he did spot that car,' said Rosie, 'he mentioned it tried to dodge his signal to stop because it was in a hurry.'

'Reasonable,' said Polly.

'I suppose so, if it wanted to get out of the area as quickly as possible,' said Boots.

'Daddy, the policeman told me there were four people in it, three men and a lady,' said Rosie.

'The woman again,' said Boots reflectively, 'the one Captain Arnold glimpsed sitting next to the driver. So there were two men in the back, were there, poppet?'

'That's what the traffic policeman said, Daddy.'

'I think your theory's just been blown up, Boots old scout,' said Polly.

'Yes, if it was still in a hurry,' said Chinese Lady. 'Well, that would of meant they weren't thinkin' of hidin' Edwin away in Guildford.'

'Or that they were simply in a hurry to get to where they were going,' said Boots, 'which could be this side of the city.'

'Boots, I don't like all these ifs and buts,' said Chinese Lady.

'I think one thing's certain,' said Boots, 'and that's that wherever they were going, they're there now. I don't favour chucking Guildford away. Let's search the streets this side of it.'

'I think we all need a break,' said Polly, 'let's find an oasis where they serve food and drink to the weary wanderer.'

'Yes, what d'you think, Daddy?' asked Rosie.

'I think your Nana could do with a break,' said Boots.

'I could do with my life like it was before all this happened,' said Chinese Lady.

'Yes, it's all a blessed worry, Nana, and that's only half of it,' said Rosie. Borrowing a phrase from Chinese Lady's book, she added, 'But we've still got to keep body and soul together.'

'I propose an uplifting drink first, reviving and slightly intoxicating,' said Polly, as Boots began a new search on wheels, this time for a licensed restaurant.

'I know we're all in a state about Edwin,' said Chinese Lady, 'but I hope no-one's goin' to make that an excuse for gettin' drunk.'

'I'm not, Nana, I'm under age,' said Rosie, and patted Chinese Lady's hand and then gave it a little squeeze. 'Daddy will find Grandpa, I'm sure he will.'

'Bless you, Rosie.'

Food and drink were all very well, but the thought of a banquet itself wouldn't have changed what they all felt, that they really had no idea where to look for the missing person. Boots also felt a call on Sir Henry Simms might become necessary. But for the moment, he still wanted to keep the problem to the family in the hope that a real clue would suddenly show itself.

Rachel, arriving at the offices of Adams Enterprises in the middle of the afternoon, did not announce herself but went directly to Boots's office. Finding him absent, she knocked on Sammy's door and showed herself.

'Hello, Sammy, how'd you like this unexpected picture of me?'

Sammy, looking up from his desk, decided that if he hadn't had Susie as the permanent picture in his eye, he'd settle for a large photograph of Rachel, inclusive of her remarkable legs.

'Well, what can I say, Rachel old love, except it's a pleasure?' he said.

'Could you manage a smile?' asked Rachel.

Smiles, thought Sammy, were a bit hard to deliver at the moment. The family had serious worries, and of the kind that didn't make sense. Tommy and Vi, who'd been told, and Emily and Susie simply couldn't believe that Chinese Lady had lost her better half in the space of a few minutes, which was what it amounted to. Boots had talked about the possibility of him being in some car or other, but Boots, Sammy thought, had something on his mind that he was keeping back. Boots was the sort of bloke who could always keep his cards close to his chest.

'Well, you know me, Rachel. When I'm up to me ears in me business affairs, me commercial responsibilities get the better of me sociableness. That doesn't mean I ain't pleasured to have you walk in like the Queen of Sheba. Mind, I say that as a respectable married husband with no thoughts of upsettin' the apple cart.'

'Same old Sammy, ain't you, lovey?' smiled Rachel. 'Where's Boots?'

'He's out on specialized business,' said Sammy.

'That's your department,' said Rachel.

'He's still out,' said Sammy. 'Might I ask why you want him?'

'Oh, we all want a bit of Boots,' said Rachel. 'Me, Susie, Emily, Vi and I daresay several others.'

'Not Em'ly,' said Sammy, 'she's had all of him since they got churched. Might I mention this female weakness for my eldest brother is gettin' indecent?'

'Oh, some of us have got a very indecent weakness for you, Sammy,' purred Rachel. 'Well, I'll see Boots another time. I was just passing and it's not important. Would you like to take me to Lyons now, for tea and a bun?'

'We'll get talked about,' said Sammy, 'and if 'Is Majesty the King finds out I won't ever get me knighthood. Still, I'll chance it and tear meself away from me work for fifteen minutes.'

So he took her to Lyons, which was close by, and they had tea and a buttered bun. They were very old friends and very compatible, but Rachel said nothing to him about what she was doing for Boots, and Sammy said not a word about his missing stepfather.

Mr Finch had a quiet day, and spent most of the time reflecting on his situation. It was impossible, of course, to accept there was no option but to have these people inform Maisie of his accomplishments as a German agent during the war. The shock would destroy their life together, particularly as he had recruited Elsie Chivers. To go to Germany for a week and then return to act as a double agent, would he be able to live with that? And would British Intelligence find his return credible? He could dismiss the threat of being tried as an accomplice to murder. Anything Elsie Chivers might have told the Germans would never stand up in court, not while she was being treated for disorders of the mind. The rest, however, would disillusion Maisie. How true it was that skeletons in cupboards were always liable to come to light.

The senior man sat in the room with him, the other man sleeping, apparently. His guard said nothing to him, immersing himself in a book, a biography of Bismarck, the virtual founder of the German Empire, the Empire that had crashed in 1918.

Mr Finch had only very faint hopes of being found. He wondered if Boots had made contact with the Whitehall office, rather than with the police. He'd give it careful thought, but Mr Finch fancied he'd come down on the side of Whitehall. He'd favour the more discreet line. He wouldn't have the faintest notion of what caused his stepfather to disappear, but he'd know it would be the work of professionals to try to trace him.

Dan was home a little earlier than usual. Not finding the girls anywhere downstairs, he armed himself mentally before going up to face Tilly. He heard Bubbles and Penny-Farving giggling in her bedroom. He put his head round the open door. There they were, in Tilly's bed, cuddling their dolls.

''Ello, Dad,' they said.

'Half a mo',' said Dan, crossing the floor and looking down at them, 'what're you doin' in Tilly's bed?'

'She put us 'ere,' said Bubbles.

'A tin of pins fell off 'er table,' said Penny-Farving.

'There was 'undreds on the floor,' said Bubbles, blue eyes angelic.

'Bubbles made it fall,' said Penny-Farving.

'It sort of tipped up and fell,' said Bubbles.

'Well, me awkward sausages, I hope it doesn't mean I'll get me head knocked off,' said Dan. 'Stay there for a bit.'

He knocked on Tilly's living-room door.

'All right, I know it's you,' called Tilly, 'so come in.'

Dan opened the door with caution, and just wide enough to put his head in, the while preparing himself for having her chuck something heavy at him. Nothing of a dangerous kind arrived, however. Nor did anything else. Tilly was at her sewing-machine, feet working the treadle, hands sliding material under the fast-moving needle.

'Um – Tilly – sorry if the girls—'

'Pick them pins up,' said Tilly.

'Beg yer pardon?'

'You 'eard,' said Tilly. 'And your gels knocked them there.'

Dan looked. The lino of the floor beside the table glittered with a multitude of scattered pins.

'Um, listen, wouldn't it be better if we made the girls pick 'em up as a punishment?' he suggested.

'The way them young mites be'ave ain't their fault,' said Tilly, 'it's the fault of their parents. They've got a selfish mother who's off her rocker, and a dad who's easy-come, easy-go. So you pick them pins up, I'm busy makin' the dresses for the gels.'

'Ruddy rockcakes,' muttered Dan, 'what a terror.'

'What's that you said?' demanded Tilly.

'Nothing much,' said Dan, and went down on his knees. 'I've been thinkin' lately it wasn't too clever, fallin' for Elvira on account of how she looked in her tights and spangles.' He began placing pins in the empty tin. 'A bloke ought to have some sense, but I suppose a bit of heavy love and passion knocks it out of some of us.'

'A bit of what? Don't you talk indecent to me, Dan Rogers, or you'll get the toe of me shoe in yer eye. I'm proud of my integrity, I'll 'ave you know.' On the other hand, she thought, isn't my integrity a bit old at twenty-six?

'I'm proud meself of what you've got, Tilly,' said Dan, picking up pins, 'and all the time you're our lodger I'll guard it with me life. If Elvira had had a fair amount of it, she'd have married me before we – well, you know what I mean. Oh, sod that, I've stuck a pin in me thumb.'

'Serve yer right,' said Tilly. 'And pardon me, but what d'you mean? You'll guard what with yer life?'

'Your integrity,' said Dan.

'I'll guard that with me own life,' said Tilly, 'I don't want you anywhere near it. I told you, I've met some of your kind.'

'It's a hard life for a woman like you, Tilly,' said Dan, moving about on his knees. 'Havin' accident'lly seen you lookin' as 'andsome a lady as ever graced me eyesight, it occurred to me then that some disrespectful geezers probably aggravate you by tryin' it on—'

'You're aggravatin' me something chronic,' said Tilly, 'I never 'eard more saucy talk in all me life. What with lumberin' me day after day with them motherless gels and talkin' the way you do, I'll be after new lodgings while I'm still sane.'

'I think that's the lot,' said Dan, coming to his feet with the tin full of pins. Advancing to stand beside her chair, he placed the tin on the open lid of the sewing-machine. 'There we are, Tilly.'

Tilly looked up at him. The blind was down in the window opposite, shutting out the light that flooded into her own window and brightened her eyes and face. Cheerful Dan, an outgoing and extrovert bloke, acted on impulse. He kissed her on her mouth. Tilly stiffened with outrage. Dan lifted his head. 'Now what made me do that?' he asked. 'Sorry, Tilly, the old Adam came over me.'

Tilly sprang up and darted for her egg saucepan. She was fond of a soft-boiled egg occasionally. She grabbed the saucepan. Dan left at speed. She flew after him. Down the stairs he leapt and tripped halfway. The stairs gave him a walloping, and he hit the passage floor on his back.

'Got yer!' cried Tilly. Dan, bruised and winded, played possum, his eyes closed. The noise had brought Bubbles and Penny-Farving out to the landing, and they peered down through the banister rails. Tilly stooped, the saucepan a threat in her hand. Dan kept his eyes shut and let a groan escape. 'I'm not fallin' for that,' said Tilly. 'Get up and take a bashin' like a man.' Dan, wisely, refused to move. 'Oh, come on,' said Tilly, 'you're not 'urt, are you?'

'It's just me broken back,' said Dan weakly, and Bubbles and Penny-Farving came scampering down the stairs.

'Dad, what you doin', lyin' there?' asked Penny-Farving fearfully.

'Oh, our dad ain't goin' to die, is 'e?' asked Bubbles even more fearfully.

Dan opened his eyes. He saw the anxious faces of his angels. He smiled and winked at them.

'It's all right, me loves,' he said, 'it's sort of more comfortable here than gettin' me head knocked off. I'm surprised you managed to upset Tilly's pins all over her floor when you promised me this mornin' you'd be as good as gold. You can't blame Tilly for bein' cross.'

'Oh, the aggravation I'm gettin' would make a saint weep,' breathed Tilly. 'I'm leavin' these lodgings as soon as I can find a new place.'

'But me and Bubbles like yer, Tilly,' said Penny-Farving. 'Can you make our dad get up, please?'

Dan got to his feet, picked up his girls, cradling them together, and said, 'No damage, sausages. Now thank Tilly for lookin' after yer this afternoon, and say sorry for upsettin' her tin of pins. She's makin' the new dresses for you, y'know.'

'Sorry, Tilly,' said Bubbles.

'Fanks for havin' us,' said Penny-Farving.

'Bless you,' said Tilly, and gave Dan a vexed look before going up to her room. What a shocker that cheerful Charlie was. Pinching a kiss and making sneaky reference to what she looked like in her underwear. If she didn't watch him, she'd have another George Rice on her hands. Still, she had to admit he was a very affectionate dad, even if an irresponsible man. Anyone could see Bubbles and Penny-Farving were the light of his life. Why he couldn't have made Gladys Hobday marry him in the first place, as soon as he knew she was in the family way, was something he'd live to regret if she wouldn't get spliced to him now. He was big enough and strong enough to give the woman a shaking and to carry her off to a registrar and make her go through the ceremony on pain of cutting her legs off. That would keep her off her tightrope for good. The trouble was, of course, he couldn't say boo to that woman. Blow it, thought Tilly, I ought to get up and leave and find other lodgings, but I'm stuck with the feeling that if I don't get him to marry the girls' mother, no-one else will.

She heard the girls downstairs in the kitchen. They were shrieking with laughter. He was playing games with them, of course, as if he didn't have a care in the world, nor his illegitimate young daughters either.

Tilly thought, why should I worry?

I'm daft, that's why.

Apart from the information gleaned from a traffic policeman, the long day had proved fruitless for Boots and the others. They'd discovered not the slightest sign of the car in Guildford. Chinese Lady was mentally worn out. She'd said more than once to Boots that he'd have to go to the police. Give it a little while longer, that was his response. Yes, give it a little longer, Nana, Rosie had said. Polly had been a stalwart in going along with all Boots's suggestions and actions. Well, Boots was an ex-Tommy of the trenches and she an ambulance driver, and that made them comrades of a very particular kind, never mind that he had a hundred ways of avoiding making love to her. In Guildford during the afternoon she'd bought herself a new dress and some lingerie, saying she was beginning to feel grubby. Rosie whispered to Boots that she felt a bit like that too. Rosie liked to be immaculate, to wear fresh undies every day. So Boots gave her the money to buy what she felt she needed, since they intended to return to the hotel just in case any real clues had turned up or Captain Arnold might have remembered something he'd forgotten. Polly and Rosie were against going back there feeling grubby. Chinese Lady was not conscious of feeling grubby. Her only need was for her life to be as ordered and undisturbed as it had been two days ago. She would have asked for the police to be contacted and for Boots to drive her home had she not had unspoken faith in what her eldest son might still accomplish.

As it was, they left Guildford at six o'clock and returned to the Hog's Back Hotel.

*   *   *

A colleague, about to depart for his home, looked in on George Simmonds, who was clearing his desk in his Whitehall office.

'Finch hasn't turned up again today?'

'I think Mrs Finch persuaded him to take a further day's leave of absence.'

'Must be the weather.'

'If it's like this again tomorrow, I'll take a day off myself,' said George Simmonds.

'Well, things are all quiet on the Western Front.'

'Simmering, old man, simmering.'

'Goodnight, I'm off to enjoy some simmering braised steak.'

'Goodnight,' said George Simmonds, who had no worries on his mind concerning Edwin Finch taking a second day off.

Well, in this particular Whitehall department, no-one was strictly employed on an unimaginative nine-to-five basis.

'Oh, Mr Adams.' Miss Jordan came out of reception as Boots and his party entered the hotel.

'Something to tell me?' enquired Boots.

'Oh, crikey, have you, Miss Jordan?' asked Rosie.

'Just that Captain Arnold hoped you'd be back before now,' said Miss Jordan. 'He wanted to see you. He's out now, but will be back about nine. He hopes to see you then.'

'We'll wait, certainly,' said Boots, 'and have dinner.'

'Did you have any luck in Guildford?' asked Miss Jordan.

'Rosie found a point-duty policeman who saw the car yesterday, and was able to tell her it contained four people, three men and a woman,' said Boots.

'One of the men could have been your stepfather?'

'Could have been, yes,' said Boots.

'Had to be, old sport,' said Polly, 'and that's not wishful thinking.'

'Did Captain Arnold mention what he wanted to see me about?' asked Boots of Miss Jordan. 'Something he'd forgotten to tell me?'

'He didn't say, Mr Adams,' said Miss Jordan.

'Well, I wish he'd left a note for us,' said Chinese Lady. 'Still, you're very kind, Miss Jordan, I must say.'

'I'm only too pleased to be as helpful as possible,' said the receptionist. 'Did you go to the police in Guildford?'

'We're giving things a little while longer,' said Boots.

'Can we go to our rooms?' asked Chinese Lady. 'I'd like to freshen up before dinner.'

'I'm in favour of that,' said Polly.

'Aren't we all?' said Rosie, who was inwardly dying for Boots to come up trumps, to discover something that would mean restoring Grandpa to Grandma. It was the most awful crisis the family had ever faced, and she was sure everyone, all her aunts and uncles, were expecting Boots to perform miracles. She had once asked Uncle Sammy why he sometimes had a soppy look on his face when he was listening to her father. Well, Rosie, said Uncle Sammy, it's not a soppy look, it's the look I get when I feel I'm listening to the One Above. Rosie, not at all put out, said oh, yes, Uncle Sammy, I've heard about Daddy starting life as Lord Muck, so I suppose it's only natural for him to have been promoted.

They left Miss Jordan and went upstairs to their rooms.

Cassie, round at Freddy's that evening on the instinctive grounds that if she didn't keep a permanent eye on him he might make some other girl his best mate, informed him that Mrs Harper had said yes, two parrots probably would fight if you put them in a cage together.

'I'd bet on them peckin' each other to death,' said Sally, Freddy's sister, who worked in one of the Adams' ladies' shops.

'So if I bought another parrot, I'd 'ave to buy another cage as well,' said Cassie. 'Of course, if I bought the parrot, I expect Freddy might buy the cage, then we could call it our parrot, couldn't we, Freddy?'

'I don't know what's 'appening to me lately,' said Freddy, 'I'm gettin' so 'ard of 'earing I think I'm what they call deaf.'

'Clever, you mean,' said Sally.

'You could always go to a doctor, Freddy,' said Cassie.

'Well, lovey, about parrots and cages,' said Mrs Brown, 'Freddy's savin' up to buy himself something for 'is bike.'

'Yes, a new dynamo for his lamp,' said Mr Brown.

'Oh, is he really?' said Cassie. 'Is it to lighten 'is darkness more when I'm ridin' with 'im?'

'What else?' said Sally.

'Freddy spends a lot of what he keeps of his wages on clothes,' said Mrs Brown, fondly proud that her younger son always looked nice. 'He likes bein' a credit to us.'

Mr Brown coughed. Sally rolled her eyes. Freddy grinned.

'Yes, you do dress nice, Freddy,' said Cassie.

'I'm goin' to sell him a pretty Sunday frock when he comes to the shop,' said Sally.

'Oh, she's not, is she, Freddy?' said Cassie, alarmed.

'With some sisters, yer know, Cassie, it's a boon to be 'ard of 'earing,' said Freddy. 'Otherwise, you go off yer chump before you're ten.'

'Freddy, I'll always be beside you if you ever get mental deficient,' said Cassie with heart-warming loyalty. 'Mrs 'Arper told me this mornin' that her 'usband's 'ealth is a bit deficient. He's in bed, poor man, and 'is brother 'as got the sack, and Mrs 'Arper said they might 'ave to go back to 'Oxton.'

'If that means we wouldn't 'ave to go and talk to 'er potty parrot any more, I might come over all grateful,' said Freddy. 'Like a bike ride, Cassie?'

'Love it,' said Cassie. Away they went a little later, Cassie perched sideways on the carrier. 'Freddy, do yer like me better as yer girlfriend than as yer best mate?'

'What's that you said?' asked Freddy loudly.

'Freddy, I can't shout, not now we're out on your bike,' protested Cassie, 'and why do I 'ave to?'

'I keep goin' deaf, that's why,' said Freddy.

'Hello, is that you, Emily?' asked Rachel over the phone.

'Yes, who's that?' asked Emily.

'Rachel. Is Boots there?'

'No, he's out, he's away for a bit,' said Emily.

'Oh, yes, Sammy said he was out on specialized business,' said Rachel. 'I called in at the offices this afternoon to talk to Boots, and as he wasn't in, I thought I'd phone him this evening.'

'Is it important?' asked Emily, who could only

think of one thing that was important at the moment. She'd heard from Boots again, but not to any cheerful extent.

'Oh, it's just a little job I'm doing for him,' said Rachel.

'Oh, yes, I think I know about it,' said Emily, 'I'll tell him to get in touch with you soon as he's home.'

'Thanks,' said Rachel. 'Tell him it's all been a pleasure. Love to Rosie and Tim.'

'Love to your two,' said Emily. Rachel had two little girls, and a professional nursemaid.

'Bye, love,' said Rachel, hanging up. She was intrigued by the possible sale of the scrap metal business, by Boots's opposition to it, and by the little part Boots had asked her to play.

As far as Sammy was concerned at the moment, the subject was out of his mind. He was giving it no thought whatever.

Chapter Eighteen

They had had dinner and were in the residents'
lounge. Only four other people were present, playing
whist at a table in the far corner. Polly, having
attended a college for young ladies before the war, was
able to associate the further strain of waiting for
Captain Arnold again with Pelion piled on Ossa.
Rosie, because of family forthrightness, said Captain
Arnold seemed an acceptable gentleman, but was a bit
of a dirty stop-out. Chinese Lady, still showing
fortitude, said she didn't like to hear Rosie using
dubious words. I could use some myself, said Polly,
a source of strength from the moment she had offered to
drive Boots to Guildford. Rosie said I know it's not
being much of a lady to call Captain Arnold a dirty
stop-out, Nana, but Miss Jordan said he'd be back by
nine and it's now gone half-past and it's fraying my
ladylike nerves. That raised a faint smile in Boots.

'I share your feelings, Rosie,' said Polly, 'and I'm
not sure we can always afford to be ladylike, so
where's the dirty stop-out got to?'

'Oh, dear, Miss Simms, I don't like us givin' in to
common language,' said Chinese Lady.

'It's a jolly old help sometimes, Mrs Finch,' said
Polly, and Boots thought it extraordinary how well
Polly got on with his mother. Chinese Lady not only
admired Polly for doing her bit so courageously during
the war, she also liked her. The liking was mutual.

'I think we can let it go, old girl, as long as Rosie and Polly don't start throwing things,' he said. 'I could swear a bit myself.'

'Not in French, I hope,' said Chinese Lady. 'Boots picked up some very disreputable French words in the war, Miss Simms, which grieved me a bit as I never brought him up to be Frenchified.'

Polly, thinking of the language she'd heard the men of the trenches use, wanted to smile.

'Penny for them, Aunt Polly,' said Rosie.

Polly, wearing her new dress, a very sleek and silky creation of violet blue, said, 'I'm thinking, Rosie, of how much time we seem to have spent looking for the invisible.'

'Lord 'elp us,' said Chinese Lady, eyes showing strain, 'I don't want to think that Edwin's turned invisible.'

'Ah, there you all are.' Captain Arnold had suddenly materialized. 'Miss Jordan said you were in here. Good evening, ladies. Mr Adams? Pleasure to see you again. I'll join you, shall I?' He pulled up a chair and sat down with them. 'I understand from Miss Jordan, who's hovering about in case you need her, that you've had a fairly blank day in Guildford. The bounders probably drove straight through the city.'

'Did you have something to tell us?' asked Chinese Lady.

'Something you've remembered?' said Rosie. 'Is that what you mean?'

'No, not at all,' said Captain Arnold. 'I rarely let details slip my memory.'

'But didn't you tell Miss Jordan you wanted to see us?' asked Boots.

'I did, old man, and I do,' said the healthy-looking

Captain. 'A guest who checked out this afternoon, a lawyer by the name of Osborne, approached me a little while before he left.'

'Oh, he had something to tell?' said Rosie.

Captain Arnold recounted the conversation. Mr Osborne had learned of yesterday's odd incident, and of the fact that Captain Arnold had offered the only clue, namely the hurried exit of a certain car. It seemed that Mr Osborne was in his room earlier. He was standing at his window, using its light to examine a very old will on behalf of a client. He noticed an attractively coloured car arrive. Two men and a woman alighted and looked around. They did not, however, make any move to enter the hotel, but got back into the car after less than a minute. The car stayed there, and he thought they were probably awaiting the arrival of friends. He moved from the window and five minutes later went down to enjoy a light tea. He gave the car and its occupants no further thought.

'I'm sorry, old sport,' said Polly, 'but where does that get us?'

'It tells us that at that stage, there were two men and a woman,' said Boots. 'Later, when the car was driving through Guildford, there were three men and a woman according to a traffic bobby. I'd say it confirms our suspicions, Captain Arnold, but doesn't give us any idea of how to get on their tail.'

'Well, old fellow,' said Captain Arnold, 'you've a description of the car, and Mr Osborne was able to give me descriptions of the two men and the woman. Both men were tall and well-built, both were wearing caps and not hats, and what Mr Osborne thought were ordinary grey serge suits. The woman was wearing a brown costume and a brown hat. He thought the men were in their thirties, the woman in her late twenties. Would your mother perhaps recognize these as descriptions of people with whom her husband was acquainted?'

'I'm afraid I wouldn't,' said Chinese Lady.

'Is he in business?' asked Captain Arnold.

'Grandpa's a civil servant,' said Rosie.

'Is he now,' said Captain Arnold, and rubbed his chin. He obviously thought the people described did not look like civil service acquaintances.

'If they were people he knew, that would explain why they were able to get him to join them in their car,' said Polly. 'While he waited for you, Mrs Finch.'

'Damn good shot, Miss Simms,' said Captain Arnold, 'bang on target, I'll wager.'

'Except that when my stepfather found himself being driven away before my mother had appeared, he'd have been raising hell when the car passed yours,' said Boots. 'He'd have done everything he could to attract your attention.'

'Yes, he would,' said Rosie, 'he'd have been furious with those people.'

'Yet I wouldn't discount the possibility that he knew them, and that you're right, Polly, in thinking it the reason why he joined them in their car,' said Boots. His stepfather probably knew all kinds of people, dubious and otherwise, none of whom he would have thought of bringing home to meet Chinese Lady. 'What's suspicious is the act of allowing them to drive him away. If I know your grandpa, Rosie, he'd have had the back door of the car open before it began to pass Captain Arnold's.'

'Edwin never had suspicious acquaintances,' said Chinese Lady, fidgeting and frowning.

'Well,' said Captain Arnold, 'Mr Osborne's exact

267

description of the woman's hat was brown with two green feathers, Mrs Finch. Would you have met any lady acquaintance of your husband who had a hat like that?'

'Beg your pardon?' said Chinese Lady.

'Sounds frightfully old-fashioned,' said Polly.

Boots sat up. Something had clicked.

'Can we be clear about that, Captain Arnold?' he said. 'Mr Osborne definitely referred to a brown hat with two green feathers in it?'

'He was definite about it to me,' said Captain Arnold.

'But you didn't notice the feathers yourself when you caught your glimpse of the woman beside the driver?'

'My glance was too brief,' said Captain Arnold, 'and in any case, old fellow, I imagine the feathers would have been touching the roof of the car.'

'It's not possible,' said Boots. The comment was reflective, spoken to himself. His mind began to work overtime, drawing for him a picture of Cassie riding in his car with him in King and Queen Street and suddenly pointing out to him a lady who had a parrot, a lady called Mrs Harper who, with her husband and brother-in-law, had taken up occupation, according to Cassie, of the house that had once been the home of the witch-like Mrs Chivers and daughter Elsie. The picture, becoming clearer while Rosie gazed at him with the eyes of a girl who was closer to his mind than even his wife was, took in the hat Mrs Harper had been wearing, a brown one with two feathers. It was the kind of hat some cockney women would stick with however old-fashioned it was. But could he seriously consider the possibility that the woman in the car was Mrs Harper? What were the odds against two women owning identical hats? Then there was the brown costume. Mrs Harper had been wearing one of that colour when he saw her in King and Queen Street, coming from the market. Could a coincidence of that kind, identical hats and costumes, be credible?

'Daddy?' said Rosie, a little excitement showing.

'I'm thinking, poppet.'

'Daddy, you're on to something.' Rosie's blue eyes were alight with the hope that he was going to perform his miracle.

'Share your thoughts, Boots old scout,' said Polly.

There was something else to think about, something that Cassie had said about Mrs Harper, the woman who had a talking parrot. Boots fastened on to it and its peculiar factor, feeling it could be made relevant if he gave it enough thought.

'We're going home,' he said.

'What, now?' said Chinese Lady. 'But it's gone ten o'clock.'

'The answer's not here,' said Boots, 'nor in Guildford. It's nearer home. Well, that's my feeling now and I'm sticking with it until events blow it apart, which I hope they won't. Captain Arnold, thanks very much for everything, a pleasure to have met you and to have had so much help from you.'

'You're able to get on the track of the bounders?' said Captain Arnold.

'We're able to get on the track of a hopeful conclusion,' said Boots.

'Well, tell us, for God's sake,' said Polly.

'I'll talk on the way,' said Boots, 'and I'd like us to be on our way as soon as I've settled our bill.'

'Oh, golly, Daddy, you're the One Above all right,' said Rosie, eyes shining.

'Rosie, Rosie, that's nearly blasphemy,' said Chinese Lady in shock.

'Nearer our God art thou, Boots,' said Polly, close to laughter despite the traumatic nature of events and the fact that they were now going to ride on the back of what he'd referred to only as a hopeful conclusion.

'I don't like anyone saying such things,' said Chinese Lady. All the same, she was a new woman. Boots, to her way of thinking, knew where to find Edwin. She'd talk to him afterwards about letting himself be called the One Above. When all was said and done, he was a music hall comedian most of the time. Still, he wasn't her only oldest son for nothing, he was the most thinking one in the family.

They all said goodbye to Captain Arnold, and while Boots settled the bill the others went up to their rooms to freshen up for the journey home. It would be midnight at least by the time they got there.

Mr Finch, having thought everything through and made up his mind which way to jump, composed himself and went to sleep. His guard, the senior man for this the second night, stared at him. The traitor to Germany had fallen asleep without an effort? Did he think, then, that they weren't serious about getting him aboard the German merchant ship if he refused to cooperate, not serious about informing his wife of his origins and his years as a German agent? He would find out just how serious everything was when, after a secret trial in Berlin, he was due to be executed by a firing squad. Better for him if he did cooperate and went freely back to Germany in civilized companionship with them. Better for them too, for a cooperative return would please their immediate superior in the Nazi secret police.

270

The senior man showed a faint smile then. Here was a man, German-born, who, in falling calmly to sleep when his life was under threat, must be an asset to the new Germany. Perhaps, if he did refuse to cooperate, he would not be shot, after all. He was too impressive a man. Himmler, perhaps, would have someone go to work on him.

The woman came up.

'Does he want anything?' she asked.

'He's asleep, sound asleep.'

'Blimey, what a character,' she said in English, and the senior man looked at her in some distaste. She could not be left to her own devices. She was too fond of gin. She would have to be disposed of. They could fill her with gin and drown her in a horse trough when they left this place late tomorrow night. She'd been useful as a cockney woman ostensibly living with her husband and having his brother as a lodger. It had been a macabre gesture, using this particular house, although it had not had the expected disturbing effect on the renegade. He had accepted it as calmly as all else. It had disturbed the woman more. She'd complained there were noises. In her coarse inbred cockney way, she talked about bleedin' things going bump in the bloody night. Drink less gin, they told her. Because of her German father and the way he'd suffered at the hands of an anti-German mob, it had been easy to recruit her services for the purpose of trapping a traitor and holding him until they could make him do their bidding one way or another. The original plan had been to first take a good look at his house, then for the woman to knock on his door just as darkness fell one evening. She was to ask to see him if he did not answer the door himself. No, she would not come in, she would speak to him on his doorstep and

271

in private. And when he did appear they would appear themselves, and take him swiftly and silently. It was seeing him when they were looking at the house that caused the change of plan, the temptation irresistible. They followed him and his wife all the way to Farnham, waited by the Red Lion Hotel during lunch, hoping to eventually catch him on his own, and then shadowed them on a shopping expedition before following them to the Hog's Back Hotel, where the opportunity of taking him occurred. They brought him to this house at well gone midnight, after motoring around for hours although they had hastened during the early stage of their departure from the hotel car park. The woman, who was an idiot whenever the sharpness of her mind failed her, had complained about leaving her parrot all day. That bird was due to have its neck wrung. It repeated things they had said to it in German.

Mr Finch slept on. The German lit a candle and turned out the gas lamp. Only a very faint light touched the drawn blind.

They were driving through summer darkness, and Polly was in a state of disbelief.

'My God,' she said, 'you're pinning your hopes on a woman because she was wearing a hat with two green feathers? There must still be fifty thousand hats with feathers in London alone. My stepmama has one that she refuses to throw away.'

'It's not the kind we're talking about,' said Boots. He had explained why he thought the woman in the car could be Mrs Harper, he had explained who Mrs Harper was and where she lived along with two men, one supposedly her husband. He had also talked about the murder that had taken place there in 1914, when Mr Finch lodged with the Adams in a house two doors away. Chinese Lady, from the back of the car, said she wished he didn't have to mention that. Boots said the mention was to remind her that Mr Finch and Elsie Chivers enjoyed a quietly affectionate relationship, that he was a staunch witness for the defence when Elsie was tried for the murder, and that eventually he and Elsie disappeared.

'Oh, yes, we all thought they'd eloped and gone to live where she couldn't be gossiped about after she was found not guilty,' said Chinese Lady. 'But they didn't get married, after all, and poor Elsie went out of her mind after a bit. It was very sad, Miss Simms.'

'Yes, I've heard about it,' said Polly.

Boots had said that if the woman was Mrs Harper, and if she and the two men had taken Mr Finch to the house of soul-destroying memories, it was probably because they felt it would have a demoralizing effect on him. Chinese Lady said she'd never heard anything more wicked, it would upset him enough to make him ill. Boots said he doubted that, but perhaps the men felt it would give them a mental advantage. In any case, the woman in the hat and costume had to be investigated. It was then that Polly expressed her disbelief in his conclusions.

'And why would the men want a mental advantage?' she asked. 'What's their quarrel with your stepfather?'

Boots, driving through an almost deserted Guildford, said, 'My stepfather wasn't always a civil servant.'

'No, he was a river pilot for ages, wasn't he?' said Rosie. 'And he sailed the seas as a young man.'

'Boots, do you mean he may have made enemies?' asked Polly. Out of Guildford, the car's headlamps projected beams of light into the darkness.

'It could have happened,' said Boots.

'I can't take kindly to that,' said Chinese Lady, who had never seen her second husband as anything less than a gentleman.

'What exactly do you intend to do?' asked Polly of Boots.

'Raid the house,' said Boots.

'Oh, ye gods,' breathed Polly. She smiled. 'What fun, old soldier.'

'Boots, stop talkin' like you're goin' to raid it yourself,' said Chinese Lady, 'you know I don't hold with hooliganism. I remember you once got into a fight with two boys at Peckham Rye on account of them messin' about with Lizzy and Em'ly.'

'Oh, did he do that, Nana, did Daddy set about them?' asked Rosie, excitement and hopes as high as they could go.

'I nearly died of shame at me only oldest son fightin' with boys in public,' said Chinese Lady, 'and I came close to boxin' his ears.' Very much a new woman now because she had this maternal trust in Boots being right about his conclusions, she added, almost with a smile, 'Still, Em'ly did go around saying he'd been very heroic. All the same, you listen to me, Boots, don't you go into that house thinkin' you can kick those men to death.'

'It seems a suitable place to do murder,' said Polly, tongue in cheek.

'Miss Simms, I wish you wouldn't say such things – oh, and must you drive so fast in the dark, Boots?'

'It's not fast, old lady,' said Boots, 'it only seems as if it is.'

'Anyway, go, Daddy, go,' said Rosie.

Boots drove on, mentally active. He was talking to himself.

I'll hit yer, I'll hit yer, I'll hit yer.

He was trying to make something else of it, something he felt he would recognize as being relevant.

It happened when they were passing through Sutton.

I'll hit yer, I'll hit yer, heil hit yer, heil Hitler.

Bloody hell, he thought. Cassie, you dreamboat.

Chapter Nineteen

Chinese Lady had been persuaded to go to bed. So had
Rosie, due to return to school in the morning. Emily,
out of bed and in her dressing-gown, was making a pot
of tea. Polly, in charge of her own car again, was
outside the house in Red Post Hill, free to return
home at last. Not that she was in any hurry, even
though it was well past midnight. Frankly, her
adrenalin had been high throughout the apparently
hopeless search for clues and pointers. Now Boots was
saying goodnight to her.

'What a very good friend you are, Polly,' he said.

'You may think that, I think it's a curse,' she said,
seated in her car. 'Friendship's platonic. I'm not made
for that kind of stuff, not with you. You'll find that
out one day, and when you do you'll think you need to
call out the fire brigade.'

'Sounds as if it might be fatal,' said Boots, 'but it'll
be a famous way to go.'

'Oh, we'll drop off God's demented world together,
darling,' murmured Polly, 'because where you go I'll
be right behind you. When are you intending to make
this raid?'

'Before the night's out,' said Boots.

'Then I'm coming with you, you crazy man.'

'You're not. You're going home. You've already
been a tower of strength, and a very decorative one.
The friendship we enjoy might have its frustrations—'

'Might have? It does have.'

'But I'd miss if it fell to pieces. Goodnight, Polly.' Boots bent his head and kissed her, with the light of the nearest street lamp too distant to reach them. Polly, naturally responsive, kissed him back.

'Do that again,' she breathed.

'Goodnight, Polly, all my thanks,' he said and faded away from her.

'Take care,' she said. Strangely, she was smiling as she drove home. Well, he cared for her, which was something to treasure. It wasn't enough, but it was something.

'What's the idea?' Tommy over the phone sounded as if he still had sleep filling his mouth. 'D'you know what the time is?'

'Yes, close to one o'clock,' said Boots. 'Come to, Tommy.'

'Wait a bit, me brain's lightin' up,' said Tommy. 'Is this something to do with Dad?'

'Who else? Dress yourself and put plimsolls on. Then wait for me and Sammy to pick you up. Tell Vi you'll be out for quite a while.'

'If we're all goin' to be out for quite a while in the middle of the ruddy night,' said Tommy, 'I want to know why.'

'Not now, Tommy. When we're on our way.'

'To where?'

'To Walworth, to bring Chinese Lady's better half home. I think.'

'What d'you mean, you think?'

'I hope,' said Boots.

'It 'ad better be more than hope,' said Tommy.

'Well, say a prayer, then,' said Boots. 'We'll be armed, by the way.'

'Armed?'

'I'm bringing three cricket stumps,' said Boots. 'That's all for now, Tommy. Stand by.'

'Talk about the Lord of Creation,' said Tommy, 'but if – hello?' No answer. Boots had hung up. He rang Sammy next, and Sammy left his legal wedded place in the marital bed to answer the call. He shook himself fully awake.

'I'm guessin' that's you, Boots.'

'Good guess, Sammy. I think we might be able to find our stepdad. Dress yourself and wear plimsolls. I'll be picking you up in a few minutes. Then we'll pick up Tommy. Give yourself a cold wash to get rid of any sleep. We all need to be wide-awake. Further, flex your muscles, we'll probably want to use them. By the way, we'll only be going as far as Walworth.'

'If it's not askin' too much,' said Sammy, 'are we on to a cert?'

'No, a hunch.'

'I don't like hunches,' said Sammy. 'Em'ly's old dad, God rest him, used to get hunches on horses called also-rans.'

'Don't argue, Sammy, just get ready. I'll bring you and Tommy up-to-date when we're on our way. Plimsolls, don't forget, not hobnails.'

'I heard you first time,' said Sammy, 'and d'you mind not talkin' like a sergeant-major?'

'Sergeant-major? Watch your lip, Junior, that's too much of a come-down from the Lord of Creation.'

Sammy grinned as the line went dead. You couldn't get much change out of Boots, any more than out of a wedded female wife like Susie. But if he knew Boots, there'd be a good reason for acting on a hunch. He went back into the bedroom. Susie was awake, her bedside light, an electric boon, switched on.

'Sammy?'

'That you, Susie love?' said Sammy, peeling off his pyjamas. 'So it is. Bless me soul, don't you look a charmer when you're in bed? Beats all the cigarette cards I ever collected.'

'Sammy, who was that on the phone at this time of night, and what're you doin'?'

'It was Boots on the phone, and I'm dressin',' said Sammy.

Susie sat up, loose hair a softly bright cloud of gold.

'It's my dad-in-law, isn't it?' she said.

'I think Boots thinks he knows where he is,' said Sammy, looking very athletic in his brief white pants and singlet.

'You think he only thinks?' said Susie.

'Well, you know Boots,' said Sammy, 'he's got a modest way of showin' off. If he says he thinks he knows, he knows enough to make me dress meself seriously at this time of night.' Sammy, trousers in place, pulled on his shirt, tucked it in and brought his braces up over his shoulders.

'Sammy, are you dressin' to go out?' demanded Susie.

'Well, Susie love, it seems that Boots, Tommy and me need to go to Walworth immediate if not sooner.'

'That's now, at one o'clock in the mornin'?'

'Well, I'm not dressin' seriously for anything but now, Susie.' Sammy, socks on, fished for his plimsolls at the bottom of the wardrobe. 'Boots'll be here in a few minutes. You go back to sleep.'

'How can I?' said Susie, the bodice of her flimsy black nightie floating delicately about over her rounded turrets. Blow me, thought Sammy, is she worrying about me? Has me lawful wedded wife got a slightly agitated bosom? Bless her. 'Sammy, are you

279

and Boots and Tommy up to anything dangerous?'

'Not on your Nelly, Susie. Chinese Lady wouldn't stand for it. It's just a short trip to Walworth on be'alf of your respected dad-in-law.'

'Boots must know where he is, then,' said Susie, 'and if it's not dangerous, why are all three of you goin' and in the middle of the night?'

'I'll ask Boots and let you know soon as I get back, but if you're asleep I'll wait till breakfast,' said Sammy, his plimsolls tied.

'I don't want any of your flippancy, Sammy Adams.'

'Ain't it curious?' said Sammy. 'There's my Susie, fond daughter of Mother Brown, soundin' just like my dear old Ma.'

'I'm not laughin', Sammy.'

'Believe me, Susie, nor am I. Boots is comin' the old sergeant-major stuff, and I'm havin' to go down now to wait for him outside on our doorstep. I don't want him ringing the bell and wakin' our little man and our infant plum puddin'.'

'Wait a minute, has anyone told Lizzy what's happening?' asked Susie.

'I'm leavin' that to Boots,' said Sammy. 'Lizzy's been a bit fretful each time I've phoned her, imputin' that him and me and Tommy's been responsible for mislayin' our stepdad. Well, that's it, Susie love, like a kiss before I go?'

'Boots, I'm scared,' said Emily. They were in the hall, Boots about to depart. 'I mean, if these people 'ave got hold of Dad for some peculiar reason, mightn't they have guns or something?'

'No, I shouldn't think so, Em.'

'What's goin' to happen if you've guessed wrong and Dad's not there?'

'I'll feel like an idiot,' said Boots. He kissed her and left, carrying three cricket stumps and a torch.

Mrs Harper, so-called, woke up again that night, conscious of those disturbing sounds. Such things coming on top of the trying nature of the day did her no good at all, and this time she went agitatedly upstairs to arouse the man who was sleeping in one of the bedrooms. Shivering, she hissed there was a bleedin' ghost walking about in the kitchen. The man said nothing, but he got up and went downstairs with her. Using a torch, he examined the floor of the kitchen and then the scullery.

'Come here,' he said eventually, and she joined him in the scullery. She was still agitated. 'Look, woman,' he said, shining the beam on the stone floor. 'You've got rats, not ghosts.'

'Me, I've got rats? They ain't mine, and they're bloody 'orrible.'

'It's because the house has been empty and because it now smells of food. Go back to bed.'

'I 'ate rats.'

'You won't be here much longer. We'll all be moving out late tomorrow night. Go back to bed.'

She went. Well, there was a bottle under her pillow with a small amount of gin in it. She'd spent the whole of yesterday without any. Very trying, that had been. But she'd done a good job putting on the style when speaking to the man Finch, the German traitor, in that hotel car park. She ought to have been given a drop of what she fancied after that, but there wasn't any in the car. She took a couple of mouthfuls now to help her get back to sleep. The gin worked. It sent her back to sleep and it laid the ghost of the unfortunate Mrs Chivers.

Tilly was dreaming uncomfortably of a fat woman in spangles and tights dancing about like a stuffed balloon on a high wire. She fell off, and Tilly woke up.

'Oh, me gawd,' she breathed, 'did I come 'ere to be haunted by that Gladys Hobday? No, I didn't. I'm leavin', never mind me soft heart. I'll go lookin' for new lodgings tomorrow. Well, over the weekend, say. Saturday afternoon, say. I'll put up with the aggravations till then. I can lock me door at night in case cowboy Dan takes it on 'imself to try his luck at gettin' into me bed. Oh, lor', what'm I doin'? I'm talkin' out loud to meself in the middle of the night. Tilly Thomas, this 'as got to stop. And so's thinkin' about them little gels, that's got to stop too.'

She turned over, shut out thoughts of cheerful Charlie and the problem of his daughters and drifted back into sleep.

It wasn't long before the fat woman appeared again, still looking bloody ludicrous in tights. She began to prance about on a tightrope, which kept springing up and down. It sprang up once too often, and the female fatty was catapulted high into the air, turning somersaults. Then she began to spin slowly slowly down.

Tilly, of course, woke up again.

She fumed.

If Dan at that moment had had the lecherous gall to sneak in on her, Tilly would probably have done him the kind of injury that virile blokes don't like thinking about.

Boots made Sammy and Tommy bring torches. When they were all in the car and it was heading for Camberwell Green, Tommy asked why Boots hadn't mentioned a torch when he phoned.

'It slipped my mind,' said Boots.

'You forgot, you mean?' said Sammy. 'You're fallin' apart.'

'Sad, that is,' said Tommy. 'Never thought it would 'appen. Anyway, I'd like to be put in the picture.'

Driving through the junction into Camberwell Road, Boots explained why he'd come to the conclusion that their stepfather was in the hands of two men and a woman presently living in the house once occupied by the late Mrs Chivers and her daughter Elsie. Tommy said some conclusion, it was all pie in the sky. Sammy said never mind, let's all have a look at the pie.

The night was empty of sounds, Camberwell Road empty of traffic except for Boots's Riley. Street lamps cast their light over vacant pavements.

'How do we get into the house?' asked Tommy.

'Do we knock and say we've come to empty the gas-meter?' asked Sammy.

'Not a very good idea, Sammy,' said Boots. 'Let's see first if we can get into the yard and in through one of the back doors.'

'Pardon me for mentionin' it, but the back doors'll be bolted if you're right about these geezers holdin' Dad there. So will the front door.' Tommy had some thinking ability of his own. 'And would yer mind tellin' me how we're goin' to get into the yard in the first place?'

'By way of the adjoining yard of the house next door,' said Boots.

'Are you thinkin' that's where me in-laws live?' asked Sammy. 'Only they don't, they're two doors away.'

'No, I'm thinking of the house next door,' said Boots. 'I don't know who lives there now, but every

283

house had its latchcord in our day and few families drew it in at night or bolted the door.'

'You're goin' to use the latchcord, walk through the passage to the back door by the kitchen, go into the yard and then climb over the ruddy wall?' said Tommy.

'Sounds all right,' said Sammy.

'Sounds a corker,' said Tommy, 'providin' we don't wake anyone up. Now I see why we're wearin' plimsolls.'

A bobby on his night beat, checking shop doors in the Walworth Road, gave the car a glance as it passed. An all-night tram, humming along from the direction of the Elephant and Castle, slowed and stopped at East Street. The bobby watched two people alight. Boots's car travelled on to Browning Street.

'I can point out,' said Sammy, as Boots turned into Browning Street, 'that the people livin' in the next-door house are me in-laws' neighbours, a quite decent bloke with two little girls.'

'Well, suffer little girls to come quietly unto us if they wake up,' said Boots, slowing down.

'Bloody 'ell,' said Tommy, 'he's playin' Jesus now, Sammy.'

'Don't ask me where he gets it from,' said Sammy, 'ask the Archbishop of Canterbury.'

Boots changed into neutral as he entered Caulfield Place. He let the car run. It had just enough impetus to glide silently past the house that had once known Mrs Chivers and her daughter. It crawled to a stop beside the kerb. Its lights were out. Boots had switched them off before going into neutral gear.

Chinese Lady's three stalwart sons sat in silence for a moment. Tommy broke it.

'You still feel he's got to be there, Boots?' he whispered.

'I still feel we've got to look,' murmured Boots. 'If he is there, it'll be upstairs. Downstairs in these places is open house to neighbours. Right, let's see if there's a latchcord available to us at the house next door, and let's hope we don't come up against any bolted back doors if we manage to get into the yard that counts. If we do, we'll have to force the kitchen window open. That's going to be tricky, because there's bound to be one man awake on watch. My only real worry is if they've already moved our stepdad out or didn't actually bring him here, after all.'

'What 'appens if we only find three people mindin' their own business?' asked Tommy, the whispered dialogue too low to be heard outside the car.

'We'll ask them if they'd like to buy three cricket stumps,' said Boots. 'But once we're in we'll make straight for the stairs. Go up with your feet well to one side. That'll help to make sure the stairs won't creak. There are three rooms. We'll take one each, cricket stumps at the ready, torches switched on. That's if there's no sign of them having an all-night game of cards in the kitchen. Got it?'

'Got it, Boots,' said Tommy.

'You can read the lesson next time Chinese Lady makes us all go to church,' said Sammy.

They alighted carefully from the car then, closing the doors silently by retracting the locks. Boots led the way, with each of them carrying a torch and a cricket stump. Reaching the front door of Dan Rogers's house, Boots felt for a latchcord and found one. Despite the overall tension, he allowed himself a little smile. The street, a cul-de-sac, offered not a sound. It was essential for the opening of the door to be just as

285

soundless. The man who lived here might be as decent a bloke as Sammy had said, and his two little girls might be cherubs, but if they were woken up by intruders at this time of night, uproar would follow.

Boots applied a slow cautious pull. The latch moved, the door opened and the night air of the street silently entered the passage. Neither the stairs nor the floor were visible, but Boots and his brothers knew the lay-out of these Victorian terraced houses as well as they knew whose face was which. Boots let the latch ride slowly back into place, then stepped in. Tommy followed, Sammy after him. They paused to listen.

In the downstairs bedroom, Dan was sleeping the sleep of a man whose ownership of two precocious infants made him feel he couldn't ask for much more, apart from a marriage certificate. His sleep, therefore, was less disturbed than Tilly's, for Tilly, much to her disgust, was worrying far more about that certificate than he was. In the bedroom next to hers, Bubbles and Penny-Farving slept like perfect cherubs. Tilly, for her part, turned over again.

Hearing nothing, Sammy closed the door very quietly. Something, however, made Tilly sit up. Boots and his brothers ghosted noiselessly through the passage to the back door that was next to the kitchen, the door dustmen used to get into back yards to pick up dustbins. Again the intruders paused to listen. Upstairs, the shapely lodger, a young woman with a warm heart and formidable spirit, sat in her bed, listening. She thought she might have heard one of the girls sigh aloud in her sleep. The poor mites both had something to sigh about. But it was probably her subconscious that had been disturbed by the sighing intrusion of night air through the open front door. Hearing nothing more, Tilly sank back, turned on her side, put her face into the pillow and sought new slumber in the hope that if the female fatty appeared again, she'd fall off her tightrope and break her neck.

Boots groped for the door handle. He turned it, gently pulled, and the door opened. He smiled again. Locked or bolted doors were foreign to Walworth families. He stepped into the dark yard, the June night soft and balmy, the air free of the sooty elements of winter. Tommy and Sammy followed, Sammy again making himself responsible for the quiet closure of a door. It meant they'd left no trace of their intrusion.

The rooftops of the clustered houses, swallowed up by the moonless sky, were invisible. Not so the very faint light touching a blind drawn down over the window of the bedroom above the kitchen of the adjoining house, the house that counted. It was the darkness itself that made such a faint light perceptible. Boots touched Tommy's arm and pointed. Tommy looked up, and so did Sammy, and all three brothers took in the fact that there was a tiny light in the room shielded by the blind. They knew which room it was, the upstairs back. They knew too, without having to say so, that if Chinese Lady's better half was in that house, he was almost certainly in that particular room.

Sammy and Tommy left the next move to Boots. He gave his torch and stump to Tommy, placed his hands on the top of the thick dividing wall, and levered himself up. Over he went, landing on his plimsolled feet. Tommy handed him two stumps and two torches, then up and over he went too, with no more sound than that made by clothes and body brushing stone. Sammy followed, and all three of them moved to the back door that was to the left of the kitchen. They moved with extra caution, nail-bitingly conscious of the need to avoid touching any obstacles. A switched-on torch would have helped, but now was not the time to show a beam of light.

Boots, reaching the door, tried the handle. It turned, but the door failed to yield. It was bolted. That, thought Boots, was either unusual or, if dirty work was going on, not unexpected. He said nothing. He began to move again, along the yard to the back door of the scullery, Tommy and Sammy behind him. If Sammy considered himself a businessman with a sharp eye, and Tommy considered himself a bloke who could master the mechanics of machines, they rarely failed to allow Boots the initiative in matters seriously affecting the family.

Tommy's foot brushed a running rat. He was conscious of the contact, light though it was, and he froze for a moment, though not because he knew the thing was a rat. No sound ensued. Boots reached the scullery door. Again they all paused, ears acutely alert. Boots found the handle after a few moments and slowly turned it. The door opened. Silence greeted them. Boots did not consider this a time to dwell on memories, but they rushed into his mind all the same. Here was what had once been the home of an acidulous, complaining mother and her gentle-mannered daughter whose soft myopic eyes hid her need to be a living breathing woman. If he had loved anyone when he was young, it had been Elsie Chivers, despite her age being well in advance of his. Time had not erased the affection he still felt for her.

Tommy nudged him. The light of a torch was necessary now. Boots knew the three of them could not negotiate the scullery and the kitchen in this kind of darkness. The kitchen would be full of obstacles. Would it also contain a watchdog? He thought not. His feeling that Edwin Finch was here strengthened, for a parrot that paid a tribute to Adolf Hitler, star of the increasingly powerful Naxi organization in Germany, was a bird that had heard it from the lips of a German, surely. And it was Germans, of all people, who might claim the right to quarrel with a man who had once been a singularly successful German spy.

Boots stepped into the scullery and, transferring his stump from his left hand to his right, he switched on the torch, retained in his left hand. The beam of light guided him. He turned left into the kitchen, Tommy and Sammy close behind him. The torchlight revealed a table and chairs. On the table stood a hooded birdcage. Boots took the light away from the cage and noted that the door to the passage was open. Now, he thought, where does the woman sleep? Upstairs with one of the men? Cassie had said one man was her husband, the other her brother-in-law. All the same, he had to assume the downstairs bedroom might be occupied, even if both men were upstairs. Leaving the kitchen, with Tommy and Sammy still close behind him, he switched off the torch. The ascending banisters were on his right, the bedroom on his left. Inside, in her bed, Mrs Harper, the bitter daughter of a semi-crippled German father, slept heavily, her breathing slightly bubbly. If the two men wanted her for anything in a hurry, one would come down and wake her. That had not happened yet, neither tonight nor last night. The prisoner's behaviour had been completely untroublesome. Lucky for him, or he might have got his arm broken. In her sleep, the woman was triumphant and ghost-free as Chinese Lady's quiet-footed sons passed her door. They turned in the passage and faced the stairs. The silence could have denoted that every occupant was asleep.

Problem, thought Boots. Should he change his idea about all three of them committing themselves to the upstairs rooms? Would the woman be in this downstairs bedroom with one of the men? No, not on your life. If they had Edwin here, then both men would be close to him, one man with him, watching him, the other resting or sleeping in an adjacent room.

Boots began a slow careful ascent of the stairs, keeping close to the wall. Tommy and Sammy followed, each with a cricket stump in his right hand, a torch in his left. Despite their slow careful tread, a stair faintly creaked, and they checked and held their breath as they clearly heard the feet of a chair scraping lino. But it was a natural sound, made by someone getting up or by shifting the chair, someone with no awareness that a stair had lightly creaked. Bless me lawful wedded wife and her agitated boz, thought Sammy, there *is* a bloke up there who's awake in the middle of the night, and what's he awake for when honest Walworth citizens should be asleep? Unless they're nightwatchmen.

They tensed to complete stillness as the door to the upstairs back opened. They discerned light, small light, the light of a candle, and out of the room walked a man. Tommy took a tighter grip of his cricket stump. The man went straight to the lavatory on the landing, opened the door and walked in. The door closed.

Boots moved fast. The opportunity couldn't have been sweeter if it had been the result of one of Chinese Lady's prayers. Up he went, and up went Tommy and Sammy. On went their torches. Boots ran into the back room, Sammy into the front, Tommy into the middle, all doors being open. Boots saw who was in the back room, his stepfather, legs chained. Mr Finch came awake.

'Won't be a tick,' said Boots, and out he went, just as the lavatory chain was pulled. Sammy came out of the front bedroom, the beam of his torch running ahead of him. It preceded him into the middle room, where Tommy, beside the bed, had his cricket stump angled, its point planted in the chest of a man lying recumbent in the bed, blanket drawn back. The man's face was a study in astonishment edged with fury.

'Don't move, mate,' said Tommy, 'or I'll make a nasty hole in yer armoury.'

'Don't make him bleed,' said Sammy, 'it's messy. Hope we haven't hit a blank.' Out he went. Boots was on the landing. Framed in the open lavatory door was a tall, square-shouldered man, the beam from Boots's torch flooding his livid face.

'Fair cop, I think,' said Boots. The man's right arm executed a lighting-fast movement, and down came his hand to chop. It hit a cricket stump raised in a movement just as fast. The stump cracked and split, but the impact of hand against hard wood instead of the side of a neck broke fingers.

'You ruddy 'ooligan,' said Sammy, and hit the man in the solar plexus. He doubled up. 'How we doin', Boots?' asked Sammy.

'Not bad,' said Boots, watching the groaning man.

'But what've we got out of it?' asked Sammy. 'Who's in there?' He pointed his torch at the back room. 'Anyone?'

'Yes,' said Boots, 'your Ma's better half.'

'Well, I'll admit it,' said Sammy, making for the room, 'you ain't just a pretty face, Boots.'

Mrs Harper slept on.

Chapter Twenty

Emily was on her third pot of tea. I'll be awash in a minute, she thought, and then it'll be sink or swim. Still, if I go back to bed I don't suppose I'll get to sleep. I mean, how can Boots possibly think his step-dad is actually being held in that house where that witch, old Mrs Chivers, used to live? Oh, now I'd better do penitence or something for speaking ill of the dead. I hope all this tea isn't making me drunk. Oh, gawd, look at the time, it's gone two.

The kitchen door opened and Rosie looked in.

'I knew it,' she said, 'you're still up, Mum.' Wearing her nightie, she came in.

'Rosie, go back to bed,' said Emily, 'you've got school in the mornin'.'

'Oh, I keep waking up,' said Rosie, and sat down at the table. 'I'll have some of the tea if it's still hot, may I?'

'You really ought to go back to bed, lovey,' said Emily, dark-auburn hair glinting with touches of fire, 'or you won't be fit for school.'

'Oh, I never suffer morning tiredness,' said Rosie, pouring herself some tea and modestly sugaring it. 'Mum, you're sitting and waiting for Daddy, aren't you?'

'I'm sittin' and waitin' in the hope that your grandpa's goin' to come home to your grandma.'

'Well, he will,' said Rosie, 'he and Daddy will arrive together.'

'Rosie, we can't be sure of that.'

'Daddy's sure,' said Rosie.

'No, he isn't,' said Emily.

'Well, I am,' said Rosie.

'You shouldn't expect too much from Boots,' said Emily, 'he's only gone to Walworth in hope.'

'Mummy, we've got to have faith,' said Rosie. 'Nana's got faith. That's why she went to bed and didn't stay up drinking tea.'

'She went to bed because she was all worn out,' said Emily, 'and, anyway, if you've got faith yourself, what made you keep wakin' up?'

'Excitement,' said Rosie. 'I'd have a piece of cake if I didn't feel excited. Were you able to eat cake on your wedding day?'

'Lor', what a question,' said Emily. 'I can't remember if I did or not.'

'Did Daddy have lots of girlfriends before he became engaged to you?'

'Well, I'm blessed,' said Emily, 'don't tell me you came down 'ere to ask me these kind of questions, you funny girl.'

'But I like knowing all about you and Daddy.'

'You're at the age of curiosity, you are,' said Emily, fidgeting and giving the kitchen clock another look.

'Well, it can't be helped,' said Rosie, 'so did Daddy have lots of girls?'

'He knew lots,' said Emily, 'and they all knew him, but he never had anyone steady, he was too busy learnin' how to grow up a bit superior so's he could get a good job.'

'Well, he failed, thank goodness,' said Rosie.

'No, he didn't,' said Emily, 'he got himself a nice respectable clerkin' job.'

'I mean he failed to become a bit superior,' said Rosie.

'Still, he did get a bit posh, lovey.'

'Crikey, Mum, Daddy's the most natural man in the world,' said Rosie.

'We're all natural, like God made us,' said Emily. 'Anyway, your grandma wanted your dad to grow up a gent, she was always very set on all her children learnin' to speak proper and behave proper.'

'Well, Daddy doesn't behave very proper at parties, not when he's in charge of Forfeits,' said Rosie, casting a covert look at the clock herself. 'Mum, was it sort of sublime when you were engaged? I mean, knowing then that you'd been Daddy's one and only?'

'Was it sort of *what*?'

'Sublime,' said Rosie.

'Well, I think I liked it, if that's what you mean,' smiled Emily.

'Oh, jolly good,' said Rosie.

Boots, Tommy and Sammy were in the upstairs front bedroom, Boots standing at the window and looking down at the cul-de-sac. Its single lamp-post, outside the printing factory, cast the street's solitary patch of light. His parked car was in darkness.

Mrs Harper, very conveniently, was still heavily asleep. Sammy had checked.

Mr Finch, out of his chains, was still in the room in which he'd been held, and so were the two Germans. He'd asked to have time alone with them, after Tommy had searched them for weapons. Neither had been armed. Sammy and Tommy thought it peculiar, their stepfather wanting to talk to the men in private. Boots thought otherwise, but didn't say so. Once the two men had been revealed as German, he had a fairly good idea of why they had laid his stepfather out in the hotel car park and brought him here. He'd eat his damaged cricket stump if the reason didn't relate to Edwin's years in German Intelligence and his switch of allegiance to the British. It was on the cards that Edwin was now negotiating a mutually satisfying end to the matter. He would prefer no publicity, the kind that would come about if the men were handed over to the police. He had secrets to keep, and Boots himself had always thought it wise to keep them.

'What's he up to?' asked Tommy, wanting to get back to Vi. His adrenalin was still high, and it made him feel like enjoying a bit of healthy lovey-dovey with Vi. She might say it was a funny time for that sort of thing, but then she'd say oh, all right, I don't mind now I'm awake. 'I hope those geezers 'aven't jumped him.'

'It still beats me why they kidnapped him,' said Sammy.

'Blackmail, that's what I think,' said Tommy.

'Yes, I think our stepdad's got money in the bank,' said Boots.

'Case for the police,' said Sammy.

'Only if he says so,' remarked Boots.

'Aunt Victoria won't like that,' said Tommy, 'a case of blackmail in the fam'ly. She'll have kittens.'

'See what you mean,' said Sammy. 'Not a case for the police. Chinese Lady won't like it, either.'

'So leave it to her better half to decide,' said Boots.

'How you worked it out that he was 'ere, just on account of the woman wearin' a brown hat with feathers in it, I'll never know,' said Tommy.

'It's what his education did for him,' said Sammy with a grin.

295

'Guesswork and hope, Sammy,' said Boots. 'Education didn't make me psychic.'

'Stop talkin' like a professor,' said Tommy, 'it's hurtin' my ears.'

'No good complainin', Tommy,' said Sammy, 'be like me and live with it. Hello, something's happening.'

Footsteps on the landing preceded the arrival of Mr Finch. He had a smile on his face as he entered the front bedroom, where a bedside candle showed its yellow flame.

'We can go now,' he said.

'Pardon?' said Tommy.

'There's no point in staying longer,' said Mr Finch.

'They're not goin' to be charged?' said Sammy.

'I think not, Sammy. Your mother would prefer to – ah—'

'Keep it in the fam'ly?' said Tommy.

'Exactly,' smiled Mr Finch.

'You could invoice them for any bruises,' said Sammy, 'and if you added a bit for overheads, you could come out with a profit. Take cash, not a cheque.'

'It's a thought,' said Mr Finch, glancing at Boots.

'Let me get this straight,' said Tommy. 'We're goin' to push off now and leave those geezers 'ere?'

'Yes, do you mind?' said Mr Finch.

'If it suits you, Dad, it suits me,' said Tommy. 'What's your opinion, Boots?'

'Let's get moving,' said Boots, 'and before some night bobby decides that a parked car in the Place is a bit suspicious.'

Down they went. Sammy quietly looked in on Mrs Harper. She was still sound asleep, her slack mouth bubbling away. Sounds like a boiling egg, thought

Sammy. Boots went by and entered the kitchen. The beam of his torch picked out the hooded birdcage. He lifted the cover, and Percy the parrot blinked.

'Hello, sailor,' he said.

'How's yourself?' said Boots.

'Heil Hitler,' said Percy.

'Saucy, are we?' said Boots, and covered the bird up again. He was the last to leave the house. He closed the back door on the sleeping woman and the two Germans, one of whom was winding a bandage around the other's broken fingers, using a pencil as a splint.

'What the hell have you got there?' asked Tommy of Boots.

'A covered birdcage and a parrot,' murmured Boots, handing the cage to Tommy in the back of the car before sliding into the driving seat.

'You've nicked it,' said Sammy.

'As a present for Chinese Lady,' said Boots, using the self-starter. The engine jerked into life. 'It needs to be taught to speak more proper.'

'A suitable task for your mother, Boots,' said Mr Finch, who seemed little the worse for his ordeal.

'What d'you mean, more proper?' grinned Tommy, as Boots set the car in motion.

'It needs to be taught to say "Rule Britannia",' said Boots.

Very little was said on the journey. Mr Finch confined himself to thanking his stepsons for their timely and efficient intervention, and to expressing a hope that no-one minded the fact that he'd settled things without fuss. Sammy said a bit of blackmail, was it? You could say that, yes, you could, said Mr Finch. Well, I like it that it doesn't get the family in the papers, said Tommy. Yes, in the family you don't ask questions unless you're invited to, said Sammy.

That was as much as was said.

Tommy, dropped off at his home, thought about making himself a cup of tea, but decided against it and went up to rejoin Vi in bed. Vi woke up, wanted to know what had happened, and was told Boots had been right and that their stepdad was on his way home. Oh, that's good, you can tell me more at breakfast, said Vi, and you can come back to bed now. I am back, said Tommy, move up, love. Vi made room, Tommy snuggled and said something. Vi said something in response. Tommy said something else. Vi said oh, all right, if you're sure you've got the strength at ten past three in the morning.

Boots delivered Sammy back to Susie, who was delighted at the turn of events and to know Sammy was all in one piece. Sammy said the whole thing was a blackmail stunt, and Susie said she couldn't think what anyone could blackmail her dad-in-law about. Boots said let it rest, Susie love. Tell him to come and see me when he's passing, said Susie.

'What for?' asked Sammy, back in bed with her.

'He's me 'ero,' said Susie, trying out her cockney.

'Sufferin' winkles,' said Sammy, 'I'll do things to you in a minute, Mrs Susie Adams.'

'Yes, please,' said Mrs Susie Adams.

There was a celebratory air about some of the Adams between three and four in the morning. Well, there was on this particular morning.

Boots also delivered his stepfather back to his mother, and himself to Emily, with an account of events. Emily said all of it was still unbelievable.

'There's something else,' said Boots.

298

'Oh, me gawd, what else?' asked Emily, who had finally gone back to bed at twenty minutes to three, and had sent Rosie back too.

'It's downstairs on the kitchen table,' said Boots.

'It's not a bomb, is it?'

'No, a parrot,' said Boots.

'A what?'

'A parrot, a talking one,' said Boots, 'a present for Chinese Lady.'

'Boots, you're crazy.'

'Well, Em old girl,' said Boots, slipping into bed, 'it's that kind of world, or haven't you noticed?'

'I've noticed you've always got an answer for everything,' said Emily.

'Is that good or bad?' asked Boots, turning out the bedside light.

'I suppose it's sort of sublime,' said Emily, and giggled like a girl. 'Anyway, bless you for bein' a clever old thing. Rosie's goin' to be extra proud of you, and I expect Chinese Lady might even go round tellin' everyone in the fam'ly that you've turned out a credit to her, after all. I'll talk to Dad at breakfast – Boots? Boots?'

Boots was asleep. Well, thought Emily, there's me and Rosie been up half the night on account of all this bother, and I expect Vi and Susie have too, and what does he do himself? Brings a talking parrot home, comes to bed and drops off just like that, as if no-one's had anything to worry about.

I don't know, some husbands.

Still, this one is me one and only.

Chapter Twenty-One

Bright morning arrived. Boots treated himself to a lie-in while his family had breakfast, and Rosie went up to talk to him before going off to school.

'Daddy?'

'I'm asleep,' said Boots from the depths.

'Yes, I can see you are,' said Rosie, 'and no-one minds. We all think you're a deserving case for a lie-in. I just wanted you to know Mummy's very pleased with you, Nana's saying you've turned out a credit to the whole family, which she never thought you would, and Tim says he'll play cricket with you any time you like.'

'And have you got something to say yourself?' asked Boots.

'No, nothing,' said Rosie, 'you'll only get a swollen head. Aunt Polly's downstairs. She dropped in on her way to school to find out what happened last night and if everyone was still alive. Your better half is telling her. Oh, and Grandpa told Nana it was a case of mistaken identity, that those men thought he was someone he wasn't, and that he decided not to have any hard feelings about it because he didn't want the family to get notorious.'

'Notorious?'

'Yes, mentioned in the papers,' said Rosie.

'Mistaken identity would explain it,' said Boots.

'Mummy said you didn't mention it, but yes, it would explain it nicely, wouldn't it?'

Boots turned his head, opened his sound eye and regarded his daughter, a young lady managing to look demure.

'Yes, wouldn't it?' he said.

'I'm not simple, you know,' said Rosie, 'there's something between you and Grandpa. But I don't mind, I trust you both. Well, I can't stand here gassing. And Polly's giving me a lift to school, so I'm afraid I've got to dash.'

'Right, off you go, poppet, regards to your Aunt Polly.'

'It's actually Miss Simms today. Oh, Nana likes the parrot, by the way. 'Bye.'

Later, Mr Finch departed for his office, where no recriminations awaited him for taking an extra day off. And Boots got up and managed to dodge being cornered by Chinese Lady's inquisitive tongue before going to work himself.

'Tilly?' It was five minutes past eight when Dan knocked on her door.

'Come in,' said Tilly, a threat in her voice.

Dan entered, dressed to go to work. Tilly eyed him broodingly.

'Mornin', Tilly, how's yer good-lookin' self today?' he asked.

'Cut it out,' she said, 'I'm not in the mood for all that soft soap. I 'ad a bad night last night, and it's doin' harm to me health and beauty this mornin'. I kept dreamin' about that fat Gladys Hobday—'

'I'd not actu'lly call her fat, Tilly.'

'Well, she was as fat as a balloon in me dreams,' said Tilly, 'and dancin' about on 'er tightrope. I take it unkindly, Dan Rogers, that my association with you and yer gels has given me 'orrible dreams that keep wakin' me up, and I want to know if that woman's answered the letter you sent about marryin' her.'

'Not yet,' said Dan, 'but I'm livin' in optimistic expectation.'

'Well, your expectation 'ad better come true,' said Tilly, 'because why should I spend hours worryin' about what's goin' to 'appen to Bubbles and Penny-Farvin'?'

'Tilly, I don't want you to worry at all,' said Dan, 'not now you've been a real treasure to them. If you could—'

'Don't say it.'

'No, I'm not goin' to ask you to put yerself out,' said Dan. 'I've told the girls that you'll be up here after Cassie goes home at one, and they'll be able to use their paint boxes knowin' they ain't alone in the house.'

'Oh, yer crafty bugger,' said Tilly, 'that's lumberin' me with them again.'

'No, I've got their promise to be really good,' said Dan.

'Marvellous, I don't think,' said Tilly, 'there'll be paint over everything in the kitchen.'

'I'll talk strict to them if that happens,' said Dan. 'Anyway, thanks a lot if you'll listen out for them—'

'You've got a hope,' said Tilly, 'I'm pluggin' me ears with cotton wool.'

'You've got nice-lookin' ears, Tilly, did you know that?'

Whether Tilly knew it or not, she chucked the armchair cushion at him, and it sent Dan into retreat down the stairs and back to the kitchen.

★　　★　　★

'But where's me bleedin' parrot?' asked Mrs Harper
for the third time. Rising late, having overslept,
she'd been greeted with the news that the conspiracy
had been called off. The men were brusque and more
straight-faced than ever. She asked questions, of
course, but the only answers she received referred her
repeatedly to the fact that the operation was over, the
traitor released. They did not tell her the tables had
been turned, that Mr Finch had made it quite plain to
them they would not get a public trial wherein the
nature of his work for Germany could be made known
to the British people, including his wife and family.
The British Government would take care to ensure the
trial was *in camera*. Mr Finch, calm and collected, as
he invariably was, applied himself persuasively to the
argument. Accept the alternative of going back to
Germany within twenty-four hours, he said, for it's a
very agreeable alternative compared to inevitable
imprisonment. No, they said, it would still be possible
for his wife to be informed of his past or for German
Intelligence to lay other hands on him. No, if I let you
go, he said, I'll expect you to act as German men of
honour. They weren't men of honour, of course, any
more than he or anyone else was who dealt in
espionage, where all means justified the end.

Let me make things clearer, he said, and pointed
out that British Intelligence was extremely systematic
and far-reaching. You have seen how efficiently and
quietly they effected my release. From now on I shall
be guarded and watched by the Secret Service of this
country, and so will you be, and any other German
agents. We now know you, and you will be on our
records. If anything happens to me again, or if my past
is ever revealed, be quite sure something quite

terrifying will happen to you. Further, your superiors will be informed how inefficient you are.

A charge of inefficiency? That and all else made the Germans wince. If their top man hated anything as much as failure, it was inefficiency.

They accepted Mr Finch's terms.

Mrs Harper expressed her disgust at cancellation of the plan in voluble German, a language she had inherited from her father. But as far as her parrot was concerned, she delivered her sense of outrage in plain East End cockney.

'Where the bleedin' 'ell is it?'

'Taken.'

'Who bleedin' took it?'

'The prisoner.'

'You mean that when you let 'im bugger off, you didn't stop 'im takin' my parrot?'

'Buy yourself another, woman, and stop your screeching.'

They gave her money. It wasn't as much as they'd promised, but it was enough to mollify her.

She shook the dust of Walworth from her feet halfway through the morning. Neighbours saw her go, together with the men, one of whom they thought her husband, the other her brother-in-law. All three departed by taxi, with their bags and baggage. The neighbours didn't sorrow. Well, she'd come from the East End, which was very low class, and her husband and brother-in-law hadn't been a bit sociable.

She was unaware of the fact that cancellation of the operation saved her from being drowned in a horse trough in the darkness of night. But she did ask what had happened to the fingers of the senior man. He told her they were bandaged because he'd caught them in a door.

After they had left, the house was empty again, and the rats returned to it.

It was unfortunate that men who had laid their plans so well, and accomplished the abduction of their quarry by a stroke of luck, should have come to grief by reason of a brown hat with two green feathers. It was also unfortunate that on their return to Germany they had to report not to an understanding government figure, but to a man called Heinrich Himmler. Himmler, who had a receding chin and looked like a bespectacled chicken farmer of mild disposition, certainly seemed quite understanding as he smiled and nodded all through their explanation of failure, but he nevertheless passed them on to the leader of the Brownshirts, a thug by the name of Ernst Roehm. Roehm successfully arranged for them to have a fatal car accident.

Rachel emerged from the side door that led up to the spacious apartment above shops in Lower Marsh. She looked extraordinary in a round black straw hat common to Piccadilly flower girls, a black shawl, grey blouse and dark grey skirt. Gone was her look of sumptuous allure, such as some full-bodied stage ladies were noted for. Rachel needed only a flower basket to look as if she was about to go off to Covent Garden to fill it before taking up a pitch in Piccadilly Circus.

Mr Eli Greenberg, waiting for her in his pony and cart, beamed at her as she made her way between two stalls.

'Vhy, if you ain't a remarkable lady, Rachel, ain't it?' he said. 'Who vould know you're a lady and not a seller of sveet violets?'

Rachel climbed up into the seat beside him, showing legs in lace-up black boots and black yarn stockings, one with a hole in it.

'Well, ain't I kindly receptive of yer compliments, Eli?' she said.

'My life, and all done for Boots?' chuckled Eli, tickling the pony, which began to pull the cart.

'For my friends,' said Rachel, perched happily on the cart.

'Ah, Rachel, vhile you and me and your respected father know business ain't to be despised, since ve must all eat and pay our rent, don't ve also know ve can't do vithout friends?'

The pony trotted into Waterloo Road. A street corner boy whistled at Rachel, then called.

'Meet yer in Battersea Park wiv the lights out, shall I?'

'Not if I see yer first,' called Rachel, and laughed. 'Eli, we're rich.'

'Are ve?' said Mr Greenberg cautiously.

'Yes, ain't it a fact our best friends are the Adams? Ain't it a fact, Eli, that they love us? Who could be richer?'

'Vell, sometimes Sammy's friendship comes a little expensive,' said Mr Greenberg with another chuckle. He turned left to cut through to Blackfriars Road. 'But vhat a friend, ain't he? I might have beggared my poor self by purchasin' a small brewery if Sammy hadn't had a long talk with me. But here ve are, ain't it, vith the intention of callin' in on more of Johnson's scrap yards, vith you lookin' like a vorkin' lady with a husband thinking of buyin' metal?'

'And ain't I appreciative of how you're transportin' me?' smiled Rachel.

'Out of friendship, Rachel, and for vhat I owe to the

kindness of your father, who made me the vun and only loan I ever had to ask for. But all this for Boots, eh, and not Sammy?'

'Boots is a gentleman, Eli, Sammy an adventurer, and could a woman say no to either? And it's for the good of the family in the long run.'

'I ain't askin' to be told vhat it's all about, Rachel, though I ain't saying it don't hurt not to be told.'

'I'll tell you in time,' said Rachel, not disposed to betray a confidence from Boots, not even to Mr Greenberg. 'By the way, do you know anything about Johnson's and their business?'

'A little, Rachel, a little,' said Mr Greenberg, not disposed to ignore the fact that some friends understood information wasn't always available gratis. Such friends were the best friends.

Rachel began to ask questions.

Bubbles and Penny-Farving climbed the stairs. Penny-Farving knocked on Tilly's door.

'I know who that is,' called Tilly. The time was twenty to two, Cassie had gone at one, and that meant the little angels had had forty minutes in which to commit some act of minor destruction. 'What's up, then?' She opened the door. Bubbles and Penny-Farving looked up at her. Well, she thought, if they were mine, I'd do me level best to turn them into real angels, for I never saw two infants that looked the part more. 'All right, tell me the worst,' she said.

'Please, Tilly, there's a smell,' said Penny-Farving.

'What d'you mean, a smell?'

'It's 'orrid,' said Bubbles.

Tilly had a sudden fearful thought. Out of the room she ran and down the stairs. The smell met her the moment she began her descent. Gas. She whipped her hankie out of the waistband of her skirt and thrust it against her nose. She rushed into the kitchen and through to the scullery, and she saw at once that one brass tap was on, a gas ring tap. She switched it off, opened the scullery door and then the kitchen window. She put her face out of the window and breathed in warm air. Out to the passage she ran and opened the front door. From the landing above, the girls peered down at her.

'Is it all right?' asked Bubbles.

'It is now.' Tilly looked up at them. 'Who turned the gas on?'

'Did us do it?' asked Bubbles of her sister.

Penny-Farving looked down at Tilly.

'Us don't remember,' she said.

And they probably don't, thought Tilly.

'All the same,' she said, 'can you remember if you wanted to light the gas?' Penny-Farving was tall enough to.

'I 'member we was playin' in the scullery,' said Bubbles.

'Was we?' said Penny-Farving.

'Well, you was,' said Bubbles.

'So was you,' said Penny-Farving.

'I don't 'member I was,' said Bubbles, tall enough to switch the tap on, but not to apply a lighted match.

'Were you playin' with matches?' asked Tilly.

'No, Dad don't let us do that,' said Penny-Farving.

Well, he's shown that much sense, thought Tilly.

'Where are the matches?' she asked.

'Dad keeps them in the larder,' said Penny-Farving, 'where we can't reach 'less we stand on a chair.'

Oh, yes, that's right, thought Tilly, remembering using the matches herself and putting the box back in the larder.

'Stay there,' she said, and took a look in the larder, thinking Cassie, perhaps, had used the box and forgotten to put it back. But it was there, on an upper shelf. Cassie was an amusing girl, but she had her share of commonsense. Tilly went back upstairs. Bubbles and Penny-Farving eyed her cautiously. 'Little gels that play with gas taps ought to get smacked,' she said. 'Don't ever do it again, d'you 'ear? I'm just relieved you 'ad the sense to come runnin' up to me. Didn't you realize it was gas you could smell?'

'Wasn't it 'orrid?' said Bubbles.

'It was makin' us feel a bit sick,' said Penny-Farving.

'Well, come on,' said Tilly, 'my window's open and you can sit at my table for a while. Listen, I thought you were usin' yer paint-boxes this afternoon, your dad said you were.'

'Oh, we was makin' paper-boats first and sailin' them in the scullery sink,' said Penny-Farving.

'We was goin' to do paintin' after,' said Bubbles.

'Well, go down and bring the paint-boxes up, with yer drawin' books,' said Tilly, 'and I'll make some room on me table that you can use. Go straight down and come straight up, because I don't want you spendin' even ten seconds tryin' to do something you shouldn't.'

'Yes, Tilly,' said Penny-Farving, 'we like bein' with you in the afternoons, don't we, Bubbles?'

'Dad told us you 'ad a heart of gold,' said Bubbles.

'Well, I'm goin' to tell yer dad my 'eart of gold is 'aving a very tryin' time lately,' said Tilly.

'Oh, is someone upsettin' yer?' asked Penny-Farving.

'Go and get your paint-boxes,' said Tilly. 'Then later on, I'll see to the first fittin' of your new frocks.'

'Crumbs, will yer really?' said Bubbles excitedly.

'If you manage not to spread paint all over the furniture,' said Tilly, and down the two girls went. For once their concentration on what they'd been told didn't fail them, and they were up again, with their paint-boxes and drawing books, in quick time. Tilly cleared part of her table for them, sat them down and let them apply themselves to their hobby, a harmless one unless they ate the paints. She sat down herself to do some hand-stitching, her window open. Across the adjoining yards the blind at the Harpers' window was down.

With Rosie and Tim at school, and Emily, Boots and Edwin at their jobs, Chinese Lady was alone in her kitchen, the hub of her existence. Well, a kitchen was where a woman was queen, where she provided for her family and ordered their lives, without suffering a lot of contradiction. Family members knew a woman's kitchen wasn't the right place for being contradictory, not when it was there that they had to pay homage to her cooking and baking.

Mind, she wasn't quite alone in the kitchen today. She had a talking parrot to keep her company. She'd cleaned its cage and gone out during the morning to buy fresh birdseed. She thought it liked its new home, because it kept saying things like 'Hello, sailor,' and 'What a nice day.' She talked to it from time to time. Fancy Boots bringing it home for her, even if he hadn't told Emily where he bought it. She accepted it as a thoughtful present to make up for Edwin's disappearance having been a sore trial to her. Edwin had explained that those men had mistaken him for someone else. She wasn't sure they should have been let off, but when Edwin said he'd been sure she wouldn't want the family mentioned in the news-papers, she couldn't have agreed more. Boots had told Emily the parrot's name was Percy.

Rolling dough, she said, 'Percy? Percy? D'you like the birdseed I bought for you?'

'Watcher, missus,' said Percy.

'My, you're a funny parrot,' said Chinese Lady.

'Who's got red drawers, then?' asked Percy, hopping about on his perch.

'What's that?'

'Knickers,' said Percy, sounding as if he was chortling.

'Well,' said Chinese Lady, 'I'm not havin' any parrot saying things like that, not in my kitchen I'm not.' And she dropped the hood over the cage. 'That Boots, the sly devil, he would go and pick a vulgar music hall parrot. Just wait till he comes home.'

When Polly arrived home from school, her stepmother introduced her to a huge bouquet that had been delivered by the Dulwich Village florists. With the bouquet was a message from Boots.

Thanks for all your help, Polly. United we stand, divided we fall.

'What does that mean?' asked Lady Simms.

'It means I'm expected to be friends with him for ever,' said Polly.

'How nice,' said Lady Simms.

'Nice? It's filthy,' said Polly. 'If you were my age could you be friends, just friends, with a man like Boots for ever?'

'I don't answer questions like that, Polly my dear.'

'Well, I'll tell you this much, old darling,' said Polly, 'I'll have that man one day, even if I have to hire two hairy gorillas to tie him down.'

'Really, Polly, you do have the most extravagant ways of expressing the most ridiculous ideas,' said Lady Simms. 'Do be sensible, and don't forget to send Boots a sweet note of thanks. Oh, and have you thought of accepting a proposal of marriage from Captain Nigel Burke?'

'Not bloody likely,' said Polly.

'Your language, Polly dear, is sometimes very reminiscent of your father's.'

'Hooray,' said Polly.

She didn't send Boots a sweet note of thanks. She knew he wouldn't want her to. Emily wouldn't like it. In any case, Polly had thoughts of sending him a clandestine note of fire and passion, describing exactly what they could do to each other during a weekend in Brighton.

Emily, Tim and Rosie were home in advance of Boots. Chinese Lady's queenly domain, her kitchen, became alive.

'Nana, you've got the parrot covered up,' said Tim.

'Yes, he's been talkin' too much,' said Chinese Lady.

'Still, I can have a look at him,' said Tim, and took the cover off.

'Hello, sailor,' said Percy.

'Hello yourself,' said Tim.

'Hello, Percy,' said Rosie.

'Heil Hitler,' said Percy.

'What was that he said?' asked Emily.

'Yes, what was that you said?' asked Rosie.

'Who's got red drawers, then?' asked Percy. Rosie shrieked with laughter. Chinese Lady put the cover back over the cage, and Percy lapsed into confused silence.

'It's nothing to laugh at, Rosie,' said Chinese Lady.

'No, Nana, of course not,' said Rosie.

'That's a saucy parrot, that is,' said Emily.

'Yes, trust Boots to bring one like that home,' said Chinese Lady. 'I don't know what the vicar's lady wife would say.'

'Why, does she wear red ones?' asked Tim.

'Em'ly, speak to that boy,' said Chinese Lady, 'and when Boots gets in, I'll speak to him.'

'Should you, Nana, when he's the family hero?' said Rosie.

'Never mind him bein' a hero,' said Chinese Lady, 'I'm not goin' to give him any medals for givin' me a parrot that talks vulgar. I just hope the parrot he bought for Cassie speaks a lot more proper than this one.'

Oh, crikey, Daddy's going to catch it over supper tonight, thought Rosie. What a lark.

'Stay there, you gels,' said Tilly, when she heard their father entering the house. Down she went to have several private words with him, in his kitchen.

'Hello, Tilly,' he said, taking his cap off, 'nice to see you as soon as I come in. Never thought a lodger could be as pleasin' as you.'

'Dan Rogers, if you don't stop bein' so self-satisfied, I'll stick pins in you all over,' said Tilly. 'You nearly lost your gels today.'

'Eh?' said Dan. 'Don't tell me Elvira turned up and tried to take 'em away.'

Tilly drew a breath and counted to ten. Then she said, 'If you want to see that woman 'ere, you'll 'ave to go and fetch 'er. No, what I'm talkin' about is your gas stove. One of the taps got turned on and left on.'

'Christ,' said Dan, 'what happened, and where are the girls?'

'They're alive, I can tell you that,' said Tilly. 'They could have gassed themselves, but thank goodness they had the sense to come up and tell me about the smell. When I came down the smell was sick-makin', so I opened doors and windows after turnin' the tap off.' Tilly went on to say she'd settled Bubbles and Penny-Farving at her table with their paints, that a little later on she tied them to their chairs while she popped out for five minutes just to see for herself how Alice Higgins's fractured foot was. It was bad news. The fracture was having to be re-set, and Alice was in a state about it, waiting for the ambulance to come and take her to the hospital. So what was Mr Dan Rogers going to do about things now?

'I'm too upset just this minute to think about anything except me girls nearly gassin' themselves,' said Dan. 'I've got to go up and see 'em.'

'Not yet,' said Tilly, putting herself in his way. 'First you've got to think serious about gettin' some kind woman to look after them all day, a woman who's brought up kids 'erself and could do with the money you'll pay 'er – oh, yer swine!'

Tilly gasped. Dan had put his hands on her waist and bodily lifted her out of his way. He plonked her down, and out of the kitchen he went to run up the stairs. Tilly could hardly believe it. Handsome of figure and not a skinny line anywhere, she'd been lifted like a baby. For a moment she thought of going after him with his own frying-pan. Then she mentally gave him his due for acting like a man at last, and for showing so much concern over his girls. She went up after him with no thought of knocking his head off for manhandling her. He had the girls up in his arms, cradling them and kissing their noses and talking to them. Tilly credited him then with the virtue of being a caring and loving dad, even if he had been daft enough to become infatuated with a woman who thought more of her circus life than she did of her little daughters. For the first time Tilly thought what man would be fool enough to marry a woman like that when she'd never make the slightest attempt to be a mother to her children? Dan Rogers might, for the sake of his girls. I suppose he should, thought Tilly, the daft idiot is still infatuated enough to make Gladys Hobday his lawful wedded wife.

Dan took the girls down to the kitchen, made a pot of tea, gave them a cup each with a slice of shop cake, told them to sit there and not move from the table, then went upstairs to talk to Tilly again. He said that after he'd given the girls their supper, he'd do the rounds of the neighbourhood, calling on people he knew to find out if some homely mother whose kids were grown up would take on the full-time job of looking after Bubbles and Penny Farving while he was out at work. That is, if Tilly would keep an eye on them while he was doing the rounds.

'I'll do it for you,' said Tilly.

'What, knock on doors and talk to the women?' said Dan.

'You stay with them gels,' said Tilly, 'they like 'aving you with them of an evening when you've been workin' all day. Talk to them about not doin' things that could be fatal, and be serious. Don't talk to them with that grin of yours all over yer face. Bein' the right kind of dad 'as got to 'ave its serious side. I've 'eard you tryin' to be strict with them, and the way you do it only makes them giggle. Never mind about Gladys Hobday for the time bein', your important job is to

315

make sure your gels obey you, then when you do 'ave to leave them I won't 'ave to worry about them givin' me 'eart attacks.'

'I've got sense enough to know you're givin' me good advice, Tilly.'

'Well, that's something,' said Tilly, 'and I'll forget the way you laid yer mitts on me and chucked me about. Pity you didn't do a bit of that with your circus freak. A woman might not like bein' manhandled, but it tells 'er the bloke who's doin' it is a man and not a wet weekend. I fitted the gels with their first new frocks this afternoon, and I'll now be able to 'ave them finished by tomorrow. It'll cost you five bob.'

'For two new frocks? Is that all?' asked Dan.

'Cash on deliv'ry,' said Tilly, 'and then I'll start their second ones.'

'Where's their first ones?' asked Dan, and Tilly showed him. Both dresses were short, both blue with daisy patterns. Dan thought them delicious. Tilly said the girls would need nice new socks, and some new vests, and that she'd get them for him, if he liked. Dan said he'd be very obliged, that it was ruddy good of her, and he couldn't think why he'd been lucky enough to get a lodger like her. She didn't go to pubs and get drunk, nor carry on with dubious characters. Well, as far as he knew she didn't.

'I should say not,' said Tilly, 'what d'you think I am? I was engaged once to a very respectable bloke, and I'd be a very respectable married woman by now if I 'adn't changed me mind.'

'Sorry about that,' said Dan, 'I expect you had a good reason. Still, a fine-lookin' woman like you, Tilly, shouldn't 'ave to wait long to find someone else.'

'Don't know someone tall, dark and 'andsome, I

suppose, do you?' said Tilly with a bit of a larky smile.

'Well, actu'lly, yes, I do,' said Dan. 'One of the mechanics at the works. Gus Bradley. I'll invite him along one evenin' and get him to meet you. He's a bachelor and might just be lookin' for someone like you, Tilly. Well, you've got a warm heart and a womanly figure and then there's yer fine limbs—'

'Watch it,' said Tilly, 'it still 'urts me integrity to know you caught me only 'alf-dressed, and if you keep remindin' me of it, Dan Rogers, I'll wreck your hooter. You sure this tall, dark and 'andsome Gus Bradley is a bachelor?'

'I'm sure all right,' said Dan, 'he's my chief mechanic and I know him well.'

'What's wrong with him, then, if he's still a bachelor?' asked Tilly.

'I ain't cognisant with what's wrong with him,' said Dan, 'he seems all right to me and he's a sound motor mechanic. Like me to invite him here one evenin'?'

'Look,' said Tilly, 'I don't feel I'm all that 'ard-up, I don't feel I need people to bring blokes along for me to inspect.'

'No, of course not, Tilly, it's your say-so,' said Dan.

'Still, all right,' said Tilly, 'I'll 'ave a look at this Gus Bradley.'

'I'll see if he can come tomorrow evenin',' said Dan.

'Wait a minute,' said Tilly, suddenly feeling irked, 'you in a hurry to get rid of me?'

'Blimey O'Reilly,' said Dan, 'anybody who wanted to get rid of you in a hurry would need his best friend to hit him with a hammer. Straight up, Tilly, ain't you as good as me best friend yerself?'

'Strike a light,' said Tilly, 'ain't you kind and ain't I honoured? Fancy me bein' as good as the best friend of Gladys Hobday's Man Friday. I don't know 'ow

you can still be in love with a fat selfish woman like
'er.'

'I've never thought she was fat,' said Dan.

'No, well, I suppose 'er spangles and tights blinded
you,' said Tilly.

'Hope I'll get a reply to my letter,' said Dan.

'You're off yer silly chump, wantin' to marry that
kind of woman,' said Tilly.

'But you keep sayin—'

'I know what I've kept sayin'. I know it's for the
sake of them gels, but any man wantin' to marry
Gladys Hobday 'as to be right off 'is rocker.'

'It's only—'

'Push off,' said Tilly. 'I've got me supper to get
before I go out and try to find a good woman for you.'

'Well, look, take this,' said Dan, and gave her a ten-
bob note. 'That'll pay for the first new dresses and
leave enough to buy new socks and vests, and thanks
for bein' so warm-hearted, Tilly, bless yer.'

'You're makin' a weak woman of me, you are, Dan
Rogers,' said Tilly.

Chapter Twenty-Two

Sammy, home from the office, spent a rib-tickling time with his young son and infant daughter before interfering with Susie in her kitchen.

'If I have an accident with this saucepan, Sammy Adams, there'll be ructions you've never dreamed of.'

'Susie, I'm only makin' known to you me pleasure in comin' home to me fam'ly,' said Sammy. 'Believe me, with your dad-in-law back in the bosom of his own fam'ly, the whole day's been highly pleasurable. I've been able to concentrate me brainbox on me business, particularly concernin' the future prospects of your dad and Freddy.'

'You mean if the scrap metal business is sold, you'll still keep the one yard?'

'Well now, Susie—'

'You're up to something I'm not goin' to agree with,' said Susie.

'Susie, would I?'

'Yes, every time you start off saying well now, Susie, you're up to something fishy.'

'Might I inform you that as a highly reputable businessman, I've never shaken 'ands with anything fishy? That sort of thing gets around, Susie. Now, while I'm not in a position to promise all the yards won't be sold, I am in a position to say I'm workin' on a speculative proposition that will look after Jim and Freddy, and your brother Will too.'

'What's a speculative proposition if it's not fishy?' asked Susie, straining fresh garden peas, cooked to shining greenness, through her colander.

'It's a proposition I'm workin' on, Susie, along with gettin' Johnson's to dot some more eyes and cross some more tees.'

'I want to know more about it than that,' said Susie.

'Well, of course you do, Susie, you bein' my legal spouse and with shares in the business. Just let me get everything tied up first, then I'll guarantee you'll recommend me for me first knight'ood.'

'Your first? Sammy, you can't have two knighthoods.' Susie buttered the hot, new potatoes she'd tipped into a tureen. 'One's your lot, if you ever get near it.'

'That a fact, Susie? I was thinkin' I could award me second one to you. I like the sound of Sir Susie Adams.'

'Sit the children up, Sammy, and stop playin' about in your fairyland,' said Susie.

'Still, it's been a happy day, Susie,' said Sammy, tucking little Bess into her high chair.

'Yes, I told my hero so,' said Susie.

'You did what?'

'I phoned Boots at the office. He said hello, Susie, and I said hello, me 'andsome 'ero, thanks ever so much for rescuin' me one and only dad-in-law.'

Sammy grinned at young Daniel.

'Don't mind your mum, Daniel, she's had a long day,' he said.

Supper at the house in Red Post Hill came to the dining-room table from the kitchen via the hatch. For five years Chinese Lady and her husband had lived here with Boots and his family, and she still didn't like to mention dining-room to old friends whom she occasionally visited in Walworth. She was sure that

320

only people who were stuck-up talked about dining-rooms. Often enough all meals were taken in her kitchen, but now and again she would get it into her head that as her husband was a gentleman, only the dining-room was suitable if she'd cooked a roast, say, or expensive pork chops with apple sauce. It was pork chops this evening.

With everyone seated and served, the supper began, and so did Chinese Lady's dialogue with Boots, who'd noted the covered birdcage was on the sideboard.

'I don't think I've seen much of you today, Boots,' she said.

'Sorry about your hard luck, old lady,' said Boots, 'but I think you were making beds and dusting ornaments when I finally got down to the kitchen this morning.'

'Yes, I made a note that you slipped off before I could talk to you about one or two things.'

'Nana, isn't he a perisher sometimes?' said Rosie. 'He's always slipping off whenever I want to talk to him myself, about me having a dress allowance.'

'That's funny,' said Tim, 'I was goin' to ask him the other day about me havin' my own cricket bat, only he wasn't where I'd seen him.'

'He saw you comin', Tim,' said Emily. 'He does that to me sometimes.'

'If someone wants a dress allowance, and someone else wants a cricket bat, and someone like my better half wants me to mend a chair leg,' said Boots, 'I'm available for interviews by appointment.'

'Oh, we'll all queue up,' said Emily.

'I'm available myself if Boots is called away,' said Mr Finch, whose return had been accepted without fuss. If Emily and Chinese Lady thought there were loose ends that needed tying up, they hadn't said so.

Emily had gone along with Boots's suggestion to let the matter rest, and Mr Finch had managed to blind Chinese Lady with science. 'In other words,' said Mr Finch, 'I'll stand helpfully in for Boots.'

'I was speakin' about Boots slippin' off this mornin',' said Chinese Lady, 'I wasn't askin' for a lot of unsensible remarks.'

'Oh, sorry, Nana, carry on,' said Rosie.

'I won't refer to one of the things I had on my mind,' said Chinese Lady. That, of course, was on account of young Tim being present. The boy had been kept ignorant of the traumatic family dilemma. 'I just want to speak about that parrot you brought home as a present for me, Boots.'

'Don't mention it,' said Boots. 'Cassie's very fond of her bird, old lady, and I hope you'll get very fond of yours. It'll keep you company when we're all out. Why's it in here, by the way, and covered up?'

'You might well ask,' said Chinese Lady.

'Yes, Daddy, not half you might,' said Rosie.

'It's not fit to inhabit my kitchen,' said Chinese Lady. 'I don't know where you bought it, Boots, but it's a vulgar disgrace.'

'Well, poor old Percy,' said Boots, helping himself to more apple sauce. 'Has he said something he shouldn't?'

'Well might you ask,' said Emily.

'What I want to know is who's been learnin' it vulgarities?' said Chinese Lady.

'Good question, Maisie,' said Mr Finch.

'I think everyone's looking at me,' said Boots.

'Well, everyone knows what you're capable of,' said Chinese Lady. 'Even your children blush for you at times.'

'Me?' said Tim, appalled. Only girls blushed.

'I'm not children, Nana,' said Rosie. 'Mind, I do still blush for Daddy. He's wicked sometimes.'

'Yes, I expect he learned that parrot how to talk vulgar,' said Emily.

'Well, if I'm goin' to keep it, he'd better unlearn it, and quick,' said Chinese Lady.

'I could say I'm innocent,' said Boots, 'but all right, let's hear the bird. Take the hood off, Tim.'

'Oh, you bet,' said Tim, putting his knife and fork down and darting to the sideboard. He uncovered the cage. Percy blinked, hopped about, pecked at his seed and cocked an eye.

'Speak up, Percy,' said Boots.

Percy said not a word.

'It's ashamed of itself, I shouldn't wonder,' said Chinese Lady.

'Who's a pretty girl, then?' said Percy.

'What's wrong with that?' asked Boots, and Tim spoke up.

'But, Dad, in the kitchen he said—'

'Never mind repeatin' it, Tim,' said Chinese Lady.

'Maisie, we have to establish the cause of the upset,' said Mr Finch with due gravity. 'Perhaps you'd like to repeat what was said?'

'I'll go to me grave before I get into the habit of repeatin' vulgarities,' said Chinese Lady firmly.

'Percy, see what you've done?' said Emily.

'Bleedin' Amy,' said Percy.

Boots coughed. Chinese Lady shuddered.

'Well! In my own house and all,' she said, 'and the creature brought for me by my own son.'

''Orrible,' said Emily, 'I never heard the like except from hooligans.'

'Oh, lor', Daddy,' said Rosie, who thought the whole thing a riot.

'There's a solution,' said Boots. 'Your grandma can teach it to say "Rule, Britannia".'

'Oh, you think so, do you, my lad?' said Chinese Lady. 'Let me tell you, if that bird says one more vulgar thing, I'll cook it and serve it to you for your Sunday dinner.'

'All right, old lady,' said Boots, 'let's say with sage and onion stuffing.'

Rosie collapsed with laughter. Chinese Lady eyed Boots stiffly, but her mouth twitched.

'It's like I always thought,' she said, 'you're headin' for perdition, Boots. I can't hardly believe sometimes the way you've grown up.'

'How's yer knickers?' said Percy.

It took Chinese Lady quite a while to restore order.

'Freddy, I've got news for you,' said Cassie later that evening.

'For me?' said Freddy. 'D'you mean Tottenham 'Otspurs want me for their football team?'

'No, course not, you daft thing. Freddy, you really are gettin' daft lately.'

'Talk about the pot callin' the kettle black,' said Freddy.

'I'm sure I don't know what that means,' said Cassie. 'Anyway, I 'ad a letter today from the flower shop, and I'm startin' work on Monday.'

'Well, I'm pleased for yer, Cassie. I like the idea. You'll be able to do your share of payin' when we go to the flicks.'

'Freddy, don't be silly, girls don't treat boys.'

'But mates treat each other,' said Freddy.

'Freddy, if you don't stop sayin' mates, I'll kick you,' said Cassie. 'Oh, and Mr Rogers 'as had Tilly lookin' after Bubbles and Penny-Farvin', ain't that nice for him? I like Mr Rogers, don't you? I wonder if Tilly likes 'im as well? Me dad knew a lady called Tilly once, he met her on a horse-bus on his way to Buckingham Palace, and she wanted to marry 'im, only me dad couldn't, because he'd just got married to our mum. By the way, Freddy, did yer know Mrs 'Arper and her 'usband and brother-in-law have moved? I saw them gettin' into a taxi with all their luggage this mornin' when I was takin' Bubbles and Penny-Farvin' out. I called hello to Mrs 'Arper as she got into the taxi, but she didn't answer, she didn't look very 'appy. Freddy, we won't be able to take Cecil to see Percy any more.'

'Won't we?' said Freddy. 'That's goin' to break me heart, that is.'

'Oh, you've still got me, Freddy love.'

'Have I, Cassie? Well, I daresay I can grin and bear it.'

Dan came out of his house then. Seeing Cassie and Freddy at the gate of Freddy's house, he approached.

'Oh, how'd you do, Mr Rogers,' said Cassie, 'the girls were ever so good this mornin'.'

'Glad to hear it, Cassie,' said Dan, and told her that Tilly had solved the problem of getting the girls looked after on a full-time basis by making contact with a woman called Mrs Brooks. Did Cassie mind that he wouldn't need her any more? Cassie said she didn't mind a bit, that she'd been going to tell him tomorrow morning that she was starting work as an apprentice in a flower shop on Monday. Dan said the news was uplifting for everyone, and that he'd like to pay her for tomorrow morning, in any case. Cassie said how kind, but no, she couldn't really take anything.

'How about just a bob, then?' suggested Dan.

'Well, if it pleases you, Mr Rogers, all right, then,'

said Cassie graciously, and Dan happily gave her a bob. He was never short of money, his job paid him well.

'And thanks for bein' a great help,' he smiled.

'Oh, I was born to be a great 'elp,' said Cassie. 'You can ask me dad. And Freddy.'

'Well, I'll say this much, Mr Rogers,' said Freddy, 'it's me honest opinion that when she's older, Cassie could be a great 'elp as a plumber's mate.'

Cassie gave a little yell, and Freddy had to run then, Cassie flying after him.

Mrs Brooks arrived at eight the next morning, and Dan summed her up at once as just what the doctor would have ordered for Bubbles and Penny-Farving. A buxom woman with a distinct air of motherly warmth, she declared she'd never seen two sweeter little angels. Dan cautioned her that they had their moments.

'Well, what little girls don't, Mr Rogers? I know about little moments, and little girls. And little boys too, which are a lot more of an 'andful than girls. That's Bubbles, is it, and that's Penny-Farvin'? My, I never knew such a pretty way to call girls. You leave them to me, Mr Rogers, I'll give them kind but sensible motherin'. Just show me where everything is before you go off to your work, like.'

When Dan did leave, he had a feeling Tilly had found him a real treasure.

Rachel came through to Boots on his office line.

'Won't keep you a moment, Boots.'

'Make it a little longer,' said Boots.

'Oh, I only need to know when you'll be taking me to lunch again.'

'You've finished finding out?'

'I've some very interesting information for you.'

'I'm not surprised,' said Boots, 'you're a very interesting woman.'

'My life,' purred Rachel, 'haven't I said a hundred times that your mother had no right to produce three sons like you, Tommy and Sammy? Is it fair on weak women?'

'What weak women?' asked Boots. 'Never met any myself, only the normal kind, and I've had to run from some of them. Am I to receive the interesting information over lunch with you, and not before?'

'Yes, d'you mind a little blackmail, lovey?'

'Not from you,' said Boots. 'Next Tuesday, then? Trocadero?'

'I should say no to Chinese Lady's son and heir?'

'Twelve-thirty, then, next Tuesday,' said Boots.

Emily, of course, when she was told five minutes later, said, 'What's goin' on? It's bad enough watchin' Polly Simms eatin' you with her eyes.'

'Imagination, Em.'

'Don't make me laugh,' said Emily, 'Polly Simms'll get you one day with your trousers down.'

'God, I hope not,' said Boots, 'you know what Confucius says. "Woman with skirts up runs faster than man with trousers down."'

'Oh, yer comic,' said Emily, and burst into laughter. 'All the same, I hope I don't have to start watchin' Rachel.'

'Rachel isn't that kind of woman, Em. She's an orthodox wife and mother.'

'So am I,' said Emily, 'so watch yourself when you're havin' lunch with her. I might just be behind you. D'you think the information she's got might make Sammy think twice about callin' a shareholders' meetin'?'

'It might,' said Boots.

'You still don't want to let the scrap metal business go?'

'Not yet,' said Boots. He had no real desire to be rich. He always felt life had given him as much as he deserved. He had survived the trenches, even the first horrendous battle of the Somme, and found Emily waiting for him, Emily the godsend to the family. His sight had been restored, even if his left eye was of very little use. Rosie had appeared, little five-year-old Rosie, who had sat on his doorstep with him and taken hold of so much of his affection. Then Tim had come along, a boy of eager friendliness who now shared his love of cricket. And there were other people, his indomitable mother paramount among them, while not forgetting the two men he admired more than any others. One, his company commander, Major Harris, was gone, shot to pieces on the Somme. The second was Edwin Finch, his stepfather. Polly, the woman, he kept out of any analysis or any reflections. Because he had survived, because he had been given so much, Boots never experienced moments when he wanted more. He and his sister Lizzy were alike in that respect.

'It's not really a question of an itchy palm, Em,' he said, 'it's a question of good business. Is it better to sell now or to wait? I'd say wait. Also, I'm very curious as to Johnson's real reasons for wanting to buy.'

'I see,' said Emily, 'that's what's taken your fancy.'

'That's a clever girl,' said Boots.

'Same to you,' said Emily.

When Dan arrived home he found everything in perfect order, including the girls. They'd enjoyed a full day, been taken out and about by Mrs Brooks, had their faces and hands washed regularly, and been given a very appetizing midday meal. And they had been dressed in the late afternoon in their new frocks, socks and vests, with the result that when Dan came in he was confronted with a vision of two little angels indeed. He thanked the good lady and paid her for the day, her preference being for a daily setttlement.

Tilly came down as soon as Mrs Brooks left.

'Well?' she said.

'Look at my little sausages,' said Dan.

'I've looked at them.'

'Look at their hands and faces.'

'I've seen them,' said Tilly. She had been up and down several times to see how Mrs Brooks was coping. She couldn't think why she kept bothering, but she did, and each time she had to admit she'd recommended the perfect solution to a serious problem. 'Well, say something.'

'What can I say?' said Dan.

'What about their frocks?'

'Lovely, Tilly me treasured friend,' said Dan, and looked so delighted with everything that Tilly, correctly, thought he was going to give her a kiss of robust manly gratitude. Dan, however, held the impulse in check in case she landed him one in the eye. 'I've got to say it, Tilly, it was me lucky day when you turned up, strike me if it wasn't.'

'Yes, Tilly's nice, ain't she, Dad?' said Penny-Farving.

'I've never asked before,' said Tilly, 'but where do your parents live?'

'Greenwich,' said Dan.

'Don't you take the gels to see them?'

'Not much,' said Dan.

'You mean they don't approve of them bein'—' Tilly wanted to say born out of wedlock, but stopped herself.

'It ain't that,' said Dan, 'it's more that they've both taken to drink.'

'Well, I'm sorry for you, Dan Rogers,' said Tilly, 'I don't know many men daft enough to choose a woman like Gladys Hobday and parents that 'ave taken to drink.' She smiled at the angels. 'When you two are older, you'll 'ave to keep an eye on yer dad or he might get barmy enough to fall down a coal-hole and never be seen again.'

'Oh, crumbs,' said Bubbles.

'Don't worry, sausage, it won't happen if you keep yer fingers crossed,' said Dan, and both girls crossed their fingers immediately.

'When does Penny-Farvin' start school?' asked Tilly.

'September,' said Dan, 'at St John's.'

'Well, by then you might 'ave been unlucky enough to get Gladys Hobday to a church,' said Tilly.

'Well,' said Dan, and moved out of the kitchen, taking Tilly with him.

'Well what?' said Tilly.

'A letter came by the midday post,' said Dan.

'From 'er?' asked Tilly.

'Yes, Elvira.'

'Elvira my eye,' said Tilly forthrightly. 'What did she say?'

'No.'

'No?'

'Yes, just that. "No" in capital letters.'

'I see,' said Tilly.

'And underlined,' said Dan.

'So now what're you goin' to do?' asked Tilly.

'I thought of goin' down by train and givin' her a good hidin',' said Dan. 'Well, all your other advice has made sense.'

'You're actu'lly goin' to put 'er over your knees?' said Tilly.

'Well, no. I only thought I would, then I decided I wouldn't.'

'Oh, yer dozy 'a'porth,' said Tilly.

'Still, it 'asn't been a bad day,' said Dan, 'and I've arranged for Gus to come round this evenin'.'

'Gus? Gus who?'

'Gus Bradley, one of our best mechanics.'

'The tall, dark and 'andsome bloke?' said Tilly.

'That's him,' said Dan. 'I didn't make a mistake, did I? You'd like to meet him socially? It's my opinion a fine woman like you, Tilly, ought to be able to enjoy some sociable get-togethers with a sound upstandin' bloke like Gus.'

'Well, 'ow thoughtful of you,' said Tilly, 'but I wish you wouldn't be so bloody cheerful about it.'

'But it's a cheerful prospect, ain't it?' said Dan. 'He'll be along about half-seven.'

'Listen, you 'aven't told 'im I'm dyin' to fall over meself, 'ave you?'

'Haven't said anything about you, except I've got a lady lodger he might like to meet. I'll bring him up after I've split a bottle of beer with him.'

'Well, thanks very much, I'm sure,' said Tilly, 'I can 'ardly wait.'

The sound upstanding bloke turned out to be as described: tall, dark and handsome. Dan, having introduced him to Tilly, left them to get to know each other. Tilly looked him over, and Gus, a man of thirty, eyed her with interest.

'Nice to meet yer, Tilly,' he said.

'Well, you look all right,' said Tilly. 'Mind me askin' why you ain't married?'

331

'Pleasure,' said Gus. 'It's just that I never wanted to rush into permanent wedlock, yer know, not till we was sure we'd found the right woman.'

'We?' said Tilly. 'Who's we?'

'Mother and me,' said Gus.

That was the end of Gus as a proposition. Tilly asked him to kindly leave the room. Gus said he didn't need to, he'd gone before he left home. Tilly said what she meant was thank you for coming up, but good night. I've got things to do, she said. I don't get it, said Gus. So long, said Tilly. Gus left, looking puzzled. He reported to Dan that the lady lodger was a bit peculiar. Dan, of course, went up to see Tilly after Gus had departed.

'No go, Tilly?' he said.

'Do me a favour, would you?' said Tilly. 'Close the door nice and quiet when you leave.'

'Wait a bit,' said Dan, 'I thought you were lookin' for someone like Gus.'

'I was, I am,' said Tilly, 'but not 'im and 'is mother both.'

'Come again?' said Dan.

'I don't know how it's escaped your notice, seein' you work every day with 'im,' said Tilly, 'but 'is dear old mother is the reason why he's not married, nor ever likely to be. But if he ever is, by some wondrous reason, 'is would-be wife will 'ave to marry 'is mother as well.'

Dan laughed his head off. Tilly wasn't impressed.

'Think it's funny, do yer, Dan Rogers?' she said.

'Not half,' said Dan. 'Oh, blimey, marry his mother as well? You're killing me, Tilly.'

'Oh, I am, am I? Well, try this at yer funeral!' Her egg saucepan came flying at him. It hit the door. Dan bolted for his life. He knew what was good for him. Plain honest cowardice.

★　　★　　★

It was twilight and Boots was out in the garden, watering the sweet peas he and Edwin always liked to grow. The blooms could be prolific, and Emily and Chinese Lady delighted in having vases of them around the house.

Rosie came out.

'Pot of tea's nearly ready,' she said.

'Count me in,' said Boots.

'Daddy, that parrot's a lark.'

'Is it?'

'You spoofer, you know it is. And did you also know it can say "Heil Hitler"?'

'I did think your grandma could teach it to say "Rule, Britannia" instead.'

'Daddy, where did you get it from?'

'D'you really want to know?'

'Yes, of course I do.'

'I acquired it,' said Boots, 'from the house we raided. I thought we could improve its manners.'

'I bet,' said Rosie. 'Daddy, you're ever so deep sometimes. Hitler's that peculiar German character whose followers say "Heil Hitler" to him.'

'Well, what I'd like and what you'd like, poppet, is for Percy to say "Rule, Britannia" to him. Wouldn't we?'

'Is Hitler dangerous?' asked Rosie.

'Let's say he'd be a lot safer if he were locked up,' said Boots. 'On the other hand, you and I know someone who's more than a match for him.'

'Who?' asked Rosie.

'Your grandma,' said Boots.

Rosie laughed and cuddled his arm, and they entered the house together.

Chapter Twenty-Three

Mrs Brooks, in taking charge of the welfare of Bubbles and Penny-Farving, enabled Dan to go off to his daily work in a whistling mood, and allowed Tilly to attend to her dressmaking orders without worrying. She was also able to get out in the afternoons and go down the market. She liked the East Street market with its boisterous cockney atmosphere, where stallholders quickly became your friends, even if you still had to watch that some of them didn't slip a bit of a dud apple in with a pound. The market, generally, enriched cockney spirits. Everyone knew it didn't hurt the pocket as much as shops with marble counters or stores with posh-looking floorwalkers.

But for all that she didn't have to worry any more about Bubbles and Penny-Farving, Tilly found she couldn't stop herself looking in on them from time to time, just to see how they were getting on in the care of Mrs Brooks. The motherly lady's understanding of how to deal with high-spirited children was such that little accidents and alarming moments were becoming a thing of the past.

I've done Dan Rogers a really good turn in bringing Mrs Brooks to look after his girls, thought Tilly. Next time he offers me a box of chocolates, I might accept.

Boots and Rachel enjoyed another companionable lunch in the plush surroundings of the Trocadero, which provided an almost perfect background to Rachel's lush beauty and colourful hat. Boots commented on her eye-catching appearance, and Rachel said she was glad he'd noticed. She had never had any difficulty in communicating easily with all the members of the Adams family, particularly with Sammy of the electric blue eyes, and in a special way with Boots, whom she saw as the very personable elder of the tribe.

Happily, she imparted to him that which she had referred to as very interesting information, which so tickled Boots that he asked her if she'd like to share a second bottle of wine with him.

'Love to, my dear, but I daren't, unless you offer to drive me back home,' she said. 'Too much wine goes to my head, and I don't want to get arrested for dancing the Charleston in Piccadilly Circus.'

'Of course I'll drive you home,' smiled Boots.

'And I'll be able to trust you on the way?'

'Give you my word,' said Boots.

'One must put up with some disappointments,' said Rachel. 'Order the wine, lovey.'

They shared it very enjoyably. Rachel asked if the shareholders' meeting had been called yet.

'Yes, for next Tuesday evening in the offices,' said Boots.

'Will you pass this information to Sammy before the meeting?'

'I think it would have more effect if I presented it to everyone at the same time, during the meeting,' said Boots.

'Well, lovey, it's been a pleasure gathering it for you, with the help of Eli Greenberg,' said Rachel.

'What, in return, can I do for you?' asked Boots. 'Lunch isn't much of a reward.'

'My life, there's a sweetie, ain't you?' said Rachel. 'How many shares do you have in Adams Enterprises?'

'Two-fifty,' said Boots.

'Sell me fifty, ducky, and get me elected to the board.'

'I'll consider that,' said Boots.

'Seriously?'

'Is that what you'd seriously like?'

'Yes,' said Rachel.

'Have some more wine,' said Boots.

With Sammy plotting a fairly honest campaign which, he hoped, would ensure a smooth and relatively uncontentious sale of the scrap metal business, and with Boots keeping some very interesting information close to his chest, confiding it only to Emily, Chinese Lady took it upon herself to pay Sammy a call. Cornering him in his office, she let him know she was generally disapproving of all this money-making. Sammy pointed out he hadn't made it yet, and in return Chinese Lady pointed out she didn't like being contradicted, specially not by her youngest son. There's enough money as it is to go round for everyone, she said, and I don't like anyone getting covetous for more, so that they can hoard it like a miser. Sammy assured her he wasn't going to hoard it, he was going to spend it. Not all at once, but gradually, while keeping enough in his wallet – well, his bank – to look after any unexpected family overheads. Sammy, you're going to get addicted to money if you keep on like this, said Chinese Lady. Well, I've got to be honest, Ma, said Sammy, I started life addicted. Yes, but there was no need to make a bad habit of it, said Chinese Lady. If you've got a business, it's best to keep it, she said. We've got three businesses, Ma, three companies, said Sammy. I don't know why you're so argufying, said Chinese Lady. Just remember that I'm not going to stand for any of Susie's family being put out of work, not when they're as good as part of our own family. I'll see to it, said Sammy. You'd better, my lad, said Chinese Lady.

By Friday, more than a week after Mrs Brooks had become Dan's daily help, Tilly was suffering dissatisfaction with what was going on. Actually, nothing at all was going on as far as she was concerned, for her pleasant and creative routine was free of all interruptions. So it was sickening to realize the lack of any little incidents was the cause of her dissatisfaction.

I must be barmy, she said to herself. I'll go out to a tea dance one day at that hall in Brixton. Yes, one Saturday afternoon, when there might be a spare bloke that's just waiting to catch sight of me in me best dance frock, the short one with a fringed hem. I wouldn't mind a spare bloke interrupting some of me evenings or Sundays.

She had to admit Mrs Brooks kept the girls behaving themselves. On the other hand, she'd found out that the motherly lady used the constant threat of a policeman to sober them up. Once or twice was all right, but not all the time. Or so Tilly thought. It occurred to her that she wasn't displeased at finding what could be called a chink in the lady's armour. Well, it would be a chink if Dan Rogers didn't like his girls being kept under that kind of threat.

But no, she couldn't tell him. She'd never been a telltale, and why should she tell on Mrs Brooks of all people? She was a friend, and Tilly had recommended her herself. So why was she a bit pleased at finding the lady wasn't perfect?

The light suddenly dawned for Tilly.

'You called me, Tilly?' Dan was home from his work, and with Mrs Brooks having left for her own home, he was up on the landing in response to a verbal summons from Tilly.

'Come in, me door's ajar,' she said, and Dan entered. He blinked pleasurably, for Tilly was adjusting the top of her left stocking. She was seated on the arm of her fireside chair and wearing a shimmering silky creation with a fringed hem. Gladdening, that is, thought Dan. Tilly, having teased his appreciative eyes, said, 'I didn't know you was goin' to come in as quick as that, and anyway, you should 'ave knocked first.'

'Lucky for me I didn't,' said Dan, grinning.

'What d'you mean, lucky?' said Tilly. 'It's not lucky to embarrass a respectable lady, it's downright indecent. Were you lookin' through the keyhole?'

'Me?' said Dan.

'Don't come the old acid,' said Tilly. 'Were you or wasn't you?'

'Well, I won't say I wouldn't've been tempted, if I'd known what the magic lantern slide was showin'.'

'What a piece of impudence,' said Tilly.

'Can I help bein' admirin' of your legs?' said Dan. 'And your dress? Blimey, you're a charmer, you are, Tilly.'

'This dress is just an old thing that I've just put on to see if it's 'ad its day,' said Tilly. 'D'you think it's got too short?'

'Well, if it was twelve inches shorter, it 'ud be a knockout,' said Dan.

''Ow disgustin',' said Tilly, 'I'll start lookin' for me egg saucepan in a minute. Anyway, how's them gels of yours?'

'Fine,' said Dan, 'and might I say you look the same?'

'Is that a compliment?' asked Tilly.

'It's meant to be,' said Dan.

'I thought you liked fat women,' said Tilly.

'I don't dislike 'em,' said Dan, 'they're sort of jolly.'

'I didn't notice Gladys Hobday was a laugh a minute.'

'Well, as a circus performer, she takes herself very serious.'

'You still in love with her?'

'Hardly,' said Dan.

'What d'you mean, hardly?'

'I've gone off her,' said Dan.

'All the same, something's still got to be done about givin' your gels a proper mother. Mrs Brooks is bein' useful, but it's not enough. You've got to get married.'

'Tilly, I told you, Elvira said a great big "no" in capital letters.'

'Never mind that,' said Tilly, 'leave it to me. I'll arrange something.'

'Will you?' said Dan.

'Yes, I've been thinkin' about it,' said Tilly. 'Meet me outside the town 'all on your way 'ome from work tomorrow. You leave your work at 'alf-past-twelve, don't you? Well, you could be at the town 'all by a quarter to one. Meet me then.'

'Blimey Bill,' said Dan, 'are you goin' to get Gladys Hobday there?'

'Just meet me,' said Tilly. 'You can tell Mrs Brooks you might be a bit late gettin' in. She won't mind.'

'Listen—'

'That's all, Dan Rogers. Them gels are callin' you.'

Dan arrived at the Southwark town hall in the Walworth Road just before fifteen minutes to one the following day, Saturday. Tilly was waiting for him, looking modestly fetching in a linen dress and a nice hat.

'Now what?' said Dan. 'Where's Elvira?'

'We don't need 'er,' said Tilly, 'we're goin' in to see the registrar or 'is clerk, and arrange for him to marry us as soon as possible. Someone's got to make sure Bubbles and Penny-Farvin' have married parents, and that someone's me. Otherwise you'll just carry on as if everything in the garden's lovely. Once we're married we'll see what we can do about gettin' over the problem of the gels bein' born out of wedlock, like findin' someone in the East End who can supply us with birth certificates for them, even if they cost you a quid apiece. Birth certificates showin' you and me as their parents.'

'Could you say all that again?' asked Dan, looking as if her egg saucepan had caught him a wallop.

'I could, but I ain't goin' to,' said Tilly. 'You need me, Dan Rogers, and so do your little angels.'

'I won't say I don't,' said Dan, 'but you sure you know what you're doin'?'

'Yes,' said Tilly. 'We all ought to do one good deed in our lifetimes.'

'You've thought serious about what you're takin' on?' said Dan.

'I'm takin' on two little gels that need a proper mother, and a bloke who needs a decent wife,' said Tilly. 'And if you turn out to be a decent 'usband, you might get to see me in tights and spangles.'

Dan laughed.

'Well, I fancy you, Tilly Thomas, and that's a fact,'

he said. 'This way.' He took her arm and led her into the town hall in manly fashion, which was only right and proper, and saved Tilly having to knock him out and drag him in.

Saturday high tea, always a favourite with Chinese Lady and her family, was over. Boots, looking casual in his weekend cricket shirt and grey flannels, answered a ring on the doorbell.

'Good evening, sir,' said the caller, a tall slim boy nicely dressed and devoid of pimples, 'are you Mr Adams?'

'By the grace of God or the imps of perdition, yes, I am,' said Boots. 'My parents also had something to do with it.'

'Oh, well put, sir,' said the boy. 'I'm the first son of my own parents, I'm Peter Clark. I'm in my last year at West Square School and a friend of your daughter Rosie, who's at the girls' school, and a ripper, sir. But she said she won't allow me to take her out unless I first called to introduce myself to her mother and father. I think I've got to have your approval. I'm just turned sixteen and can honestly say I don't have a police record.'

Boots let a smile show, a smile more resigned than whimsical. He saw this boy as the first inevitable step towards losing Rosie, a lovely and endearing girl, whom he had always regarded as particularly his own. But nothing was unchanging, nothing ever stood still, apart from entrenched affections. In a few years, Rosie would be a young woman, looking outward, not inward, and thinking, as all young people did in time, of a life of her own, a home of her own, and a family of her own. He and Emily could not keep her for ever, any more than they could keep Tim.

'Come in, young man, come and meet Rosie's mother, and her grandparents. And her brother.'

He introduced the boy to the family, then went to find Rosie. She was upstairs, in her room, getting ready to go out and spend the evening with Lizzy's eldest daughter Annabelle, her adoptive cousin and best friend.

'Who was that at the door?' she asked, her fair hair burnished from brushing, and he thought how extraordinarily enchanting she was for her age.

'Your young man,' he said.

'My what?'

'A young gentleman called Peter Clark.'

'Who?' said Rosie.

'Peter Clark.'

'Oh, Peter,' said Rosie. 'What's he up to, coming here?'

'I think he's up to the prospect of taking you out, providing your mother and I approve,' said Boots. 'He explained the position.'

'What position?'

'That you said you wouldn't let him take you out until he'd met us and we stuck an approved label on him.'

'Oh, that,' said Rosie. 'That was only to put him off. Daddy, he's only another boy.'

'Well, that's how it goes, doesn't it?' smiled Boots. 'One more boy meets one more girl?'

'Daddy, I hope you're joking, I hope you haven't said he can take me out. He hasn't grown up yet. Boys don't grow up until they're at least twenty-one, and then it's still a struggle for some of them.'

'Well, this one seems a nice young man,' said Boots.

'Crikey, whose side are you on?' said Rosie.

'I'm on the side of what comes naturally, poppet.

342

You can't fight it, and parents can't fight it. Life for the young should be fun, Rosie. Enjoy it.'

'Daddy, I enjoy every moment of my life, so stop thinking I need to go out with young boys.'

'So what are you going to do, now he's here?' asked Boots.

'Oh, all right, now he's here I'll take him with me to Aunt Lizzy's and show him to Annabelle. She knows him too, and he's more her age than mine. Daddy, you shocker, trying to pair him off with me.'

'Fell flat on my face, did I?' said Boots.

'Well, none of us are perfect all the time, are we?' said Rosie, and laughed. A little later, she took Peter with her to Aunt Lizzy's to palm him off on Annabelle. Rosie, who had her own ideas about her future, was already one too many for boys of sixteen.

Tuesday evening. The shareholders of Adams Scrap Metal Ltd were all present in Sammy's office. Tommy and Vi, Sammy and Susie, Boots and Emily, Lizzy and Chinese Lady, were seated around Sammy's large desk. Sammy was in the chair, and he opened the proceedings.

'Friends, shareholders, brothers, sisters-in-law and so on—'

'I'm not so on, nor's Mum,' said Lizzy.

'Beg pardon, Lizzy, a small oversight in me address,' said Sammy. 'Consider yourself importantly included, and Ma as well. It's my pleasure to have brought us all together on an occasion which could rightly be called auspicious, seein' it might result in a highly profitable transaction for all concerned.'

'He's off,' said Tommy.

'Yes, and suppose Boots gets started as well?' said Lizzy.

'Well, with Sammy, you only 'ave to put up with him usin' twice as many words as he needs to,' said Tommy. 'Boots'll say a lot less, but we'll have to watch every one of his words.'

'Order,' said Sammy. 'Now you all know why we're gathered together in the sight of the lord of business, which is St Peter—'

'Don't be irreverent,' said Chinese Lady.

'I note that, Ma,' said Sammy. 'I'm just pointin' out you've all got copies of Johnson's proposition in front of you. I can tell you I've made 'em iron out every paragraph, which means the moment we concur and sign, Johnson's are committed to make immediate payment for the shares, a payment which you all know amounts to forty thousand lovely smackers.'

'I'm against it,' said Chinese Lady.

'We ought to listen first, Mum,' said Lizzy.

'I don't want to listen,' said Chinese Lady, 'all the talk's goin' to be about money. We've all got enough, and we don't need more.'

'It's your privilege, Ma, to vote against the motion,' said Sammy. 'I take pleasure in lettin' everyone know Johnson's proposed fifty per cent payable on signature, and the balance in six months, and that actin' on everyone's behalf, I hit them over the head in a manner of speakin'. This forthwith brought forth—'

'Can you say forthwith brought forth?' asked Emily.

'Oh, lor', I couldn't,' said Vi, 'but Sammy's managed it.'

'My arguments,' said Sammy, 'brought forth an amendment which entitles us to collect in full immediately. That's if the meeting votes for the sale.'

'Excuse me,' said Vi, 'but don't I understand Johnson's have been makin' losses? I mean, if they

344

have, where they goin' to find the money to pay us?'

'Bless me ears,' said Sammy, 'was it Vi who said that, Tommy?'

'Yes, and out loud,' said Tommy.

'Good question, Vi,' said Boots.

'My feelings exactly,' said Sammy. 'I compliment you, Vi. The money's comin' from Johnson's directors, not their profit and loss account, and if it doesn't the sale's null and void.'

'Carry on, Sammy, we all like null and void,' said Susie.

'I'm against it,' said Chinese Lady, very suspicious of null and void.

'Noted, Ma,' said Sammy. 'Now, there's been some natural worry about what might happen to our scrap metal employees if Johnson's take over, particularly certain employees close to the fam'ly.'

'Like Freddy,' said Emily.

'And his dad,' said Lizzy.

'And Freddy's brother Will,' said Emily, 'he works for the scrap metal company too.'

'All taken care of,' said Sammy. Boots smiled, knowing Susie had fought for her family as much as Sammy always fought for his. 'It so happened that our old friend, Eli Greenberg, was in a bit of a fix. Mrs Greenberg, his lady wife of a few years, was treadin' on his plates of meat about buyin' a small South London brewery as a business for his three stepsons, which purchase would've damaged his wallet fatally. So I negotiated to do him a good turn by takin' up the proposition myself, leavin' Eli to inform his trouble and strife that he'd been beaten to the deal by an interferin' interloper. Yours truly, ladies and gents, is now the owner of a brewery, havin' laid down half the purchase price and half in three months time, when I hope I won't be as poor as I am now.'

'I'm against it,' said Chinese Lady, 'I didn't bring any of me fam'ly up to take to drink, which is what ownin' a brewery means.'

'Oh, it's all right, Mum, I'll see to it that Sammy doesn't drink any of what he brews,' said Susie. 'And I know why he bought it.'

'Yes, there's good jobs there for Susie's dad, and her two brothers, Will and Freddy,' said Sammy. 'I'll be havin' an encouraging word with them once the proposal to sell the scrap metal company has been voted for, which I hope it will be or the sacrifice of me hard-earned money to buy the brewery will be what you'd call heart-breakin'.'

'It'll still make a profit,' said Boots.

'I appreciate Boots havin' faith in me,' said Sammy, 'seein' we all respect him as our Ma's eldest. Might I now suggest we get on with puttin' the motion to the vote?'

'Before we do, Sammy, I'd like to make a few points,' said Boots.

'Go ahead,' said Sammy.

Boots questioned what lay behind the proposed purchase, since Johnson's had been losing money regularly. He produced figures relating to balance sheets. He questioned why a firm, running a business at a loss, should want to purchase an identical business, since the Adams company was only making a small profit and the market generally was depressed. Further, Johnson's were conducting their company in a very odd way, selling only inferior quality stocks. Their yards held plenty of first-class scrap metal which they weren't offering for sale.

'How'd you know?' asked Sammy.

'From visits to their yards,' said Boots.

'Boots, you've been goin' the rounds of their yards?' said Susie.

'I must say Boots shows a bit of sense sometimes,' said Chinese Lady, 'which is always a nice surprise to me.'

'Granted, old lady,' said Boots, evading answering Susie. If, he said, Johnson's acquired the Adams' yards, was it for the purpose of also acquiring and holding the best of Adams' scrap? In their position, how could they afford to? The Adams' yard would immediately become loss-making.

'Still,' said Tommy, 'why should we worry? We'll have shared out forty thousand quid by then.'

'I'm against it,' said Chinese Lady.

'My feeling is that Johnson's are hoarding,' said Boots.

'Well, Boots,' said Sammy, 'as Tommy's just pointed out, why should we worry?'

'There are three directors running Johnson's,' said Boots. 'One of them is a bloke called Berger. He's a German who's the London agent of a family firm called Bergers in Dusseldorf. It makes machinery.'

'But does it matter, Boots?' asked Lizzy.

'It will matter if one day Germany gets short of raw materials,' said Boots.

'Hold on, Boots,' said Sammy, 'if as soon as Johnson's take over our yards, this German firm puts in an order for all our top quality scrap, what's it to us?'

'I don't think they'll do that,' said Boots, 'or they'd have already bought what Johnson's are holding. Or tried to. But there's a limitation on certain commodities Germany would like to import. It's a limitation imposed by the Allies since the end of the war, to stop Germany from re-arming.'

'What do they want to re-arm for?' asked Tommy.

'For another war,' said Boots.

'Is Boots serious, Emily?' asked Susie.

'I think he's got certain ideas about that bloke Adolf Hitler,' said Emily.

'Hitler's potty,' said Vi.

'My feeling,' said Boots, 'is that we shouldn't give a helping hand to the leader of a German political organization that's as aggressive as he is. I think Johnson's is in German hands, that their best scrap metal is being hoarded for export, and that they're after ours and all that both firms continue to buy in. The limitation doesn't apply to scrap metal imports.' Boots was dealing in what he knew himself and in the information he'd had from Rachel, some of which had been passed to her by Mr Greenberg, including the fact that Berger was a representative of the family firm in Dusseldorf. 'Let's hang on. If the market ups in a few years, it would pay us to.'

'Boots old lad,' said Sammy, 'I'm sorry to mention it, but you're all ifs and buts. I trust you don't mind me sayin' so?'

'Not if you're sorrowful,' said Boots.

'No hard feelings, I hope,' said Sammy.

'None,' said Boots, aware that if Sammy and others regarded the information as irrelevant, the vote would probably go in favour of the motion.

'I don't like any talk about that man Hitler,' said Chinese Lady, 'nor don't I like selling anything to him or what he might get up to with it.'

'Don't lose any sleep over him, Mum,' said Tommy, 'he's off his chump.'

'Might I now propose we accept Johnson's offer?' said Sammy.

'Seconded,' said Tommy.

'Tommy, didn't I say I was against it?' said Chinese Lady fretfully.

'Well, you've got the privilege of voting that way,' said Tommy.

'I'll take your votes,' said Sammy, and addressed the shareholders individually and clockwise, beginning with Chinese Lady on his left. 'Ma?'

'You know I'm votin' no,' she said firmly, and on a slip of paper Sammy noted down the number of her shares. Fifty. Then he asked Tommy.

'For,' said Tommy, and on another slip of paper, Sammy pencilled in Tommy's holding. One hundred.

'Boots?'

'Against,' said Boots, and down went his holding under Chinese Lady's. Two hundred and fifty.

'Em'ly?'

'Against,' said Emily, standing with Boots, of course.

'H'm,' said Sammy, pencilling the number. 'Lizzy?'

Lizzy had spoken in earnest to Ned before leaving for the meeting. She wanted his serious opinion. Ned said although he couldn't fault Sammy as a businessman, on a matter like this he'd always side with Boots.

'I'm against it, Sammy,' she said.

'Pardon?' said Sammy, confident until then that Lizzy would be in favour.

'Against,' she repeated, and with the kind of smile that always made Boots think his sister richly brunette.

Ruddy hell, thought Sammy, totting up, that makes four-fifty votes against. I could be facing defeat. Me, Sammy Adams. Never mind the spondulicks, what about me pride? I've got Tommy's hundred and my three-fifty, but now I need Vi's and Susie's. And that

Susie, she's been getting the better of me and dotting me in the eye for years now.

'You, Vi?' he said.

'For,' said Vi just a little shyly and hesitantly, because although she thought a lot of Boots and his opinions, she simply couldn't go against Tommy.

Five hundred for our side, thought Sammy. Now, you Susie.

'Susie?'

'Um, er,' said Susie, never more teasing than when she had Sammy wriggling.

'Susie?' said Sammy, quavering a bit.

'For,' said Susie. Well, Sammy had acquired a new business that would look after her dad and her brothers, so how could she not support him? Besides, she still thought her children's dad a lovely bloke generally.

'Well, friends, fam'ly and shareholders,' announced Sammy, 'the motion's passed five-fifty to four-fifty. All rise.'

'What d'you mean, all rise?' said Lizzy, who at least knew now she could have the conversion done that would give Ned a billiards room.

'Just to show respect to St Peter,' said Sammy, 'the lord of business. Don't forget he was in charge of the fishin' fleet.'

'Sammy, you've gone and sold one of the fam'ly businesses and you're bein' irreverent as well,' said Chinese Lady.

'All fair and square, Ma,' said Sammy, 'and no hard feelings in anyone, I hope.'

'All right, Sammy,' said Lizzy, and glanced at Boots. He smiled.

'Fair and square,' he said, and Emily liked him for taking defeat so well.

350

'It's been a privilege,' said Sammy.

'Winnin' the vote?' said Tommy.

'No, makin' you all feel a bit rich,' said Sammy.

Chinese Lady frowned, not liking what Boots had said about Germany.

Boots poured himself a beer on arrival home and took it into the garden to stand and muse. Rosie, learning from Emily how the vote had gone, came out to stand beside him.

'Daddy, you lost,' she said, and felt upset for him.

'It's not fatal, poppet.'

'But you're disappointed, aren't you?'

'I don't think so. Life's not always about winning, Rosie. You have to lose sometimes. If you didn't, if you always won, you'd begin to think you were God. And what would that do for you? Make you think you could never be bowled out at cricket. And what would happen if your own daughter did bowl you out? Thunder and lightning.'

Rosie laughed. Looking at him she thought he seemed at peace with everything, that he wasn't even thinking about the argument he'd lost with Uncle Sammy, that his mind was on something else.

'Penny for them, please, Daddy.'

'Is it worth double a penny, Rosie, to let you know I think myself a very favoured bloke in my family, my friends and everything else I have?'

'Bless you, Daddy, you're the best ever.'

'Well, bless you too, poppet,' said Boots, 'and you owe me tuppence for my thoughts.'

'Oh, do I, Daddy?' said Rosie.

'I'll settle for a penny,' said Boots.

'Crikey,' said Rosie, 'now we've both made a profit again.'

Sunday afternoon.

'Freddy, Freddy?' Cassie, having made use of the latchcord, danced into the Brown family's house. 'You there, Freddy?'

'Unfortunately, yes,' said Freddy.

Into the kitchen danced Cassie, beaming and alive.

'Freddy, what d'you think? I know now why Cecil 'asn't ever said much. It's because he was broody.'

'Broody?'

'Yes,' said Cassie in delight, 'he's just laid an egg.'

Collapse of Freddy.

THE END